Dinner at Rose's

Dinner at Rose's

DANIELLE HAWKINS

ARENA
ALLEN&UNWIN

Arena Books, an imprint of
Allen & Unwin
Sydney, Melbourne, Auckland, London

83 Alexander Street
Crows Nest NSW 2065
Australia
Phone: (61 2) 8425 0100
Fax: (61 2) 9906 2218
Email: info@allenandunwin.com
Web: www.allenandunwin.com

Cataloguing-in-Publication details are available
from the National Library of Australia
www.trove.nla.gov.au

ISBN 978 1 74331 557 6

Text design by Ruth Grüner
Set in 12/15 pt Granjon by Post Pre-press Group, Australia
Printed and bound in Australia by Griffin Press

10 9 8

Chapter 1

I TURNED UP a steep rutted driveway ten kilometres south of town, navigated around a huge pothole and a wheelbarrow full of marrows, and pulled up on the dusty gravel beside the house. Instantly a pack of dogs appeared, barking hysterically.

Opening the car door a crack I bellowed, 'Get out of it!' and they sank to their bellies in a servile and unattractive manner, panting hard. Now that they were stationary I counted four.

'Sweetest of peas!' cried Aunty Rose, sailing around the corner of the house with a half-grown ginger piglet at her heels. 'How are you, my love?'

'Very good,' I said. 'It's lovely to see you.' Aunty Rose was six foot two and built like a tank, and I had to reach up to hug her. I don't have to reach up to hug many people, being almost six foot tall myself, so this made a pleasant change.

She smiled at me fondly. 'Likewise,' she said. Her

I

voice was as rich and plummy as a fruitcake, every vowel beautifully rounded. It made one think of elocution lessons and cucumber sandwiches and tea with the vicar. Come to think of it, it made one use the word 'one' in one's thoughts. Accents are terribly contagious.

'Have you been doing anything exciting?' I asked.

'I've been *frightfully* busy. That incompetent library committee has taken most of my time this week, and the garden is running amok. I shall enlist your services, dear child.'

'No worries,' I said. 'You can pay me in marrows.'

'Bloody marrows!' said Rose. 'Every year I plant just a couple of tiny, feeble zucchinis, and they spend the first two months trying to die and needing half-hourly watering. And then I go out to buy milk and they transform into triffids.'

'Why keep planting them?'

'It's a sickness,' she said gloomily. 'I probably need counselling.'

'Perhaps you could go to meetings. You know – "Hello, I'm Rose Thornton, it's been two days since my last courgette."'

'A fine idea,' she said. 'Come in. It must be time for a G and T by now.'

WE STRETCHED OUT side by side on the veranda in a pair of ancient deckchairs, drinks in hand. Rose's house was the original homestead of a station long since split into several smaller farms. Set on the crest of a ridge, it's an old villa with high ceilings and a steep roof, utterly charming but decayed beyond the point of repair. There is an alarming tilt in the veranda which matches the sag in the kitchen floor, the door in the living room has to be wedged shut with a 1972 copy of the *Woman's Weekly* to block the draughts whistling down the hall, and little piles of borer dust accumulate in every cupboard. The paint is peeling, the fretwork is decidedly tatty and there are at least three leaks in the roof. But there is also a huge crimson climbing rose taking over the veranda and the view out over the ranges is spectacular. In the four years since I'd last been here nothing had changed, which gave me a nice warm feeling of security.

I took a large mouthful of my gin and tonic, and choked. 'Is there *any* tonic in here, Aunty Rose?'

'A dribble,' she said, taking a cautious sip of her own drink. 'Hmm, perhaps I was a tad heavy on the gin. How are your parents?'

'Mum's got a quality-control audit tomorrow, so she's cleaning the milking shed with a toothbrush. Dad's good.'

'Is he still playing the guitar?'

'Yes,' I said sadly.

'It could be worse. Imagine if he'd taken up the bagpipes.'

'It's the singing. He's completely tone deaf, bless him.'

'Your parents are marvellous people,' said Rose. 'Mad, both of them.'

The piglet climbed up onto the deck and collapsed beside her chair, and she picked up a fork from the table by her elbow and scratched his stomach.

'Do you keep that fork especially for pig-scratching?' I enquired.

'I do. You don't need to point out that I'm mad as well. You really should consider becoming an eccentric yourself, young Josephine; it makes life so much more interesting.'

'I will,' I said, then took another mouthful of neat gin, enjoying the way it evaporated on my tongue before reaching the back of my throat.

After several drinks I suggested we make tea.

'Dinner, Josephine, please,' said Rose reprovingly as we made our way, weaving slightly, to the kitchen. (My parents have never given me a satisfactory answer to the question of why they thought 'Josephine' was a good name. It's not; it sounds like a nineteenth-century governess. Nobody else was allowed to use it, but somehow I rather liked it from Aunty Rose.) 'It's not tea, it's dinner.'

'I'm a beastly colonial, Rose, and you're just going to have to come to terms with it,' I said.

'You're as bad as Matthew,' she said, removing a somewhat limp carrot from the pantry and pointing it at me for emphasis. 'Years of nagging, and he still says "New Zullind" and "moolk".' Matt was Rose's proper legitimate nephew – Rose being his mother's elder sister – whereas I was only an honorary niece. Rose came out from England in the seventies as a freshly qualified nurse, taking advantage of a bonding scheme the New Zealand government was running to get staff for small rural hospitals. She promptly (and some would say inexplicably) decided Waimanu was the best place in the world and stayed. Her sister came out to visit her a few years later, married a local dairy farmer after a whirlwind courtship lasting about three weeks, and then spent the next twenty-five years lamenting his lack of polish and refinement.

I grinned. 'How is Matt?'

'He's well. Working far too hard, but he seems quite happy. That reminds me, he's coming for dinner.'

'Very cool,' I said. Although slightly scary. 'Now, are you going to cook that carrot or just wave it about?'

'Go away and stop distracting me,' said Aunty Rose. 'In fact, why don't you unpack and freshen up?'

When I re-entered the kitchen half an hour later Rose was grating cheese with such reckless abandon that I feared she might lose a finger.

'Ah,' she said. 'There you are. Now, how about pouring us a glass of that lovely wine you brought with you?'

'A week of this and I'll develop cirrhosis of the liver,' I remarked.

'Nonsense,' she said. 'The liver requires exercise, like all muscles.'

'I'm almost certain the liver isn't a muscle.'

She waved her hand airily. 'The principle, Josephine, is the same. I hear a vehicle – that must be Matthew. Why don't you trot out and say hello?'

That sounded like a fine idea, and besides I was keen to put off the pouring of any more drinks until tea (or dinner) was served. Aunty Rose was a somewhat erratic cook at the best of times, and when half-cut she was liable to decide that prunes would make a delightful addition to the risotto. I wandered out the kitchen door in time to see Matt climb out of a battered red ute, fend off the dogs with the skill of long practice, and walk across the gravel. The piglet flopped onto its back in front of him and he paused to scratch its stomach with his foot.

'Hey, Matt,' I said. He hadn't changed much to look at – he was still tall and lean and brown-haired and slightly scruffy – but four years of farming had made him tougher-looking. The last time I'd seen him was at his father's funeral, dazed with grief and jet lag and pale from the British winter. Now he was sunburnt and cheerful, and had that classic dairy farmer's tan: brown legs that turned lily-white below the gumboot line.

He looked up and grinned at me. 'Hey, Jo.' The piglet grunted indignantly as he stopped scratching and he prodded it with his toe. 'That's enough now, Percy, bugger off. You look good.'

I assumed the last sentence was meant for me rather than the pig. 'So do you. How are things?'

'Good. And you?'

'Fine.' This was followed by a slightly uncomfortable silence, and I tried hard to think of something witty and casual and friendly to say. 'How's the farm?' I asked at last, coinciding with his, 'How are your parents?'

'Good,' we said together, and smiled at one another ruefully.

'It's good to see you,' he said, and put an arm around me in a friendly hug. 'Do you think you'll be able to handle the hustle and bustle of Waimanu?'

'I hope so.' Three weeks ago I had been living in inner-city Melbourne; Waimanu has a population of four thousand. 'It was a bit of a shock to see you've got a McDonald's.'

'I know,' said Matt. 'We're practically a metropolis.'

'WHAT WOULD THIS BE, Aunty Rose?' Matt asked, poking at an unidentified wedge of orange stuff on one side of his plate.

'It's a carrot and apple bake,' she said, adding quite unnecessarily, 'My own recipe. How about another drop of wine, Josephine?'

'Better pour me some too, to wash it down,' Matt said, and I had to disguise a laugh with a cough.

'You used to be such a nice boy,' said Rose plaintively.

'When?' I asked, and Matt threw a pea at me, hitting me on the nose.

'Children!' said Rose. 'Behave yourselves!'

'Isn't it nice being called "children"?' I said dreamily. 'It makes me feel young again.'

'I didn't realise you were teetering on the brink of the grave,' Rose remarked.

'I'm going to be thirty in two months.'

'I'm alright,' said Matt. 'I've got another whole year. Don't worry, Jose, you're not looking all that bad for your age.'

'Thank you,' I said, and poured the wine.

'HE'S A DEAR boy,' said Rose, letting herself back in the kitchen door after waving Matt off.

I was washing the dishes – she appeared to have used every pot in the house in the preparation of this evening's meal – and as I scrubbed grimly at the roasting dish I agreed, 'He is. He's one of my very favourite people.'

'He's seeing a girl who sells fertiliser, I believe,' she said.

'Good on him,' I said. And though I meant it, a small cold weight settled in the pit of my stomach at this further piece of evidence that everybody in the entire world had somebody – except me. By the time I was thirty, you see, I was supposed to be happily married and thinking about babies. I was *not* meant to be emerging from the wreckage of the relationship I'd thought would be providing said babies. A poor attitude for a girl who grew up with Rose Thornton as a shining example of making singleness into an art form, but there you go.

'Leave that to soak, sweet pea,' said Rose. 'I'll wash it in the morning.'

I WOKE UP ridiculously early, mostly due to having spent the night bent like a staple. The bed in the Pink Room was about sixty years old, with a kapok mattress on a wire-woven base. Outside the sky was pale lemon and green, and I could hear a disconcerting snuffling sound that I hoped was being made by the piglet. I got up and went to look – it was, and the mist wreathing up off the bush-clad hills behind the house was so lovely that I threw on a pair of shorts and a T-shirt and went out to commune with nature.

When I came back down the hill, accompanied by a retinue of four dogs and one pig, Aunty Rose was breakfasting on the veranda in a crimson satin dressing-gown with her long grey hair loose down her back. As I came through the little wooden gate under the walnut tree she waved the butter knife at me and called, 'The toast is hot, sweet pea, and I've just refreshed the teapot.'

'This is all very civilised,' I said, sitting down and reaching for the marmalade.

'I suppose you've fallen into the modern habit of breakfasting on black coffee and eating a lettuce leaf for lunch?'

'Do I *look* as if I live on lettuce leaves and black coffee?' I asked.

Aunty Rose looked me up and down. 'You look very nice,' she said firmly. 'You've inherited your mother's legs, lucky girl. When do you start this new job of yours?'

'I'm going into town this morning for Cheryl to take me through the computer system, then starting properly on Monday. Lovely marmalade.'

'The secret is to slice the oranges finely. Some people –' her tone implied that these were not the type of people she wanted anything to do with – 'actually use one of those food-processor things.'

'Does it matter?' I asked.

Rose sighed. 'Sometimes, Josephine, I despair of you.'

I had a leisurely breakfast, followed by an invigorating

run around the back lawn after a brace of escaped chickens and a very quick wash under the world's most pathetic and under-pressured shower. Then I got dressed in a selection of what I hoped were professional yet flattering clothes, left Rose heaving marrows over the back fence and set off into town.

Chapter 2

WAIMANU IS IN the middle of the King Country, about halfway down the western side of New Zealand's North Island. It's only a little place, run-down and distinctly lacking in cafe culture, but it services a large area of farmland. Consequently, although you can't buy a pair of shoes any self-respecting woman under a hundred and ten would even *consider* wearing, it has a base hospital, a decent-sized supermarket, an enormous Farmlands store and a freezing works.

I parked about halfway along the main street in front of Heather Anne's Fashions (where you could find any number of blouses made of peach-coloured polyester but almost nothing else), and opened the door of the physiotherapy clinic next door.

Behind the counter a girl in her early twenties with very prominent pale-blue eyes and no chin looked up, sniffed and wiped her nose with the back of her hand. 'Can I help you?' she asked.

'Hi,' I said. 'I'm Jo. You must be Amber.'

'Oh,' said Amber, with only mild interest. 'You're going to work here. Cheryl's in the loo.'

After a few minutes there was a gurgle of plumbing and Cheryl appeared in the doorway. She was looking hugely pregnant. A small woman, she looked like a beach ball balanced on a pair of toothpicks.

'Morning, Jo,' she said cheerfully. 'I was half expecting you not to show up.'

'Thanks a lot,' I said.

'Oh, not because you're unreliable; it's just that I've lined up three locums in the last two months and they've all got cold feet at the last minute.'

'Bloody hell, Cher, what's wrong with the place?'

'Nothing,' she said with dignity. 'Is there, Amber?'

Amber was staring vacantly into space and winding a strand of limp blonde hair around her right index finger. Hearing her name she started, sniffed and asked, 'What?'

Cheryl sighed and turned back to me. 'Come and look around, Jo.'

'When are you due?' I asked as I followed her down a beige-carpeted hall.

'Ten days.' She put her hands to the small of her back and rubbed it tiredly. 'You've come not a moment too soon.'

'So I see. Congratulations.'

'Thank you. Right, here's the consulting room – it's all computerised. Amber's in the process of getting all the files onto the computer; I expect it'll take her about another five years.' She lowered her voice and added, 'You'll have gathered she's not one of the great minds of our age.'

I smiled. 'So she's mostly ornamental?'

To my surprise, Cheryl shook her neat auburn head. 'Nope. I've never in my life seen anyone as good at getting money out of people as Amber is. You know they've tightened up the ACC laws?'

'Has it hurt you very badly?' I asked. The old Accident Compensation Corporation system was scarily easy to take advantage of and was, to be honest, well overdue for an overhaul, but the drastic cuts to physiotherapy subsidies had been pretty rough on anyone in private practice. It's amazing how few appointments people need when they suddenly have to pay for them.

'It's okay,' she said. 'I was just on the verge of expanding and getting someone else to help before the new system came in, and it's taken us back to a nice workload for one. Now, what else? Braces and straps and things are all in this cupboard – I see lots of shearers with lower back problems. Hypochondriacs and the people who just come in because they're lonely have a red dot inside their files, but Amber'll tell you who they are anyway. I don't think I've got any creeps at the moment. You know – the greasy, hopeful ones who tell you they think they've pulled a muscle in their groin.'

'You don't get nearly as much of that in a hospital,' I observed. 'For the last eighteen months I've mostly been doing rehab with stroke patients.'

'I'm sure it will all come back to you,' said Cheryl. 'You'll be fine.'

I was mildly amused and just a little annoyed by this; I'm good at my job, and I work reasonably hard to keep getting better. Also, I remember pulling an all-nighter in our third year of university to help Cheryl get to grips with some pretty basic anatomy before the next day's exam. 'Thanks,' I said.

'Have you sorted out somewhere to live yet?'

'Not yet. I'm staying with Rose Thornton in the meantime.'

'The new accountant at Horne and Plunkett's is looking for a flatmate,' said Cheryl. 'I'll pass on your number if you're interested.'

I wrinkled my nose doubtfully. 'I was thinking more of somebody's farm cottage. I don't know if I want to go flatting again.'

'Josie, hon, you can't leave your fiancé –'

'He wasn't,' I protested.

'As good as,' said Cheryl impatiently. 'Anyway, you can't move from the middle of Melbourne to downtown Waimanu and live by yourself in someone's farm cottage. You'll go into a decline and slit your wrists.'

❦

AS I TURNED the corner of the house, lifting one side of the lawnmower to stop it scalping the edge of a flowerbed, I saw Rose appear at the back door and wave her arms wildly. I turned off the mower and she carolled, 'Josephine! Phone!'

'Hello?' I said breathlessly, taking the portable phone and leaning back against the veranda railing. Rose's lawn sloped steeply away from the house in every direction and mowing involved spending most of your time shoving the mower up hills and over the roots of fruit trees.

'Hello!' a woman said in a bright, chirpy little voice like a sparrow. 'It's Sara Rogers here. Cheryl called me yesterday and mentioned you might be after a flat?'

'That's right,' I answered.

'Well, Andy and I – Andy's my flatmate – have a room spare if you'd like to look at it.'

'I would,' I said. This was not strictly true, but on reflection I'd decided that perhaps Cheryl had a point. 'Thank you.'

'You don't smoke, do you?'

'No.'

'Any pets?'

'Nope.'

'And do you listen to loud music?'

'No,' I said. 'Of course I do play the tuba, and I like to cook naked.'

There was an anxious silence while she digested this statement.

'Sorry, I'm just being an idiot,' I said. 'How about I come round and we have a look at each other?'

'Okay,' said Sara, sounding a little wary, and not quite as chirpy. 'When would suit you?'

'WELL?' ROSE ASKED as I climbed out of the car the following morning.

I bent to pat a dog with one hand and the piglet with the other before making my way across the gravel to where she was taking sheets off the washing line.

'All sorted.' I took two corners of the sheet she was holding out and we doubled it over. 'The house is fine, and they seem like fairly normal people. I'm moving in some time next week.'

'It's lucky I'm not easily offended, or I might assume it's my cooking that's driving you away so quickly.'

'Not at all,' I assured her. 'Some may feel olives and broccoli are an unusual combination, but personally I think it's a bold stroke of culinary genius.'

'Thank you,' she said graciously. 'It's nice to have one's genius recognised. Oh, and I've just been speaking to your mother – if you can't live without the tin of hair goo please let her know, and she'll send it up.'

'I can live without it. It turned out to be an inferior type of goo,' I said. 'What are you planning to do with the rest of the day?'

'Ah,' said Rose. 'Yes. I'm glad you asked me that. What are *you* doing, sweet pea?'

'Something nasty, by the sound of it.'

'It doesn't matter if you'd rather not, but Edwin and Mildred are feeling the heat terribly, poor dears. Matthew is so busy I don't like to bother him.'

I turned and looked over the back fence to where Edwin and Mildred, a pair of obese pet sheep, lay slothfully under an apple tree. 'I'll try,' I said doubtfully, 'but it won't be pretty.'

'I shall sharpen up the combs for you after lunch,' said Aunty Rose happily. 'Isn't it marvellous to be such a multi-talented young woman?'

Multitalented is not the word that would spring to the mind of anyone watching me shear. Long, smooth blows with the handpiece are utterly beyond me, so I just chip off bits of wool at random in a performance with no flair or style. And Rose's rotten sheep were not only bigger than me but had no manners whatsoever. The climax was reached with Edwin lying on top of both me and the hand-piece, kicking me repeatedly in the stomach. Aunty Rose was no help at all. Overcome with laughter, she merely leant on the fence clutching her sides.

'I hate you,' I told her as the horrible Edwin staggered to his feet and lurched off, his rolls of fat wobbling and little tufts of long wool I had missed fluttering in the breeze.

'Oh, sweet pea,' gasped Rose when she was finally able to speak. She dabbed at her eyes with a scrap of white lacy hanky. 'I wish I had a video camera. You've made my year.'

I wiped my streaming face on the hem of my singlet. 'I always suspected you were a nasty person. Sunday is supposed to be a day of rest, you know.'

'Come and sit on the veranda and have a cold drink,' she said.

After a bottle of Corona (complete with lemon wedge, as Rose was feeling guilty) on the veranda, shaded by the big magnolia and surrounded by fragrant crimson roses, I felt sufficiently revived to go and shower under that pathetic dribble of water. I spent two hours stretched at ease with *Cheaper by the Dozen*, which I had found in the Pink Room's bookcase, and then rolled to my feet and went in search of Aunty Rose.

I ran her to earth under a large shrub in the back garden. 'Can I borrow your gumboots?' I asked.

'Of course you can. Are you going to go and help Matthew milk?'

'I thought I might.'

'Take him a beer,' said Aunty Rose. 'Have fun.'

In Rose's gumboots, which were three sizes too big for me and made me feel like a yeti, I slogged down the steep driveway, across the road and diagonally up through three paddocks to reach the Kings' cowshed. This was a charmless structure built of concrete bricks painted mustard yellow, with a sweeping view down over the effluent ponds. Now, in late summer, the cowshed caught the breeze and was cool and pleasant to work in, but in winter and spring the wind whistled off the mountains to the south and slid icily down the back of your collar.

Near the top of the hill I paused and looked back towards Rose's place, the house crumbling gently in its overgrown garden and the scrub reclaiming the little paddocks that ran down to the road. It was still and very peaceful in the hot afternoon sun and the only sign of movement was one lazily circling hawk.

From where I stood I couldn't see the house I'd grown up in because it was around the brow of a hill. Five years ago my parents had had some sort of rush of blood to their heads, sold up and moved down to Nelson to milk goats.

They didn't make any money, but as ex–sheep farmers they were quite used to that.

I was glad I couldn't see our old house because the new owners were very energetic, apparently, and had added a conservatory, a retaining wall and swathes of yuccas. It may have been delightful (although I doubted it), but it's hard to view the improvements somebody else has made to a place you love. I could see just a corner of the back paddock and the creek where a wily old brown trout used to live, and these looked reassuringly the same. Turning away, I walked quickly up the last slope to the shed.

When I let myself in through the gate at the top of the pit Matt was teat-spraying a row of cows with a little Cambrian sprayer and singing along loudly to 'Smells Like Teen Spirit' on the radio, only slightly out of tune. The cows shifted uneasily at the sight of a stranger and he looked up.

'Afternoon,' he said.

'Hello,' I said. 'Beer?'

'It would be rude not to. Let the row go, would you?'

I did, and the cows began to drift out. I removed a bottle of beer from each of my pockets and handed one over. 'Bugger. I forgot to bring a bottle opener.'

'Don't worry. Pass it here,' said Matt, whereupon he twisted the two tops together and opened them both.

'Slick,' I remarked.

'It's almost my only skill.' He handed one of the bottles back and took a long swig from his. 'Jose, you're a legend.'

'I know,' I said modestly. 'The cows look nice.'

'How would you know?'

I grinned at him, unoffended. 'Condescending prat.'

'They *are* looking pretty good. I've been getting all serious with feed budgets. What have you been up to today?'

'I've been highly productive,' I said. 'I've found somewhere to live and shorn the two most disgusting sheep on the planet.'

'Mildred and Edwin? I've been putting that off for months.'

'I hate to break it to you, but you're doing it next time. It nearly killed me.'

'I'm not surprised,' he said. 'Revolting overfed animals. Good effort.'

'They don't look very pretty,' I admitted.

'Who cares?' He reached up to shut the gate at the front of the bail and the first cow shuffled into position. 'It's nice to have you home, by the way.'

'Thanks.' And a large aching lump in my throat, which had in the last month or so begun to appear at the most embarrassing times it possibly could, decided that now was an appropriate time to turn up. I took a hurried mouthful of beer to dissolve it, which was not a well-thought-out move because I promptly choked and Matt had to pound me on the back. 'Th-thank you,' I spluttered.

'No problem.' He removed the cups from the front cow on the left and began deftly to slip them onto the udder of the front cow on the right, a great fat red thing that looked about a hundred years old. With his eyes fixed on the cow he asked casually, 'Been having a rough time, Jo?'

'A little bit.' I put down my bottle of beer and began to change over the next set of cups, the cow twitching indignantly at my unfamiliar hands. If I expanded on the subject I would probably cry, and that would just embarrass us both. 'I'm not really being any help, here; you'd be quicker without me.'

'Rubbish,' he said. 'Anyway, it's kind of nice to have you around.'

Chapter 3

I MET ONE of Cheryl's hypochondriacs on my first day at work, a pudgy fellow in his thirties who worked, he informed me, as caretaker at the high school – when the rod of fiery agony that was his spine allowed him to. He couldn't *bear* doing nothing; he was one of those blokes who would go to work even if he was at death's door rather than let people down.

On his way out he told Amber he would fix us up next week, that he was heading to the doctor's for the ACC form and he would drop it off at his next visit without fail. She smiled at him with chinless charm and said that would be lovely; there would be no problem at *all* with refunding him and in the meantime that would be forty dollars, please. Eftpos or cash, Ron? Now, you have a *lovely* day and make sure you take *really* good care of yourself.

'Plonker,' she said dispassionately as the door closed behind him.

'You have a gift,' I said with some awe. 'That was brilliant.'

'Nah,' she said. 'He's as thick as two short planks. Never done a day's work in his life.'

'I sort of gathered that.'

'I heard you say that you could tell he was normally really active, and that it was lucky because it would be so much better for his back than sitting still,' she said accusingly.

'Do you reckon it'll work?' I asked.

'Oh,' said Amber with slow-dawning comprehension. 'Were you doing that reverse psychology thing on him?'

'That was the idea, anyway.'

I MOVED INTO my new flat on the outskirts of town on Wednesday night, having purchased from Cheryl's sister-in-law a bed that *didn't*, unlike the one for sale at the Waimanu Second-Hand Palace, have suspicious dark patches in the middle of the mattress or a faint smell of urine. 'But you'd be putting a sheet over it!' the lady running the Palace had protested. 'And it's such a reasonable price, dear.' I declined to purchase it anyway and reflected that perhaps big-city living had made me a bit precious.

Cheryl's husband (his name is either Ian or Alan; I never can remember which) kindly brought my new bed around to the flat on the back of his ute and helped to manhandle it up the front steps and in through the sliding door to the sitting-room. 'Where to now?' he asked.

'Right down the hall to the end and then left,' I said.

'I hope you haven't bought any more furniture,' he remarked, propping the mattress against the wall. 'This isn't a bedroom, it's a cupboard.'

Sara, who was small and plump with a large bust only barely contained by her low-cut singlet, came and leant in the doorway as I dropped my two bags on the floor next to a little stack of towels and bedding lent to me by my mother. Everything else I owned was, hopefully, on its way between Australia and New Zealand by sea. Although according to my friend Stu, who had shipped his possessions from Britain to Melbourne a few years before, my belongings were more likely on a random wharf in Papua New Guinea, either uncovered in a tropical thunderstorm or being chewed by rats – or both.

'Is this all your stuff?' Sara asked, no doubt looking surreptitiously for tuba cases.

'Yep,' I said. 'It's a bit minimalist, isn't it?'

'I'm cooking tonight,' Sara said. 'Do you like chicken chow mein?'

Dinner turned out to be a stir fry made from bottled sauce, chicken pieces and frozen vegetables, served in a cereal bowl over boil-in-the-bag rice. There was nothing the matter with it, but it made me feel I had gone wrong somewhere. My ex-boyfriend, when he cooked, would whip up a squid-ink pasta and prawn dish and serve it with a glass of pinot gris on the deck. Yet here I was on someone's shabby couch watching *Shortland Street* with my bowl on my knee, while outside the boy racers drove laps around Waimanu's residential area.

Andy, the other flatmate, was in his early twenties and a stock agent. He said almost nothing over dinner and vanished into his room with the phone as soon as he had eaten, not to reappear for the rest of the evening. As Sara kept a firm grip on the remote, watched dire reality-TV shows and crunched boiled sweets steadily until she went to bed at ten, I completely saw his point.

AFTER THE FIRST fortnight, I was starting to get used to the way things were done – or not done, in Amber's case – at Waimanu Physiotherapy.

On Tuesday afternoon I was typing up the notes from my three-thirty appointment (a delicate blonde girl called Cilla who'd strained a muscle in her shoulder; she informed me proudly that she had fallen from the roof of a barn at a particularly good party) when someone put their head around the door and said, 'Josie?'

I turned in my seat to see a round-faced girl with dimples and glossy dark brown hair cut in a long fringe over her eyes. She wore a Waimanu High School uniform and swung a battered leather satchel.

'Kim!' I said. 'Crikey, you've got pretty. But don't you go to boarding school in Hamilton?'

'Not anymore,' said Matt's little sister with satisfaction. 'I told Mum that if she didn't let me come home I'd drop out and work at Woolworths. So I transferred last week.'

I grinned. Even when Kim was little her mother was no match for her at all. Of course, neither was anyone else.

I should know – I used to babysit her. 'Does this decision have anything to do with Aaron Henderson?'

'No,' she said. 'It's just that single-sex schools aren't good for social development.' She spoilt this speech somewhat by adding, 'How did you know that?'

'Matt mentioned you were seeing someone.' His actual words had been, 'The silly kid's taken up with some pimply little git,' but I am nothing if not tactful.

Kim came right into the room and closed the door behind her. 'So,' she whispered, 'what did you think of the lovely Cilla?'

'It would be unprofessional to discuss a client,' I said primly. 'How do you know her?'

'She's Matt's girlfriend.'

'Is she?' I asked, startled. Somehow I wouldn't have thought she was his type.

'Yeah,' said Kim. 'Needs his head read, if you ask me. She thinks she's the cat's pyjamas – she's all "I'm such a good keen farm chick and I can strain up a fence and I drive a wanky big ute". I'm sure he's only going out with her because he wanted to get laid.'

'Kim,' I demurred, 'you shouldn't say things like that. Matt's a big boy – he can go out with whoever he likes.'

'Hmm,' she said darkly. 'We'll see about that. Hey, Josie, those are wicked shorts.'

'Thank you.'

'And I like your shoes. I wish *I* was all tall and blonde and athletic.'

I smiled at her, flattered, although perfectly well aware

that I was being buttered up in case she needed something in the future – probably an alibi for spending time with the pimply git. Kim always was a charmingly manipulative little horror.

'The correct description,' I said, 'is "strapping wench". Great fat men come in with bad backs and say, "Cor, *you'll* be able to straighten me out." It's very depressing.'

In moments of wild optimism I hope I achieve a sort of Junoesque elegance; at other times I console myself with the thought that if people piss me off I can wrestle them to the ground and stamp on them until they beg for mercy.

'Matt thinks you're pretty,' Kim murmured, looking at me sideways through her lashes to see how I took this piece of news.

'Is that right?'

'But you only go out with doctors, don't you?'

'*What?*'

'That's what he said when I wanted to know why he didn't ask you out.'

'He was probably trying to shut you up,' I said. He'd better have been, anyway.

'You *would* go out with him, though, wouldn't you?'

'Well, no.'

Kim looked affronted. 'Why not?'

'Bloody hell, Kim, give me a chance to get over the last one!'

'But you've been best friends your whole lives,' she argued. 'It would be so perfect.'

'I think you might be getting a bit carried away there,'

I said. 'We used to fight like cats and dogs. And besides, the man's got a perfectly good girlfriend already.'

'You didn't fight that much, did you?'

I began to list Matt's many sins, counting them off on my fingers. 'He spilt my nail polish, he pulled the insides out of my Kylie Minogue tape, he pinged my bra straps – and then to add insult to injury he said I didn't even need a bra.' Which was quite true, at age thirteen, but he didn't need to *say* it. 'He ignored me any time he had a boy over to play with . . .'

Kim giggled. 'He said you nearly turned him into a eunuch once,' she said.

'Not on purpose,' I protested.

'How do you accidentally kick someone in the balls?'

'It *was* an accident,' I insisted. 'That's my story, and I'm sticking to it. Anyway, he started it.'

Amber knocked on the door then opened it. 'Your four o'clock's here,' she said.

'Do you need a lift?' I asked Kim.

'No, I've got Mum's car. Nice to have you home, Josie.' She slung her satchel up onto her shoulder and sauntered out of the room.

I'm afraid that my next appointment and his stiff neck may not have received my complete and undivided professional attention. I was otherwise occupied with wondering just what on earth Matt King felt he had in common with that little blonde Barbie doll. Good luck to him, obviously, but shouldn't he be going for someone a bit more like – like –

Me, suggested a small internal voice.

No. *No!*

Poor Ralph Godwin let a small hiss escape between his teeth, and I pulled my mind guiltily back to his trapezius muscle, which was being massaged with excessive vigour.

Chapter 4

'HOW'S WORK?' ASKED my mother as my first month drew to a close.

'Fine,' I said, tucking the phone between ear and shoulder so as to be able to file my nails while I talked. 'It's a bit of a change working by myself, but I can call the girls at the hospital if I want to talk shop.'

Cheryl had finally produced her baby a fortnight ago. She had been almost entirely sleepless ever since, her mother-in-law had come for a long visit to advise her on correct baby-rearing, and the poor girl was in no state to discuss tricky cases.

'And your flat?'

I sighed. 'Oh, it's alright. But if my furniture ever arrives I think I'll go and look for something else. Sara follows me round the house switching off lights and making sure I only boil enough water for one cup of tea at a time.'

'How very environmentally friendly of her,' said Mum.

'Last night I left my mobile phone charging in the living room and she turned it off at the wall so it went flat about half an hour after I left home.'

'Ah, that explains it. Graeme rang us this afternoon asking how to get hold of you. He said your mobile kept going through to voicemail. I gave him your home number – you don't mind, do you?'

'No,' I said sadly, wondering what he wanted. These days my ex-boyfriend only rang me when something expensive happened – the rates were due or the bathroom ceiling had developed an ominous crack. 'How are the goats?'

'Oh, they're doing well,' said Mum. 'We had a minor panic yesterday when the tractor broke down, but luckily it was just a split hose.'

'What are you going to do when it finally blows up?' I enquired.

'Goodness only knows. Perhaps I could hire myself out as an escort.'

'I don't think I want my mother lurking on street corners in a miniskirt and thigh-high boots. I'll buy you a new tractor.'

'We cannot let our only daughter finance us. It's supposed to be the other way round.'

'That's okay,' I assured her. 'I am confidently expecting to inherit a farm worth millions in another fifty years.'

'Well, that's a thought,' said Mum. 'And it may be considerably sooner if your father continues the way he's going.'

'What's wrong with him?'

'He's been playing the guitar in bed is what's wrong with him,' she said grimly. 'If I hear "Rhinestone Cowboy" one more time I'll do him a serious injury.'

THAT EVENING I temporarily escaped the reality-TV shows and the struggle for sufficient light to read by at home and went to have tea with my old schoolfriend Clare. She married a solicitor from Hamilton five years ago, brought him back home and has been producing children steadily ever since.

Brett and Clare live on several acres on the edge of town. They have fancy chickens and ducks, pigs, alpacas and miniature ponies and a malevolent goat called Alfred. The children are all white-blond with huge blue eyes and pink-and-white complexions, and they're fairly uphill work.

When I arrived the two big boys were rolling together across the lawn, apparently trying to strangle each other. It looked like a reasonably even fight so I didn't intervene, but I did pause by the back step where two-year-old Lucy was carefully pulling up a whole row of newly planted pansies by the roots. 'Hey, Luce, that's probably not the best plan,' I said. 'Let's put them back in.'

Lucy narrowed her beautiful eyes at me and pushed back her curls with a grimy hand. 'No,' she said flatly.

'I think we'd better,' I told her. 'If you pull up the plants they won't grow and have pretty flowers.'

'Nononononono! Go 'way!'

Clare came to the door looking warm and mildly harassed. 'Lucy,' she said without any real hope, 'don't pull up my flowers. Say hello to Josie.'

Lucy threw herself to the ground and began to beat her head on the path. I took a step forward in alarm but Clare said wearily, 'Leave her. Apparently we just have to ignore her and she'll grow out of it.'

'Okay,' I said doubtfully, crouching down to poke the baby pansies back into the soil.

'Oh, leave them,' said Clare. 'I don't know why I bothered. Michael! Charlie! Please stop trying to gouge each other's eyes out – oh, never mind. Come in, Josie, and tell me all your news.'

Clare's is a nice house, or at least it looks like it was once. But the floor was four inches deep in crappy plastic toys and someone had made a solid attempt at ripping the paper off the walls up to a height of about three feet. A somewhat wild-eyed kitten observed us from the top of the microwave and the kitchen bench was entirely hidden under piles of dirty dishes.

'Have a seat,' said Clare. 'Not that one! Charlie had a little accident this afternoon. Here . . .' She lifted a pile of old newspapers and put them on the table, where they slid gently to the floor. 'Leave it,' she said. 'Honestly. Wine?'

'Yes, please,' I said, producing a bottle. 'I hope this stuff's okay – I bought it because the label was familiar and then had a horrible feeling it was familiar because we tried it once before and it tasted like turps.'

'Who cares?' said Clare. 'As long as it's alcoholic. How are you, anyway?'

'Good.' I sat at the table and began to clear enough space for two wine glasses. It was a still, golden evening and the bush-clad ranges out the French doors looked close enough to touch. They made a lovely backdrop to the two little boys, who were now digging a hole in the middle of the lawn. We couldn't see Lucy but she was still howling with impressive stamina. 'How was the kindergarten picnic?'

'Oh, it was fine,' said Clare. 'Michael threw up in the car and Lucy bit Maureen Stacey's little boy and got put in the naughty corner, but it was fine. God, this is good wine.'

'That's a relief.'

'Are you missing the bright city lights?'

'Nope,' I said. 'When you live in the city you talk lots about the restaurants and plays you could go to, and you still end up picking up takeaways on the way home and watching TV.'

'Still,' she said, 'it must be nice to be able to do it if you want to. I never appreciated how free I was before I had children. These days it's a major mission to go and buy something to wear.'

'You haven't resorted to Heather Anne's, have you?'

'Not quite,' said Clare glumly. 'The Warehouse. And I got a lovely pair of jeans at Farmlands last week.'

Michael appeared in the doorway, breathing heavily. 'I want a sandwich,' he announced.

'It's nearly tea time,' said his mother.

'Want a *sandwich*!' He kicked the white-painted door-frame with a muddy gumboot. 'Mum! Sandwich! Mum! Sandwich! *Mum!*'

'For the love of Christ,' said Clare savagely, getting to her feet. 'Alright! You'd better take one to your brother too.'

'He's done a poo in his pants,' Michael informed her gleefully. 'It's going down his leg.'

'Bloody marvellous,' said Clare.

'I'll do the sandwich if you do the poo,' I offered.

'Thanks.'

I made Michael a peanut butter sandwich, which he looked at in disgust because I had cut it into squares rather than triangles. I cut the squares diagonally across, and he rejected it again because the triangles were too small. Charlie sat on his mother's knee and grizzled steadily, holding up a book between Clare and me so we couldn't see one another. Lucy fell down the steps and grazed her knee – though you'd have thought her leg had been severed – and at bedtime Clare had to go and lie down with each of them in turn until they fell asleep.

'The joys of parenthood,' said Brett sourly, slumped on the couch with his eyes closed. Clare had been gone for three-quarters of an hour and I was beginning to wonder if she would come back at all. 'We haven't had a conversation for four years.'

'How on earth did you manage to conceive the last couple?' I asked.

'Can't remember. Must have met in the hall once or

twice, I suppose.' He opened his eyes and grinned at me – he has a particularly nice grin. 'Ah well, it'll come right in another fifteen years or so.'

'And just think – never seeing each other stops things from growing stale. It must really keep the romance and mystery alive.'

'Much easier than having an affair, I suppose,' he said, then abruptly sat up. 'Shit, I'm sorry!'

'That's okay,' I said. 'Honestly, Brett, stop looking so appalled.'

I GOT HOME at about nine to find Andy in the kitchen making himself a vegemite and honey sandwich. As you do. He raised his chin at me in greeting and muttered, 'Some bloke rang for you before.'

'Graeme, he said his name was,' Sara called helpfully, hoisting herself off the couch (it was the ad break). 'He wants you to call him back urgently.'

'Thanks.' I picked up the kettle to fill it, feeling a need for strong coffee before the fun-filled conversation to come.

'Are you filling it from the *hot tap*?' Sara demanded, horrified. 'That's such a waste of power!'

Andy met my eyes for a second in silent but eloquent sympathy, then turned and mooched out of the kitchen. Sara pulled the kettle from my nerveless grasp, tipped the hot water it contained down the sink and turned on the cold tap. I briefly considered bashing her to death with the soup ladle before reluctantly deciding that, as satisfying as that would be, it probably wasn't worth spending the next thirty years in prison. Instead I picked up the phone and went down the hall to my tiny room, vindictively switching on every light as I went.

Chapter 5

'**G**ET OUT OF it!' I shouted.

The dogs obeyed but the pig paid no attention whatsoever, instead pushing between my legs and leaning lovingly against the inside of my right knee. I scratched him between the ears and he closed his little piggy eyes, giving soft grunts of pleasure. He really was an animal of immense charm.

'Aunty Rose?' I called, putting my head around the open kitchen door.

'Out here, sweet pea.'

I wandered through the house, swinging a plastic bag from one wrist, and found her lying limply in a deckchair on the veranda. 'Hello,' I said, bending to kiss her cheek. 'I brought you some of Mum's new batch of cheese.'

'How lovely. I can't get up; I'm far too lazy. How about fetching us both a drink to have with it?'

I went to the kitchen and returned with two glasses of riesling, a knife for the cheese and an open packet of crackers unearthed from behind the bread bin. Aunty Rose accepted her wine with a sigh and lay back in her chair. 'I don't know how old those crackers are,' she said.

'Never mind. If they're stale Percy will eat them.' The pig had trotted round the outside of the house and was squatting at the foot of the steps, panting gently in the afternoon sun. 'How are you?'

'Shattered,' said Rose, taking a long appreciative drink from her glass.

'Why?'

'No idea,' she said. 'Old age, I expect. Look at the late sunlight catching the thistledown – isn't that lovely?'

I looked over the fence at the silver drift of an acre or so of Californian thistle seed head. 'It is, but I don't know if Matt would agree with you. Are you feeling brave enough to try the cheese?'

'Why not,' she said.

I cut us each a modest wedge and handed one over. We both sniffed warily – it was fairly pungent stuff – and then took a cautious bite.

'*Christ!*' said Aunty Rose, spraying cracker crumbs before hurling the rest of her portion over the veranda railing and gulping a large mouthful of wine, which she swilled around in her mouth. I responded with even less class, leaping to my feet and spitting the lot into a handy flowerbed, where Percy nosed after it with interest.

'Here you go, mate,' I said, unwrapping the rest of the round and tossing it to him. 'Bloody hell.'

'Trying to poison an old woman,' said Rose, shaking

her head. 'In my day the younger generation had a little more respect for their elders. I'm not at all sure you should have given that to Percy, either – he'll probably turn up his toes.'

'Never,' I said. 'He's made of sterner stuff. But Mum and Dad can't sell that at the farmers' market. They'll be run out of town.'

'They must have done it on purpose. What did you do to make your parents hate you so much?'

I shook my head. 'I don't know. I try to be a good daughter, honestly.'

A long and sleepy silence fell, while we drank our wine and lazily batted away the wasps.

'Blasted wasps,' Aunty Rose muttered. 'They're in the plum tree. I should pick them, but it's just too hard.'

I frowned at that. Rose is an absolutely fanatical harvester of nature's bounty – she would no sooner waste a crop than have a wild affair with a teenage Hispanic back-up dancer. 'Are you feeling alright?' I asked.

'Just tired.'

'But it's not like you to feel tired.'

She sighed. 'True. I *have* been thinking of going to see Dr Milne one of these days. Maybe I'm low in iron or something.' She smiled. 'Or maybe I just need more wine – be an angel and pour me another glass, would you?'

ON A STICKY afternoon, more like February than April, Amber handed me a file with a red dot inside.

Hypochondriac or creep? I wondered, ushering in my three o'clock appointment. 'Hi, I'm Jo Donnelly. What can I do for you today?'

'Neville,' said my new patient, extending a warm damp hand and clasping mine for rather longer than strictly necessary. 'Well, well. Little Josie Donnelly. Haven't you blossomed?'

There is no appropriate response to a comment like that, so I didn't try. 'What's the problem?' I asked.

'I did something to my leg last week at squash, and it's getting worse not better.'

'Is it worse in the morning, or after you've been up and about on it?'

'Sore in the morning, and then gets worse.' He looked at me mournfully.

'That's no good,' I said. 'Now, have you been in before? I'll just bring your history up on the screen.'

'Wharfe,' he told me. 'Neville Wharfe, Taylor's Block Road.' I turned briefly to look him up on the computer, and turned back to see him shedding his trousers to reveal thin little legs with knobbly knees. 'It's actually more in the groin, my dear. Just here. Just feel how tight it is.'

He left twenty minutes later a disappointed man – I had given him a selection of exercises and declined to massage his inner thigh. I opened the windows to dispel the lingering scent of his cologne (evidently a more-is-better man) and went out to talk to Amber.

'Bob McIntosh is coming in,' she informed me with gloomy relish.

41

'Oh, crap,' I said. Bob was a painfully shy man in his late forties with swimmy eyes, breath that could fell an ox and enormous pores. He made what must have been a precarious living by driving around the countryside peddling dodgy cowshed detergents and stock drenches – Dad used to hide behind a hedge every time his little truck came up the drive. Unfortunately he'd taken one look at me and decided I was a likely-looking lass, possibly wife material. And despite his natural bashfulness, having made this weighty decision he was not to be deterred from his courtship. 'Couldn't you have told him we're booked up?'

'I did that last time,' she pointed out.

'Well then, that I've got leprosy or bubonic plague or something, and I can't see any clients?'

She giggled and shook her head.

I HAD JUST got rid of Bob (shooting pains in his back and tickets to a jazz concert in Hamilton he knew I'd be interested in – how about making a night of it and having dinner at the Cossie Club first?) when Kim ambled in.

'Hey, Amber,' she said. 'Hey, Jo. Got any biscuits? I'm starving.'

Within seconds she'd found a packet of chocolate afghans in the tiny kitchen. She threw herself into the single battered armchair and smiled at me happily. I made the three of us a cup of tea and took Amber's out to the front desk, where instead of catching up with filing she was giving herself a painstaking French manicure with correction fluid.

'Do you need a lift home?' I asked Kim as I handed her a cup. The bus would have left half an hour ago, I knew.

'Nah,' she said. 'Matt's in town – he said he'd come and get me when he's finished his errands.'

'What a nice brother,' I said.

'I don't know about that,' said Kim, taking another biscuit and examining it suspiciously from every angle. 'He decided to give me a lecture about safe sex the other day.'

I nearly choked on my biscuit, momentarily overcome by the vision of Matt in this stern older-brotherly role. Taking a hasty sip of tea, I tried to assume a suitably mirth-free expression.

'I'm not having sex with anyone, anyway,' she continued. Then, looking at me through her eyelashes, she added provocatively, 'Yet.'

'Are you considering it?' I enquired. Cripes, she was only a baby.

'Don't know,' said Kim. 'Yeah, maybe. I'm not in love with Aaron or anything, but it'd be good practice. And yes, I know all about contraception.'

'Fair enough,' I said mildly. 'But in my experience – which probably isn't worth much – having sex with someone you're not particularly attracted to is a pretty big let-down. It's just sort of messy and embarrassing, and you end up feeling a bit depressed about the whole thing.'

'Oh,' said Kim thoughtfully.

'Not that you should listen to me, with my brilliant history of relationships,' I added, smiling at her. 'At this point it looks like I'm going to have to choose between Bob McIntosh or becoming an eccentric spinster with fourteen cats.'

'Spinster,' she said. 'Definitely spinster.'

'Yeah, that's what I thought.'

'Or –' she raised her voice as we heard the creak of the outside door, and then her brother's slow voice in counterpoint to Amber's nasal tones – 'you could just settle for Matt.'

'There's just one insurmountable problem with that,' I told her.

'Cilla's not insurmountable,' Kim protested audibly as her brother appeared in the kitchen doorway. She smiled at him with great charm. 'Hey, bro. Biscuit?'

'No, thanks.' He glared at her. 'Are you ready to go? Hi, Jose.'

'I haven't finished my cup of tea,' said Kim. 'So, Josie, what's wrong with Matt? Apart from being a complete pain in the arse, of course.'

'It's his name,' I said gravely.

'Fair enough. Matthew *is* a bit gay, I suppose.'

'Matthew I could live with, but just imagine being called Jo King.'

Matt's lips twitched. 'You could always keep your own name after we got married,' he offered. 'I'm not unreasonable.'

'Certainly not,' I said haughtily. 'I'm very traditional. So you see it's impossible. And anyway, as you know, I'm only interested in doctors.'

'Which one are you gunning for?' he asked, looking at his sister with even more malevolence. 'Milne or Oliver?'

Waimanu had two male doctors, one pushing sixty and the other a strong contender for the title of Sweatiest Man Alive.

'Doesn't matter,' I said. 'I'm not fussy. Right, Kim, get up. I've got someone to see at four.'

Chapter 6

'I DON'T SUPPOSE,' said somebody in a voice of immense softness and sweetness – the kind of voice associated with the presenters of educational TV shows for preschoolers – 'that Josie would be available?'

'Jo!' called Amber flatly. Relations between the two of us had become somewhat tense today, after I'd suggested that more time doing work and less time bidding on clothes on Trade Me would be desirable.

I put down the catalogue I had been perusing and went out the front. 'Hello, Mrs King.'

Matt and Kim's mother shuddered delicately. 'Oh, please don't call me Mrs King, Josie dear. It makes me feel so stern and old. Hazel, please.' She held out both hands and clasped mine tenderly. 'How *are* you, my dear?' Hazel was utterly unlike her sister; she was small and slight and indecisive, with a soft voice that tended to trail off at the end of every sentence as if she lacked the strength to complete it.

'Very well, thank you. How are you?'

'Getting by,' she said with a sigh. 'I've been meaning to pop in – my baby never stops talking about you.'

'How alarming,' I said.

'Nothing but the highest praise,' Hazel assured me. 'You're obviously a wonderful influence. But make sure you send that little monkey away if she annoys you, won't you?'

'She doesn't. She's good fun.'

Kim's mother looked somewhat doubtful. 'You're very sweet,' she said. 'Now, Josie, when can you come and have dinner with us?'

'Whenever you like. My social life is not terribly exciting just at the moment.'

'Well, after what you've been through you need a little time to lick your wounds,' she said.

I must have looked a little disconcerted at this, because she added, 'Rose told me about your . . . partner. That's the right word, isn't it?'

Personally I would have chosen another word, but wonderful influences probably shouldn't use that sort of language.

'How about Friday?' she said.

ACCORDINGLY, ON FRIDAY night at half past six I left Andy lying on the couch eating chips to fortify his inner man before taking his girlfriend out for tea (with all the kitchen and sitting-room lights on, since Sara had gone away for the weekend), and drove up the valley.

The King house was an unattractive place built of white

concrete bricks, with tinted windows and nasty aluminium joinery, surrounded by hot little garden beds. These were currently filled with alternate red and purple petunias and had carefully clipped yellow conifers at the corners.

Rose pulled up just behind me in her elderly Ford Falcon. 'Hideous, isn't it?' she murmured, looking at the garden before passing me a bottle of port and heaving herself out of the car.

'Yep,' I agreed. 'Whose ute is that?'

Rose looked at the great silver double-cab beast in front of the garage. 'Cilla's, I believe.'

'Ah.'

'Have you met her?' she asked.

'Yes,' I said, 'she's come into work a couple of times with a sore shoulder. She's pretty, isn't she?'

'I suppose so,' said Rose.

'Don't you like her?' I asked, curious. One of Aunty Rose's best characteristics had always been her refusal to say anything negative about our romantic partners, so this lack of warmth was somewhat unusual.

'I don't know anything about the girl,' she said and, having put me in my place, walked briskly up the path to the back door.

As I followed Rose up the hall, peals of silvery laughter sounded from the kitchen, as if two dainty elfin maidens were sharing a dainty elfin joke. 'Good evening, Hazel,' said Aunty Rose, thumping her bottle of port down on the counter. 'Hello, Cilla.'

'Rosie and Josie,' said Hazel gaily. 'Angels, you

shouldn't have.' She accepted the brown paper parcel I handed her and dropped a butterfly kiss on my cheek. 'Ooh, cheeses. Lovely.'

'*Josephine!*' said Aunty Rose.

'From the supermarket,' I told her.

'Thank heaven for that.'

'Have you two girls met?' Hazel enquired, looking from me to Cilla.

'We have,' I said. 'Hi, Cilla. How's the shoulder?'

'Getting better,' said Cilla. She was wearing a powder-blue shirt with the collar turned up and a pair of close-fitting moleskin trousers, pearl drops in her ears and a quantity of very shiny lip gloss. Pointedly rural, prettily feminine, and faintly – or not so faintly – private school. 'Hazel, give me a job.'

'Why don't you go and help Matthew with the barbecue?' said Hazel. And as Cilla vanished through the sliding door and around the side of the house she observed, 'Such a sweet girl. Her parents are charming people – they own that property north of town with the lovely avenue of flowering cherries. I'm so pleased that Matthew has found someone who shares his interests.'

Aunty Rose looked ever so slightly incredulous. 'War documentaries and eating mince pies?' she asked.

'The farm and the cows,' said Hazel reprovingly. 'I hardly think mince pies rank as a leisure activity, do you?'

'He *is* a bit of a pie connoisseur,' I said, but on seeing Hazel's stiffening expression changed the subject. 'Where's Kim?'

'Here,' said Kim, appearing in the doorway wearing an oversized T-shirt and minuscule shorts.

'Oh, sweetie, put some clothes on,' her mother implored.

'I have,' said Kim, dangerous patience in her voice.

'Lucky you've got nice legs,' I told her.

'Thank you. Where's little Miss I-can-fix-a-water-leak-with-only-my-nail-file?'

'Kimmy!' Hazel wailed. Rose and I glanced at one another and began simultaneously to laugh. 'You shouldn't *encourage* her!' she said to us.

'True,' said Aunty Rose, wiping her eyes. 'Kim, be nice. You can help me set the table.'

'THIS LOOKS DELICIOUS,' said Cilla politely as we took our seats at a table set under the large and beetle-y elm tree on the back lawn.

Kim lounged in her chair, looking as if she was about to say something unpleasant in response to this inoffensive comment. I kicked her under the table.

'What was that for, Josie?' she asked sweetly. 'Did you kick me for any special reason? Were you trying to convey anything in particular?'

'No,' I told her. 'Random muscle spasm. I'm terribly sorry.'

Matt met my eye with fleeting but sincere gratitude across the table. 'I believe,' he said, 'that muscle spasms are a common problem once you get to thirty.'

My birthday had been a week ago – I'd received a book on container-gardening from my mother, an eggshell-blue china jug from Aunty Rose, a phone call from Grandma and emails from various friends. A vague plan to have a combined birthday party with my friend Chrissie had come to nothing seeing as: a) I had left the country, and b) she'd started sleeping with my boyfriend.

'Yes,' I agreed. 'It's all downhill from here. You'd better cherish your last eight months.'

'Foolish children,' said Rose. 'You'll look back in another ten years and realise you were still mere spring chickens at thirty.'

'If that's supposed to cheer me up, it doesn't,' I told her.

'Well, if you're determined to be miserable, go right ahead.'

'Thank you. I will.'

'Now, Josie, you mustn't worry,' said Hazel. 'You're certainly not too old to find someone really lovely and have a family of your own.'

'My aunt had her first baby at thirty-eight,' Cilla added helpfully.

These comforting words nearly had me crawling sobbing under the table – there is nothing more depressing than receiving condolences over something you've resolved firmly not to worry about.

Matt grinned, not unsympathetically, and reached across the table to refill my wine glass to the very top.

AFTER DINNER KIM dragged out a selection of old photo albums. 'I thought you might like to see some pictures of Matt,' she said, plonking down beside Cilla on the sofa.

Looking somewhat surprised at this apparently unprecedented display of friendliness, Cilla smiled. She really was a very pretty girl. 'I'd like that,' she said.

'It'll give you some idea of what your children will look like,' said Kim. 'Just kidding.' She flicked rapidly through the pages. 'Bloody hell, Mum, that's the most hideous outfit I've ever seen!'

I leant over the back of the sofa to look. Said picture was of an extremely pregnant Hazel dressed in a voluminous orange smock, with her hair in a long plait down her back. She looked very young – but then, of course, she had been. She was nineteen when Matt was born.

'Fashions change,' Rose said. 'In twenty years you might even look back at those shorts and wonder what possessed you.'

'There's Matt,' said Kim, pointing at a plump infant with a disturbingly vacant expression sitting on his father's knee.

'You've improved,' Cilla murmured, looking over at Matt with a fetching grin. 'Is that your dad?'

'Yep,' he said. 'I think his shorts were even shorter than Kim's.'

'You're very like him.'

'Here we are,' said Kim. 'Matt on the tractor, Matt in the bath, Matt in the bath again, Matt with no trousers on . . .'

'That's right,' Rose put in from the armchair across the room. 'Couldn't keep clothes on the child. We used to find little pairs of pants all over the farm.'

Kim turned the page. 'Matt and Josie *both* in the bath,' she said.

The picture must have been taken at Rose's because I recognised the pink tiles on the bathroom wall. My fringe had apparently been cut by my mother with her eyes shut and I was busily wresting a rubber duck from Matt's fat little hands. His face was purple and his mouth open in a roar of fury.

'We were the ugliest children in the country,' said Matt.

'You were *not*,' said his mother. 'You were beautiful.'

'She's your mother; she's obliged to think that,' I said.

Rose laughed. 'Somewhere there should be that picture of Matthew you entered in a baby contest, Hazel. I think he's lying on a sheepskin.'

'Here's one,' said Kim. 'With no hair, in a little pair of green dungarees.'

'That's it,' said Rose. 'He didn't make it past the first round.'

'I'm not at all surprised,' I said. 'He looks like a fat white grub.'

My childhood friend gave me a really first-class dead arm in response to this comment.

'Ow-w!' I made a grab for his ear, but missed.

'Stop it!' said Hazel sharply. 'Not in my living room.'

'Yes, what will Cilla think?' said Kim, turning another page. 'Did you guys *ever* wear trousers?' She was looking

53

at two small people dressed only in T-shirts and gumboots bent with rapt interest over something on the lawn, bottoms gleaming in the sun.

'Apparently not,' Matt said.

'Well, it was the eighties,' I pointed out. 'No farmer had any money. Dad used to make us eat rabbit and duck once a week to save money.'

'God, that's right,' said Matt. 'Your mother used to make duck chow mein.'

'It was revolting,' I said nostalgically.

'This can't be very interesting for Cilla,' Hazel protested.

'It's fine,' said Cilla politely, though her smile looked a little fixed.

'There's nothing worse than reminiscences about things you weren't there for,' I said. 'Everyone else is in gales of laughter and you have to sit there and pretend to be interested in some barbecue ten years ago where Uncle Phil undercooked the chicken and gave everyone food poisoning.'

'True,' agreed Matt, giving Cilla's shoulder a gentle squeeze. 'Right, anyone want a hot drink?'

WE ALL LEFT together. (Matt, despite his mother's pleading, had declined to move back into the family home on his return from Europe. He lived next door, in the worker's cottage below the cowshed, and I'm sure that felt quite close enough.) We were accompanied out to our cars by

Kim who, in a lightning change of mood, had decided to play the role of Most Charming Hostess.

'Are you alright to drive?' Matt asked his girlfriend as she opened the door of her enormous silver ute.

'Nice try, Matthew,' she said, climbing in. Crampons would probably have helped her with the ascent. 'Lovely evening, everyone. Thanks.'

We murmured polite goodbyes, and Matt waved as he got in the passenger seat. 'Hey, Aunty Rose,' he said, 'I'll come and fix that hole in the fence tomorrow if you'll give me lunch.'

'It's a deal,' his aunt said promptly.

Cilla started the ute with a roar, gunned it twice and sped down the driveway in a little shower of gravel.

'*What*,' said Kim, 'is he thinking?'

'I don't know why you've got it in for the poor girl, she's perfectly nice,' I said, though to be honest I wasn't quite convinced that she was.

'No she's not,' said Kim flatly. 'She only likes him because he's a farmer. She thinks he makes a – a good accessory.'

'He's a big boy,' said Rose. 'He can look after himself.'

Kim sighed. 'But he's stuffing everything up. Josie'll meet someone else if he doesn't stop mucking around.'

'Just *stop* it, Kim!' I said sharply. 'You're making everything uncomfortable and embarrassing, and – and Matt's one of my best friends, and I'd like it to stay that way.'

'Sorry,' muttered Kim.

'The trouble, Kimlet, is that you're going about it in

completely the wrong way,' said Aunty Rose, opening the door of her car. 'If you keep insisting that they were made for each other the silly twits will both just dig their toes in and refuse point blank to admit it, even though you'd think it would be perfectly obvious to anyone with half a brain.'

'Oh, for Christ's *sake*!' I said furiously, storming across the gravel to my car, throwing myself into the driver's seat and shoving it into gear. This would have made for a much more dramatic exit if I hadn't found third gear instead of first and promptly stalled.

❧

I WAS STILL good and mad when I got back to the flat, and I stamped up the steps to the back door. The kitchen and sitting-room lights were still on – Andy really was rebelling to have gone out for the night without switching them off. But when I went into the kitchen he was still there, sitting at the table surrounded by empty beer bottles with his laptop in front of him. It was only nine-thirty, and the restaurant he'd booked for this evening (a terribly upmarket place attached to a boutique hunting lodge that mostly attracted overweight American businessmen who saw no shame in shooting old tame stags in a paddock) was a good forty-minute drive away.

'Didn't you go out for dinner after all?' I asked. Aunty Rose would have approved of my choice of words – although pleasing Aunty Rose wasn't high on my list of priorities just at that moment.

'Nope,' said Andy, then he tipped half a bottle of

Speight's down his throat, pushed his chair back and stood up. 'How was your night?'

'Crap.'

'Beer?' he asked on his way to the fridge, weaving slightly.

'Why not?' I said, taking the bottle he handed me and leaning back against the bench. 'So, your night was crap too?'

'Yep,' said Andy. He twisted the cap off his beer bottle and took a grimly determined swig – the action of a man who wishes to get legless in the shortest possible space of time.

I looked at him thoughtfully, wondering whether or not to enquire further. He might like to tell someone about it, or he might be pissed off by a flatmate he barely knew poking her nose into his private affairs. *Ah, stuff it*, I thought. 'What's up?'

'Bronwyn thinks we should take a break. What did she say? "It's not you, it's me." And then: "I still love you, I'm just not *in* love with you."'

'Bugger,' I said.

'She could at least have said something original,' said Andy morosely, downing the rest of his beer and squinting into the empty bottle in a slightly puzzled fashion, as though he couldn't understand how it had reached that state.

'A poor effort,' I agreed. 'You're not writing her a drunken email, are you?' Remembering in the morning that you've sent someone an ungrammatical tirade declaring your undying love or rubbishing their bedroom prowess (or possibly both) is very disheartening.

'Nah, just updating my Facebook status.' He sat down in front of his laptop again and resumed typing laboriously with his right index finger. 'Single. There.' He blinked owlishly at the screen.

I took a large mouthful of beer. 'Want to see what *I* found on Facebook today?' I asked.

'Okay.'

'Then shove over,' I said and pulled up another kitchen chair beside him. 'All done?'

'Yeah.'

I logged out of his profile and into my own. 'Now, where is it? Ah. Here.' I scrolled down to find a comment posted yesterday by Chrissie de Villiers. The profile picture beside the comment showed Chrissie peeping coyly up through a screen of streaky blonde hair, all smoky eyeliner and sharply defined cheekbones.

Thanks so much for all the birthday wishes, everyone. Wonderful weekend, wonderful party, wonderful friends, wonderful man . . . Hangover not quite so wonderful. Hard to come back down to earth after being spoilt like that.

'Read it?' I asked.

'Um, yeah,' said Andy.

'But wait, there's more.' I clicked on the new photos Chrissie had posted, in which happy, laughing people with glasses in hand squinted at the camera in the bright sunlight while leaning back in their chairs, wearing silly hats and becoming progressively more flushed of face and glazed of eye as the evening wore on.

'Friends of yours?' Andy was clearly wondering why I was inflicting pictures of drunken revellers on him in his darkest hour.

'Yeah,' I said. 'And that's my house – well, mostly the bank's house, but I pay half the mortgage. And those are all my friends, and that's my ex-boyfriend, and *that's* my ex–best friend snuggling up to him. And that was supposed to be a combined birthday party for both her and me, except that I came home from work not long ago and found them having sex in an armchair.' My favourite armchair, too, just to add insult to injury.

'That sucks,' said Andy solemnly.

'That's what I thought,' I said and logged out of Facebook with a vicious click of the mouse. 'You know what?'

'What?'

'I think we need something more serious than beer. What've we got?'

Chapter 7

I WOKE UP horribly early the next morning to the sound of some sadistic bastard operating an electric hedge-trimmer just outside the window. I lay for a while hoping this prat would be struck by lightning or washed away in a bizarre flash flood. Neither happened, so I groaned and rolled out of bed.

My skull had shrunk so that my brain was in imminent danger of being squeezed out of my ears, my teeth seemed to be covered in wool and my tongue was far too big for my mouth. I staggered up the hall to the kitchen and gulped down about two litres of water before looking dully at the empty bottles strewn across the table. Andy and I had decided, I seemed to recall, that gin mixed with chocolate milk was delicious, and when we ran out of this gourmet concoction we had opened the coconut liqueur Andy had discovered in the recesses of the cupboard above the microwave.

On my way back from the bathroom I peeped around

Andy's door, just in case he was lying unconscious in a pool of vomit. The smell of his room made me recoil hastily; the fug of beer fumes laced with old sock was so thick you could have cut blocks out of it with a spade.

'Are you alive?' I called from the safety of the hall.

'Unnghhh,' came the answer.

'Great stuff.' I left the door wide open in the hope that he might get some fresher, oxygen-containing air and went back down the hall.

I really just wanted to crawl back into bed, but I had promised to go to the beach with Clare and her kids so I swallowed two Panadol and made myself a scrambled-egg sandwich instead. Scrambled-egg sandwiches on soft brown bread were Chrissie's sure-fire hangover cure, and even though I wished Chrissie would develop some horrible, disfiguring face fungus, denying the effectiveness of the sandwich would have been childish. I put on my sunglasses and took my sandwich out to eat on the back step, ruing my stupidity. What kind of moron gets rotten drunk the night before accompanying three small children to the beach for the day?

Luckily, by the time Clare picked me up at nine I'd improved to the stage of mere mild seediness. Stopping in the driveway she leant on the horn, prompting a string of incoherent curses to issue from Andy's room.

The three children were buckled into a row of car seats in the back, each one clutching a sandwich and looking sticky around the edges. 'Aunty Jo!' Charlie crowed.

'Good morning, guys,' I said cheerily.

Lucy threw her sandwich at me in response and then, realising she no longer had it to eat, began to roar.

It took us an hour to get to the beach, along a beautiful road that winds its way through the gorge, crossing and recrossing the Waimanu River. Unfortunately, Michael began to throw up about ten minutes into the trip. Clare had clearly anticipated this possibility and had thoughtfully covered him with a towel and given him a basin. It was my job to empty this basin as it was filled, and by the time we arrived I'd relapsed from mildly seedy to quite unwell.

'Are you okay, Jo?' Clare asked as she pulled a mountain buggy from the boot and unfolded it.

'I'm not sure.' I took a deep breath and turned to release a wildly struggling Charlie from his car seat.

It was a lovely beach with an empty sweep of fine black sand stretching from the river mouth down the coast to a jumble of boulders at the foot of a cliff. There were interesting rock pools and piles of driftwood, and the wet sand was silky beneath our bare feet. The boys immediately rushed knee-deep into the sea, but Lucy decided that sand was nearly as terrifying as water and huddled fearfully in her stroller, shrieking as the little waves came in to break with a soft hiss of foam.

Clare bent to fish through a bag of supplies slung under the stroller, found a little box of raisins and passed it to Lucy. She stopped sobbing and began to extract raisins from the box with the delicate precision of a brain surgeon, pushing them through a little gap between the seat and the frame of the mountain buggy.

'Oh well, at least it's keeping her busy,' Clare said wearily.

'What's Brett up to today?' I asked.

'When we left he was looking up vasectomies on the internet.'

'Well,' I said, 'three's a pretty good effort.'

'Yeah.'

We wandered along the smooth firm black sand after the boys, who were chasing one another along the very edge of the breakers with exuberant cries. They looked the epitome of happy, healthy children enjoying themselves in the fresh air, not eating preservative-filled foods or watching mind-numbing TV programs. A sight to gladden the heart of any parent.

'Michael filled the petrol tank of the lawnmower with paint yesterday,' Clare said.

I laughed – I couldn't help it. 'Was that the deciding factor in the whole vasectomy decision?'

'Not quite,' said Clare, with a wicked smile. 'The deciding factor, I believe, was finding that the Sky card was missing from the decoder last night when he wanted to watch the rugby.' She added dreamily, 'I found it this morning in the oven drawer.'

We paddled in the rock pools and counted hermit crabs (Michael was dissuaded with some difficulty from taking home a selection in his pocket) before setting out a picnic on the dry sand at the base of the dunes. A brisk, sand-laden breeze blew up just as we unwrapped the sandwiches, and Charlie managed to upend the chocolate cake icing-side down into the sand so that it was a somewhat gritty meal. Everyone got cold and tired and grizzly and wanted to be carried back up the beach in their wet togs. Lucy found a rotten puffer fish and clutched it lovingly to her chest, then threw a tantrum when we wouldn't let her take it home in the car. But these were merely minor incidents in an otherwise excellent day's outing.

We went to McDonald's on the way home for chicken nuggets and chips (Lucy returned from the play area with suspiciously damp knickers but Clare and I are terrible people and we decided not to go searching for a puddle to clean up, on the grounds that child-friendly restaurants had to expect that kind of thing). It was nearly six when Clare dropped me back home and I let myself in the kitchen door to find Andy and two other blokes playing PlayStation with a half-empty crate of beer beside them.

'Hey!' said Andy, slurring his words just a bit. 'Hey, Jo! Beer?'

'Dear Lord, no,' I said fervently. 'How can you?' Even ten years ago I wasn't keen on serious drinking two nights in a row, and these days it would have nearly killed me.

'Hair of the dog,' he said airily. 'Wade, Euan – this is Jo. She's a cool chick.'

I spent the rest of the evening playing Gran Turismo with them as they worked their way through the crate, and it was the most enjoyable evening I'd spent in that flat yet. When the beer ran out around ten I offered to take the boys home – they declined, saying they would crash on the couch if they didn't feel like walking. So I retired to bed, taking a selection of car keys with me and feeling extremely mature and responsible. Being called a wonderful influence had evidently gone to my head.

Sometime in the middle of the night a slurred beery voice informed me from much too close to my face that the couch wasn't very comfortable and that the voice's owner thought he would share my bed instead. By the time I'd struggled up to consciousness a skinny youth wearing far too few clothes had crawled into bed beside me; I promptly evicted him but I was more grateful than annoyed at this interruption to my night's sleep. I'd been in the middle of an unpleasant dream in which Matt was explaining to me with condescending pity that it was no wonder Graeme had chosen Chrissie rather than me because she was so beautiful, and that if I ever wanted anyone to find me attractive I'd better start wearing lip gloss and tight moleskin trousers.

Chapter 8

'Is jo anywhere handy?' came a familiar voice from reception.

It was a drizzly Wednesday morning in early May and I was catching up on some paperwork.

'I'm afraid she's tied up right now,' said Amber primly. 'If you'd like to leave your number I'll ask her to call you when she's got a –'

Before she could finish I jumped up from my desk and opened the door of the consulting room. 'Hey, Matt, wait.'

Matt turned at the sound of my voice. 'I can call you later if you're busy,' he said.

'I'm not.'

'But you said –' Amber began.

'I said if *Bob* came in I was busy,' I reminded her.

'You've got to ring the hospital,' she informed me smugly. 'So you *are* busy.'

'True,' I said. 'But I reckon I can probably talk to Matt

for a minute or two if that's okay with you – I'll take it off my lunch break.'

'You don't have one today. I booked in Mrs O'Connor. Her hip's been really bothering her and she can't wait till tomorrow.'

'That was kind of you,' Matt noted.

'Thank you,' said Amber.

I repressed a sigh – I would have fitted in Mrs O'Connor too, no doubt, but Amber was depressingly generous with my time. 'Come in for a minute,' I said to Matt and led him into the consulting room.

'Have you talked to Rose in the last day or two?' he asked.

'No, not for a week.' I was currently being slightly chilly towards Rose, just to underline my displeasure at her comments on my love life. 'What's up?'

'She's got cancer.'

I stood quite still and stared at him in horror. 'Wh-what kind of cancer?' I croaked at last.

'Breast,' he said. 'Hey, Jo, don't panic. Rose reckons it's an easy one to kill off. It's not fatal or anything, and they're getting right onto it – she's starting chemo next week.'

Chemo next week. It must be real, then. 'Bloody hell,' I said blankly.

'Yeah.' He reached out and touched my shoulder very lightly. 'It'll be okay. It's not like Dad's. She hasn't waited until she's nearly dead before going to see someone about it.' Patrick King died of bowel cancer that had metastasised *everywhere* before he thought perhaps he should talk

67

to a doctor about why he'd lost twenty kilograms in six months and was passing blood when he went to the toilet.

I put my arms around Matt and hugged him. 'Aunty Rose would never let a mere detail like breast cancer interfere with her life.'

He hugged me back, resting his chin briefly on the top of my head before letting me go. 'That's what she reckons,' he said. 'Right, you'd better get back to work or you'll be in trouble.'

I followed him out to reception, where Amber was chatting over the counter to Bob McIntosh.

'Sucks to be you,' said Matt very quietly, grinning with a most unfeeling lack of sympathy as he went out the door.

THAT EVENING AFTER work (which I left late, Amber having obligingly squeezed in another two appointments after five) I went to see Rose. She was pruning the roses in a truly breathtaking pair of tartan dungarees as, with Percy trotting before me, I made my way towards her across the lawn.

'How am I to diet that pig?' she wanted to know, straightening up and waving her secateurs at me in greeting. 'He gorges on windfall apples and walnuts, and it breaks his heart if I shut him up.'

'Perhaps you could put him on an exercise program,' I suggested, leaning forward to kiss her cheek. She smelt of Ponds face cream and Chanel No. 5, as she had ever since I could remember.

'I s'pose he and I could jog together,' she agreed, tweaking my collar straight. 'So I take it I'm forgiven for my tactless remarks?'

I hugged her tightly. 'You're a horrible woman, you know. Now, what's the story with this cancer?'

Aunty Rose made a face. 'Doesn't good news travel fast?' she murmured. 'A mere nothing, my dear. I shall have it blasted with chemicals and if there's anything left they'll whip it out with a scalpel, and that will be that. I wonder if they'd be willing to do a tummy tuck at the same time? Some kind of two-for-the-price-of-one deal?'

'How long've you known?' I asked, refusing to be distracted.

'Oh, goodness, only a week or so. I went up to Waikato and they stuck needles into my armpits, among other things. Honestly, Josephine, they leave no orifice unprobed, it's all terribly undignified – and now they've decided to add insult to injury by giving me a course of nasty toxic medications that will no doubt have all sorts of unpleasant side effects.' She shook her head sadly. 'Very sadistic people, oncologists.'

'And when is your first appointment?'

'Next Tuesday.'

'Can I take you?' I asked.

'Too late. Matthew is going to be my chauffeur.' She bent down and gathered an armful of spiky rose branches. 'Let's toss these over the fence and go and have some wine, shall we?'

I THOUGHT I'D better leave Rose in peace on Tuesday evening, but on Wednesday I drove up the valley through the gathering dusk. It was a spectacularly lovely evening with just the hint of a breeze stirring the golden leaves of the poplars along the roadside and the sun setting behind the ranges in a soft glow of apricot and green.

Matt's ute was already there, and Hazel's zippy little white car. The dogs were evidently worn out from greeting this surfeit of visitors and got up rather reluctantly to wander over and sniff me. The ancient huntaway did manage to lift his leg and squeeze out a drop or two against my back tyre but you could tell his heart wasn't really in it. Percy was busy under the walnut tree behind the shed and I could only see his well-padded ginger bottom.

I let myself in at the kitchen door just in time to see Rose throw up copiously into the sink. She stood there a moment, gripping the edge of the bench with her head bowed, before looking up and saying, only a very little less emphatically than normal, 'Why are there always carrots in one's vomit even if one hasn't eaten one of the beastly things for days?'

'My friend Stu has a theory about that,' I said. 'He reckons the gall bladder is actually a carrot-storage organ, and whenever you throw up some are released.'

'Ah,' said Rose, nodding as she turned on the tap to rinse out the sink. 'That explains it.'

'Oh, *Rosie*,' wailed Hazel from the living room. 'I can't bear to see you suffering like this.'

'Then don't look,' Aunty Rose muttered, running

herself a glass of water and taking a large gulp. 'That's better. Come through, sweet pea, the whole *whānau* is here, bless their cotton socks.'

In the living room Kim was curled in an armchair, Hazel was pacing the floor in a distressed sort of way and Matt was leaning against a heavy oak sideboard crammed with dusty willow-pattern dishes. 'Hey, Jose,' he said lightly. 'Have you come to watch Rose throw up? It's great entertainment.'

'It is,' I agreed. 'I had a free evening, so I thought it might be a fun way to spend it.'

Hazel looked at us more in sorrow than in anger. 'Your aunt has *cancer*,' she said. 'It's not funny. R-remember your father, Matthew . . .' And pulling a wisp of lace from the sleeve of her cardigan she pressed it to her eyes in a touching display of grief. I looked at Matt's face and wanted to hit her.

'We might as well laugh. Much better than all sitting around sobbing. Pull yourself together, Hazel,' said Rose briskly. She sank onto a sofa and leant her head back wearily. 'Kimlet, don't look so worried. It's just the chemo; it's only temporary. It will be making those cancer cells a lot sicker than it's making me.'

Kim nodded, and smiled at her tremulously.

'Oh,' I said. 'I saw this in town, Rose, and thought of you.' I passed her a small brown paper bag and sat down on the sofa beside her.

Aunty Rose opened the bag and pulled out a bright purple Indian cotton scarf shot with silver threads. 'Josephine, it's fabulous.' She smiled.

'It won't be very warm,' I said, 'but I thought it looked nice and glamorous.'

'Darling, you shouldn't have.'

'It only cost seven dollars,' I told her.

'Stingy cow,' she said.

'Absolutely.' I squeezed her hand for a second.

'Matthew, there's a bottle of ginger ale in the fridge. Be an angel and get me a glass?' said Rose. As he went she added, 'I may as well make the most of all this sympathy, don't you think?'

'Should I make you a poached egg, Aunty Rose?' Kim asked eagerly.

'Sweetheart, I don't think it would stay down just at the moment. But thank you.'

'How much chemo are you going to have?' I asked.

'One lot down, five to go.' She sighed. 'Yippee.'

'Rosie,' said Hazel, dabbing at her eyes again, 'I'll stay the night.'

'Most unnecessary,' said Rose.

'I insist,' said Hazel.

'Well, if you like. But we're not watching *Dancing with the Stars*. I couldn't face it in my fragile state.'

Chapter 9

Any tips for getting scorch marks off ceilings greatly appreciated! In future must remember to have fondue night separate from tequila night – it's a dangerous combination. But so much fun!

TIGHT-LIPPED, I LOGGED out of Facebook. I shouldn't keep doing this – I should just remove the slapper from my Friends list – but it was like picking off a scab. You know you're making it worse and that it would heal much better if you left it alone, but the compulsion to do it is almost irresistible.

I looked at my watch and found that it was three twenty-seven. I had a three-thirty appointment but Carol Abbott was chronically late. I had intended to grab a cup of tea before she arrived, but instead I opened my email and started a message to Stu.

Hey, dude, have you been round to the house lately? According to my BFF Chrissie's Facebook updates there's a party there every evening – it all sounds much more exciting than it was in my day. I was a bit concerned to read her comments about scorch marks on the ceiling, though. If they trash the place during their high-spirited capers it won't impress potential buyers.

Life here in sunny Waimanu is ticking along quite happily, though contrary to your predictions the place *isn't* bristling with virile and rugged farming types like those seen in *McLeod's Daughters*. Or if it is, none of them need physio. I can't complain, though – just yesterday a man in his late forties with halitosis and pores like the craters on the moon brought me an African violet and asked me to go to the rugby with him on Saturday. It's nice to know I have another option apart from tie-dying my clothes, throwing away my bras and living in a shack with seventeen cats. The only thing standing between me and perfect happiness is that Aunty Rose has just been diagnosed with cancer. She is quite determined not to let a silly little thing like that slow her down, but the chemo's knocking her round quite a bit.

Anyway, must go and strap an ankle. Are you still coming to Wellington for that orthopaedic conference? It would be very cool to see you.

Love, Jo

After pressing 'send' I got up and went to chat with Amber. She was currently having boyfriend troubles (or rather, the boy that she liked but had never had the courage to even speak to in passing had started going out with Freda at the petrol station) and she needed sympathy and chocolate biscuits to get through the day without bursting into tears. Amber was pretty damp and snivelly at the best of times; in tears she all but flooded the front of the shop.

'OH GOD, TWO down, four to go,' said Aunty Rose weakly on Tuesday evening.

She was in her crimson satin dressing-gown, reclining on the chaise longue that sat under the kitchen window. This was the most magnificent piece of furniture I'd ever seen. Built of heavy dark oak and weighing about a tonne, it had great clawed feet and a leering griffon that surveyed you from above the seat's balding velvet back. When I was little I firmly believed that griffon was alive, and to be honest I still wouldn't be all that surprised to catch him stretching his wings and yawning.

'I know you feel like total poo,' I said, 'but you look very elegant lying there.'

'Total poo,' Aunty Rose repeated. 'Really, Josephine, with all the glorious adjectives of the English language to choose from, you decide on "total poo"?'

'Can I take you to chemo next week?' I asked. Matt had taken her to both appointments so far because his mother felt that visiting the oncology department at the hospital would rake up far too many painful memories. Hazel wasn't worried, apparently, about the painful memories her only son might be reliving when *he* took Rose to chemo (despite the woman – and here I quote dear Hazel herself – living solely for the happiness of her precious children).

'It's not very exciting, sweet pea. And don't you have a job?'

'Doesn't matter at all,' I said, dismissing the job with a flick of the wrist. 'We can shut for a day – it'll give Amber a chance to catch up on her computer work.' Actually, if I wasn't there for a day it would give Amber the chance to photocopy thousands of fliers for her father's Lions Club barbecue, treat herself to a pedicure and play Spider Solitaire on the computer, but never mind.

Outside, the dogs, who had been lying in a heap on the back step, began to bark hysterically. Looking out the window I saw them dash across the lawn to meet Matt's ute. Percy, hampered by his increasing girth, laboured along in the rear.

'Matthew?' Rose guessed.

'And Kim,' I said, passing her a glass of ginger ale. Kim was wearing her school uniform, which at five-forty was odd given she claimed the Waimanu High School Year Thirteen uniform had been carefully designed by an evil genius to be the most unflattering outfit on the planet.

Matt paused to scratch Percy between the ears while Kim came straight up the path.

'How are you, Aunty Rose?' she called as she came through the door.

'Seedy,' said Rose. 'But I shall live. How are you faring in your travels along the road of knowledge?'

'Poorly, actually,' said Kim, opening the fridge door and beginning to forage. 'Hi, Josie. Been asked out by any dirty old men this week?'

'Just the usual,' I told her. 'Very disappointing, really. Why the school uniform?'

Emerging from the fridge with a cold sausage in one hand, Kim said, not without pride, 'Detention. Mum'll go spare.'

'Foolish child,' said Rose. 'What did you do?'

'*Apparently*, I was rude to old Williamson, the paedophile.'

'Kim,' said her aunt sternly, 'you cannot say things like that about people – it's both slanderous and extremely cruel. Unless it's true, in which case you need to go and talk to the police.'

'Well,' Kim muttered, hanging her head, 'he *looks* like a paedophile. Anyway, he's a dick.'

'He's not, you know,' I said. 'If you can get past the hairy ears – and I admit they're not pretty – he's kind of cool.'

Kim didn't bother to reply, but merely shrivelled me with one scathing look. Oh well, I never was going to pull off the tag of trendy-Jo-with-the-wicked-city-clothes for long.

Kicking off his work boots at the door and coming across the kitchen to kiss Rose's cheek, Matt remarked, 'Being nasty to teachers isn't as cool as you seem to think it is.'

'Oh, shut up,' said Kim crossly. 'What would you know about being cool?'

'Actually, although you wouldn't think it to look at him now, Matt *was* quite cool once,' I said, risking further damage to my image.

'I'm still cool,' he protested.

I shook my head. 'Cool people don't tuck their jeans into their socks, my friend.'

He looked down. 'It stops my jeans getting all wet and muddy round the bottoms.'

'Cool people don't care about muddy hems.'

'He probably tucks his singlets into his undies, too,' said Kim witheringly.

'I don't wear singlets,' Matt said mildly.

'Or undies,' I put in.

'Jo, you're an idiot.'

'I know,' I admitted.

'Especially if you ever thought Matt was cool,' said Kim, still trying hard to pick a fight. She was in a truly foul mood.

'Define "cool",' Aunty Rose ordered. 'I'm out of touch with the younger generation. Does it have anything to do with having the crotch of your trousers hanging somewhere around your knees and not bothering to lift your feet when you walk?'

'No, no,' I said. 'That's not cool at all – that's just silly little boys trying way too hard. Real proper coolness is when you don't waste your time trying to impress people because you *know* you're awesome, so you don't care what anyone else thinks.'

'Then I was never cool,' said Matt, opening the pantry and extracting the peanut jar that had lived on the second shelf for as long as I could remember. 'I spent most of my teenage years trying to impress you.'

'*Did* you?' I asked, touched.

'Well, I didn't know any other girls. I had to practise on somebody.' He tipped about half the contents of the peanut jar into his hand and threw the entire handful into his mouth. I looked at him enviously; if I ate peanuts like that I'd be the size of a house. Damn boys and their testosterone-driven metabolisms.

Kim stopped looking cross and started looking like a girl hatching a Plan. Probably a foolproof, Matt-and-Jo-have-actually-been-in-love-with-each-other-their-whole-lives-if-they-can-only-be-brought-to-realise-it Plan, guaranteed to cause maximum embarrassment all round.

'Hey, Kim,' I said hastily, in an effort to distract her, 'it wouldn't hurt to apologise to Mr Williamson. You know, on the grounds that teachers have feelings too.' This reminded her nicely of her grievances and she ignored me pointedly for the next half-hour.

Chapter 10

'I GOT OUT *Burn After Reading*,' Sara announced, coming down the hall and leaning against the bathroom doorframe.

'You'll have to let me know what you think of it,' I said, carefully applying a second coat of mascara. Graeme and I had watched it last year and decided that it should have been called *Burn Before Watching*. I think the only movie I've ever enjoyed less was *Scent of a Woman*, which meandered on for three slow and painful hours and made me want to chew off my own leg.

'Don't you want to watch it?' she asked.

'I'm going out.'

'Oh,' she said, sounding disappointed. 'So's Andy.'

I finished my mascara and frowned critically at my reflection. I'm a bit scared of makeup, which is a ridiculous thing for a grown woman to admit. I always worry that I will look as though I've tried too hard, and as a result I apply the stuff so sparingly I may as well not bother. But I thought of Chrissie with her enormous smoky eyes and dark spiky lashes, put my shoulders resolutely back and turned away from the mirror *without* rubbing my eyeliner off again with a flannel. 'Scott Wilson's having a barbecue. You could come along if you like – I'm sure he wouldn't mind.' Instantly I wished I had bitten my tongue.

But Sara shook her head. 'The DVD's only for one night, and I've been wanting to watch it for ages,' she said.

This was a relief; Sara masks intense shyness behind a loud and crass manner in public, talking over people she doesn't know in a voice so penetrating that nobody else can make themselves heard at all. I pitied her, although had she known it she would have been deeply offended – it's got to be the most miserable feeling in the world to realise you're not a social success but not understand why.

'Fair enough,' I said. 'Well, I'd better go.' Not that I was late, but if I spent another ten minutes drifting around the flat she might change her mind and come with me after all.

Carrying four bottles of designer cider, a packet of beef and tomato sausages and a bag of Twisties I walked across town. Down the hill from the flat, past Mrs McClintock who was, for some inexplicable reason, hanging out her washing at half past six on an overcast May evening, around the back of the soccer fields and across the railway lines. One of the low fogs that plague Waimanu's residents during winter was already gathering and the town looked dilapidated and dreary. But to be fair I think that if you frequented the railway lines of Prague or Nice on a foggy autumn evening you would decide they were pretty dreary places, too.

Scott lived in a tiny little box of a house on one of Waimanu's dodgier streets (and in Waimanu we do dodgy quite well). His section was fenced in three-metre-high corrugated iron and his lawn was home to about five dead cars. I was pretty sure he lived like that mostly to annoy his parents, a prim couple who wore matching beige shoes and were leading lights of the local bridge club.

His tiny living room was overrun by small children – Clare's biggest boy Michael had wrapped himself in a Harley-Davidson flag and was running around like a small caped crusader, while Lucy was sucking hopefully on the top of an empty beer bottle. I smiled widely; it was very nice to see Scotty with his unkempt goatee and leather vest balancing a baby on his knee as he opened a bottle of bourbon and cola.

Brett and Clare were there, obviously, and Cheryl and her husband Ian/Alan. I didn't know anyone else by name, although a couple of people looked vaguely familiar.

'Aunty Jo!' Charlie shouted, and threw himself at my knees in a frenzy of welcome that gave me a little warm glow inside until I realised it wasn't me he was interested in but the junk food I was carrying.

After half an hour or so Scott returned the baby to Cheryl and wandered out to the garage to light the barbecue. All of the men went with him to supervise (although even with a whole team of barbecue experts the sausages still turned out burnt on the outside and pink in the middle), while the women stayed in the lounge to chat and wipe noses and break up the fights that broke out between overexcited preschoolers.

'It's frightening, isn't it?' I said to Cheryl, putting my bottle of cider under my chair so I could have a turn cuddling her baby. 'Look at us; you'd think we were grown-ups.'

'I know,' she said. 'I suppose our parents felt the same – like they were only pretending to be adults but they were actually still sixteen.'

'This is a particularly cute child you've got here,' I told her, letting young Maxwell chew my index finger. 'Well done.'

'Yes,' she said seriously. 'I quite like him. You should consider it yourself.'

'I'm beginning to think you're right. I just have to decide between Bob McIntosh and Dallas Taipa as potential fathers.' Dallas was grossly overweight with trousers that sat somewhere mid-bum and personal hygiene issues, and he had a severely inflamed tendon sheath in his right foot.

Cheryl spluttered a little on her glass of orange juice. 'What a depressing thought,' she said. 'Surely you can find someone a bit more useful than that.' She smoothed a strand of cobweb-fine hair off her small son's brow. 'Do you think you'll stay round here, Jo? I'm only going to want to come back to work part time, and Sue at the hospital was telling me she's keen to get you onto the staff up there.'

'No idea,' I said cheerfully. 'I've decided not to think about it for another six months.' All my life I had carefully weighed up every decision. Lamb or calf for Pet Day? Public or private practice? Come home for Christmas or pay off my credit card? Rent a house or get a mortgage? I wrote lists of pros and cons and spent weeks in painstaking research – it once took me a week to decide between a navy and a beige pair of three-quarter pants to wear to work. And my meticulous planning had led to a temporary job in a one-woman physio practice where my constant companion was a girl with the brains of a goldfish and sinuses like Niagara Falls, a flat where someone banged on the bathroom door if I showered for more than two and a half minutes and most of my income going to pay a mortgage on a house in Australia that I was never going to live in. A little bit of spontaneity seemed like a good idea.

Matt, accompanied by his pretty blonde girlfriend, arrived late and with his arm in a sling. We had all migrated out to the garage to eat burnt sausages and doubtful bean salad, and Scott called, 'Bloody hell, King, what've you done to yourself now?'

'Flattened by a cow,' said Matt serenely, accepting a beer with his slow smile. 'Could have happened to anyone.'

'It usually happens to you, though. Did you break it?'

'No, just dislocated my shoulder.' He wandered up beside me. 'So it looks like you'll be taking Rose to chemo on Tuesday, if that's still okay.'

'No problem,' I said. 'Hi, Cilla.'

'Hello.'

'If I were you I'd grab a sausage,' I advised her. 'Just avoid those funny purplish ones – they taste like warm dead pig.'

'How delightful,' she said. 'What would you like, hon?'

'I'll finish my beer first,' said Matt. 'I've only got one hand.'

'I could feed you if you like,' Cilla suggested.

'That's a very kind offer, but think of the damage to my manly reputation.'

'Have you got a reputation for manliness?' I enquired as Cilla made her way towards the food table.

'Well, I'd like to think so. Did you know you've got baby spew on your shoulder?'

'Hey, Matt, are you still interested in that V6 engine?' asked a large hairy man I didn't recognise. The two of them embarked on a long and involved conversation about split diffs and automatic chokes, and I drifted off to chat to Scotty.

By around ten I was sitting with Clare on the bottom step of Scott's deck. She was cuddling Lucy, who was fast asleep with her thumb in her mouth, and Charlie was leaning against me sleepily and playing with my mobile phone. I had to admit that the child was reasonably cute, and seeing that his parents were excellent people he would probably become quite nice, eventually.

'Matt!' I called as he went past, Cilla attached to his side with limpet-like devotion. I didn't think I'd seen her more than two feet away from him all evening.

'What's up?'

'Could you grab me a beer? I'm a bit stuck here.'

'Okay,' he said, and passed me his, which was very nearly full.

'You're a legend,' I told him.

'I know.' He sat down on the edge of the deck and Cilla sat beside him, so close their thighs touched. Kim was wrong: he wasn't just a suitably tall and good-looking accessory; Cilla was well and truly smitten.

'Your parents bought Reynolds' farm, didn't they?' I asked her.

'That's right,' she said proudly. 'We're Mountain View Angus. And Dad runs fifteen hundred Perendale ewes.'

'Psychotic animals,' Matt remarked.

'Matt, don't be rude,' his girlfriend said, placing a slim hand on his leg.

'He's very disparaging about sheep,' I said. 'Dairy farmers mostly are.'

'I spent far too much of my youth catching the bloody things for your father to dag,' said Matt. 'It put me off.'

'Have your parents retired now?' Cilla asked.

'No. They're milking dairy goats in Nelson.'

'Nice place, Nelson,' Clare put in.

'Mm,' I agreed.

Matt held out a hand for his beer. 'But not as nice as here?' he prompted, taking a mouthful and passing it back.

'Nowhere's as nice as here,' I said firmly.

He grinned. 'Here in particular?'

I ran a thoughtful eye from the rusting corrugated-iron fence around Scotty's section, past the disintegrating cars on the lawn and on to the verdant bed of thistles beside the steps. 'Yep.'

'Honey,' said Cilla, 'are you ready to go?' She slid a hand into Matt's and stroked the back of his hand with her thumb. 'I'm helping Dad pick lambs in the morning.'

'Can do,' he said. 'Want a lift, Jo? You probably shouldn't wander around town by yourself in the dark.'

NOT LONG AFTER, I clambered down from the back seat of Cilla's great silver ute and went wearily up the front steps of the house. I was tired and lonely and I'd had enough to drink to become a little bit maudlin. I could hear the TV inside but I didn't go in; instead I sank down on the top step and rested my forehead on my jean-clad knees.

I must have been mad to come back. Waimanu wasn't home anymore with Mum and Dad gone and the farm sold. It was somewhat ironic that Matt was the one who'd had to come home and take over the family farm when I was the one who would have loved to. But I'd gone and attached myself to an Australian surgical intern who had to live in a city big enough to have a decent-sized hospital. And you can't expect your father to keep wrestling with sheep indefinitely when he has two dodgy knees and a huge overdraft, just in case his offspring has some sort of epiphany and decides to give farming a crack.

'Hey!' somebody called from the street below. 'Are you locked out?' I looked up to see Cilla leaning out the window of her ute. She must have driven to the end of the road and done a U-turn. It just went to show that wallowing in self-pity only ever made you look like an idiot.

'No,' I called around the treacherous lump in my throat. My voice came out as a sort of strangled croak. 'I'm good.' I got to my feet and dug in the pocket of my jeans for the key to the door.

'Goodnight!' And off they went, the ute's engine snarling impatiently.

The door opened behind me to reveal Andy, clad in his good grey skinny jeans and with his hair artfully rumpled and stiff with wax. He must have only just beaten me home. 'Jo?' called Sara from the lounge. 'What on earth are you doing?'

'Feeling sorry for myself,' I called back.

'Dude,' said Andy gently, 'you've *got* to stop looking up your ex on Facebook.' And he put his arms around me in an awkward, Lynx-scented hug. I felt a little surge of gratitude for the sympathy – thank goodness I hadn't gone and lived by myself in somebody's farm cottage after all.

I hugged him back for a second, then pushed myself away and smiled at him. 'It's a real bugger we finished that coconut liqueur the other week.'

Sara appeared in the kitchen doorway. '*My* coconut liqueur?' she asked.

'I'll buy you some more,' I said.

'Buy me peach schnapps instead. I don't like coconut.'

Andy and I looked at one another and began to laugh helplessly.

'What?' asked Sara. 'That's fair!'

Chapter 11

'AMBER,' I SAID, coming to stand behind her and putting on my best stern-employer voice, 'I need you to chase up Craig from Waikato Medical Supplies tomorrow to make sure he's put the ultrasound machine back on the courier.' It was Monday evening and I wouldn't be in on Tuesday.

'Okay,' said Amber. 'I'll call him first thing.'

'And please clean up the reception area – wash the windows and all that. It's looking a bit dingy.' She turned to look at me with a blank stare. It was like meeting the eye of a dead fish. 'Cheryl promised she'd bring Max in to see us for morning tea, and it would be really cool to impress her.'

'I'll do it if I've got time,' she said.

'If I come in on Wednesday and find it's not done,' I told her, 'I will know you spent the entire day on the internet and I will hurt you in ways you cannot even begin to imagine. I used to do kickboxing in Melbourne.'

In response to this dire threat Amber giggled. 'Right,' she said, and wiped her nose, just for a change, on the shoulder of her blouse. 'Have a good day tomorrow.' She stood up and gathered her possessions.

'You too,' I said, barely repressing a sigh. I had never worked with anyone like Amber before. I'd pulled up a couple of physio students in the past, and once a nurse with the most appalling phone manner in the world; I hated doing it but I could if I had to. Amber, on the other hand, had obviously been sent to me as a punishment for the sin of pride in my managerial skills. She drifted along in her own happy (albeit soggy) little world, utterly impervious to reprimand or threat or disappointment. The only thing on the positive side was that she never held a grudge. I'm not sure there was room for one in her head.

AUNTY ROSE MET me at the kitchen door the next morning with a recyclable green shopping bag in her hand. As she climbed into the front of my car, Percy and the dogs watched mournfully, fearing that their goddess was leaving for good.

'It must be nice to be loved like that,' I remarked, looking at the little row of forlorn faces in my rear-view mirror.

'It is. I shall get you a piglet for Christmas.'

I grinned. 'Sara would have hysterics. How are you feeling today?'

'Oh,' said Aunty Rose. 'You know. Total poo.' She looked at me sideways. 'The phrase has grown on me – it rolls nicely off the tongue. Thank you, Josephine.'

'You're welcome. I have various other phrases if you ever need one. I've been compiling a list for cheating boyfriends.'

'Such as?'

'I think,' I said as I navigated potholes, 'that "gimpy trouser-weasel" is my personal favourite. It's not original, though; it's my friend Stu's.' I turned north onto the main road.

'Very good. And what do you use for the girl that he's cheating with?'

'Either "skank" or "hose-beast".'

'I see,' said Aunty Rose, rummaging in the bag at her feet and pulling out a large basin. 'Don't be alarmed, Josephine, it is merely a precaution.' She leant her head back against the seat and closed her eyes.

IF EVER THERE was a place guaranteed to make you count your blessings, it's the oncology ward of a hospital. While Aunty Rose received another intravenous dose of cancer-killing drugs that would make her feel even sicker than she already was, I fell into conversation with the woman in the next room. She looked about my age, although it was hard to tell because she wore a scarf over her bald scalp and had deep dark circles under her eyes. She told me she had two small children and that her husband had moved out the week before because he 'needed space'. What a marvellous chap.

We got home again just after five and Rose went straight to bed. I fed the dogs and Percy (he received three Tux biscuits every night to supplement his walnut and apple diet and carried them away carefully in his mouth to savour under his favourite shrub), emptied and rinsed the sick basin and made Rose a cup of tea that she couldn't keep down.

Matt and Kim arrived at about seven-thirty, bickering gently about Kim's driving skills as they came into the kitchen.

'Where's Aunty Rose?' Kim asked.

I had been scrubbing the floor, partly because it needed it but mostly because it was a rotten job and it suited the general rottenness of the day, and I got up to empty my bowl of dirty water. 'In bed. Asleep, I hope.'

'I'll check,' said Kim.

'Don't wake her up!' said Matt.

'*Jeez*, Matt, I'm not *stupid*.' She pattered down the hall.

'How is she?' he asked.

'Awful.'

He ran a hand over his face.

'I'll stay the night,' I offered.

'Thank you.'

'Could your mum sleep here until the chemo's over?' I asked.

'Mum,' said Matt tightly, 'is going to Thailand tomorrow with Nan Gregory. She'll be away for three weeks.'

'Oh.'

'She needs a break.'

'From what?' I asked. Sometimes my mouth runs along totally unconnected with my brain. I winced. 'Sorry.'

'It's a reasonable question. Fucked if I know.' I looked at him, surprised at the heat in his voice. Matt doesn't really do blazing mad; it's not his style.

'Maybe I should call Mum,' I said. 'The goats are dried off – she could probably come up for a week or two.'

'That'd be really good,' he said. 'I keep offering to stay but Rose isn't keen on the idea.'

'She just can't bear the thought of giving you any more work than you've already got.'

Aunty Rose believed that when a man came in from his day's work he should be able to sit down with the paper, not empty the sick bowl before starting dinner. She also took it for granted that a woman with a full-time job should be perfectly capable of cooking and cleaning for her family too – and this although she wouldn't hesitate to describe herself as a feminist. Bless her.

Kim came back down the hall. 'She's asleep,' she reported. 'Can we stay for a drink, Matt, or do you need to rush home and call Cilla?'

'We'll have a coffee, if Jo can put up with us,' he said. 'Watch it, Toad, or you'll be sleeping in the shed.'

Kim grinned at him. 'It wouldn't be much different to your spare room. His house is *dire*, Josie. I'll probably catch some horrible disease.'

'I'm babysitting while Mum's away,' Matt explained

93

with a notable lack of enthusiasm. 'And there's nothing wrong with my house. Compared to your bedroom it's pristine.'

'I like listening to you two,' I observed. 'It makes me so grateful I'm an only child.'

My mother, who I rang while we drank our coffee at the kitchen table, said, 'Of *course*. I should have thought of it myself. I'll check the internet for flights and ring you back.' She called back seven minutes later. 'How about arriving in Hamilton at two o'clock tomorrow?'

'Is there a later flight?' I asked. 'Then I could come and get you after work.'

'I'll just get a shuttle,' said Mum. 'Much easier all round.'

'You're wonderful,' I told her. 'Can you afford to fly up at such short notice?'

'Of course,' she said. 'That's what credit cards are for. I'll see you tomorrow.'

The King siblings departed soon afterwards. 'Thanks, Jo,' Matt said, gingerly shifting his bad arm in its sling as he stood up.

'Do you want me to take a look at that shoulder?' I asked.

'What? Oh, yeah, the doctor told me to have some physio. I'll make an appointment.'

'Or I could just look at it now.'

He shook his head. 'We'd better go. I'll hit you up tomorrow – you'll come up to see your mum, won't you?'

'Yes,' I said.

'Come on,' said Kim from the doorstep, 'or Cilla will throw a wobbly.'

'And why on earth would Cilla throw a wobbly?' Matt asked.

'She's that type,' said Kim darkly.

Matt rolled his eyes. 'Zip it, Toad,' he said, following her out the door.

❀

WHEN I GOT to work the next morning I found that Amber had indeed made a praiseworthy effort to wash the windows. Whether they looked any better was, however, open to debate – instead of being fly-spotted and dusty they were streaky and smeared, as if she'd cleaned them with her tongue. Curious, I snatched twenty seconds to ask her just what she'd washed them with.

'Soap and water,' she said.

'Not window cleaner?'

'We didn't have any.'

'How about you take five dollars out of petty cash and grab a bottle at lunchtime?' I suggested.

'Oh,' said Amber. 'Well, if you want.'

'I want,' I said. 'Mr Hopu, come on through.'

❀

I DROVE STRAIGHT up to Rose's after work, and Mum came out to meet me as I waded through the canine reception committee. She wore a pair of faded jeans and one of Dad's ancient bush shirts with her greying fair hair bundled up at the back of her head. My mother is quite startlingly beautiful but is happiest when dressed like a homeless person. 'Josie, love,' she said affectionately.

I threw myself at her with a spasm of the same kind of relief you experience when you're four and lost in a department store, and then your mother finds you again. Mum would know exactly what to do to make everything better. 'It's *wonderful* to see you,' I said against her comforting shoulder.

She patted me on the back. 'I like your hair like that, sweetheart. And your father sends his love.'

'He does?' I asked sceptically. Dad, although a truly excellent person, is the kind of man whose idea of expressing affection is to pat my shoulder and say briskly, 'Right, then, Jo.'

'Well, he told me to make sure you're not working too hard and that you should be sure to wring every cent possible out of that slimy prick Graeme.'

I smiled. 'Is he still practising "Rhinestone Cowboy"?'

'No, thank the Lord. He hasn't touched the guitar in a couple of weeks; he's training for a long-distance cycle race with Maurice from next door.' We began to walk up the brick path to the kitchen. 'It's brilliant. His cholesterol's down, he fits into his favourite pants again *and* I don't have to put up with that godawful strumming.'

'Great,' I said. 'How's Rose today?'

'She assures me she's feeling better,' said Mum. 'I expect she's lying, but you know Rose.'

Aunty Rose was dressed today, and busying herself

around the kitchen. As Mum and I came back in she said, from the depths of the ancient fridge, 'Josephine, are you planning to stay for dinner?'

'What is it?' I asked warily.

'I'm making a quiche.'

'Out of what?'

'Edith, it's a terrible shame you never managed to instil any manners in your daughter,' Rose said. She emerged from the fridge holding a block of cheese in one hand and half a cabbage in the other.

'I'm just remembering the Marmite omelette,' I defended myself.

IT WAS SUCH a nice meal. We drank ginger ale all round so as not to torment Aunty Rose (alcohol and chemo don't mix, and she said not having wine in the evening was harder to bear than the nausea), and with profound relief I reverted from the role of anxious caregiver to child allowed to stay up and have tea with the grown-ups. After the quiche, which was happily devoid of Marmite or olives or any of the other peculiar things Aunty Rose is liable to add to her dishes, I washed up while the two of them sat at the kitchen table and gossiped.

Matt arrived just before the coffee stage.

'Matthew,' said Mum warmly. 'I swear you've grown another foot. Come here and give me a kiss.'

He obeyed. 'Thanks for coming up, Aunty Edith.'

'Most unnecessary,' said Rose, holding up her face to be

kissed in turn. 'Not that it isn't nice to see you, Edie.'

'Unnecessary to you,' Matt told her, 'but it makes Jo and me feel better, so you can just put up with it.' He came over to the sink beside me and picked up a tea towel. 'Hey, Jose.'

'Hey, Matt,' I said. 'Where's the toad?'

'At home, texting some pimply youth.'

'Ah.' There's no mobile phone coverage at Aunty Rose's. 'Aaron, or a new pimply youth?'

'This one's called Jonno. He works at the mill and has a car with lowered seats. Aaron's been kicked to the kerb.'

'A working man with a car,' said Mum. 'That sounds ominous.'

'Doesn't it just,' said Matt grimly. Then to me, 'What are *you* sniggering about?'

'Matthew King, stern older brother. How ironic.'

'Do tell, sweet pea,' said Aunty Rose. 'I always suspected that Matthew was not always the fine and upstanding member of society we see before us.'

The fine and upstanding member of society gave me a long, flat stare.

'I can't,' I said. 'He'll break my arms.'

He grinned. 'Watch it. I could tell the odd story about you, too.'

'Please don't,' Mum said hastily. 'I have absolutely no desire to know what you got up to in your misspent youth.'

'Nothing very bad,' I told her, setting the last pot on the draining board. 'I was a geek, remember. Matt, if you sit down I'll look at your shoulder for you.'

Chapter 12

TWO WEEKS LATER, in a masochistic sort of mood, I logged into Facebook. I used to be a very sporadic Facebook user, but lately I had been checking my home page with anxious regularity. Today it told me that Todd was sad because it was raining, Cath's baby slept nine hours straight last night, Suzie's had colic and didn't . . . Ah, here was Chrissie's daily gem.

> How spoilt am I? A weekend away, flowers, long walks on the beach, a romantic candlelit dinner – is he wise to be setting a precedent like this for future anniversaries?

Anniversary? Of *what*? Just how long did I spend in happy ignorance of the pair of them having sex in cupboards at parties? Something had been going on since September, Graeme had admitted on that last horrible evening. 'It's not like we meant for it to happen, Jo. Chrissie feels so awful about it.' And then his eyes had gone misty at the thought of poor Chrissie's suffering. I wish, in hindsight, that I'd thrown something at his head, but at the time I was dumb and passive with shock.

She'd changed her profile picture again and was now sitting on his shoulders, with her hair whipping round her face and her eyes alight with laughter. She looked like a bloody model in an ad for panty liners.

Amber put her head around the door. 'Your five o'clock's here,' she said. 'Goodnight.' And off she toddled – without, I discovered, locking the back door, shutting down her computer or clearing away the little collection of used mugs from her desk.

AFTER MY LAST appointment I went home, showered and made toad-in-the-hole, it being my turn to cook. The atmosphere in the flat was still somewhat frosty after Saturday night's fracas. (Andy had come home drunk and decided he needed a nice hot snack, then had forgotten to turn off the oven after heating and devouring four frozen pies. Did he have any *idea*, Sara had demanded the next morning, how much power the oven uses? Andy, hungover and short-tempered, had told her to shut up and piss off, and things had deteriorated from there.)

After dinner I left the two of them to their Cold War and went, as usual, to Rose's. It was raining in a dreary, persistent sort of way and a car I didn't recognise was parked in front of the woodshed.

This was the night after Rose's fifth chemo appointment. She had begun to lose her hair a few days earlier. She'd looked at the long grey strands covering the cushion she was leaning against with no expression whatsoever for a moment and then said, 'Well, wouldn't *that* just rip your nightie?'

'I called Rob Milne,' my mother told me as I let myself into the kitchen. She was cleaning the oven, scrubbing grimly at the blackened concrete-like residue of years of cooking. 'She's had no sleep for the last three nights. She can't go on like this.'

'I didn't think you could get a house visit from a doctor unless you were the Queen of England,' I said, wiping my wet face on my sleeve. Mum handed me a stack of charcoal-coated oven racks; I dropped them into the big kitchen sink and got out a pristine new block of steel wool with which to attack them.

'Well, I tried calling the medical centre, and they told me to take her to Hamilton. Honestly, a two-hour drive through the gorge when she's too sick to sit up? So I called Rob at home.'

'You legend,' I told her.

'I have my moments,' Mum agreed.

Dr Milne is a small man with a dry sense of humour and an uncanny resemblance to Radar from *M*A*S*H*. He came down the hall from Rose's bedroom holding a proper old-fashioned leather doctor's bag, sighed deeply and peered at us over the tops of his bifocals. 'I've given her a bit of a cocktail,' he said, 'and she'll at least get a night's sleep. Don't worry if she doesn't make a lot of sense – it's just the drugs. Call me in the morning and let me know how she is, will you?'

Mum got to her feet and smiled at him gratefully. 'Rob,' she said, 'you're a wonderful man.'

He smiled back. 'Just you wait till you see the bill. I'll be able to spend a week in the Islands.'

'I *was* planning to pay you in goat's cheese,' Mum said.

'Then I'll send it to Josie,' he said promptly. 'Physiotherapists are all overpaid and underworked, aren't you?'

'No,' I said, a vision of the gormless Amber rising before my eyes, 'you're thinking of their receptionists.'

Dr Milne gave a little snort of laughter. 'Ah, well,' he said. 'You may be right. Goodnight, girls. Nice to see you again, Edith.'

He had just reached the door when it opened and Matt came in, looking damp and dishevelled. His jeans, however, were not tucked into his socks. 'Is she worse?' he asked, looking at the doctor in alarm.

'Just nauseous and miserable,' Dr Milne told him. 'I've given her a couple of shots so she can have a bit of a break from trying to bring up her stomach lining, the poor woman.'

'Oh,' said Matt. 'Thank you. Send me the bill, won't you?'

The doctor patted him condescendingly on the shoulder. 'I still remember the day I gave your teddy bear an injection to show you it wasn't so bad, and you screamed the place down. Never injected a bear since. Goodnight.'

Mum sighed as the door shut behind him. 'I think I'd

better change my flight,' she said. 'You two are doing a great job, but Rose really needs someone here all the time.'

'Mum'll be home tomorrow,' Matt said. 'And I can sleep over here – Rose doesn't really rate my nursing skills, but she'll cope.'

'Why don't I stay for the next couple of weeks?' I offered. 'Just till the chemo's finished and she's feeling a bit better.'

'Thanks,' he said, and smiled at me tiredly. 'She'd be much happier about you doing it.'

'I *do* feel I should go home and check up on your father,' Mum confessed. 'A diet of tinned spaghetti on toast can only support a man for so long.'

'And eggs,' I said. 'He can fry eggs. But you should go home – he sounded all wistful on the phone yesterday.'

'If you can't cope you'll ring me, won't you?' said Mum.

'Promise,' I told her. Putting down my block of steel wool I looked at the oven rack I'd been scrubbing. I couldn't discern any improvement at all. 'I really don't think I'm making any progress here.'

'Move over. Let me try,' my mother ordered – she is a very managing woman. She must have always been a bit like that, but after thirty-odd years spent organising my father, the King of Dither, she has become almost totally incapable of letting anyone finish a job without elbowing them out of the way and doing it properly herself. 'Go and see if Rose is still awake. She might like a cup of tea.'

Matt and I went down the draughty hall to the end bedroom and peered around the door. It was beautifully warm thanks to a little oil heater in the corner, and Rose was lying back on her pillows with her grey hair spread out around her like a fan and her eyes shut. Her face, in the soft light of a truly hideous brass bedside lamp, was all hollows and shadows and looked frighteningly old. I hadn't realised just how much weight she had lost in the last month.

'She's asleep,' I whispered.

'No I'm not,' said Aunty Rose, her voice soft and slurred. 'Come in. Who is it?'

'Me,' said Matt, 'and Jo.' He went into the room and sat beside her on the edge of the bed. 'How are you feeling?'

'Good,' murmured Aunty Rose. She groped for his hand and held it.

I leant my head against the doorframe and watched them – two of my very favourite people. I was lucky to have grown up with Matt to play with and fight with and stop me turning into a brattish only child, and even luckier to have had Aunty Rose's eccentric loving presence only two paddocks away throughout my formative years.

'Pat,' said Aunty Rose suddenly, opening her eyes.

'No,' he said gently, 'it's Matthew.'

'Pat, you shouldn't be here.' She closed her eyes again and moved her head restlessly on the pillow.

Matt looked at me, alarmed.

'Dr Milne said she might be a bit out of it,' I said softly. 'It's just the shot he gave her.'

'You know we talked about this,' Aunty Rose continued. 'She'll find out and she'll take Matthew back to England and you'll never see him again.' She grimaced painfully, a travesty of a smile. 'And let's face it, that child is going to need *some* sort of sensible presence in his life – he sure as hell won't get it from Hazel or my parents.'

There was a thick, dense, appalled silence. Very gently, Matt detached himself and stood up. I moved aside for him and he went blindly past me down the hall. I looked from Aunty Rose's still face to his departing back, turned and went after him.

'Matthew, love,' Mum was saying as I reached the kitchen door, 'are you alright?' She had turned from the sink and was looking at him with concern. 'She'll be okay. Your aunt's as tough as old boots, you know.'

'Yeah,' he said. He opened the back door. 'I'd better go . . .'

Evidently assuming Rose's appearance had been truly frightening, Mum reached for a tea towel, wiped her hands and went quickly out of the kitchen to check on her.

'Matt,' I said helplessly, so sorry for him – and for Rose – that it hurt.

''Night, Jo. See you tomorrow.' He bent to pull on his work boots.

Not knowing what to do but wanting to do *something* I went across the room to him and touched his shoulder. 'It's okay.' What a bloody stupid thing to say. I took my hand away again.

'Did you know?' he asked.

I shook my head. 'I won't say anything.'

'I know that.' He stood up straight. 'Don't look like that, Jose, it's not the end of the world.'

I put my arms around him and hugged him fiercely and he sighed, hugging me in return. He was very warm and he smelt nice – like soap and clean cotton and something faintly spicy. It occurred to me after a little while that smelling somebody else's boyfriend isn't all that cool, and I let him go.

'Are you doing your shoulder exercises?' I asked.

'Hmm? Oh, yeah. Sometimes.'

'Twice a day, please, or you'll be really unhappy in a couple of months when you're supposed to be heaving calves around.'

'Yes, Jo,' he said obediently. He smiled and flicked me lightly on the nose. 'Hey, thank you.' And he let himself out into the rainy dark.

Feeling suddenly about a thousand years old I closed the door behind him and turned to tackle the oven racks once more. What a thrilling way to spend an evening.

'Jo?' Mum asked cautiously, coming around the doorway from the hall where she must have been lurking.

'Yes?'

'Have you and Matthew been arguing?'

'No,' I said.

'Ah.' It's amazing what delicate shades of meaning can be infused into a single syllable; she managed concern and gentle enquiry and a truly noble reluctance to poke her nose in where it might not be wanted.

I chose to ignore these subtle undertones. 'Look,' I said, 'bugger these oven racks. They're never going to come clean, and Rose couldn't care less anyway.'

'I expect you're right.' A brief silence fell, until she said with real anguish, 'Josie, love, please tell me what's wrong.'

I sank wearily onto the chaise longue, under the griffon's sardonic eye. 'Rose thought Matt was his father, and she told him he mustn't keep coming over or Hazel would find out about it and take Matt away from him.'

'Oh,' said Mum. 'Shit.' She sat down beside me and leant her head back against the balding velvet. 'Poor Matt.'

I nodded.

'Will he say anything to her?'

'No,' I said definitely.

'Are you sure? Rose would be so upset – she's never forgiven herself.'

'You mean you knew about it?' I stared at her.

Mum sighed. 'It was so sad. Patrick had never really met Rose before he married her sister, you see. None of us had. She moved in different circles. And of course Hazel's the most painful woman on the planet, and Rose is kind and warm and intelligent and – well, you know how wonderful Rose is. I think poor Pat realised he'd picked the wrong sister within a few months, but by then Hazel was already expecting Matthew, and he just wasn't the type of man to leave his pregnant wife for another woman.'

'So why did Aunty Rose buy this place?' I asked. 'Why on earth wouldn't she move to the other end of the country and try to get over it?'

'She did,' said Mum. 'She moved to Christchurch. But then Matthew was born, and Hazel fell completely to pieces.'

'What – post-natal depression?'

'I suppose so,' Mum said. 'At the time we just thought it was typical Hazel behaviour, but that's probably a bit unfair. Anyway, there was no way she could manage the baby, and Pat was trying to run the farm and look after Matthew and keep his wife from doing herself an injury, so Rose came home to help.'

'What a lousy, miserable balls-up,' I said softly.

'Yep,' said Mum. 'We wondered if Pat might leave Hazel when Matthew got a bit older, but then Kim came along. Hazel always insisted that Kim was an accident, but I'm not at all sure.'

'You think Kim was a husband-detaining strategy?'

'Yes, I suspect so,' Mum said. 'Matthew was – what? Ten? Eleven? – and I can't imagine Hazel would have been able to get him away from his father without an almighty battle. And almighty battles aren't Hazel's style; she prefers to guilt people into doing what she wants.'

I recalled Patrick King's funeral with a new clear-sightedness. Hazel had been prostrate with hysterical grief while Aunty Rose comforted Kim and Matt, organised undertakers and eulogies and the catering and a thousand other details, just quietly trying to make things a little bit easier for Pat's children.

'God,' I said violently. 'What a bitch that woman is.'

Mum smiled a bit sadly and shook her head. 'No,' she said. 'She's just selfish, and not very bright.' She reached out to tuck a strand of hair back behind my left ear. 'I don't know how much of this you should tell Matthew – she *is* his mother.'

'I cannot imagine, in any circumstances, talking to Matt about his father's love affair with his aunt,' I said flatly.

'Well, if he talked to anyone about it, it would be to you.'

'No, I expect it would be to his girlfriend.'

'Josie, sweetheart,' said my mother tenderly, 'have you considered telling him how you feel about him?'

I stiffened. 'What *are* you talking about?'

'He cares about you, too,' she assured me.

'Oh, stop that,' I snapped. 'We're just friends.'

Mum smiled and kissed my cheek, and only the knowledge that she would twist anything I said into further proof for her little theory kept me quiet.

❧

'HOW LONG DO you reckon you'll stay with your aunty?' Andy asked. He leant a shoulder against the doorframe of my cupboard-bedroom and watched with an expression of deepening gloom as I threw clothes into a bag.

'A couple of weeks? She's got one more chemo appointment, and then it'll take a little while for her to stop feeling like crap.'

He grunted in that eloquent way boys do – I've met some who could carry on entire conversations without articulating a single word – and dug his hands into the pockets of his jeans.

'If you pick out a new girlfriend you can spend all your time at her place,' I suggested. According to my source (i.e. Amber, who was part of the group that spent their Friday nights at the Frisky Possum, Waimanu's leading – and only – cafe-bar) both Anna Williams and Ngaire Swainson were showing signs of interest in my young flatmate.

'Yeah, but then you've got to talk to them.' He shook his head as he considered the unreasonable demands of girlfriends. 'Pretend to be interested in their new haircut, tell them they look skinny – all that crap.'

'Andy, you're such a gentleman,' I said. 'So sweet and sensitive. It warms my heart, it really does.'

'Thank you,' he said, and grinned.

'I'd have thought that getting your leg over would have made up for having to talk about clothes and hair.'

'Man, you're crude,' said Andy admiringly.

'Thank you,' I said in turn.

***

'HEY, JOSIE,' SAID Kim as I opened Rose's kitchen door. 'Need a hand?'

'No thanks, I'm good.' I put my bag down and turned to scratch Percy behind the ears. It seemed the least I could do, considering he had got up out of his warm bed in the woodshed to escort me from the car to the house. 'Hi, Hazel. How was your trip?'

'Come *in*, Josie dear,' she said reproachfully. 'There's a cold draught blowing onto poor Rose's feet.'

I closed the door, shutting out a wistful pig, and Aunty Rose looked at me from her seat on the chaise longue with just a flicker of a smile.

'The trip was good, thank you,' Hazel went on, 'although the heat was a little trying. And Nan's not the easiest of women. Very selfish and demanding.' Well, maybe. And maybe not.

'Your room's all ready, sweet pea,' said Aunty Rose.

'Thank you.' I went across the kitchen to kiss her hello and got a waft of Chanel No. 5. 'You smell so nice. I wish I had a signature scent.'

'You do,' said Kim. 'That anti-flamme stuff. Sort of pepperminty.'

I grimaced – not really a fragrance redolent of feminine beauty and allure.

'Your mother called,' Aunty Rose told me. 'She had a good flight home, and she says your father and the dog have both put on about a stone in her absence.'

I smiled. They would have, too – Dad and Toby the Jack Russell, when left to their own devices, spent their evenings sitting side by side on the couch and eating chips by the jumbo-sized packet. Dad flicked every second chip up in the air and Toby caught it. 'Poor things,' I said. 'She'll have them both on skim milk and salad for a month.' It really was lucky that my father tolerated and even enjoyed being micromanaged. I asked him once how he put up with it and he smiled sweetly and said, 'I can get my own way if I need to, young Jo, don't you worry.'

'It was kind of her to come,' said Hazel. 'But perhaps a little exhausting for you, Rosie, to have someone coming for such a long visit when you're unwell.' She looked at me sternly, just to make sure I was taking the hint. I looked back with my very best blank expression, and she added, 'I'm afraid, Josie, that you won't be able to expect Rose to cook and clean for you while you're here.'

'*Mum!*' Kim protested.

Aunty Rose smiled. 'That's right, Josephine,' she said. 'I won't have you just lazing around the place demanding Marmite omelettes. Now, my chickens, I'm going to be a truly awful hostess and totter off to bed.' She pushed herself to her feet and her sister gave a little breathless shriek of horror.

'Rosie. Oh, *Rosie*, your *hair*!' A good handful of silvery strands glinted against the dark green velvet of the chaise longue.

'Yes, Hazel, it's falling out,' Rose said calmly. 'I shall be as bald as an egg in about a week.' And she stalked out of the kitchen and down the hall.

Hazel looked after her with the wounded, puzzled expression of a kicked puppy. Then a look of saintly forbearance crossed her face and she looked gravely from Kim to me. 'Girls,' she said, 'Rosie needs all our patience and understanding just now. This nasty chemotherapy is making her feel very low.'

THE WEEKEND PASSED pleasantly, in a quiet and uneventful sort of way. Aunty Rose managed to sleep quite a lot of the time – when she was up we played Mah-jong at the kitchen table with the country and western station on the radio as background noise and drank multiple cups of tea. Aunty Rose's kitchen was the homiest place in the world. It had red velvet curtains (only a little bit tatty) at the windows and the walls were painted pink. She had a huge wood stove and about an acre of scrubbed wooden table, sheepskin rugs scattered at random across the floor and the griffon overseeing the lot from his perch on the back of the chaise longue.

'I really do admire Dolly Parton,' she remarked, as 'Jolene' drew to a close. She was wrapped in her crimson dressing-gown, and had wound her remaining hair into a loose chignon that cunningly disguised the large bald spot at the back where her head pressed against her pillow as she slept. 'I saw her interviewed on the television a few weeks ago – she looked at the interviewer with a wicked little glint in her eye and told him that it cost a lot of time and money to look as cheap as she does.'

'Graeme thinks she's a classless bimbo,' I said, and shook my head. 'You'd think that would have set off a few alarm bells, wouldn't you?'

'Indeed,' said Aunty Rose gravely. 'You had a narrow escape there, my girl.'

I grinned at her. 'Didn't I just?' And it occurred to me for the first time that perhaps I had. Being shafted by my boyfriend *and* my best friend had hurt so horribly that for months I couldn't bear to think about it (although, unfortunately, I couldn't think about anything else either, which meant the inside of my head really wasn't the happiest place). But actually I wasn't at all sure I'd have wanted to spend the rest of my life with Graeme the Snob. And that had to be a fairly major breakthrough. Not on the scale of Newton and his apple, I know, but still.

'Hurry up,' I said. 'It's your turn.'

'Where's the book?' Aunty Rose asked. 'I'm sure I've got an Imperial Dragon, or something really exciting.'

'I'm sure you haven't.' The woman cheated like you wouldn't believe; she was always inventing new combinations of tiles and claiming that they were worth vast numbers of points.

Chapter 13

MATT TOOK AUNTY Rose to her final chemo appointment on Tuesday. They were late home, and Aunty Rose, her face grey, crept straight into bed. Back in the kitchen Matt rubbed his face with his hands. 'Thank God that's the last one,' he said.

'When are they going to check her again?' I asked.

'Two weeks' time.'

'And with any luck, that'll be that.'

'Yeah. I don't know why I'm so knackered – I haven't done anything all day.'

'Well, hanging out in the oncology ward doesn't really top my list of fun things to do either,' I said.

'It's somewhere up there with shovelling out the calf sheds,' he agreed.

'Or massaging Dallas Taipa's feet.'

'Now that would be pretty bloody grim.'

'His socks . . .' I said dreamily. 'They're sort of crunchy.'

He grinned. 'You're really living life on the edge, aren't

you? Dallas's feet during the day, emptying the spew bowl by night . . .'

'I expect it's character building,' I said. 'We can feel all noble and superior about what great people we are. That's always nice.'

'Well, you can, anyway. All this housework and nursing and feeding that horde of animals – you shouldn't have to be doing all this, Jo.'

'I want to,' I said. 'I want to help. But if I'm getting a bit carried away and intruding you'll tell me, won't you?'

'Intruding?' he said. 'Don't be an idiot. I thought you were smart enough not to listen to my mother.' Hazel had yet to do anything even vaguely helpful, as far as I could tell, and had instead taken to making gentle comments about the extra work a house guest was giving poor dear Rosie.

'But it occurs to me that I might grow up into *my* mother, if nobody tells me to pull my head in.'

'Your mother's a legend. But you're nothing like her.'

'Gee,' I said drily as the phone started to ring. 'Thanks.'

'Hello?' Matt said, picking it up. 'Hang on – she's just here.' He handed it over.

'You never answer your mobile,' was Graeme's greeting.

'No,' I agreed. 'There's no service here so I keep it switched off most of the time.'

'Which would seem to defeat the purpose of having a mobile,' he said.

'What's up?' I asked, seeing no point in discussing my mobile phone usage with Graeme.

'Why didn't you pay your share of the mortgage on the first?'

'Didn't I?' I asked, taken aback.

'No, Jo, you didn't.' He was using his patient and superior voice, the one that always set my teeth on edge.

'I'll look into it tomorrow,' I said. 'Sorry.'

'It's not good enough,' said Graeme. 'I shouldn't have to run around checking up on you.'

'Look, I said I was sorry. It's on automatic payment – it should have gone through. I'll check it out.'

'As soon as possible, please. I've had to cover it – I had a call from the bank.'

'When are you having an open home?' I asked.

'Had one on the weekend.'

'Just last weekend?'

'No,' said Graeme testily. 'The one before.'

'As in nine days ago?'

'Yes, Jo, as in nine days ago.' There it was again. Superior.

'And how did it go?' I asked sweetly.

'Not bad – a couple of people looked interested.'

'Graeme,' I said, 'this is a fascinating little story, but I happen to know you were wandering up and down some beach on a romantic getaway that Sunday.' Thank you, Chrissie, for publicising every minute detail of your life on Facebook.

'What are you talking about?' he spluttered.

'You must think I'm really, really stupid. But I've got to say I'm getting pretty bloody tired of subsidising your love nest. If you want the house you can damn well buy me out.'

'I see,' he said. 'So you decided you'd just stop your half of the payments?'

'No,' I said angrily. 'I didn't. Although maybe if I *did* stop paying you'd stop sabotaging every offer anyone makes.'

'You just make sure you put that money in tomorrow. I'll get a lawyer if I have to, Jo. Don't think I won't.'

'*Man*, you're a prick,' I said, and slammed the phone down.

'That sounded like fun,' Matt remarked. He had withdrawn tactfully to the sink and started to concoct a cup of Milo while this happy little conversation was taking place.

'Yep,' I said. I swiped my eyes crossly with the back of a hand – I would *not* cry over this anymore. They were mostly tears of rage, anyway.

'Drink?'

'Yes, please.'

'How many sugars?' he asked.

'Three,' I said firmly.

He smiled. 'Does sugar help?' he asked.

'Of course. Didn't you know that?'

'I think it might be a girl thing. I've always preferred whisky.'

'Tempting,' I said, 'but not worth it when you've got to go to work the next day.' I sat down cross-legged on the chaise longue. 'I think I'm going to have to go to Melbourne and kick him for a while, and I really don't want to.'

'Can't you get a friend to do it for you? Or a lawyer?'

'I suppose so,' I said. 'We were just going to halve everything rather than pay a lawyer thousands of dollars to do it for us, but I'd really like to get the house sold and he seems to have decided he doesn't want to.'

'So you can just keep on paying half the mortgage while he moves the next model in?' said Matt. 'What a guy.'

'What *really* pisses me off is that he'll be getting Chrissie to pay half his share of the mortgage. He's insanely tight.'

'Jo?'

'Mm?' I accepted the cup of exceedingly sweet Milo and took a sip.

'Why on earth did you stay with this loser for five years?'

'Stupid, probably,' I said morosely. 'Oh, I don't know. He's very charming when he wants to be . . .'

'*And* he's a doctor.'

'Contrary to what you seem to think, I don't go out with people because they're doctors.'

'The last couple have been.'

'I've only ever *had* two boyfriends,' I protested. Surely the nice boy in my physio class with whom I spent a few excruciating weeks about ten years ago didn't count. 'I'm not sure that's a large enough sample size for you to be making these sweeping generalisations.'

'Perhaps not.' He yawned, stretching his arms above his head. 'So what happened?'

'Haven't you heard the dread tale?' I asked, surprised.

'Only Mum's version, and that probably bears more resemblance to *Days of Our Lives* than to anything else.'

I smiled. 'Actually, it *was* all fairly dramatic. I got home from work early one day and found him and my best friend having wild sex in a chair.'

Matt laughed. 'Sorry,' he said. 'I don't want to sound like an unsympathetic prat, but I've always wondered what happens in a situation like that.'

'You mean, do you politely withdraw and wait for them to finish up, or start screaming and throwing things?'

'That's the one. Which did you do?'

'I just stood there with my mouth open. Probably drooling in shock.' I started to laugh a bit hysterically. 'He saw me first, and he went purple, and she didn't notice . . .' I lost it completely and had to bury my face in a cushion until I recovered from a fit of the giggles. 'I've never seen anyone look so stupid in my whole life.'

'What a dickhead,' said Matt.

'Who? Me?'

'No, you muppet. Him. You're pretty great, you know.'

A great surge of heat rose from the soles of my feet to the tips of my ears. It must have been appallingly obvious; I may as well have waved a sign saying I AM CURRENTLY RECALLING EVERY DETAIL OF OUR NIGHT TOGETHER. Repressing with some difficulty the urge to bury my face again I said hastily, 'I think the worst thing is feeling like there's no place for me in my own life anymore. For months I was telling Chrissie about how he was all grumpy and stressed out, and she was pouring me glasses of wine and being sympathetic and sleeping with him every time I turned my back. They're apparently besotted with each other, and they're living in *my* house and having all the people I thought were *my* friends over for drinks, and everyone thinks it's all just wonderful. It's like I never existed at all.'

'People are just miserable cowards,' said Matt, eyes fixed firmly on the floor. He too was looking a little warm around the ears. 'They probably think it's pretty crappy, but no-one has the balls to say anything. So they just rewrite history and decide you guys were never particularly good together and you've probably been wanting to leave and come home for years anyway.'

'Only one person ever gave me a hug and said the pair of them deserved to be strung up,' I said. That was Graeme's English friend Stu from work, the campest gay man I have ever met and also one of the kindest people in the world. I wrinkled my nose. 'Sorry. You shouldn't look all nice and kind – it just encourages me to bore you to death.'

'You're not. And I asked.'

I smiled at him. 'That'll teach you.'

He smiled back. 'Well, I'm sorry your life has fallen apart, but it's very convenient that it happened when it did.'

'That's *very* consoling. Thank you so much.'

'You're welcome,' he said cheerfully. 'I'm good like that.'

He let himself out and I threw myself down flat on the chaise longue.

So I wasn't over Matt after all, I thought drearily. The only reason I had ever thought I might be was that I had forgotten, not having seen him for years on end, how great he was. And he was attached to a lip-glossed, pearl-earringed Farmer Barbie, and I was only his old mate Jo, a good stick but about as appealing as Shona at the Four Square who weighs a hundred kilos and has a mole with a long hair growing from the middle just below her right eye. *Crap*. I *hate* having to admit that my mother is right.

Matt and I never had one of those idyllic childhood friendships that gradually deepen into love. I suspect those friendships only exist in romantic novels, anyway. We played together at home but ignored one another at school, fed the calves and went eeling and swam in the creek and pestered Aunty Rose, and we used to fall out at least once a week. We developed periodic crushes on one another in our teens, although never at the same time, and by the end of high school had decided that we were probably quite good mates after all. And then when he was twenty and I was twenty-one we had a *spectacular* one-night stand, and he went to Scotland the next day, and with the exception of his father's funeral we hadn't managed to be in the same country at the same time since.

Chapter 14

The night before Matt went to Scotland

FROM MY BEDROOM at the end of the hall I heard someone pounding on the door, followed by my flat-mate Neil's voice raised in complaint. 'I'm coming, keep your hair on!' Then, 'Jo! Visitor!'

I marked my place in *Pathology of the Spine* with a pen, and rolled off my bed.

Neil had lost interest in the guest and vanished, leaving him standing in the hall with his enormous pack leaning against the wall beside him.

'Matt!' I cried.

'Hey, Jose.' He grinned at me. 'I'm flying out tomorrow morning – can you put me up for the night?'

'Of course.' I put my arms around his neck and hugged him. 'Crikey. You've got all muscly.'

'Thank you,' he said, detaching himself to heave his

pack onto one shoulder. Lucky he *had* got muscly, if he was planning to carry that thing any distance.

I led the way down the hall. 'You can leave your pack in my room. Where are you off to tomorrow?'

'Scotland.'

'*What?*'

'I got a scholarship for a rural exchange program. Six months on a sheep farm in Scotland, and then Scotty's coming over and we're going to cruise around Europe and the Middle East for a while.' He dropped his pack just inside my bedroom door with a thud.

'You and Scotty let loose in Europe,' I said. 'The mind boggles. Now, would you care for a cool beverage of some sort?'

'That's a bloody brilliant idea,' said Matt gravely.

I fetched us both a beer and we went outside to drink it in the pale winter sunshine. 'Not that one!' I said as he pulled up a grubby folding chair. 'Someone peed on it last weekend.'

'Why not wash it?'

I shrugged. 'It'll rain eventually. Here.' And I pushed an uncontaminated chair his way before perching on the porch railing.

'Your standards have slipped,' he noted.

'I live with three slobs. I had to decide whether to clean up after them all the time and get bitter and twisted or turn into a slob myself and stay cheerful, so I went for slobby and cheerful.'

'Very wise,' said Matt.

I looked at him surreptitiously over my bottle of Tui and decided he was looking quite disturbingly attractive these days.

It was Friday, and some of Neil's friends were having a flat-warming party that night. We moved from the porch to the untidy lounge when the sun vanished behind next-door's high wooden fence, ordered Thai takeaways for tea and eventually walked down the road to the party.

As I recall, it wasn't much of a party. A large group of journalism students in op-shop suede coats and hand-painted Doc Martens had taken over the lounge, and another group were drinking yardies on the back lawn. Watching someone throw up into his yard glass and then attempt to continue drinking is only fun for a while, and the journalism students were playing peculiar Indonesian music very loudly on the stereo.

Wandering through the kitchen sometime around midnight I discovered Matt leaning against the fridge and fending off an extremely drunk girl wearing a bright green polyester pinafore and brown tights. She looked like a tree.

'Jo!' he said, with just a hint of desperation in his voice. 'Beer?'

'I was actually thinking of heading home,' I said.

'I'll come with you. Lovely to meet you.' And putting down his can of Rheineck (by far the best thing to be done with a warm can of Rheineck) he fled ahead of me out the front door.

'Do you really want to come, or were you just escaping?' I asked.

'I want to come. Besides, you shouldn't walk around Auckland by yourself at night.'

There was a bite to the air and we walked briskly. 'It's much nicer out here,' I said, digging my hands into the pockets of my jeans to keep them warm.

'Mm,' he agreed absently. 'Your flatmates are good sorts, Jose.'

'They are, aren't they?'

'Neil seems like a nice bloke.'

'Yeah,' I said. 'He is.' And I added casually, just in case he might have thought I had any interest in Neil, 'His girl-friend's nice, too. She's gone up north for the weekend to see her parents.'

Matt said nothing in response to this, and we walked the next block in silence. As we went up the porch steps to the back door I fished in my pocket for the key, and fitting it into the lock said with a fairly pitiful attempt at nonchalance, 'You can sleep on the couch or have half my bed, whichever you'd rather.'

'Half your bed, please.'

And as I turned the door handle he reached for my other hand and held it. He had big, rough hands, callused from spending the last week rehanging gates; Patrick King liked to use the periods between university holidays to make lists of little jobs for his son, to be started about five minutes after his arrival home.

Be cool, I told myself fiercely, *he's your friend, that's all*. 'Do you want a coffee or something?'

'No, thank you,' he said, shutting the door behind

us. And by the sickly orange light of a streetlight shining through the window in the hall he took my face in his hands and kissed me.

Oh, thank God, I thought. *It's not just me.* I slid my arms around him and kissed him back.

My romantic experience, by the age of twenty-one, had consisted of kissing Tane Jones in the car park outside the Waimanu High School ball at age sixteen (followed closely by throwing up on his feet, having consumed an indecent amount of extremely nasty vodka mixed with even nastier orange cordial) and one awful month spent going out with a very nice boy in my class whom I didn't fancy in the least. Having observed the relationships and hook-ups of my flatmates and friends I had begun to think that there was something wrong with me – considering that I wasn't avoiding sex on any moral grounds, surely I should have been having some of it. I went out twice a week and encountered *packs* of boys my own age, and if I still couldn't find anyone to sleep with I was obviously well on the way to a lonely and eccentric spinsterhood.

Kissing Matt had not a single thing in common with kissing the nice but undesirable Marcus. He tasted faintly of beer, he was lean and hard, and his mouth was hot against mine.

'Jo,' he said thickly after some time, pulling his mouth away.

'Y-yeah?'

'I've been wanting to do that all night.'

'Do it some more,' I said breathlessly, and pulled him down the hall into my bedroom.

'Okay.' And then some time later, 'Hey . . .'

I removed my hand from the hard bulge in his jeans and blushed in the near-darkness. 'Sorry.'

'I like it,' he said. 'I *really* like it. But I have to go to Scotland tomorrow.'

'Sorry,' I muttered again. 'You should be getting some sleep.'

He took me by the shoulders and shook me gently. 'I couldn't give a rat's *arse* about sleep,' he said. 'But we might not see each other again for a couple of years.'

'So why did you kiss me?' I asked, made brave by half a dozen bottles of beer.

'Couldn't help it.'

'That's nice.' I reached up and kissed him again.

'God, Josie, you're beautiful,' he said shakily. And sighing as he lost his short battle to be noble and gentlemanly he slid his big warm hands up under my tight top.

This was absolutely nothing like letting a nice boy fumble with my breasts and grunt damply against my neck during a few mercifully brief encounters. That had been just sort of sticky and embarrassing, and I was never sure whether to try to gasp and writhe convincingly or just lie there and wait. I mostly decided on something between the two and ended up feeling both dispirited and like a horrible fraud.

Matt was in an entirely different league. He pushed me gently back on the bed and came down with me, peeling off my clothes between kisses and sliding a hand between my legs.

'Matt . . .' I whispered, arching up against him.

'Okay?'

'Yes – come here.' I wrestled with his belt.

'Hang on,' he said against my mouth. 'I'll do it.' Then, 'Jose, if you don't stop doing that I'm going to lose it completely.'

'That was kind of the idea.'

He laughed, caught my hands in his and held them firmly, and put his mouth over my right breast.

'*Matt!*'

'Don't you like it?'

'*God*, yes! Have you got any condoms?'

He let me go, tugged his wallet out of the back pocket of his jeans and shed the rest of his clothes at close to the speed of light. I sat up to take the condom out of his hand and rip open the little foil packet, and he laughed as he reclaimed it and put it on. I pulled him down again, wrapping my legs around his waist and sparing just a fraction of a second to be deeply thankful I'd shaved them that morning. 'Just slow *down*,' he whispered.

'Can't. I mean, don't want to.'

'Fair enough,' he muttered, and put his arms around me tightly. 'Me neither.'

AFTERWARDS I LAY flat on my back, looking at the zigzag crack in the ceiling and trying to breathe.

Matthew sat up and looked down at me. 'Should we get under the covers?' he suggested.

'I would,' I said, 'but I don't think I can move.'

'Is that a good thing or a bad thing?'

'Good.' I pushed myself up on my elbows with some difficulty and he leant down to kiss me softly. 'Matt?'

'Yeah?'

'Thank you.'

He kissed me again. 'You're welcome.' He sighed. '*Bugger* having to go to Scotland.'

'When do you have to go?'

He looked at the face of my little fluorescent alarm clock. 'In about seven hours.' He pulled at the edge of the duvet and I wriggled aside to let him tug it out from under me. We curled up underneath it and I rested my forehead against his shoulder.

'We have the worst timing on the planet,' I said sadly.

He tightened his arm around me. 'We have seven hours,' he pointed out.

We spent them talking, cat-napping and using up the remaining three condoms in his wallet. Then we got up and I drove him to the airport, dropped him at International Departures ('Don't come in, Jose, it'll just make it worse') and went home. I had to take an exit I didn't want off the motorway so that I could park up a side street and bawl my eyes out for half an hour without endangering myself or my fellow motorists. I seem to remember that I picked a street down which a constant stream of pedestrians passed within a foot of my car, but that I was too busy wallowing in misery to care.

130

MATT SPENT NEARLY five years overseas. My sources (that is, Clare, whose brother was in London at the same time) informed me that he was partying extremely hard and working his way through a never-ending procession of girlfriends. He decided after a year or two that he'd better try to see a bit more of Europe than the inside of a pub and went travelling – he drove tractors in France and operated ski lifts in Switzerland and even somehow ended up running a motel on Corfu for a year.

I was nowhere near as adventurous. I thought I'd work for a year or two and then explore the world, going on some sort of voyage of self-discovery in the process, but I never got there. I finished my physiotherapy degree and spent a year's internship at Middlemore Hospital in Auckland, where I fell heavily for a sandy-haired anaesthetist, and I only made it as far as private practice in Greenlane.

Matt and I used to ring each other sporadically, but I didn't see him again until his father's funeral. He stayed home after that to run the farm, and about a month later I moved to Melbourne with boyfriend number two.

We'd never spoken of that night in all the years since; presumably it had meant so little to Matt he'd all but forgotten it. But I hadn't.

Chapter 15

'GOOD AFTERNOON, MISS Donnelly,' said Bob with his special brand of slightly ponderous gallantry. He was a nice man, but even had I been able to overlook the halitosis, and even if I wasn't currently restraining myself from dreamily practising 'J.M. King' signatures around the margins of newspaper crossword puzzles, he was so pedantic that I'd have had to hit him over the head with a pot after a week of his company.

'Hi, Bob,' I said, gathering up bits of paper and stuffing them into my shoulder bag in a pointedly hurried fashion. 'I'm running a bit late.'

'I brought you a few recipes.' He pulled a wodge of those glossy, tear-off Food-in-a-Minute recipes you can get at the supermarket from his back pocket and handed them to me proudly. 'You said you needed some meal ideas.'

Ah, yes. The last time he had popped in I was ushering out Mrs Clarke, chatting idly about food that somebody who is nauseous and miserable from chemo might find tempting. 'Thank you very much,' I said, trying to sound suitably grateful. 'That's very thoughtful. Look, I've got to head –'

But he waved me to silence with an imperious gesture. 'Just one moment of your valuable time, my dear.' Behind him Amber was sniggering gently at her computer keyboard in a distinctly unhelpful way. 'There's a wine and cheese do at the Workingman's Club this Friday. Don't you think that sounds like a bit of alright?'

'I can't go out in the evenings at the moment,' I said.

'That's right, your dear honorary aunt. But surely a couple of hours of rest and relaxation would do you nothing but good.'

'I couldn't leave her,' I said firmly. 'I just wouldn't be able to enjoy myself. Thank you so much for the invitation, Bob, but I really do have to run.'

'I think it's marvellous,' he murmured, beaming at me fondly. 'A young woman like yourself with such a delightfully old-fashioned sense of duty.' No doubt he was envisaging me cheerfully wiping his bottom in another twenty years or so. What a truly revolting image.

'Amber, you can lock up, can't you?' I said. 'See you, Bob – thank you again . . .' And I bolted from the building like a startled rabbit.

Safely in my car I rested my head for a moment against the steering wheel. This was getting ridiculous – I couldn't just keep using Rose as an excuse. Perhaps I would have to make a flip chart, complete with graphs and professional-looking red arrows, comparing my likelihood of ever going *anywhere* with poor Bob with the chance of hell freezing over. Somebody tapped on the driver's window and I looked up wildly. Right, that was it, I was going to lose it and start shouting at the man – but it was Kim, dressed in her school uniform with her satchel over one shoulder. I wound down the window.

'What on earth are you doing?' she asked.

'Escaping from Bob McIntosh.'

'Right. Can I have a lift home?'

'Sure,' I said. 'Did you have detention again?'

'No,' said Kim, sounding offended. 'Guitar practice.'

'Since when do you play the guitar?'

She trotted around the front of the car and hopped in beside me. 'Two weeks. I can do three chords now. Jonno's in a band and I'm going to be back-up singer and guitarist.'

'Awesome,' I said solemnly.

'HOW DID IT go?' I asked, letting myself in the kitchen door a couple of days later to find Aunty Rose beating eggs in a china mixing bowl. She was wearing a fetching little green satin cap with a spray of artificial cherries sewn onto one side, one of a boxful of hats and wigs given to her by Mary-Anne Morris at the chemist's. Mary-Anne had lost her own hair in a battle with cancer a few years before.

'Well, the rotten thing has shrunk, anyway,' she said. 'So they're going to whip it out next week.' Her check-up appointment had been that morning, and she'd stubbornly resisted all offers to drive her, claiming that Matt and I were just looking for an excuse not to do any work and she couldn't condone that sort of thing.

'Good. They'll hit it with a bit more chemo after that, won't they?'

'Yes, but not such nasty drugs this time.'

'So you won't start puking your guts out again?' I put the grocery bags I was holding on the kitchen table and began to unpack them.

'Josephine, you use these expressions solely to annoy me, don't you?'

'Yes,' I admitted, and grinned at her.

'I did hope that was the case. No, the nausea should be much better.'

'Just think of all the wine you'll be able to drink.'

She sighed happily. 'I know.'

Outside the dogs began to bark, and Aunty Rose peered out the window. 'Ah,' she said. 'Kim, with a face like thunder. Honestly, that child is as good as a soap opera.'

Kim flounced in, shutting the door with what came perilously close to a slam. She was taking her new role of rock chick very seriously; today she wore Doc Marten boots, shiny black tights and a very short tartan skirt. You could barely see its hem peeping out from underneath a worn black T-shirt that I thought I recognised as one of Matt's – it was far too big for her and had SEPULTURA written across the front, the words wreathed in flames and topped by a leering skull.

'Nice outfit,' I said appreciatively. Teasing Kim was one of my very favourite hobbies.

'Hi, Aunty Rose,' she said, ignoring me and kissing her aunt's lined cheek. I was looking forward to seeing Rose fatten up a bit. Losing so much weight had aged her horribly and fifty-three is *much* too young to look old and drawn.

'Hello, my love,' said Aunty Rose. 'How was your day?'

'Sucked,' Kim said, perching on the edge of the kitchen table and swinging her booted feet.

'That's a shame.'

'Hey, Jo, chuck me an apple?' I did, and she bit into it with relish. 'Those dicks at school are so far up their own bums you wouldn't believe it.'

'Kim Amanda King!' said Aunty Rose sharply. 'That sort of language just implies you're too stupid to speak proper English. If you *were* stupid I wouldn't mind, but you're not.'

'Sorry,' Kim muttered.

'Which dicks at school?' I asked. 'That is, which people have provoked your displeasure?'

'Dean and deputy principal. And they *are* di–... idiots.'

'What did you do?' Aunty Rose asked with some misgiving.

'There was a cigarette in my bag.'

'Oh, Kim, don't start smoking,' Aunty Rose said. 'If only because of the expense, let alone that insignificant little statistic of smoking killing one person in two.'

'I won't, I won't,' said Kim. 'But honestly, what a fuss

over nothing. Mum's having hysterics, and I've got to go and be hassled by the disciplinary committee.'

'For a cigarette?' I asked, deeply sceptical.

'Well, actually it was a joint. But still . . .'

'*What?*' said Aunty Rose, fingers gripping her whisk so tightly that her knuckles went white. She drew herself up to her full six foot two and glared at her niece. 'You took marijuana to school? Have you lost your *mind*?'

'Aunty Rose, it was just one tiny little joint –' Kim started feebly.

'I don't want to talk to you,' said Aunty Rose. 'I might say something I'd regret.' She removed a dog roll from the fridge and stalked outside into the dusk, slamming the door behind her.

There was a dismayed silence, and then Kim said, with a slightly shaky attempt at bravado, 'Well, that wound the old girl up.'

'Shut up,' I said flatly, putting away the last of the groceries and shutting the pantry door.

'It's not like you can talk!' she cried. 'I don't believe *you've* never smoked a joint.'

Actually, in my sheltered life I'd only ever shared one with Chrissie, one night when Graeme was working late, and it had sent us both to sleep. Not really a prime example of living life on the edge. 'In my stupidest teenage moments I'd never have taken drugs to school,' I snapped. 'You might be expelled, you moron – then what'll you do?'

'School's a waste of time anyway. I might chuck it in.'

'Brilliant. You can go and pump petrol for the

minimum wage. And if you're *really* lucky you can find some dropkick – that one you're going out with would do – to get you pregnant. You might as well fuck up your life completely while you're at it. But don't worry, if you smoke enough dope you won't really care.'

Kim burst into tears, threw her half-eaten apple at me and ran out of the house.

I found, as I bent to pick it up, that my hands were shaking. *Well done, Jo*, I thought. *You couldn't have handled that worse if you'd tried – now you've lost any influence you might have had over the poor kid.* I waited until I heard her roar down the drive in her mother's car before going outside.

'What did you say to her?' Aunty Rose asked, straightening up from where she was attending to the itchy spot between Percy's ears. He grunted indignantly, sighed and waddled off.

'I stuffed it up completely,' I admitted. 'I told her she was an idiot and asked why didn't she just drop out of school and get herself pregnant while she was at it.'

'*Ex*cellent.'

'Huh?' I asked blankly.

'That child thinks you're the most marvellous thing since sliced bread.'

'Not anymore, she doesn't.'

'Let me finish,' said Aunty Rose. 'She thought you'd be amused and instead you came down on her like a tonne of bricks. It might actually shock some sense into her.'

'Or she might rush off and mainline some heroin,' I said.

'Of course she won't.' Rose sighed. 'Well, I hope not. I do hope we can get her through the next few years. Matthew had his moments, but at least he had a useful father.' She added as she turned back towards the house, 'And then, of course, you don't have to worry about boys coming home pregnant.'

Chapter 16

KIM'S DISCIPLINARY HEARING was held on Monday afternoon, after school. According to Matt she had been threatened with suspension and reduced to a small and pathetic heap before receiving her sentence of recataloguing every reference book in the Waimanu High School library. She would tackle this task every afternoon from three-thirty until the cleaners finished and locked up at five.

'I'll bring her home,' I offered. Matt had wandered into the physio clinic during Amber's lunch break and was leaning against the front counter digging thistles out of the pads of his fingers with his pocket knife. Getting out prickles is such a satisfying pursuit – I was itching to have a go but since the unhappy day, about fifteen years earlier, when I lanced his infected toenail and hit a fairly major artery, I had never been allowed anywhere near him with a sharp instrument. 'Although she'd probably rather walk than go anywhere with me just at the moment.'

He grinned. 'Poor little sausage,' he said. 'You yelled at her, I yelled at her, Rose yelled at her, Mum sobbed broken-heartedly for about an hour last night about the shame she's brought upon the name of King . . .'

'*Poor* Kim,' I said with feeling.

'She's not allowed to go to guitar practice anymore and Mum's banned her from spending time with Jonno the dropkick.'

I rubbed my nose thoughtfully. 'You don't think that'll just encourage her to rush off and sleep with him?'

'Probably,' he said morosely. 'Rotten little bastard. I bet he gave the stuff to her in the first place.' He sighed. 'It was bloody thoughtless of Dad to go and die just as she hit her teens.'

'You're doing a good job,' I said. 'She's lucky to have you.' I felt my face getting warm and added hastily, 'When does she start her detention?'

'Today,' said Matt. 'I've already told her she'd better come round here afterwards and grovel until you give her a lift home.'

'I hope she turns up.'

'She will,' he said. He straightened up and put his pocket knife back in his pocket, evidently satisfied with his thistle progress. 'Hey, Jo – thanks.'

'I'm going that way anyway,' I pointed out.

'Not just for that. For – well, everything.'

I barely stifled a sigh. Being viewed by Matt as Good Old Jo, although undoubtedly better than Jo the Interfering Pain in the Neck, was profoundly depressing.

KIM APPEARED AT ten past five, cloaked in gloom. Amber had gone for the day – she'd even shut down her computer, which was little short of miraculous – and I was sorting through a box of ancient tag ends of Elastoplast rolls. Why Cheryl felt that keeping the last two inches rather than wrapping it around the client's ankle was a useful saving was beyond me.

'Matt said you might take me home,' Kim muttered, looking at the ground.

'Of course I will.' I put the box back in its cupboard and shut the door. 'Hey, Kim?'

'Don't!' she said hysterically. 'Just don't lecture me anymore – I can't stand it.'

She looked so small and so miserable that I hugged her before it occurred to me that I probably wasn't high on her list of potential comforters at the moment. However, she buried her head in my shoulder and burst into tears. I patted her soothingly for a while, and when at last she stopped sobbing and began to hiccup I passed her the box of tissues I had strategically placed on the front counter to encourage Amber to stop wiping her nose on the backs of her hands. (It hadn't worked; Amber used the tissues solely to remove polish from her fingernails. Clients of Waimanu Physiotherapy waited for their appointments in a haze of acetone fumes.)

Kim took the tissues and blew her nose. 'Sorry,' she whispered.

'Me too. I had no right to yell at you – sometimes I forget you're not actually my sister.'

'I wish I was,' said Kim.

'That may be the nicest thing anyone's ever said to me,' I told her. I fished in my bag. 'Here, I got you something.'

She unwrapped the little package, looked at the pair of silver hoop earrings I had purchased that afternoon during the ten-minute lunch break Amber had allowed me and began to cry once more. 'They're b-beautiful,' she sobbed. 'And they're real silver – oh, *Josie*.'

'Steady on there, Kimlet. Come on, let's go home.'

HAZEL, ACTING LIKE an early Christian martyr, took Aunty Rose to Waikato Hospital for her mastectomy. The rest of us were strictly forbidden to visit.

'What an incredible waste of your time,' Aunty Rose said. 'I'll only be there a day or two. It will be a pleasant change to have a little time to myself, rather than having to constantly try to instil a little decorum in you three hoodlums.'

Matt grinned at her. 'If I were you I'd give up on Jo and me,' he said. 'We're far too old to discipline properly. Concentrate on the toad.'

She stayed in hospital three nights, and Hazel brought her home again on the Saturday – it transpired that Hazel's new bedroom curtains were finished by then and waiting in Hamilton for collection. I was finding it very hard to look at Hazel's motives with anything approaching charity these days.

They arrived at around six, having waited hours to

be discharged, and Aunty Rose made her way shakily across the gravel and up the kitchen path. She was surrounded by an anxious retinue of four dogs and one pig, all of them needing reassurance that she wouldn't leave them again.

'I see you've mistreated the animals in my absence, Josephine,' she said.

I crouched down to help her off with her shoes. 'Spud slept in the kitchen in front of the stove last night, and I scratched Percy's stomach for about an hour. Don't believe a word they say.'

Aunty Rose touched my head lightly. 'Of course your flaws are too numerous to count, child, but you do mean well.'

'Thank you,' I said. 'Cup of tea?'

'Does the Pope wear a funny hat?'

Hazel sank into a kitchen chair with an air of exhaustion. 'What a day,' she murmured. 'And *now* who's coming to bother you, Rosie?'

Aunty Rose was lowering herself carefully onto the chaise longue. I heard the familiar splutter of Matt's decrepit ute through the dogs' chorus and said, 'It's just Matt.'

'Where is Kimmy, dear?'

'At home,' I said. 'I dropped her off about half an hour ago.'

'How is our young miscreant?' enquired Aunty Rose.

'Bowed by remorse,' I told her. 'I hope it wears off in a day or two. It's pitiful to see.'

'I hope it doesn't,' said the young miscreant's mother tartly. 'How she could be so insensitive as to worry us all at a time like this – and think of the repercussions for your health, Rosie dear.'

'Good God,' said Aunty Rose. 'I hope you didn't say that to Kim.'

'Well, she needs to know how her thoughtlessness affects others.'

'Oh, for Pete's sake,' Aunty Rose muttered. 'Josephine, remind me to ring the poor child. Hello, dear boy.'

'Yeah, g'day,' said Matt in a low, flat Kiwi drawl specifically designed to provoke his aunt. 'It's nice to have you home.' He came across the kitchen and kissed her cheek, Farmer Barbie at his heels. This evening Cilla was wearing a snow-white top and a delicate primrose cardigan over her jeans. Her hair was loose down her back and she looked, I thought bitterly, like a little porcelain doll.

I was a bit taken aback by the intensity of my resentment, and to make up for it said, 'Hi, Cilla. You look beautiful,' far more warmly than was really necessary.

'*Doesn't* she just,' said Hazel. 'What a lovely little cardigan. And *such* flowers, dear.'

'Thank you,' said Cilla demurely. 'Miss Thornton, it's so nice to have you home.' She handed Aunty Rose a bunch of chrysanthemums, yellow and cream – they went delightfully with her cardigan.

'They're very nice,' said Aunty Rose. 'Thank you.'

'So thoughtful,' murmured Hazel. 'Such a dear girl.'

For Christ's sake, she got them at the petrol station, I thought, as sour as a whole vat full of acid. *It's not like she grew them from seed*. 'Anyone else for tea?'

'No,' said Hazel. 'I must head home. I've a shattering headache from the driving.'

Cilla looked sympathetic, which made one of us. Matt merely smiled faintly on his way to the peanut jar and I turned away to fetch a vase for the flowers. 'Aunty Rose,' I said, 'can I possibly interest you in a scrambled-egg sandwich?'

'Hmm,' she said. 'You know, Josephine, what I would *really* like is a very soft boiled egg with toast soldiers.'

As I made dinner according to Aunty Rose's precise instructions – 'Butter to the very edges of the toast, love,' and, 'Leave them in for four minutes and twenty seconds from when the water comes to the boil' – Matt vanished outside with the empty wood basket and Cilla made extremely polite conversation.

As soon as he reappeared she tucked a hand into his and murmured, 'Honey, your aunt will want to rest.'

'I'll be over tomorrow morning,' Matt said. He kissed Aunty Rose, smiled at me and went out with Cilla still clinging to his hand.

I blinked hard once or twice, said silently, *Don't even* think *about it* to the lump in my throat and asked, 'I don't suppose you should have a glass of sauvignon blanc with your egg?'

'Probably not,' said Aunty Rose, 'but I can't think of anything nicer.' She was silent for a moment as I carefully sliced the tops off our eggs and retrieved the wine from the fridge, and then she said gently, 'Josie, my love, come here.'

I went, sinking to the floor beside her and leaning my head against her knee. I wasn't sure whether Mum had told her or if she'd seen it herself, but I was unexpectedly comforted that she knew. She stroked my hair while the griffon stared over our heads in a bored fashion, and at length she said, 'I suppose it might get us in trouble if we put those flowers straight onto the compost heap.'

I gave a little gulp of laughter, got to my feet and poured us each a glass of pale, crisp wine to go with our eggs. 'Matt would never notice,' I said, 'but his mother would.'

Aunty Rose got slowly and painfully to her feet to take her seat at the table. 'They're almost exactly alike,' she said. 'Cilla and Hazel, I mean.'

'Mm,' I said thoughtfully. They were indeed. Soft and sweet and clingy, just like fragrant pink leeches.

Chapter 17

I HAVE NO doubt that mastectomies are painful and unpleasant, but compared to the hideous crippling nausea of the chemo, Aunty Rose said, a mere surgical wound was an absolute doddle. She had a little stash of pain medication and drove herself down to the medical centre in town every afternoon for a change of dressing, but as early as Sunday morning she was better than she had been since the chemotherapy began.

On Monday night after work I met Andy in the supermarket, pushing a trolley containing two boxes of beer, a wide range of frozen pies, hash browns, chips and fish fingers, and a token bunch of bananas.

'Howdy, stranger,' I said. 'That's a health-giving and nutritious selection you've got there.'

'All the food groups,' said Andy. 'Alcohol, fat and protein.'

'You forgot sugar.'

'I haven't got to that aisle yet,' he explained.

'I see. Hey, I'm coming home in a day or two.'

'I wouldn't,' he advised. 'The bush pig has found herself a boyfriend.'

'Crikey,' I said in surprise. 'Who?'

'Some dickhead who drives for Hayden Judd.' Hayden ran Waimanu Transport, a small down-at-heel trucking company that operated out of a grotty shed next to the sale yards.

'Huh. Well, good on her.'

'Just you wait,' said Andy. 'They have long showers together and lie on the couch groping each other and making sucking noises.'

'I can hardly wait. Long showers, did you say? What about the power bill?'

'It's disgusting,' Andy continued. 'Having to get in that shower knowing they've been having sex all over it. I can't take it anymore – I'm moving in with Chris.'

'Gee, thanks,' I said.

He grinned. 'You can come and hang out there if you want,' he offered.

❧

I ENTERED AUNTY Rose's kitchen half an hour later hung with bags of groceries like a Christmas tree and found her sitting at the table.

'It's a lovely evening,' I announced. 'Full moon, and lots of little tattered clouds streaming across the sky – you should go out and look. It would be a perfect night for witches.'

'Excellent,' said Aunty Rose in a tight little voice.

I turned and looked at her properly and saw that she was clasping her hands together so firmly that the knuckles were white.

'What is it?' I asked.

'The hospital called,' she said. 'They want me to have another CAT scan tomorrow before they start the next round of chemo.'

Oh, God. 'Another one? Why?'

She sighed and pushed herself up to stand, palms flat on the table. Her knuckles were far too big for her hands now, and the old-fashioned amethyst ring she wore slid freely between the joints. 'The margins weren't clear,' she said. 'And they want to find out where else the bloody thing has popped up.'

I was appalled – they'd already taken her right breast and several lymph nodes. It had seemed horribly drastic but Matt and I had told each other that at least they'd be sure to have got the whole rotten thing, and that would be that.

'Oh,' I said weakly.

Aunty Rose sighed. 'Well,' she said, 'I can only think of one thing to do, and that's to have a glass of wine. Might as well make the most of it while I'm not feeling like total poo.'

Several glasses of wine later, curled in one of the big overstuffed armchairs in the living room, I asked, 'Would you like me to move back into town for a bit and let you have your house to yourself?'

'Josephine,' said Aunty Rose with the slightly pompous solemnity that descended on her when she was tiddly, 'the reason is almost impossible to fathom, but I would actually miss you if you weren't around.'

'Good,' I said. 'Then I'm around.'

She looked at me, suddenly serious. 'My dear, is it too hard for you?'

I wasn't sure if she meant my housekeeping duties or the proximity to Matt, but I shook my head. 'Nope. I'm very grateful, to be honest. I ran into my nice flatmate Andy this evening and he told me the dread Sara had found herself a boyfriend and they've been lying all over the lounge sucking each other. He can't take it anymore – he's moving out.'

'That does sound fairly dire,' Aunty Rose agreed.

'I think I'll move out too. When you're better I'll look for something else.'

The words 'when you're better' hung between us like smoke from a snuffed candle – what if she wasn't going to get better? Well, she just had to. I got up and divided the remaining dregs of wine in the bottle between our glasses.

IT NEVER RAINS but it pours – especially when it comes to bad news. The next day I was in the consulting room when Amber called, 'Jo! Phone!'

I got up with some relief. I had been reviewing notes on acupuncture and just after lunch is not the ideal time for review; I tend to go to sleep on my book.

'Who is it?' I mouthed as I took the phone, but Amber merely shrugged and turned back to her computer screen. 'Hello, Jo speaking.'

'Jo, my angel,' said a rather high-pitched and very camp male voice with an upper-crust British accent.

'Stu!' I cried delightedly. 'Hello! How are you?'

'Not bad at all. Now, I'm planning my little hop across the ditch. If I popped up for a night to see you do you think you could find me a spare floorboard and a crust of bread?'

'I'm almost sure we could manage that,' I said. 'When?'

'Last weekend in July. This conference goes from Tuesday till Friday – I thought on the Saturday I might hire a car and meander north to this dreary little hamlet you're frequenting.'

'Waimanu,' I said haughtily, 'is *not* a dreary hamlet. It's a bustling epicentre of culture and excitement.' Stu's manner of speech is catching.

'Oh good,' he said. 'I can hardly wait.'

'Me neither. Thank you so much, Stu.'

'How are you doing, angel?' he asked. 'You sound a bit flat.'

'Aunty Rose had her mastectomy last week and the margins weren't clear,' I said gloomily. 'She has to have another round of chemo, and the last lot nearly killed her.'

'Cancer's just a total bitch,' said Stu. 'I'm sorry, hon. I thought maybe you'd heard Graeme and Chrissie's news . . .'

152

Someone should expose the whole wedding industry. I swear things are three times more expensive if they're for a wedding than if they're just for a party. I'm thinking about starting a one-woman crusade.

She'd changed her Facebook profile picture again. Today it was a close-up of an enormous glittering diamond ring and part of a hugely magnified hand. What a show-off. And how on *earth* had she managed to get him to fork out the thousands of dollars that ring had cost? Deciding abruptly that this was doing my mental health no good at all I moved the mouse and deleted Chrissie de Villiers from my Friends list.

A tear trickled down my cheek and I left it there, rather enjoying the effect. Surely it's reasonable to cry just a little bit when your ex-boyfriend cheated on you, he's marrying the new one although he said loudly for years that marriage is just a snare and a delusion, your next appointment is with Bob bloody McIntosh, your favourite aunt is wasting away before your eyes, you're working late and when you get home you've got a good couple of hours of household chores waiting for you *and* you have a nasty case of unrequited love.

'Bob's here,' said Amber, putting her head around the door and looking at me with a complete lack of interest. 'And the fax machine's broken.'

'Open it up,' I said crisply, taking a savage swipe at my wet cheek with the back of one hand. 'Take *out* the bit of jammed paper. Shut it again. And send Bob through.'

'Okay,' said Amber vaguely, and drifted out again.

'Good afternoon, young Josie,' said Bob, peeping coyly around the door. 'I need you to work your magic on this bally vertebra of mine.'

'Come on in,' I told him, metaphorically stiffening my upper lip. Enough was enough. Today was going to be the day I finally put my foot down.

I *did* put my foot down – quite hard, actually – but the man was utterly unsquashable. Like a human cockroach. He invited me to dinner, and then to lunch when I refused.

'Bob,' I said, 'look, I'm very flattered, but it's just not a starter.'

'I'm sure your aunt would be pleased to see you getting out and about,' he said imploringly.

'I'm sure she would,' I said. 'But *I don't want to go out with you*. I'm sorry to be rude, Bob, but I'm really not interested.'

'Such a sense of duty,' he murmured. 'You're a sweet girl, Josie.'

'*Bob!*' I said crossly.

He motioned me to silence with a wave of his hand. I considered, for a second, lunging at him and biting it, but it looked none too clean. 'Josie,' he said kindly. 'Josie, Josie. A little bird has told me your faith in men has taken a few knocks recently. You can rest assured I won't rush you. I'll just be here quietly waiting and hoping in the background until you feel ready for more than friendship.'

I gave up. 'Go away,' I said tiredly. 'Just go away.'

I was beating my head gently against my desk when Cheryl, a baby capsule over one arm and an enormous nappy bag over the other, put her head around the door. 'Oh, no,' she said in alarm. 'Don't tell me it's all got too much for you and you're going to hand in your notice. I warn you I'll burst into tears.'

I sat up straight. 'It's Bob. He has just assured me he knows I've been badly hurt but he's prepared to wait as long as it takes.'

'You lucky girl,' she said. 'Have you got time for a cup of tea?'

'Only if you let me cuddle Max,' I said, and followed her out the back of the clinic to the tiny kitchen.

'You can keep him,' Max's doting mother told me. 'He screamed for two hours straight last night.'

'Why?' I asked, looking at the baby. He had inserted one fat hand into his mouth up to the wrist and was chewing it – he looked plump and rosy and the picture of childish contentment.

'Who would know?' Cheryl said. 'Just felt like it, I think.'

Well, fair enough, I thought. *Me too*.

Chapter 18

THE FIRST SUNDAY in July was a perfect winter's day – crisp and tangy with the air so clear you'd have sworn you could reach out and touch the ranges with their coat of shaggy dark bush. Mount Taranaki behind them was pure white and looked from this angle like a storybook mountain, an improbably perfect cone. I looked at the washing line with satisfaction – a whole row of clean white sheets gives you such a fulfilled and housewifely feeling – and, picking up the washing basket, turned back towards the house. Across the road Matt was putting up a fence in front of his cows and I waved as I crossed the gravel. He held up an electric fence standard in return.

Aunty Rose, who had just begun round two of chemotherapy, was sitting in a deckchair wrapped in a blanket and wearing a bright orange woollen hat with a bobble on top.

'Cute,' I remarked, sitting down on the top step of the porch.

'Thank you. I thought myself it was a fetching look.'

It was, in fact, coupled with deathly pallor and great dark circles under the eyes, a horrific look, but we were both being very bright and positive today in the hope we'd fool each other.

There was a soft grunting noise and Percy waddled around the side of the house. He paused at the bottom of the porch steps and looked up with his head on one side. 'Come on up, dear boy,' said Aunty Rose, and he trotted up the steps to sit beside her chair. 'You're a fine figure of a pig, aren't you, Percy?'

Percy sighed contentedly and turned his snout up to the sun.

'He is indeed,' I said. 'Have you noticed he looks almost exactly like Ronnie Barker?'

Aunty Rose looked at him critically. 'So he does. Now there's a compliment, Percy.'

The pig laid his head in her lap and looked at her with concern as she reached for the basin beside her, took a couple of deep breaths and laid it aside again. It occurred to me that if this round of chemo didn't work he was going to waste away and die of a broken heart, and I had to get up and weed the patch of garden around the steps to hide my face.

ONCE THE SUN moved down behind the hill Aunty Rose got up stiffly from her deckchair and went inside to lie down. When I went to check on her a little later she was asleep. I wondered whether I should wake her for dinner and decided it would be unnecessarily cruel.

At around six Matt let himself into the kitchen, a bottle of Monteith's Winter Ale in each hand. 'Beer?' he asked, opening a drawer to hunt for the bottle opener.

'Yes, please. That's very upmarket stuff you've got there.'

'I splashed out,' he said solemnly. 'Apparently the pay-out's going to be good next season. How's Rose?'

'She's asleep,' I told him. 'Have you had tea?'

'Dinner,' he said reprovingly. 'No. What've you got?'

'Leftover macaroni cheese?'

'Sounds better than what's on offer at my house.' He crossed the kitchen and handed me a frosted bottle. 'Your car needs a wheel alignment, by the way.'

I had borrowed his ute yesterday so as to move my bed from the flat to Rose's and thus finally escape the spine-deforming horror of the kapok mattress in the Pink Room, lending him my car in return.

Now I rolled to my feet – I had been stretched full-length on the chaise longue with the entertainment section of the Sunday paper. 'I know. I'm just slack. You don't feel a burning desire for vegetables, do you?'

'You don't have to eat vegetables on the weekend,' said Matt.

'Good.' I removed the half-eaten dish of macaroni cheese from the fridge, slung it into the oven and turned it on.

We talked a bit as we waited for dinner to heat, but mostly drank our beer and passed the big weekend crossword puzzle between us in silence. I was never quite sure, after he had left, how I felt about being alone with Matt – never quite sure whether the pleasure of his company outweighed the strain of trying not to wind strands of hair around my index finger and stare at him like a besotted teenager. But when he was there I generally decided that if friends was all I was going to get it was a hell of a lot better than nothing.

I got up to check the temperature of the macaroni cheese, found it was still only lukewarm in the middle and, turning back to the crossword puzzle, saw Matt cautiously shrug the shoulder he had dislocated as he wrote in a word. 'Four down is "eyrie",' he said.

'Well done. How much trouble is that shoulder giving you?'

'Not much,' he said. 'It's my own fault. I decided to carry about three hundred standards up a hill this afternoon and I was too lazy to make two trips.'

'Hmm,' I said suspiciously. 'How long *did* you do your exercises for?'

'I did exactly what you told me,' he said, but he looked shifty.

'Liar,' I said. 'Don't worry, you're not the only one. According to an article I was reading last week only about twenty per cent of people do their exercises properly.'

'I admit nothing,' he said, and grinned at me. 'It's pretty good, really – it only worries me when I do something stupid.'

'Take your shirt off,' I said.

He looked pained. 'Must you, Jo?'

'Come on, don't be a baby. It'll only take a minute to have a look at it, and you're going to be unhappy if it's still not right by calving.'

Matt sighed but pulled off his jumper and T-shirt. The body underneath them was lean and wiry and indecently attractive. 'Anything to stop you nagging, woman,' he said.

I pulled myself together – drooling on one's patients is such an unprofessional look. 'You're just full of charm. Shrug your shoulders.'

He did, and I scowled, mostly for effect.

'What? It needs amputation at the neck?'

'Yep,' I said. 'It's going to wither and waste away. Probably go black too. Should I just cut it off now?'

'Well,' said Matt, 'why not? The stump will have three weeks to heal before the cows start calving. What *is* wrong with it?'

'It's just not moving very freely.' I took his upper arm in one hand and felt the joint with the other as I moved his arm around. 'That's pretty tender, isn't it?'

'Only if you go on prodding it,' he said acidly.

'If you can bear it, how about coming in and having some ultrasound?' I suggested. 'If you don't want me to do it you can talk to the girls at the hospital.'

'Of course I want you to do it. I'm just complaining because it makes me feel manly.' He turned in his chair and smiled at me. 'I'll make an appointment.'

From outside came a volley of barks.

'It's probably Kim,' Matt said as he started to pull his

shirt back over his head, but three seconds later the kitchen door was flung wide to reveal Cilla. She was wearing a white trench coat over her jeans and a little pink cashmere scarf around her neck; her cheeks were flushed and her eyes very bright. She looked ridiculously pretty.

She paused on the doorstep with her chest rising and falling quickly, as though she'd been running.

'Hello,' said Matt. 'What are you doing here?'

'What am I doing here? Don't you think that's the question *I* should be asking *you*?'

It was suddenly clear that the flush was due to emotion and not exercise, and that the girl was on the verge of hysteria.

'Hey,' Matt said feebly. 'Settle down, would you?'

How on *earth*, I wondered, had the man got to nearly thirty years old without realising that telling one's girlfriend to settle down is almost as bad as telling her she's put on a bit of weight?

I turned away to busy myself at the sink, and Cilla said sharply, 'And *you* don't need to stand there grinning, bitch.'

I spun around to look at her, startled – it's normally only in soap operas that people actually say things like that. Most of us, when in the middle of these dramatic situations, are curbed by convention and can't actually bring ourselves to be nasty to casual acquaintances.

'What the hell is your problem?' Matt demanded, heaping fuel upon the flames of his girlfriend's wrath. Honestly, his lack of tact was staggering.

'How could you do this to me, Matthew?' Cilla asked, going abruptly from belligerent to tearful. 'With *her*?'

Well, that was hardly flattering. You'd have thought I was pushing sixty with a club foot and personal hygiene issues.

'I have no idea what you're talking about,' he said, bewildered, and Cilla burst into tears.

'Hey,' I said, seeing as Matt showed no signs of imminent speech, 'I was just checking his dislocated shoulder, Cilla.'

'All night?' she spat at me, tears rolling down her cheeks.

'Huh?' Matt asked.

'Y-your ute was here *all last night*,' she wept. 'I'm not *stupid*.'

'Oh, for Christ's sake,' he said. 'I lent it to Jo so she could go and pick up her gear from her flat in town.'

'But you n-never answered your phone . . .'

'You knew I was watching the rugby at Scott's,' he said. He was looking embarrassed and annoyed rather than conciliatory – Matt the Sensitive New Age Guy would rather have his teeth pulled than discuss relationship stuff in public.

Cilla snivelled gently. 'You didn't answer your mobile either.'

'Left it on the tractor when I fed out yesterday.'

'Oh,' she said in a very small voice. 'S-sorry.' She came across the kitchen and rested a little pink cheek on the top of his head.

Matt patted her on the back in a half-ashamed fashion that reminded me of my father's approach to female emotion, and stood up. 'Look,' he said, 'I'll just go and see if Rose is awake, and then we'll head off.'

'Okay,' Cilla whispered.

Left alone with her there appeared to be no possible subject for conversation. I sat down at the table and pulled the crossword puzzle towards me, and after a minute or so of dense uncomfortable silence she murmured, 'I'm sorry.'

'It's fine,' I said coolly. The 'With *her*' still rankled.

'It's just – he spends so much time here, and you know each other so well . . .'

'We're just friends,' I said. 'Probably more like brother and sister than anything else. We fought like cats and dogs when we were kids.'

Matt reappeared in the kitchen doorway. 'Rose is still asleep,' he said. 'Let's go.'

'Bye,' said Cilla sweetly to me.

He followed her across the kitchen, pausing at the door to pull on his work boots. ''Night, Jose,' he said.

I could hear the crunch of their feet across the gravel and Cilla's voice asking with professional-sounding interest, 'How was the quality of those last couple of silage bales? I thought they looked a bit wet.'

I got the macaroni cheese out of the oven, spooned some into a bowl and sat down at the table to let it go cold again while I tortured myself with pointless recollections.

Pointless recollections

We were lying facing one another on our sides, not talking, and my eyes had drifted closed. I was nearly asleep when Matt reached out and stroked the hair back off my face to tuck it very gently behind my ear, and I opened my eyes and looked at him in the muted orange glow of the streetlight outside the window.

'Sorry,' he murmured.

'For what?'

'Waking you up.'

'You didn't. Anyway, sleeping's a waste.'

He smiled crookedly. 'Jo, my friend, I have a feeling you're going to be hard to get over.'

'Really?' I asked, ridiculously pleased.

'Oh, hell yes,' he said, sliding a hand down my back and pulling me up against him.

'So are you.' I could feel him breathing in and out and his skin was very warm against mine. 'This may not have been the smartest idea.'

He sighed. 'No.'

There was a longish pause, and then I said slowly, 'Maybe it's best you're going away. It would be so awful to have it turn to custard.'

'You're going to want to watch this wild optimism, Jose.'

'I mean – you have to go, and I have to stay here, and it's nobody's fault so there are no hard feelings.' I sat up and looked down at him. 'And maybe the next time we see each other the . . .' I paused, searching for the right words, and borrowed a phrase from Aunty Rose, 'the circumstances will be more auspicious.'

'Maybe.' He ran a fingertip very lightly down the side of my left breast. 'You've filled out very nicely, by the way.'

'You too,' I said, and he pulled me down on top of him, and we didn't talk anymore.

Chapter 19

PERCY HAD SHRUNK to the size of a chihuahua and was perched on the kitchen table watching me make a bacon and egg pie. I was trying to be surreptitious about the bacon but I could tell he'd noticed, which made conversation somewhat awkward.

'Put in some of those olives,' Aunty Rose called from the next room. 'Graeme likes olives.'

'But Chrissie doesn't,' I answered as the oven timer went off.

It shrilled and shrilled – and after some time I realised it sounded more like the phone. It must be Graeme to say they were running late. There was a creak as Aunty Rose's bedroom door opened and then the sound of her footsteps hurrying past the Pink Room.

'Hello?' she said breathlessly.

By now I had managed to fight my way up to semi-consciousness and realised there was no oven timer, no Percy, no pie and – thank Saint Peter and all the

Apostles – no Graeme and Chrissie. I rolled out of bed and stumbled out into the hall.

Aunty Rose, hairless and swathed in folds of white nightie, had reached the phone. She looked impressively ghoulish in the wavering light of the forty-watt bulb that dangled on a long flex above her head.

'Slow down,' she ordered. 'Where are you?' There was a pause as she listened. 'Sweet pea, calm down. She's just here, I'll put her on – it's *alright*, Kim.' She held out the phone to me, her face creased with concern.

I took the phone, shivering despite flannelette pyjamas and two pairs of socks. Aunty Rose's hall couldn't have been draughtier if it had been designed specifically as a wind tunnel.

'J-Josie,' Kim wept. 'Oh, J-Jo, I'm s-sorry, I –'

I could hardly make out the words – her breath was catching in little hysterical gasps and the music in the background was insanely loud. Some parent was going to be unhappy tomorrow when they discovered that the speakers of their stereo had blown out.

'Kim!' I roared over the din. 'It's *alright*. Where are you? I'll come and get you, it's okay.'

'I – I shouldn't b-be here, I –'

She said something else, I think, but at that point a thunderous drum solo broke out. Yep, those speakers were definitely going to be toast.

'It doesn't matter. Just tell me where you are, hon, and I'll come and get you.'

'J-Jonno brought me,' she gasped. 'But he . . . he –' At

that point she lost it entirely and sobbed.

I always thought I was pretty easygoing, but I was abruptly filled with murderous, blazing fury. I was going to *flay* that little prick when I caught up with him. '*Kim!* Where *are* you?'

There was a brief scuffle at the other end of the line and I had a horrendous vision of Kim being attacked by multiple drunken youths. But then a different voice said, 'Hey, Jo, it's Andy here.'

I sagged with relief. 'Andy! What on earth is going on?'

'She's a bit upset,' said Andy unnecessarily. 'I don't think her mum knows she's here, and she's had too much to drink.'

'Is she okay?'

'Yeah,' he said. 'Well, except that she's going to throw up any minute – yep. There she goes. Spewing like a maggot.'

Hopefully all over Jonno's guitar, which apparently was worth more than my car.

'Can you keep an eye on her until I get there?' I asked.

'Don't worry about it,' said Andy cheerfully. 'I'll take her home. It's a bloody awful party.'

'Are you okay to drive?'

'Been on ginger beer all night,' he said. 'Here, you'd better tell her I'm not a serial killer.' Over the background din – by the sound of it someone was now doing shots, spurred on by the crowd – I heard him say kindly, 'Finished chundering? Talk to Jo again – you'll be right.'

'Andy's going to bring you home, okay?' I shouted. 'He'll look after you. He's a friend of mine.'

'Not home!' said Kim hysterically. 'Josie! Not h-home . . .'

'*Okay*, Kim. Here. Aunty Rose's.'

'And you c-can't tell Matt!'

I was surprised at the panic in her voice. Her brother wasn't going to be thrilled about this evening's performance but he's really not that scary. 'Okay. Okay, just go with Andy.'

Aunty Rose, her nightie billowing in the draught, stalked into the kitchen and bent to throw another log into the stove. 'I suppose we should be thankful that she called,' she said.

I made a little trip back down the hall for Aunty Rose's dressing-gown, the orange hat and a pair of woolly socks. Re-entering the kitchen I passed them over and switched on the kettle. 'And I think Jonno's going to be a thing of the past, which can only be good.'

'What did he do?'

I shook my head. 'No idea. Probably took her there and then went off with someone else. Poor Kim.'

Ten minutes later we heard the snarl of Andy's company car climbing the hill. It woke the dogs from a sound sleep and they began to bark hysterically.

Aunty Rose pulled the door open and shouted into the frosty darkness, 'That's enough!'

It was a very small and bedraggled Kim who crept into her aunt's kitchen. She was wearing another knee-length

T-shirt over her jeans, her eyes were pink and swollen and the makeup had run so she looked like an unhappy raccoon.

'I'm cold,' she whispered, sinking onto the chaise longue and resting her head against its velvet back.

'You'll be better after a cup of tea,' said Aunty Rose. 'Would you like one, young man?'

Andy had paused uncomfortably in the doorway. 'Um,' he said, 'yes, please. Hey, Jo.'

'Hey.' I went across the room and kissed his cheek, which made him look even more uncomfortable. 'Thank you.'

'Pleasure.' He looked doubtfully at his hostess in her woolly hat and crimson satin dressing-gown. 'Look, I should get out of your hair.'

'What hair?' said Aunty Rose briskly. 'Sit down – you're making the place look untidy. Now, Josephine, what did you do with that rather more-ish sticky chocolate thing?'

At the mention of something sticky and chocolate Kim groaned.

'Serves you right,' I told her.

'Really, Kim, why anyone would *choose* to feel nauseous is beyond me,' Aunty Rose remarked.

'I'm sorry,' she whispered piteously. 'Aunty Rose, I'm sorry.'

'When *I* was your age,' said Aunty Rose, 'we nursing students used to place intravenous catheters and tape them in before we went out on the ran-tan. And then when we got home we would run in a litre of saline before bed – marvellous hangover prevention.'

'Awesome,' said Andy.

'It backfired once. The cap came off my catheter and I bled all over someone's carpet. It looked like the scene of an axe murder.' She smiled nostalgically, and then looked at her niece, her expression stern. 'However, even if I had a catheter, I haven't put one in for twenty years, so you'd better drink a litre of water and take two paracetamol.'

Kim curled herself into a miserable ball and sobbed gently. *Good*, I thought, pouring cups of tea, but Andy went and sat beside her.

'Hey,' he said gently, 'you're okay. No-one's mad at you.'

'Speak for yourself,' I said, and received a very reproachful look.

'Don't listen to Jo,' said Andy. 'I've seen her so drunk she could hardly stand up, teaching people the mamba.'

That treacherous rat-fink – *he* couldn't talk. That was the evening of the gin and chocolate milk, and he had demonstrated his own special interpretation of River-dance, which had ended when he fell over a chair.

'Mam*bo*,' I corrected him. 'The mam*ba* being a type of snake.'

'Whatever,' said Andy. 'The point is that you do dumb things too.'

'Be that as it may,' said Aunty Rose, 'Josephine is neither eighteen years old nor sneaking off to a party without telling her mother where she is.'

'I keep saying I'm sorry,' Kim muttered.

'Where does your mother think you are?'

'Rachel's. Are – are you going to tell her?'

Aunty Rose sighed. 'I expect not,' she said. 'Although I should.' She accepted her tea. 'Thank you, Josephine.'

'And *please* don't tell Matt.'

Outside the dogs began their welcome chorus – they were having a busy night. I passed Kim a mug and said, 'You can tell him yourself.'

Matt's ute gave its characteristic unhealthy splutter as it stopped. Kim jumped about a foot and burst into fresh tears, slopping tea over her jeans.

'Asked you not to go to this party, huh?' I said.

'Y-yes . . .' The tea wobbled again and Andy sensibly took it out of her hand.

'Oh, *Kim*,' sighed Aunty Rose.

Matt opened the kitchen door and stared at his sister. His hair was rumpled from sleep, his sweatshirt on inside out and his lips folded in a grim line. I didn't think I'd ever seen him angrier; not even on the terrible day I dropped his new fishing reel and filled its delicate innards with sand.

'You're alive, then,' he snapped.

'Matt, I didn't mean to,' she whispered.

'You didn't mean to be at a party you promised me you wouldn't go to, where you threw up all over Brian Mallard and then pissed off with some random bloke?'

'I'm *sorry*!' Kim cried.

'I couldn't give a flying *fuck* whether or not you're

sorry!' He was nearly incandescent with rage. 'I've just been rung by Brian and driven halfway to Orua to be told by that little prick of a boyfriend of yours that you've left with some unknown man. You weren't answering your phone – I was on my way home to see if you were at Mum's before I called the police. For God's *sake*, Kim!'

Kim hid her face in a sofa cushion and sobbed. Her brother looked at her for a second, turned on his heel and went out of the house, closing the kitchen door behind him with an exaggerated softness that was far more shocking than a slam would have been.

There was an awed hush in the room, broken only when the engine of Matt's ancient ute coughed into life.

Aunty Rose sighed and stood up, abandoning her cup of tea. 'I'm going back to bed,' she said. 'You can sleep in the end room, Kim. The bed's not made up but there are blankets in the cupboard.' She nodded to Andy on her way out of the kitchen. 'Thank you for returning her.'

I fished in a drawer for Panadol, filled the largest glass I could find with water and carried it to Kim. 'Come on, stop it. You'll make yourself sick.'

From the depths of the cushion came a strangled gulping sound as Kim made a truly heroic effort to pull herself together. I was touched despite myself and added more kindly, 'He's mostly mad because you scared him, Kimlet; he'll have settled down by tomorrow.'

'I –' Kim gasped. 'I'm so s-*sorry*, Josie.'

'We've all done it,' Andy told her, and patted her shoulder awkwardly.

'But Matt n-*never* tells me what to do, and he asked me specially not to go because the guy whose party it was is a crazy druggie, and I – I did anyway!' she wailed.

'Well, why did you?' I asked.

'Jonno said I was a silly little k-kid, and that he really wanted me to go with him.' She wiped her wet face on one sleeve of the enormous T-shirt and added bitterly, 'But then I found Megan Nichols giving him a blow job in one of the bedrooms.'

Andy grinned. 'Classy.'

'It was *not*. It was gross.'

'Yep,' I agreed, handing her the glass and two tablets. 'Shame you didn't throw up on him instead of poor old Brian.'

Chapter 20

I WAS SEATED behind the front desk at work during Amber's lunch break on Monday, idly looking through her extensive nail polish collection as I waited for my next appointment to arrive. Had it not been the middle of winter I'd have been tempted to try the Tangerine Dream on my toenails.

The little bell above the door jingled and I looked up. 'Hey.'

'Hey,' said Matt, closing the door behind him.

'Which do you prefer?' I asked, holding up two little bottles. 'Pale pink with glitter, or bright pink without?'

He gave it some thought. 'Bright pink.'

'Hmm,' I said. 'I agree. Although it's never as nice on your nails as it is in the bottle. What's up?'

'You told me to come and make an appointment,' he said. 'So I am.'

'Good man.' I dropped the nail polish back into its

drawer and swivelled in my seat to look at the computer screen. 'When is good for you?'

'You haven't got a slot now?'

I shook my head. 'The next person's due shortly, and the afternoon's full. Sorry. Tomorrow, maybe – oh, no, you're taking Aunty Rose to chemo. Wednesday?'

'Afternoon would be better,' said Matt.

I scrolled down Wednesday's appointment list. 'Two?'

'Okay.'

I reached for a card to write the time on the back.

'I'll just lose it,' he said. 'Don't worry, I won't forget.'

'Very good,' I said. 'Forgiven your sister yet?'

Matt smiled his slow smile. 'There was a mince and cheese pie on the tractor seat this morning when I went to feed out,' he said.

'She feels really, really bad about letting you down,' I said. Anything more pitiful than Kim at the breakfast table on Sunday morning would have been hard to imagine – tears had trickled steadily down her face and dripped into her Weet-Bix.

'I know.'

'And at least she's not going out with that useless little toe-rag anymore.'

'Rotten little shit,' said Matt. 'I've never been so close to smashing someone's nose into his face in my life.'

'Why didn't you?' I asked.

'Well, I did punch him in the stomach.'

'You legend,' I said admiringly. 'Hard, I hope.'

'Dropped him,' he admitted.

'That's *brilliant*.'

'I didn't think you condoned violence, Jose.'

'I make an exception for people who take their under-age girlfriends to parties, get them plastered and then vanish into a back bedroom with someone else.'

Matt looked mildly disgusted for a moment, and then brightened. 'With any luck that means he wasn't getting any from my baby sister. She's far too young for that kind of carry-on.'

'You hypocrite,' I told him. 'If I remember rightly – and I'm pretty sure I do – you were doing all kinds of dodgy things when you were Kim's age.'

'I was not!'

'Well, you were lots dodgier than me.'

'Jose,' he pointed out, 'there'd have been nuns dodgier than you were at high school.'

'True,' I admitted sadly.

'Remember that New Year's party at Wilson's where you drank about half a can of Lion Red and fell into the wool press?'

'Was that the party where you spent the whole night with Alicia Beaumont attached to your face? *Man*, she was annoying.'

'It wasn't her personality I was interested in,' he said mildly.

'Is she still around?' I asked.

Matt nodded. 'I see her in town every now and then. She's really let herself go. And she's got at least three kids.'

'None of them yours?'

He merely looked pained.

'That was during your Kurt Cobain phase,' I reminisced. 'When you used to lighten your hair with Sun-In and rip holes in your jeans.'

'And Aunty Rose bloody patched them up again and gave me a short back and sides.'

'Did Alicia still put out when you didn't have sexy sun-bleached hair anymore?'

'Of course,' said Matt. 'I was awesome.'

'Mm,' I agreed, and then realised in horror that I'd said it aloud.

He smiled widely. 'Thanks. You've gone the same colour as that nail polish.'

'A nice person,' I said bitterly, 'would pretend not to notice.'

'Quite likely.' He went across the waiting room and opened the door. 'You were fairly awesome yourself, by the way.'

So it was his fault that my next appointment, when she finally arrived, told me it was probably a dietary imbalance making my cheeks so red and advised me to try chelation therapy.

AUNTY ROSE GRIPPED the arms of the brocade wing chair in the lounge and pushed herself to her feet. I was wading through the hobbits' visit to Tom Bombadil in *The Lord of the Rings* and finding it even more painful than

I had remembered, and I looked up to see her catch her breath with a little grunt of pain. 'What hurts?' I asked.

'Back,' she said through her teeth.

'Can I give it a rub for you?'

She shook her head and straightened fully with an effort. 'It's not a muscle problem. It wouldn't make any difference. I shall feed it a couple of pills.'

I grimaced in sympathy. 'Nausea *and* a bad back seems a bit unfair. High or low spine?'

'Low,' said Aunty Rose.

'There are a couple of stretches that might help.'

'Physiotherapy is doubtless a noble profession, Josephine, but it's unlikely to help a growth on a vertebra,' she said drily. She went slowly out of the room, and I heard the groan and shudder of elderly plumbing as she ran the bath.

A growth on a vertebra? Holy *crap*. I let my book slide to the floor, got up and fetched the portable phone from the coffee table. Stu's phone was either turned off or the battery was flat, and it went straight to voicemail. ''Ullo, Stuart 'ere, leave a message and h'I will h'endeavour to get back to you.' This week, it appeared, he was showcasing his rural Yorkshire accent – which was surprising, considering Stu thinks it would be no loss if the whole of northern Britain fell into a deep hole. I gnawed my bottom lip indecisively for a moment and then dialled Graeme's mobile number.

He answered on the third ring. 'Graeme Sunderland here,' he said. I'd forgotten what a nice voice he had – deep and rich, like caramel.

'Hi,' I said. 'It's me.'

There was a longish pause. 'What can I do for you?'

'I need your professional opinion.'

Another pause. 'Go ahead, then.'

Calling him had been a mistake. Somehow when *he* rang *me* I had the moral high ground. But I'd done it now, so I asked, 'If a breast cancer metastasises to the spine while you're getting chemo, what's the prognosis?'

'That's not my area of expertise,' said Graeme.

'I know, but you've got a far better idea than I do. Aunty Rose had a six-week course of chemo and then a mastectomy, and then they found that the margins weren't clear, and now she's got back pain because of a growth on a vertebra.'

'Look, Jo, I don't know what kind of cancer you're talking about –'

'Ductal carcinoma.'

He carried on as if I hadn't interrupted, '– or what chemotherapy regime she's on, or what type of surgical margins they took. I can't just speculate on a case I know nothing about.'

'Graeme,' I said tiredly, 'for just half a minute could you pretend to be a nice person? I know you can't say exactly – I just want a bit of an idea.'

Graeme sighed. 'Had it metastasised before they started the chemo? Did she have an initial CAT scan?'

'Yes. It was clear, as far as I know.'

'Then I wouldn't have thought there was a whole lot of hope.'

'That's what I thought.'

'I'm sorry, JD.'

His tone had gone from pompous and professional to quite kind, and hot tears rose in my eyes. 'Yeah, life's a bitch. Thanks.'

'You're welcome. And Jo?'

'Yes?'

'I'm sorry about everything else, too.'

I nearly fell out of my chair in shock. This coming from Graeme, the man who would rather pull out his own carefully groomed fingernails than apologise for *anything*. 'Um, thank you.'

'I'm having an open home this weekend. I'll let you know how it goes.'

'That'd be good,' I said. 'Talk to you later, then.'

'Yeah,' said Graeme. 'Miss you, JD.' And he hung up.

It's funny how things change. A few months ago I would have spent many hours that would better have been devoted to sleep in thinking about the ramifications of 'Miss you, JD'. Did it mean he'd seen the light? Was he regretting the whole sorry mess? Did he wish he hadn't replaced me with a woman who refused to leave the house without makeup? Was he on the verge of rushing to Waimanu to cast himself at my feet and beg me to take him back? And so on and so forth.

But who the hell cared about Graeme and his apologies if all this chemo and nausea and – and *bullshit* was for nothing?

'HOW ABOUT POPPING on a pair of gloves for chopping onions?' Hazel suggested. 'It saves you from getting that smell all over your hands.'

Or you could just wash your hands afterwards. But I said, 'That's a good idea,' because it's easier to agree with Hazel.

Kim was lying full-length on the chaise longue with her hands folded across her stomach, like an effigy on a medieval tomb. 'What're you making?' she asked.

'Liver and bacon.'

'Gross.'

I smiled at her. 'I just do what I'm told.' I rinsed my hands and added a generous knob of butter to the frying pan.

'So *much* butter, Josie?' Hazel asked gently. 'You know what they say: An instant on the lips, a lifetime on the hips.'

'She doesn't *have* hips,' Kim protested.

'That's right,' I said. 'Rub it in.'

'It was a compliment!'

'Being rectangular is no laughing matter, I assure you. Do you have any idea how hard it is to find trousers that fit properly?' I added the onions to the pan. 'I reckon the more calories we can get into Aunty Rose the better.'

Hazel sighed. 'This ghastly disease,' she said. 'Rosie, how are you feeling today?'

Aunty Rose had just come slowly into the kitchen. 'Not bad,' she said. It was quite obviously a lie – she was an unpleasant shade of yellowy green and had deep shadows under her eyes. 'Kimlet, move over.'

Kim rolled to her feet. 'Would you like a glass of ginger ale?' she asked eagerly.

'I would adore one.' Rose sank onto one end of the chaise longue and rested her head back. 'Who's that, Josephine?'

From the window above the sink I saw a little blue truck mounting the hill. The dogs arose in a body from the back porch and sped to meet it. 'Bob McIntosh,' I said. 'Oh, dear Lord, *no*.'

'What do you suppose he wants?' Hazel asked.

'Josie,' said Kim, and sniggered.

'Lucky me. Can you get the door?' I turned away from the window to fetch the lamb's liver from the fridge, pretending not to have seen his coy little wave.

'Good evening, ladies,' said Bob, nodding from the doorstep. 'How are we all?'

'Very good, thank you,' said Kim demurely. 'How are you?'

'Oh, not bad at all.' He advanced into the room with a crab-like sidle. 'Something smells wonderful, Josie.'

'Liver and bacon,' said Aunty Rose briskly. 'What can I do for you, Bob?'

She may as well not have spoken. 'Liver and bacon,' he repeated. 'Delicious. Real old-fashioned cookery. Is there anything Josie *can't* do?'

'Shear,' Aunty Rose said, accepting her drink.

'That was uncalled for,' I told her. 'I didn't want to shear your revolting sheep in the first place.' Taking out a sharp knife I began to shave wafer-thin slices off the side of the liver. Liver's never going to be high up on my list of favourite foods, but if you slice it so fine it's almost transparent and then cook it in about half a pound of butter with plenty of bacon and onion, it's actually not too bad. Especially compared to my grandmother's recipe, which consisted of large dense cubes of ox liver in Bisto gravy. I remember being about eight and looking down at a plateful of the stuff with the strong conviction that even if I somehow managed to get it down it would come straight back up again.

'Well,' said Hazel, 'we'd best be off, Kim, and get our own dinner.'

'May I stay?' Kim asked.

'I didn't think you liked liver,' I said.

'I could have spaghetti on toast.'

Aunty Rose smiled at her. 'Fine by me,' she said. 'Now, Bob, is there anything we can help you with?'

Bob coughed nervously. 'I *was* wondering if young Josie might like a little jaunt this weekend,' he said. 'Perhaps a meal out. I know she prefers not to leave you in the evenings but lunch may not be out of the question?'

'No thanks, Bob,' I said, and with a superhuman effort I prevented myself from adding, 'But that's very kind of you,' which would only be taken as encouragement.

'Oh,' he murmured sadly. 'Oh, well, perhaps another time. Now I can see I'd best leave you ladies to your dinner . . .' He paused hopefully, just in case anyone was going to press him to stay, and then sagged when nobody did. 'Well, goodnight.'

As he went back across the gravel to his little truck Hazel said, 'Poor fellow.'

'You reckon?' Kim asked. 'I think he's pretty creepy.'

I sighed. 'He's harmless, but I wish he'd leave me alone.'

'Sit him down,' Hazel advised, 'and explain that you're just not interested.'

'I *have*,' I said. 'I've made it crystal clear.'

'Don't you feel too sorry for him,' Aunty Rose said. 'He knows perfectly well he's making you uncomfortable – it's a rather subtle form of bullying. Now, Hazel, are you staying for liver?'

'No, no,' said Hazel. 'Kim, love, haven't you got homework that needs doing?'

'Hardly any,' she said. 'Don't worry, Mum, I'm on it.'

'Are you sure you want this monkey on your hands, Rosie?'

'I rather like her,' said Aunty Rose. 'Goodness knows why.'

'I'll return her when we get sick of her,' I said.

WE ATE AT the kitchen table, and then Kim and I did the dishes while Aunty Rose supervised with her feet up. 'This is lovely,' she remarked. 'Watching the pair of you work is quite delightful. Kim, my sweet, the table needs a wipe.'

'You haven't fed the dogs yet, have you?' I asked.

'No. You may do it, if you like.'

I fetched a new dog roll from the cupboard above the wood box and began to slice it up. 'Some for Percy, or is he dieting again?'

'Perhaps he'd better. The poor fellow's on the verge of morbid obesity.'

Matt's ute came up the hill as I handed out chunks of dog roll (and one carrot to a pig who looked at me with deep reproach).

'Hi,' he said as he crossed the gravel.

'Hi. Isn't it lovely?' It was icy outside and breathlessly still. A thin trickle of smoke from the wood stove rose straight upwards and the sky was alight with stars. I had forgotten, living in the city, about winter nights like this where the stars swing in blazing arcs across the sky and the air is sharp and crisp. The kind of night where you imagine fancifully that you can hear the stars singing in high pure voices and you vow to take up astronomy and moonlit walks. And then you go inside and watch *Master-Chef* and forget all about it.

'It'll be a killer frost unless the wind picks up,' said Matt. 'There was ice on top of the troughs this morning.'

'I think there was ice on my pillow, too.'

'I wouldn't be surprised,' he said. 'This is the coldest house in the world.'

'I particularly like the way the wind whistles through the walls and lifts the wallpaper from underneath.' I scratched Percy between the ears and turned to go back inside. 'I'm thinking of getting myself a onesie.'

'A what?'

'Those cool pyjama-things made of polar fleece, with feet and a zip up the middle. Like a baby's stretch-and-grow. And you can get them with a flap at the back so you don't even have to take them off to go to the toilet.'

'Jo,' said Matt, 'you're all class.'

We went back into the warm shabby kitchen to find Kim had set out four teacups on the table and was standing on tiptoe in the pantry to reach down a packet of chocolate biscuits. 'Tea, Matt?' she asked.

He blinked in surprise. 'I should yell at you more often.'

'But if you overdo it you'll desensitise her,' I said. 'It's hard to get it just right.'

'You won't need to yell at me at all,' said Kim. 'I'm off men. Probably for good.'

'Excellent,' he said. 'I expect it'll only last for a week, but it will be a nice relaxing week.' He kissed Aunty Rose and she laid a claw-like hand against his cheek.

'Are the cows behaving, dear boy?' she asked.

'Two heifers calved last night,' he said. 'That's five cows in already – I'm not feeling mentally prepared just yet.'

'When are they due to start?'

'Not for another ten days.'

'I'll take you to chemo next week, then,' I told Aunty Rose.

'I can do it,' Matt said.

'I was talking to Cheryl the other day. She'd be quite keen to start doing a bit of work and her mother-in-law's dying to have Max for a day, so it'll be no problem at all.'

'It's alright,' he said. 'I won't be really busy for another couple of weeks.'

'Sweet peas,' said Aunty Rose. 'I won't be going to chemo.'

We both stared at her. 'What do you mean?' Matt asked.

'I'm not going to have any more chemotherapy,' she said quietly.

'But you've got four weeks to go,' he said.

'No.'

'But . . .' I started, and then stopped.

Aunty Rose smiled at me. 'You see, chickens,' she said, 'it's really only palliative now, and what on *earth* is the point of a few more weeks or months if it's spent feeling, as Josephine so aptly puts it, like total poo?'

There was a horrified silence, broken only by the hiss of falling embers in the wood stove. Finally Kim, eyes enormous in her white face, whispered, 'What does "palliative" mean?'

'That they can't fix it; they can only alleviate it a little.'

Kim gulped and hid her face in her hands.

'Oh, sweetheart,' said Aunty Rose. 'Come here.' And holding out her arms she gathered Kim up against where her bust used to be.

'Look,' said Matt angrily, 'you can't just give up. There are plenty of other specialists – I was reading on the internet about this new protocol in America with really impressive results.'

'No,' she said again.

'But –'

'Matthew, hush.' He hushed, with an effort that hurt to watch. 'We've given it a good solid try, but the rotten thing has spread right through my lungs now, and into the bone. I would so much prefer to enjoy the time that's left, rather than dashing all over the country to be told the same thing by a dozen different oncologists.' She held out a hand to him, and on taking it Matt, who I had never seen anything but stoical in the face of bad news, sank abruptly onto the kitchen floor beside her and hid his face in the skirt of her dressing-gown.

I slid to my feet from where I had been perched on the edge of the table and went blindly across the room. Kim and Matt should have some time alone with her. They'd already lost their father and now they were going to lose the woman who had provided all the useful mothering they'd ever had. Of all the lousy, miserable, *unfair* bloody set-ups – I just wanted to get away and find something to kick.

'Josephine,' said Aunty Rose gently as I reached the door to the hall. I looked back over my shoulder and she beckoned with the hand that she had been using to stroke Kim's sleek brown head. Going slowly back across the kitchen I sank down beside her and rested my head against her spare knee, breathing in the familiar scent of her perfume. Kim was crying quietly with her face buried in a cushion and Matt sat quite still on her other side. I touched his hand because I couldn't help it, and he reached out without looking to grip my fingers hard in his.

Aunty Rose patted us in turn for a while, and then she said, 'My darlings, this is terribly flattering, but you're starting to make me quite damp.'

'Tough,' said Matt thickly, but he sat up straight and swiped the sleeve of his shirt across his wet face. I got up and fetched a roll of paper towels off the bench, taking one to blow my nose before passing them along.

'That's it,' said Aunty Rose encouragingly. 'Good little sausages.'

I gave a slightly hysterical sob of laughter that Matt and I, at six foot four and five eleven respectively, could ever be described as good little *anythings*.

'Josephine, have we got any of that sherry left?'

'N-not the good stuff. Only that awful cooking sherry.'

'Never mind,' said Aunty Rose resolutely. 'It will be better than nothing. We'll have one all round.'

'It'll probably finish us off completely,' I said, but I got it out of the cupboard above the microwave and poured a slug apiece into four of the best crystal tumblers.

'Christ,' Matt muttered, sipping dubiously. 'Are you sure it's not paint stripper?'

'It's not good, is it?' Aunty Rose agreed. 'Never mind – bottoms up.'

'How long have you known?' Kim asked, shuddering as the sherry went down.

Aunty Rose sighed. 'I didn't tell you, but the prognosis never was very good, and then the last scan showed that quite a few secondaries had popped up during that first course of chemo. I really did feel that was a case of adding insult to injury. So I had a long talk with the specialist last week, and he agreed that we weren't making much progress and that it was a reasonable decision to stop wasting a lot of expensive drugs on tumours that weren't responding to them.'

'How long?' Matt asked.

'Who knows?'

'Rough estimate.'

'A few months. Perhaps.'

'And how long if you finish this course of chemo?'

'Six months, they thought,' said Aunty Rose. She sighed again. 'It's all terribly inconvenient, I must say. I would have liked to see your children. Although no doubt they'll be an ill-disciplined rabble with permanently runny noses and sticky hands.'

'Please stop trying to cheer us up,' I said, mopping my eyes again on my paper towel. 'It's unbearable.'

Aunty Rose smiled at me fondly. 'Ungrateful wench,' she murmured.

Chapter 21

'HOW ARE THE goats?' I tucked the phone between my ear and shoulder and bent to feed another log into the wood stove. Matt had been over while I was at work and stacked about half the wood pile inside the back door, which I suspected had taken up all of the time he might otherwise have used to have breakfast.

'Fine, fine,' said Mum dismissively. 'Kidding like mad. How's Rose?'

'Not that great. Her back's giving her quite a lot of trouble, and she's still nauseous from the chemo. Although she pretends she feels fine so we won't worry.'

'You sound so tired, sweetheart,' said Mum. 'Are you bearing up alright?'

'I'm okay,' I said bravely, and then had the grace to feel ashamed of myself. It's not *that* noble to produce the odd omelette for a woman who used to make you cat-shaped biscuits and who suffered through every one of your school plays.

'You don't sound okay. You sound exhausted.'

I felt a little warm glow inside – maternal sympathy is such a comforting thing. 'Well, Hazel came over this evening and wailed for about an hour about the unfairness of a God that would let such a thing happen. That was enough to exhaust anyone.'

'That *stupid* woman,' my mother said.

I lay down on the chaise longue and looked up at the griffon, who stared haughtily out over my head. 'And then there's a new leak in the kitchen ceiling, and Amber was stunningly useless today even by her low standards, and one of the dogs went over to the neighbours' place and dug a hole under their fence, and dinner burnt to a crisp while I was retrieving him.' It had been one of those days where a thousand little insignificant things go wrong and you start to wonder if it's payback for having sinned in a previous life.

'Jo, love,' said Mum, 'you're not going to be able to work full time and look after Rose indefinitely.'

'She's been talking to the district nurse and they think they can get her a bed in the hospital here once she can't manage anymore, rather than going to the hospice in Hamilton. But she'd much rather be at home, and – and it won't be forever.'

'Hmm,' Mum said. 'And what is the lovely Hazel doing to help?'

I smiled. 'She made a blancmange yesterday.' Nasty, pale, washed-out quivery thing – it was enough to make someone in the best of health feel unwell, let alone a person dying of cancer. The dippy woman had also, for some inexplicable reason, presented her sister with a morbid little book of poems written by people dying of terminal illnesses. Aunty Rose had just smiled faintly, slid it down behind the sofa and continued with the third *Twilight* novel.

'Josephine,' she had said later when I brought her a cup of Milo in bed, 'they're *not* well written, the woman only appears to use about three adjectives and all the characters ever do is stare into each other's eyes. And I read the damned things until two in the morning.'

'WHAT ELSE DO you need?' I asked, adjusting the tray table at Aunty Rose's elbow so she wouldn't have to stretch for it. 'Cup of tea?' I wasn't at all sure that going out for the evening was a good idea.

'For pity's sake, Josephine, would you just go away?' she said plaintively. 'I could probably even stagger across the kitchen and make my own cup of tea, if the worst came to the worst.'

'I know. I'm sorry.'

Aunty Rose straightened her startling purple turban. She looked like a dowager countess. 'You're going to want to watch yourself, sweet pea, or you'll grow up into your mother.' Seeing me open my mouth to protest she added, 'I adore your mother, but I think one is enough. Go on, chicken, have fun.'

The last time I visited Clare she had sobbed gently into

her coffee because Moira the pig was even then being converted to bacon, while an unsupervised Charlie cut Lucy's hair and then tried to glue it back on in the next room. But this evening as I went up the back steps I heard only Sarah McLachlan assuring me earnestly that it simply wasn't good enough.

Clare came to the door with her hair loose down her back, wearing long dangly earrings and eye makeup. 'Guess what?'

'What?'

'We're child-free,' she announced gleefully. 'Mum's taken them all away for the night.'

'When was the last time you had a night to yourselves?' I asked.

'Um . . . just before Charlie was born.'

'How about I go away again so you can enjoy it all by yourselves then?'

'No way,' said Clare. 'We're going to have a proper grown-up dinner party with no tomato sauce. Come and have some wine.'

She had cleared the dining table and surrounding floor of toys (presumably with a shovel – there was a bright plastic mountain around the corner on the floor of the formal lounge).

'Evening, Jo,' said Brett, wandering down the hall with his hair still damp from the shower. 'Can't we turn off that revolting noise? It sounds like someone dying of stomach cancer.'

'*Brett!*' said his wife.

'Well, it does – oh, shit, Jo, I'm sorry.'

'It's fine.'

'A few months ago he told Laura Kennedy she looked like Alice Cooper,' said Clare.

Brett opened the fridge door and extracted a bottle of beer. 'She does.'

Clare giggled. 'She does, actually. She's had her eyelids tattooed with permanent eyeliner. But you didn't need to *say* it.'

'You'd want to trust your tattooist,' I said. 'Imagine if they slipped.'

'It wouldn't be good, would it?' She handed me an enormous glass of red wine, the approximate size of a potty. 'How *is* Rose?'

'She's amazing. She keeps thinking of things she wants to put in her will and writing them down on post-it notes, and she wants them to play "Another One Bites the Dust" at her funeral.'

'She's so cool,' said Clare, pouring herself a glass of wine the same size as mine and thus emptying the bottle. I calculated that if I drank my half very slowly over the next few hours I *might* be able to drive home.

'Who else is coming?' I asked, seeing four places set.

'Scotty,' said Clare. 'That'll be him now.' There was a distant roar, which grew nearer with alarming speed and gave the impression a jet fighter was about to land on the roof. 'I wish he wouldn't drive like that. He'll stampede the alpacas.'

'Good,' Brett said. 'Horrible bloody things. He's not

going to appreciate your stomach-cancer lady – sorry, Jo.'
He went down the hall to open the door.

'Poor boy,' said Clare tolerantly. 'His vasectomy's on Monday and he's scared of needles.'

'Clare,' Scott called, 'your music's crap.'

'Better than that German death metal,' she retorted.

'Are you a Rammstein man, Scotty?' I asked as he came into view.

'Damn straight. Are you a fan?'

I shook my head. 'I'm sorry. I prefer Sarah McLachlan.' Scott turned to take off his leather bike jacket.

'Scotty, *what* is that at the back of your head?'

He put up a hand to stroke the neatly plaited two-inch rat's tail brushing the neck of his Def Leppard T-shirt. 'Cool, eh?'

'No,' said Clare. 'No, Scott, it isn't.'

He grinned widely. 'I'm growing it specially for my sister's wedding. She'll go nuts.'

'Good stuff,' I said. Scott's sister Rebecca is a deeply painful snob, or at least she was ten years ago. 'Has your mother seen it?'

'Not yet,' he said. 'You'd have heard the screams. Hey, where are the sprogs?'

It was a nice dinner party. We had chicken breasts stuffed with ricotta and mushroom risotto followed by crème caramel, and then sat around the table eating after-dinner mints and solving the world's problems.

Clare gulped the last of a large glass of port and shuddered slightly. 'Sold your house yet, Jo?'

'Not yet,' I said. 'Although apparently someone was interested.'

'Think you'll buy a house here?' Scott asked. 'The place next to mine's for sale, and I wouldn't mind having you as a neighbour. You couldn't be worse than the ones there now.'

'Thank you,' I said. 'That means so much. Is it the purple railway house or the concrete-block place with all the couches on the lawn?'

'The concrete-block one.'

'Who knows? Maybe I will. Except I'm not sure I could live so close to that rat's tail.'

'What do you mean?' asked Scotty, wounded. 'It's *mint*.'

'I might grow one too,' Brett mused.

'If you do,' said his loving wife, 'you're sleeping in the woodshed from then on.'

'Then you wouldn't need the vasectomy,' I pointed out.

'Well, true,' he said. 'It'd be much cheaper than the vasectomy, too.'

'I'll have you know,' said Scott, 'that this hairdo pulls chicks like you wouldn't believe.'

'You're right,' Clare said. 'We wouldn't believe.'

IT WAS AFTER eleven when Scotty and I got up to go.

'Right,' he said. 'No kids. You'll be spending the rest of the night having wild sex, then.'

'That would just be a waste of good sleeping time,' said Clare. 'I haven't had an unbroken night for three years.'

'Bet you wake up every two hours all night,' I said.

'Thanks for that thought,' she said. 'Goodnight, guys, thanks for coming.'

I pulled on my tan suede leather boots that I love more than life itself and just don't get to wear often enough in Waimanu. 'Thank you for having us. It was great. Good luck, Brett.'

Scotty's enormous motorbike was parked next to my car. 'How's young Matthew?' he asked, tucking his helmet under his arm. 'Haven't seen him for a week or two.'

'Miserable,' I said. 'But you know him; he doesn't say much.'

'Rose being sick is pretty rough on him.'

'Yeah,' I said. 'And on Kim. The whole thing just sucks.'

'It's rough on you, too.'

'But my dad didn't die of the same thing a few years ago. I've still got two nice parents.'

Scotty grunted and played with the strap of his helmet. 'Hey, Jo, want to go out for a drink or something, sometime?'

I expect there's a way to say 'thanks but no thanks' graciously, without embarrassment or injury to anyone's feelings. I've never found out what it is, but then I suppose I haven't had enough practice. Unlike my ex-friend Chrissie I've never been troubled by men trying to pick me up every time I step out of my front door. In fact, she doesn't even need to leave the house: the bloke who came to fix her phone line last year asked her out before he left. It was always a bit humbling being Chrissie's friend, and it particularly pissed me off that with such a dizzying selection of men to choose from she had to take mine.

'Thanks so much for asking,' I said slowly, 'but maybe not. I mean – that would be really nice, but just as mates.'

Scott sighed and then grinned at me. 'It's the rat's tail, isn't it?'

I grinned back. ''Fraid so.'

'Well, I wouldn't want to go out for a drink with anyone so shallow anyway,' he said with dignity, putting on his helmet. 'So the offer's off the table.'

'Fair enough.' I opened the door of my car. 'Hey, thank you. It's a really big compliment.'

'You're welcome,' said Scotty, clambering onto his enormous bike. He started it, revved the engine loudly and roared off down the drive.

'Jo!' Clare hissed.

I turned and saw her leaning out of the bathroom window. 'Yeah?'

'Did he ask you out?'

Her face was alight with anticipation and I started to laugh helplessly. 'Yes. Was this your idea?'

'Maybe,' said Clare, looking as inscrutable as a woman can look while hanging precariously out of a window with a toothbrush in one hand. 'What'd you say?'

'No thank you,' I admitted, and winced as she pointed the toothbrush at me like a pistol.

'*Why*, you ungrateful slapper?'

'I – I don't like Scotty in that way.'

'Couldn't you go out with him and just *see*? I wasn't even slightly attracted to Brett at the start. I just thought he'd be good practice.'

'Clare,' called Brett from somewhere inside, 'you're a horrible trollop and I don't know why I married you.'

'Because you adore me,' she said over her shoulder.

'Ignore her, Jo, she's pissed,' Brett called. 'Goodnight!'

'Goodnight,' I called back, and climbed into my car.

Before I could start it, Clare opened the back door and ran across the lawn in bare feet. She opened the passenger door and got into the car beside me. 'Shit, it's freezing out here,' she said. 'Now, Jo, you listen to Aunty Clare.'

'Don't want to,' I said, laughing. She was still clutching her toothbrush and she was indeed just a little bit pissed.

'It's time you got back on the horse,' she said. 'I know you were with Graeme for a really long time and being cheated on is a massive kick in the teeth, but you're not going to get over him until you put yourself out there and start seeing someone else.'

'I am over him,' I said. 'Well, just about, anyway. I'm still pissed off, and it's not great for your self-confidence when your boyfriend decides he prefers your best mate, but I don't want him back.'

'So what's the problem? Maybe Scotty wouldn't turn out to be the love of your life, but you don't have to *marry* him. You could just hang out with him a bit and see. I reckon the whole sexual chemistry thing's crap – it's not always there from the start.'

'I agree,' I said.

'And seriously, Jo, you don't want to put it off for too long. Everyone else gets coupled up, and then you find you're already in your mid-thirties and your fertility's declining and the only single men left are gay or weird, and –'

'Stop,' I begged. 'Please stop, or I'll cry. I *know* all that – you try not to think about it because you'll turn into a sad and desperate person, but it comes and gets you in the middle of the night.'

'So go out for a drink with the man! He's had a crush on you ever since high school, for Christ's sake! I know he's a bit scruffy round the edges and needs a shave and haircut, but he's a sweetie, and he's really good with kids.' She gestured with her toothbrush for emphasis and nearly poked me in the eye.

'Clare,' I said, relieving her of the toothbrush and laying it on the dashboard, 'just settle down. I can't go out with Scotty for a drink – there's someone else.'

'*What?*' she demanded. 'You're seeing someone and you didn't even *tell* me? What kind of a friend do you call yourself?'

'I'm not seeing anyone,' I said tiredly. 'I've just got a – a stupid crush on Matt, and until I talk myself out of it I can't really go out with his best friend.'

'Huh,' said Clare. 'Matt King. I thought you were immune.'

I gave a miserable little hiccup of laughter. 'If you ever tell anyone I swear I'll hunt you down and dismember you with a teaspoon.'

She made a face. 'Messy.'

'I mean it.'

'I can tell,' said Clare. 'You're looking very fierce. So why don't you do something about it?'

'Because he's going out with Farmer Barbie.'

'You should just tell him. What've you got to lose?'

'I can't tell him,' I said. 'He's not interested.'

'How do you know?' Clare asked.

'Because he's going out with Farmer Barbie,' I repeated.

She dismissed this with a wave of her hand. 'Yeah, but probably only because he hasn't got around to cutting her loose. He's not the most organised of blokes.'

'If you liked someone else you'd get around to it, wouldn't you?'

Clare shrugged and, picking up her toothbrush, pointed it at me again. 'If you don't ask you'll never know.'

I began to get cross. 'Oh, come *on*. Even if I decided I needed that extra little bit of rejection, how could I stay at Aunty Rose's and see him every day? His aunt's dying and he's got two hundred cows to calve all by himself and his mother's entirely useless and who *knows* what Kim'll do next – the last thing the poor man needs is me telling him he's the love of my life.'

'Hmm,' said Clare. 'Crap. You have a point.'

'I know.' I leant across and impulsively kissed her cheek. 'Now, go inside and sleep it off.'

Chapter 22

'HELLO, JOSIE. HOW lovely to see you again. I don't suppose you remember me?'

I smiled. 'Of course I do. Hello, Mrs Titoi.' Bonnie Titoi was a plump, charming Maori lady who lived in town; Aunty Rose had nursed her at the births of at least three of her children. I dropped my bag on the kitchen table and crossed the room to kiss Rose's cheek and give her today's mail. Aunty Rose was the only person I knew who received actual handwritten letters rather than just bills and announcements from *Time* magazine that she had just won a sumptuous, personalised gift.

'Did you bring the paper in, sweet pea?'

I shook my head. 'Never saw it. I thought someone must have brought it up.'

'I think David aims for the ditch on purpose,' she said. 'Ah well, never mind.'

'I'll go down and have a look for it in a moment,'

I said. 'Percy can come with me for the walk. How are you, Mrs Titoi?'

'Very well, thank you, my dear. Hasn't she grown up pretty, Rose?'

'She's not too bad, I suppose,' said Aunty Rose.

I ran myself a glass of water, and perched on the edge of the kitchen table to drink it. I had spent half an hour this afternoon with Dallas Taipa's feet, and another half-hour trying hard to explain to Keith Taylor that if he didn't stop taking his newly reconstructed shoulder out on the quad bike he would stuff it up irrevocably. I was fairly sure he wasn't going to listen to me, and that he was going to regret that for the next thirty or so years.

'Josie, sweetheart,' said Bonnie.

'Mm?'

'Please get off that table – it's *tapu*. We don't put our bottoms where we put our food, hmm?'

I slid to my feet. 'Sorry. Aunty Rose, I'll just go and get the paper.'

'You mustn't be offended, sweetheart.'

'Of course not,' I murmured, although privately I reflected that after all it wasn't Mrs Titoi's table. And my bottom hygiene is excellent, thank you very much.

Outside on the porch I took one of Aunty Rose's ancient oilskin coats from its peg and slid it on cautiously in case wetas were hiding in the sleeves. It's so disconcerting when a large spiky insect crawls out across the tender skin just behind your ear. Calling up my retinue of dogs and pig I went down through the orchard to the mailbox.

I had just retrieved the *Times* from the middle of a blackberry bush a good ten metres away from the little sign the paper man is supposed to aim for when Hazel's white car came down the road and turned in beside me. The driver stamped hard on the brakes and stalled a mere foot away from Percy, who was sitting in the middle of the driveway scratching his left ear with his hind foot.

'Idiot pig!' said Kim crossly, winding down the driver's-side window. 'What's he doing in the middle of the road in the dark?'

Trevor the boxer-cross poked his nose in through the window at her and she patted him gingerly; you never knew what that dog had found to roll in since you last saw him.

'Sorry,' I said, climbing out of the blackberry bush. 'Are you heading up?'

'I'll give you a lift.'

'I might go up the track to the trig station first.'

'In the dark?'

'I feel like being outside for a bit, and the dogs need a walk.' Lately I didn't seem to have found time to walk any further than the washing line, and I was starting to fear my legs would atrophy from lack of use. Also it seemed a shame to inflict my current bad mood on Aunty Rose, who had more than enough to put up with.

'Well, okay,' said Kim doubtfully. Kim feels that the Great Outdoors is all very well in its way, but she much prefers to admire it from the comfort and security of an air-conditioned car. And exercise only counts if you're wearing a little Nike crop-top and texting as you jog on a treadmill.

It was an eerie, gusty sort of night and the wind blew little mini-tornadoes of leaves across the rutted clay track that led from Rose's back paddock up through the scrub to the trig station on the top of the hill. Percy gave up halfway and made for home but the dogs stayed with me, trotting ahead and vanishing intermittently into the fern. The air smelt nice – cold and fresh, laced with the sharp scent of crushed bracken and the lovely mushroomy smell of leaf litter. A pheasant chinked in alarm before breaking cover two steps ahead of me to fly up in a breathless flurry of wings, and I yelped in shock. I hate the way they do that, although you have to admire it as an escape strategy; the animal that might have enjoyed a nice pheasant lunch is far too busy trying to restart its heart to think about pursuit.

BONNIE TITOI HAD left when I let myself and the dogs in through the little rusting gate beside the walnut tree three-quarters of an hour later. I could see Kim at the kitchen window, frowning in concentration as she stirred something.

'Polenta and roasted vegetable stack,' she said as I opened the door.

I fished the paper out of an enormous pocket in my coat and put it on the table near where Aunty Rose sat peeling wedges of pumpkin. 'That sounds very fancy.'

'It will be,' said Kim.

'It sounds like the sort of food that should come with

a caramelised onion jus,' said Aunty Rose. 'Is a jus still the latest in modern dining, Josephine? I cancelled my sub-scription to *Taste* magazine last year.'

'No, no,' I said. 'That's *so* last week. You've got to have a pomegranate vinegar reduction if you want people to even *begin* to take you seriously. Although come to think of it, I'm out of touch – probably by now reductions are out of fashion too.'

'Hey, Josie?' Kim asked casually, spooning chicken stock powder into her polenta pot. 'You haven't got your friend Andy's mobile phone number, have you?'

I met Aunty Rose's eye and she shook her head, amused. 'About a week was Matthew's estimate, wasn't it?' she murmured. 'And it's been – what? Ten days?'

'It was nice while it lasted,' I said. 'Kimmy, he's way older than you.'

'I'm not *interested* in him!' Kim cried.

'Methinks she doth protest too much,' said Aunty Rose to the ceiling.

'Oh, don't be stupid,' said Kim. 'I just want to say thank you. And I think I was a little bit sick in his car. I thought maybe I should get him some chocolates or something to apologise.'

'He likes Picnic bars,' I told her. 'Should I give her the number, Aunty Rose?'

'Nice boy, is he?'

'Reasonably nice.'

'And unlikely to encourage her to dress like a member of Kiss?'

'I wouldn't have thought so,' I said.

'Or to impregnate her?'

'We'd have to ask him.'

'Make a note of it, Josephine, and I shall call him tomorrow.'

'You guys are not as funny as you think you are,' Kim said huffily.

VERY LATE THAT night, as I padded back up the hall from the loo in my double-sock-pyjama-and-woolly-jumper sleeping ensemble, I heard a faint rumbling noise from the kitchen. Flicking on the hall light as I passed the switch I opened the kitchen door.

Old Spud, whose arthritis troubled him on these wintry nights, had been sleeping in front of the wood stove on his Spiderman beanbag for the last week. He wasn't in his normal spot with his tail wrapped tight around his ears; he was standing stiff-legged in front of the outside door, hackles up and growling deep in his throat. It was an unnerving sound – a low continuous snarl that made the back of my own neck prickle in sympathy.

In horror movies, at this point, the heroine opens the door and quavers, 'Is anybody there?' Then she takes three hesitant steps before being startled by a passing cat. She gasps, laughs shakily and bends to stroke puss, and only then does the insane axe murderer/serial killer/mutant spider deliver the fatal blow. I saw more than my share of horror movies during five years with Graeme Sunderland, thriller aficionado, and there was no *way* I was going out-side to see what was bothering the dog.

'Spud,' I said softly. 'Hey, dude, what's up?'

Spud turned his old head and whined before resuming his fixed stare at the door. I went on tiptoe across the dimly lit kitchen and knelt on the chaise longue, twitching aside the curtain to peer out. This was a total waste of time; it was a moonless night and the darkness was complete. I couldn't even see the dark outline of the woodshed silhou-etted against the sky. Spud padded across the room to lean against my leg and looked at me expectantly.

'Well, Spud,' I said aloud, 'it's either a prowler or a pol-tergeist or a possum. I hope you're impressed by my snazzy use of alliteration there. We *could* ring Matt to come and scare it off, but he's not going to be able to do anything if it's a poltergeist and he'll be pissed off if I wake him up in calving season for a possum – and then Cilla's probably with him, and she'll think I'm trying to seduce him if I go calling him in the middle of the night. Not that I'm dressed for seduction, but still. And nothing has come up the drive, because it would have passed the dog kennels and they'd all be barking. Besides, surely a prowler would pick somewhere a bit easier to prowl than a house ten kilo-metres out of town up a long steep hill. So we'll both go back to sleep, okay?'

Spud turned and looked at the door again, and gave a short hoarse bark.

'I'm not going to go out there,' I said. 'Sorry to be such a disappointment. In your bed, mate.'

With a well-I-did-*try*-to-warn-you look, Spud yawned and went to throw himself down on his beanbag once more. I checked the door just to make sure it was still locked and went back to bed. Possum, I told myself firmly, carefully tucking in the bedclothes to keep out the draughts and the poltergeists. Definitely a possum. I would set a trap under the lemon tree tomorrow.

THE FOLLOWING EVENING I looked thoughtfully into my supermarket trolley, trying to remember what else had been on the list I'd left at work. Aunty Rose had decreed that she would prepare a gourmet meal for me and Stu on Saturday night, and had given me strict instructions not to bother coming home unless I brought capers, sundried tomatoes and brazil nuts with me. She had also requested olives, but I was going to lie brazenly and say the supermarket had sold out.

I found the other delicacies and remembered the batteries for the wall clock and the three mouse traps, but I had a niggling feeling that there had been something else. Surely it wasn't something we couldn't live with until tomorrow? I tossed two loaves of bread into the trolley and turned towards the checkout.

As I passed the end of the snacks and fizzy drinks aisle someone gave a high-pitched, breathless shriek. It was my energy-efficient former flatmate Sara, but she hadn't seen me – she had her eyes closed as a greasy-looking youth buried his head between her breasts while she leant against the Grain Waves stand. I winced – lovely that she'd found someone, and she was evidently enjoying herself, but how disconcerting for the rest of us hapless shoppers to have to witness their foreplay if we wanted snack food.

Most of Waimanu seemed to be shopping this evening; I met my high school English teacher, Mrs Palmer, beside the frozen vegetables, and Brett in the checkout queue.

'How's the wound?' I asked him.

'I've got some interesting bruises,' he said. 'I can show you if you like – meet me in the car park.'

'Tempting,' I said. 'But your wife would eviscerate me.'

He grinned widely. 'Of course she wouldn't. She would understand your interest as a health professional.'

'Maybe, but it would be hard to explain to passers-by why you were showing some other woman your scrotum. Perhaps you should just email me a picture.'

'Excuse me, sir, would you like to come into this lane?' called a woman from behind the neighbouring checkout, and off he went. I was perusing the cover of next week's *TV Guide* and hoping I wasn't actually going to receive a photo of Brett's vasectomy scars when Farmer Barbie came up behind me holding a magazine and a bottle of water.

I hadn't seen Cilla since the night of the cheating allegations and didn't really want to see her now. I'm quite sure she felt the same, but there were only three checkouts open for the evening rush and the other two queues had just been joined by families with months' worth of groceries.

'Hi,' I murmured when the silence became uncomfortable.

'Hi,' said Cilla, half turning away and letting her hair fall between us like a curtain.

Motivated not by kindness but by the desire to avoid five minutes of stilted conversation, I said, 'You go ahead. You've only got a couple of things.'

'Thanks,' she muttered, and slipped in front of me to lay her purchases on the conveyor. One bottle of mandarin-flavoured sports water (now there's a marketing scam if ever I saw one) and one *Bride and Groom* magazine.

Surely not, I thought as I began to unload my trolley. *She's probably going to be someone's bridesmaid*. But my vision went blurry, and for a hideous moment I feared I was actually going to burst into tears at the supermarket checkout.

IT WASN'T A good evening: Aunty Rose's pain was bad and Hazel popped in to bring her a healing crystal and tell us all about the insensitive behaviour of one of the women at her Pilates class. 'I simply couldn't believe she would speak to me like that,' she said. 'I can't imagine what made her so – so *hostile*.'

'Mm,' said Aunty Rose, shifting painfully in her seat. The book at her side slid to the floor and her sister bent to retrieve it.

'Well, what do you know,' she said, turning it over between her hands. 'I couldn't think where this had gone to. It's been missing for years.' And she put it in her handbag.

'I'm reading that,' said Aunty Rose mildly.

Hazel gave a little tinkle of laughter. 'Sorry, Rosie darling. Of course you may read it. It's just –' here she paused and looked soulful for a moment, like Percy when he wants your toast crusts – 'it was Pat's. His favourite, goodness only knows why. I never could get him to take an interest in any other poetry, poor dear soul.'

'That's my copy,' said Aunty Rose. 'I bought it at a Rotary book sale several years ago. *Thank* you.' She held out a hand for the book, and tucked it firmly down between her hip and the back of the chaise longue.

Just before bed, when I was locking the doors and banking up the fire for the night, I found the book and picked it up. It was a copy of *The Songs of a Sentimental Bloke* by CJ Dennis – I'd read it before, but not for years. I like it; it's a charming love story written all in verse in the Cockney slang spoken in the Sydney slums a hundred years ago, about Kid and Doreen (who was a bonzer tart).

It was a tatty old book, with faded orange cloth covers and foxed pages. I flicked through it sleepily, reading a line here and there, and then looked inside the front cover to see just when it was first published. It *was* Aunty Rose's copy, but not one she'd bought at a Rotary book sale. In a corner of the title page someone had written '*For Rosie*' in very careful copperplate with a fountain pen. I knew that handwriting – occasionally when I was small I was allowed to go to town with Matthew and his father on the twentieth of the month to pay bills, so I had seen Pat King write out plenty of cheques. I shut the book up again and tucked it under a cushion.

Chapter 23

'AAH,' SAID AUNTY Rose with satisfaction, leaning back in her chair at the breakfast table and cradling her teacup in both hands. 'This is better. Hurrah for codeine.'

'It doesn't make you feel sick?' I asked. 'I had some when I had my wisdom teeth out and then spent the next eight hours hanging over the toilet bowl.'

'Not at all,' she said. 'Of course, there *are* some annoying side effects. Pass me that piece of paper and I shall make a note to ask Rob Milne for a prescription for laxatives. And then I must get to work on my marinade.'

There was a southerly blast heading up the country this weekend; it struck at lunchtime with a seriously impressive hailstorm. The hailstones hitting the corrugated-iron roof drowned out the radio (this was a good thing – Aunty Rose insisted on listening to a special broadcast of horrible warbling songs from the forties), piled up on the window-sills and drove Percy and the dogs to take cover on the back porch. I hoped Stu would be alright driving through it; he's a city boy from the tips of his gelled hair to the soles of his expensive designer sneakers.

'There's a new leak,' I noted, digging through a cupboard to find the preserving pan, which was the biggest pot in the house.

'Is there?' Aunty Rose asked absently. 'Josephine, where did you put the sherry?'

'It's only two in the afternoon,' I protested. 'And do you think it'll go well with codeine?'

'It's for soaking the gingernuts for dessert,' she said. 'Now where's this new leak?'

'In the toilet at the end of the hall.'

'Oh, I know all about that one – it's been there for years. It will stop as soon as the wind changes direction.'

MATT FELL INTO the kitchen out of the driving rain just before seven, shaking his head like a wet dog.

'Dear boy!' Aunty Rose cried. She turned and waved a spatula at him, and drops of orange sauce flew across the kitchen. I sighed internally – the clean-up tonight was going to take me *hours*. 'You're right on time. Does that mean the cows are behaving themselves?'

He smiled, clearly pleased to see her in such fine form. 'Yep. There's only one that looks like calving tonight, and they're in the Pine Tree Paddock so there's heaps of shelter.'

'Marvellous.'

'So,' he said, 'you're cooking tonight.'

'I am,' said Aunty Rose.

He looked wary. 'Ah.'

'Matthew King, there is no need to take that tone. You'll frighten Stuart.'

'Never,' I said. 'He's very brave. Stu – Matt.'

'Nice to meet you,' said Matt. He wiped his wet face on his sleeve, put his work boots in the corner beside the wood stove to dry and held out a hand to Stu, who was standing at the kitchen table wrestling with a champagne cork. 'You must have had a fairly exciting drive up from Wellington.'

'It was,' Stu confirmed. He transferred his corkscrew briefly to the same hand as the champagne bottle so as to shake hands. 'Jo assures me this weather isn't normal, but I'm not sure I believe her.'

'I usually don't believe her just on principle,' Matt said, and got the table between us before I could kick him.

'Aunty Rose,' I said, 'are you quite sure Matt is going to be an asset to this dinner party?'

'No,' she said cheerfully. 'Throw him out.'

'Don't you dare,' said Stu, delicately levering out his cork. It hissed gently, and with the precision that I imagine he uses in surgery he began to pour out the champagne. 'I have been simply *pining* to meet Jo's first love.' He minced across the kitchen to present Aunty Rose with a champagne flute. 'Gorgeous glasses, Rose. And the champagne will go beautifully with your codeine.'

I looked at Matt and grimaced apologetically.

'JD, angel, don't tell me I've embarrassed you. I shall never forgive myself,' said Stu.

There's no point in getting cross with Stu. He just thinks it's funny.

'Yes,' I said resignedly. 'I can see you're crushed by remorse.'

Dinner that evening consisted of a Moroccan chicken dish (delicious), served with mashed potato (not authentic, but also delicious) and a vegetable medley that seemed to be flavoured mostly with vinegar and was utterly inedible.

'Never mind, Aunty Rose,' I said consolingly. 'Two out of three's pretty good.'

'I don't understand what went wrong,' she said. 'I followed the recipe to the letter.'

'You've never followed anything to the letter in your life,' Matt told her, helping himself to more chicken. 'You've been at a conference, haven't you, Stu?'

'Indeed,' said Stu, inserting a heaped forkful of vegetables into his mouth and then becoming temporarily incapable of further speech.

'My dear boy,' said Aunty Rose warmly. 'That is above and beyond the call of duty. The scrap bucket's under the sink if you'd like to spit it out.'

Eyes watering, Stu shook his natty dark head and swallowed. Then he picked up his wine glass and took a large gulp. 'N-no,' he managed. 'I'm good.'

'That was a superhuman effort,' I told him. 'So how was your conference?'

'Just the usual,' he said. 'Drug reps schmoozing and buying you expensive drinks – that sort of thing.'

'That's probably due to your boyish charm,' Aunty Rose put in.

'JD, your aunt is a woman of remarkably good taste,' said Stu. 'There were a few good lectures – some new techniques for getting into hip joints – and I found a *fabulous* pub on the waterfront.'

'Stu always finds a fabulous pub,' I explained. 'He'd discover a divine little wine bar in downtown Ruatoria. It's pretty much his only skill.'

'Well,' said Matt, 'that's not a bad skill.'

'You should be nicer to me,' Stu told me. 'I'll have you know I retrieved your iPod *and* some extremely fetching lacy knickers.'

'My pink knickers?' I adore fancy bras and knickers, especially when they come in matching sets. It's probably due to having spent my whole professional life wearing sensible sports clothes. I'm very fond of sensible sports clothes and even fonder of sports shoes (Graeme felt that my obsession with sparkly sneakers was a reasonably major character flaw), but I do like to compensate with impractical undies. '*Thank* you.'

'You're welcome. Your erstwhile boyfriend –'

'Good word,' Aunty Rose put in. 'Sorry, do continue.'

'Thank you,' said Stu. 'He asked after you – he looked all wistful. I get the feeling that life with the lovely Chrissie's no bed of roses.'

'Good,' I said. 'I hope she's insanely high maintenance and drives him up the wall.'

Stu gave a little snort of laughter. 'An enormous bunch

of flowers arrived at the nurses' station the other day –' Chrissie is a theatre nurse; I first met her at one of Graeme's work functions – 'and she rang him up and screamed down the phone because they were the wrong colour.'

'Far out,' I murmured. 'I *never* got flowers. He said they were a big waste of money because they just died.'

'Once again, Josephine, I ask myself what you were doing with this pillock,' Aunty Rose said, shaking her head.

'He's a doctor,' Matt reminded her.

I propped my chin in my hands and looked at him thoughtfully. 'Once, long ago,' I said, 'I kicked you square in the balls. I could do it again if you like.'

He grinned at me. 'Tempting,' he said, 'but I'll pass.'

IT WAS AROUND ten before the party broke up and Stu and I began to tackle an enormous pile of dishes.

'I don't know how the woman does it,' I said. 'I swear she can dirty every pot in the house just boiling water.'

'I won't hear a word against her,' said Stu severely. 'She's pretty fabulous, isn't she?'

'Yep,' I said. 'You should have seen her six months ago. She had long flowing grey hair and a bust like the prow of a ship.' I pressed the heels of my hands to my eyes to suppress the tears.

'If I ever get some fatal disease,' he said, 'I hope to be able to carry it off with one-tenth her style.'

'You'd better tell her that. She'll like it.'

There was a companionable silence while he swilled dinner plates under the hot tap and I dried them, broken only by Spud's gentle snores from his position in front of the stove. At length I asked, 'So, are you seeing anyone?'

'No,' said Stu glumly. 'I have taken most unwillingly to celibacy.'

'Apparently it's a virtue.'

'That's just what people who aren't getting any tell one another to make themselves feel better.'

'You may well be right,' I said. 'If it's any consolation, your love life can't possibly be any worse than mine.'

'Why on earth aren't you shagging the divine Matthew?' Stu demanded. 'He's *highly* shaggable.'

'Matt?' I said lightly. 'That would be almost incest.'

'You've done it before,' he pointed out. It is very dangerous to tell your close friends your secrets during late-night conversations over a bottle of wine – they remember them.

'We were young and stupid then. Anyway, he's got a girlfriend.'

'Really?' Stu asked sceptically. 'If I was her I'd be feeling very insecure.'

'What do you mean?' I picked up a plate, examined it and tossed it back into the sink because it seemed to still have about half a chicken stuck to it.

'JD, don't be dense. The man obviously thinks you're the bee's knees. Didn't you see him prick up his ears when I mentioned your knickers?'

I hadn't, and I very much doubted Stu had either. 'Ah, but you should see the girlfriend,' I said. 'She looks like a little china doll, but she can talk about feed conversion efficiency and calving spreads with the best of them.'

'I hate her,' said Stu promptly.

I sighed. 'Yeah,' I admitted. 'Me too. When are Graeme and Chrissie getting married?'

'Who would know? Chrissie's still trying to decide between an intimate ceremony on a tropical island and a huge sit-down dinner followed by a masquerade ball.'

I laughed, but it didn't sound very convincing. Stu put down his dish brush and slung a consoling arm around my shoulders. 'You didn't really want to marry him, did you?' he asked.

'No,' I said slowly. 'But it's a bit depressing that after five years he'd go and get engaged to someone else at the drop of a hat.'

'I doubt very much it was his idea,' said Stu drily. 'But I know what you mean – it's not great for the self-esteem.'

'It is not,' I said with feeling.

'The last bloke *I* was interested in decided that after all he liked girls,' said Stu comfortingly. 'Maybe being squashed flat will give us stronger characters.'

I picked up my tea towel again. 'Just how strong do our characters need to be?'

Chapter 24

'HOW DID YOU sleep?' I asked Stu when he came into the kitchen the next morning. It was still raining, but only in a half-hearted drizzly sort of way, and the wind had dropped. Outside everything looked grey and sodden and miserable.

'Fair to middling,' he said, stretching his arms above his head and yawning. 'Something came and cleared its nasal passages under my window at about two ...'

'Percy,' I explained, passing him a mug of plunger coffee.

'An elderly local rustic?'

'Aunty Rose's pet pig.'

'You've lifted a weight from my mind. And then I ran into an enormous pot when I went for a slash in the middle of the night.'

'That's for the leak in the toilet ceiling.'

'Of course. Good coffee.'

'Thank you.'

'And you were right – I did want the gloves as well as the beanie.'

'Sorry about that,' I said. 'I've been meaning to buy an oil heater.'

'No, no,' said Stu. 'I'm glad I've done it. I feel like that chap who wanders around the mountaintops drinking his own urine.'

'If you like, you can have urine instead of coffee to complete the whole survival experience,' I offered.

'I have to save *something* for my next visit.'

I smiled at him. 'Thanks for coming. I've missed you.'

Stu smiled back. 'You're welcome,' he said. 'Want me to tell Graeme you're having a wild affair with your sexy childhood friend?'

I was a little bit tempted – once, in a moment of extreme sleepiness, I did call Graeme 'Matt' in bed, and he brought it up in every argument for about the next three years. But knowing my luck Graeme would then ring Aunty Rose's to tell me the house had fallen over or exploded or something equally expensive, and Matt would answer the phone, and I would be revealed as a delusional liar. 'Nah,' I said. 'Just tell him that I'm perfectly happy and I look like a goddess.'

STU LEFT FOR the airport mid-morning. 'Thank you for having me, Rose,' he said, picking up his overnight bag.

Aunty Rose got to her feet, resplendent in her satin dressing-gown and, today, a peroxide-blonde wig. 'Dear boy, it was a pleasure.'

'I'll see you next time I visit.'

She smiled. 'In that case,' she said, 'you'll want to come back fairly soon.'

Stu put his arms around her very gently and kissed her cheek. 'I am constantly disgusted at the unfairness of life,' he said.

'I agree,' said Aunty Rose. 'However, there is almost no point in complaining about it. Now you drive carefully, young man. It won't be icy this morning but the road may well be flooded further south.'

After he left I got Aunty Rose's ancient vacuum cleaner out of its cupboard and drearily started the housework. I hate that vacuum cleaner and it hates me; it's an old Tellus that catches on every doorframe and falls over just to spite you, pulling its cord out of the wall. The house was bleak and chilly and there was a glaring contrast between scrubbing elderly toilet bowls in Waimanu and going to my Sunday morning aerobic dance class before brunching with friends in Melbourne. I had almost forgotten, before Stu's visit, that I used to shop for nice clothes and drink cappuccinos and work in a progressive hospital with witty, intelligent colleagues.

'Josephine, don't use detergent to mop the floor,' said Aunty Rose, passing the bathroom door on her way up the hall. 'It leaves streaks. There's ammonia under the sink beside the washing machine.'

I had washed floors with a little detergent in hot water for at least the last ten years without having streaking issues. It's hard to go back to being told what to do when

you're used to being a home owner and a grown-up –
these days I can only live with my mother for a weekend
before it starts to drive me insane. 'Great,' I muttered. 'So
the whole house can smell like a urinal.' I picked up the
mop bucket and went to fetch the ammonia.

Aunty Rose came into the kitchen as I tipped my mopping water down the old-fashioned concrete sink beside
the washing machine.

'Sweet pea,' she said, leaning stiffly against the doorframe. 'Don't worry about the floor; it looks fine.'

The tears welled hot behind my eyelids. 'Aunty Rose,
I'm sorry.'

'I do realise this isn't easy for you.'

I turned to face her. 'It's a hell of a lot easier for me than
it is for you, and *you* manage not to act like a sulky teenager.'

She crossed the room and lowered herself slowly onto
the chaise longue. 'Apparently that's still to come. I am
assured that I can expect bitterness, anger and depression
before we get to resignation. Won't that be fun?'

I tried to smile. 'I can hardly wait.'

'Why don't you go out for a walk? Take a stick and
whack things – you'll feel better for it.'

I opened my mouth to say something, realised I wasn't
going to be able to squeeze any voice past the constriction
in my throat and nodded instead.

I WENT UP the steep hill behind the house at a cross
between a scramble and a run. It was rough going through

the sodden mats of Yorkshire fog and last year's dead pig fern, and the hillside was all ridged and seamed with sheep tracks. My jeans were saturated to the knee after about four steps and clung to my legs in a clammy and unpleasant sort of way.

I stood on the crest of a ridge in an icy wind that whipped down off the mountains, and looked up the valley. There are at least a thousand different shades of green in those bush-clad folds of hill leading up to the ranges, and as I caught my breath and tried to count them the seething tangle of resentment began to recede. It was indeed *crap* that Aunty Rose was dying and I no longer had the right to call this place home and Matt didn't want me, but somehow mountains do tend to restore your sense of perspective. They are so enduring and grandiose and indifferent that your fleeting human troubles seem very unimportant in comparison. And away down below was Spud, toiling valiantly up the hill to keep me company. He was far too old for serious hill climbing; I sighed, kicked the top off an unfortunate foxglove and went down to meet him.

Spud was puffing hard, and when I reached him he flopped down across my feet with his tongue hanging out, evidently wishing to put a stop to any more foolish exertion. I bent to pull his ears and looked the other way, down across our old farm and over the white weatherboard house where I grew up (noting in passing that the new conservatory was indeed horrible) to the Kings' cowshed across the road.

Matt was break-feeding the springer mob through the flatter paddocks in front of the shed. He had given them today's break hours ago and they should have been sitting down by now, chewing their cuds and contemplating whatever ruminating cows contemplate (not, I suspect, a whole lot). But they weren't sitting down; they were all standing in one corner, being herded more and more tightly against the fence by one small black pig.

That pig looked like he was having the time of his life, bustling to and fro and forcing any poor cow that tried to break away back into the group. But no matter how much fun he was having you can't really have bumptious pigs intimidating your heavily pregnant cows, so I pushed Spud off my feet and started to slither and slide back down the hill.

I went down through our old place rather than Aunty Rose's. It was trespassing, I suppose, but the gully I picked isn't visible from the house. I opened a wooden gate for Spud – and was obscurely pleased to note it still sagged and had to be lifted with a little jerk in order to unlatch it – and trotted down to jump across the creek at its narrowest point. There was a small group of stubby bearded pungas on the far bank and a smooth, lichen-covered boulder where I used to sit with a book and a hand line, although I never caught the enormous eel that lived there.

Spud didn't even try to jump but sat down mournfully on the bank and looked at me. 'Useless animal,' I said, stepping back into the creek up to my knees and heaving him across. He weighed a good forty kilograms, was soaking wet and smelt like old wet sock. 'Come on, then.' And we laboured up the steep bank to the fence that borders the road.

I manhandled Spud across the boundary fence and started along the road towards the Kings' tanker entrance. The cloud had come down and it had started to rain again – that gentle persistent drizzle that soaks you to the skin. I was walking fast with my head down, and almost yelped in surprise when Matt called, 'Pleasant morning for a stroll.'

He was standing on the edge of a medium-sized lake in his front paddock, with his hands in his pockets and a pensive look on his face.

'Nice water feature,' I called back.

'Feel free to go in and unblock the culvert pipe, if you'd like to experience it from closer up.' He sighed and began to take off his waterproof leggings.

'I will, if you like. I'm wet already.'

'That's okay,' he said. 'You might get bitten by an eel and sue me for damages.'

I climbed the fence. 'Never. Tell you what – I'll unblock the pipe while you roar up the hill and deal with the pig that's mustering up your springer mob.'

'Is there one?' he asked.

'Well, there was ten minutes ago. I saw him from the top of the hill. He's not a very big pig, but the cows weren't looking too happy about the whole thing.'

He turned towards his quad bike, parked just up the

hill on the track. 'I'd better go and see. Don't worry about the pipe . . .'

I watched him disappear up around the shoulder of the hill before wading into the murky water to find the culvert pipe and remove the armful of slimy, decaying vegetation blocking its end. The things we do for love.

WHEN I OPENED the kitchen door Kim wrinkled her small nose fastidiously and said, 'Been communing with nature again, have we?'

'You should try it sometime,' I suggested. 'You might enjoy it.'

'I have,' she said. 'And I didn't. What would you like on your toasted sandwich?'

'Pineapple and cheese, please. Where's Aunty Rose?'

'Feeding the chooks.'

When I came back into the kitchen ten minutes later, showered and with an armful of wet, muddy clothes, it was full of people. Matt was riffling through the pantry, Aunty Rose was setting the table for lunch and Andy was buttering slices of bread for toasted sandwiches while Kim filled them.

'Hi, Andy,' I said, opening the lid of the washing machine and tossing in my clothes. 'How's the world of livestock wheeling and dealing?'

'Not bad at all. Have I buttered enough yet?'

'For a start,' said Kim. 'Aunty Rose, would the chicken in the fridge make a good toastie?'

'Delicious,' she said. 'We *could* have had olive and sundried tomato and cheese, if Josephine had deigned to purchase all the items on the shopping list.'

'I'd sack her,' said Matt. 'You're out of peanuts, too, which is poor at best.'

'Ah,' I said. 'I knew I wanted something else at the supermarket, but then I ran into Sara getting all frisky with her new boyfriend and my mind went blank. I can see why you moved out, Andy.'

'It wasn't just the public displays of affection,' he said. 'There are girls that look good in hot pants and singlet tops, and girls that just don't.'

'And she just doesn't?' Matt asked, replacing the empty peanut jar and taking down a bag of sultanas instead.

'Nope,' said Andy.

'That's the thing with hot pants,' Matt said. 'Most women should be forbidden by law to wear them, and just a few should be forbidden to wear anything else.'

'Andy dropped in to bring your mail,' Aunty Rose informed me. Her eyes were bright with amusement under the peroxide-blonde wig. 'Wasn't that kind of him?'

'Very,' I said. Kim looked sharply from her aunt to me, but we returned the look with matching vacuous smiles. I shuffled through the EziBuy catalogue, the postcard from *Reader's Digest* informing me I had just won a gift worth thousands and the letter from the bank offering to increase my credit card limit.

'None of it looked very urgent,' said Andy, slightly shamefaced, 'but you never know.'

'Thank you very much,' I said, noting with some amusement that the letter from the bank was dated June. 'Was that pig still there, Matt?'

'It was. It's now an ex-pig.'

'Crikey. That'll teach it.'

'I fired a warning shot,' said Matt defensively. 'Right between the eyes. You can't really have a pig with a taste for cattle-rustling wandering around the place. And now I suppose I'll have to do something with the bloody thing.'

'How big is it?' Andy asked.

'About fifty pounds. It's not a bad little pig, actually.'

'If you don't want the hassle of butchering it,' said Andy diffidently, 'I've got a mate with a proper walk-in chiller and a sausage maker and all the gear.'

'Excellent,' said Matt. 'It's all yours.'

'I'll bring it back, cut up.'

'Of course not! I was tempted to heave it into a black-berry bush, but I felt guilty. Good man – I didn't really want to spend an hour dismembering a pig.'

'I enjoy it,' said Andy. 'I used to hunt at home, but I haven't got a dog now.'

'Where is home?' asked Aunty Rose. She produced a heavy silver platter covered with bunches of wart-like grapes for the toasted sandwiches.

'Near Gisborne. Dad and my brother have a sheep farm.'

'And farming's not your cup of tea?'

Andy shook his head. 'I'm the lowest in the pecking order, so I spent all my time dagging and grubbing thistles.'

232

'I suppose the excitement of grubbing thistles would pall eventually,' said Aunty Rose. 'So you decided to make your own way. Wise fellow.'

'RIGHT,' SAID MATT, pushing back his chair. 'I suppose these gutters aren't going to unblock themselves. Do you want that pig today, Andy? It's hanging up in the meat house – Kim might show you where it is if you ask her nicely.'

Andy brightened so obviously at this suggestion that Aunty Rose had a lengthy and not very convincing coughing fit. 'Crumb,' she murmured. 'Do excuse me. Matthew, is there any reason Andy shouldn't go up to the back of the farm for a look, seeing as he's keen on hunting and the bush?'

'Not at all.'

With an endearing show of carelessness Kim said, 'I can take you if you like. But you've probably got way better things to do.'

'I'd love to,' said Andy. 'If you've got time.'

'Sure.' Kim shrugged, the epitome of nonchalance.

'You can take the ute,' said Matt. 'I don't need it this afternoon.'

'I wouldn't mind walking,' Andy said. 'You see a lot more, and this is amazing country.'

'It's a nice walk,' said Kim. 'There's a lovely view of the ranges from up the back.'

I didn't look at her, and not the merest hint of a smile

crossed my face at this unprecedented enthusiasm for fresh air. I began to pile used plates onto the silver tray that had contained the toasted sandwiches while Matt and Aunty Rose started an innocent conversation on the whereabouts of her ladder, and yet Kim raked all three of us with the sort of glare normally reserved for those found pocketing the cutlery at a restaurant.

'YOU'RE A KIND brother,' I remarked, coming back across the lawn with an empty basin under one arm. Percy had enjoyed last night's vegetables if no one else had.

'Oh well,' said Matt, jumping lightly down from the roof to the water tank, then the tank to the ground. Aunty Rose's wooden ladder had been found to be harbouring a thriving community of borers, and so he had ascended the roof via the plum tree outside the bathroom window. 'He seems like a nice bloke.'

'He is.'

He wiped his hands on the legs of his jeans. 'Thank you for unblocking my pipe, by the way.'

I sniggered at that, and he looked briefly puzzled before recognising it as a childish, pulling-the-conversation-down-into-the-gutter snigger. My sense of humour never has developed very far.

He smiled. 'As in "Hey, baby, want to unblock my pipe?" Somehow I can't see it catching on as a pick-up line.'

'Anyone you picked up with a line like that, you wouldn't want,' I agreed.

'Do you miss Melbourne?' he asked abruptly.

I considered this. 'Sometimes. Seeing Stu reminded me. I miss my job and my friends and living in my own house. And shoe shops.' I missed being half of a couple, too, and thus not having to feel guilty if I preferred spending Friday night reading in the bath to partying till dawn. I added, 'But then, in Melbourne I didn't get to unblock culvert pipes *or* massage Dallas's feet.'

'Well, there is that,' said Matt. 'Who needs bright city lights when they have Dallas's feet?'

'Exactly. Do *you* miss the bright city lights?'

'Not now,' he said. 'I always knew I'd have to come home to the farm or break Dad's heart – it was just all a bit more sudden than I expected.'

'It was very hard on you, not getting to say goodbye,' I said tentatively. Why the King family had thought they were doing Matt a kindness by hiding the severity of his father's illness from him was a complete mystery to me.

Matt's mouth twisted in what may have been a smile. 'It was very hard on everyone else watching him die. And he did write me a letter.' He smiled again, more convincingly. 'He said I wasn't too much of a disappointment, considering, and to look after my sister, and wrote me a list of all the farm jobs that needed doing while the cows were dry.'

I laughed, because if I hadn't I'd have cried.

'ROSIE, DARLING, I know you would never mean anything by it, but . . .' Hazel's voice trailed off, and she put

235

her head on one side and gave a little winsome smile. Had she been six years old it might even have looked cute.

'Mean anything by what?' Aunty Rose asked. She pulled up the woollen rug covering her knees, and I left the washing pile and went to feed another log into the wood stove. It was dark outside and raining again but Aunty Rose's kitchen, with its velvet curtains and cheerful pink walls, was a warm and happy place. I had thought our Melbourne kitchen was the essence of all a kitchen should be, sleek and shiny with a fridge that made its own ice (Graeme's specification) and a centre island with four stools (mine), but this one was a thousand times nicer. Although that could well have been because this one contained Aunty Rose, with her crimson dressing-gown and green satin cap, her heavy rings and faint scent of Chanel No. 5.

'Good gracious, Josie,' said Hazel. 'The room is like an oven as it is.' She smiled at me to show there were no hard feelings and added, 'I do realise it's very easy to be extravagant with someone else's firewood.'

'She split it,' said Aunty Rose drily. 'What's the matter, Hazel?'

'I'm not at all sure it's appropriate for my little girl to be showing a scruffy pig hunter over the farm.'

'Scruffy pig hunter . . .' Aunty Rose mused, frowning with entirely fake perplexity. 'Oh! Young Andy Morrison?'

'I didn't ask his name,' said Hazel stiffly. 'But I assume you haven't given your blessing for Kim to chauffeur more than *one* pig hunter around the place. Really, Rosie, did it not occur to you that the boy's probably scoping the place out for his gang of thieves, and he'll be back in the middle of the night to murder us all in our beds?'

If Aunty Rose had still had eyebrows, they would have risen right up to her hairline. If she had still had a hairline. 'I can't say that it did,' she murmured.

'Andy was my flatmate,' I put in helpfully. 'He's a nice guy – a stock agent for Wrightson's.'

'A stock agent?' Hazel repeated, in the sort of tone she might have used to say 'A pimp?' 'Well, I'm sorry to disparage a friend of yours, Josie, but I made it clear that it really isn't appropriate for him to be hanging around a young, innocent girl like my daughter. In the nicest possible way, of course.'

'Ah,' I said.

'Andy's one of the Hawkes Bay Morrisons,' said Aunty Rose carelessly. 'Very wealthy family – one of those large stations. Fourth generation, is he, Josephine?'

'Fifth, I think,' I said, although for all I knew Andy's father ran a hundred motley ewes on a patch of scrub and grew dope to supplement his income. If Kim was actually showing an interest in someone decent, for once, surely this was behaviour that should be encouraged.

Chapter 25

'DID YOU HAVE a good weekend?' I asked, pushing the chocolate biscuits across the table towards my receptionist.

'It was okay,' said Amber, wiping her nose on her sleeve and taking a Tim Tam. She bit off both ends and dunked it in her tea, sucking hard.

'That was quite a hailstorm on Saturday,' I remarked.

Having slurped up the liquefied interior of her biscuit, Amber began to lick melted chocolate from its dunked end. 'Was there?' she said thickly. 'Didn't notice.'

I didn't feel up to watching her enjoy her afternoon tea for any longer, so I carried my mug of tea back up the hall to drink it in reception. On the floor beside her desk was an atlas-sized cardboard FedEx box with '*Jo*' written across the front in black. I picked it up and looked at it curiously – it had been opened and taped up again, and it was addressed to M. King of Puketutu Valley Road, RD8, Waimanu, New Zealand. It had come, of all places, from Phoenix, Arizona.

Amber wandered down the hall in time to see me unwrap a truly hideous garment, made of mustard-brown polar fleece with a pattern of purple cabbages (or they may have been roses). It had a hood, feet soled with grey suede and a long zip all the way from one foot to the opposite shoulder. 'What *is* it?' she asked.

I noticed the decorative teddy-bear ears sewn onto the hood and grinned. 'It's a onesie. It's *awesome*.'

'Okay,' said Amber, looking at me doubtfully and wiping her nose on the back of her hand. 'Whatever.'

There was a note in the bottom of the box, written in Matt's cramped spidery script on the back of a docket from the Waimanu Bake House (where he had apparently spent eight dollars thirty). It read: *Jose – I couldn't find one with a flap at the back.*

LATER THAT AFTERNOON I opened the door of the consulting room to usher out Mrs MacPherson (chronic back pain coupled with complete refusal to cease picking up chunky four-year-old grandson. 'Isn't he big enough to climb up onto your knee himself?' 'But he holds up his little arms to me. How can I resist?' 'You could kneel down and give him a cuddle.' But apparently she couldn't), and Kim shot in as if she'd been fired from a gun.

'Hello, Kim, dear,' said Mrs MacPherson kindly.

Kim's cheeks were hot and her hair dishevelled in a most un-Kim-like fashion. She gave a jerky little nod of greeting.

'Shall we say the end of the week?' I asked.

'Not Thursday,' said Mrs MacPherson. 'I've got the Lyceum Club luncheon.' She eyed me sternly, in case I was going to refuse to see her at any time except on Thursday between eleven and one.

'Friday would be fine,' I assured her. 'Amber will find you an appointment.'

Mrs MacPherson nodded to me and addressed Kim once more. 'Your mother tells me you're going to university next year,' she said. 'What are you hoping to study?'

Kim made a truly heroic effort, and answered fairly evenly, 'I haven't decided just yet, Mrs MacPherson.'

'So you won't have decided on a university yet, either?'

'Otago.'

'Otago? But it's so far away!'

'Ex*act*ly,' said Kim.

Closing the door behind Mrs MacPherson I asked, 'What on earth's the matter?'

'My mother,' Kim spat, 'has asked the principal to make sure I get on the bus every afternoon after school. Like – like some *retarded* five-year-old who doesn't know the way home.'

'Or like some horny eighteen-year-old who might rush off and have sex with a pig hunter,' I suggested helpfully.

Kim scowled at me, then laughed. 'That's the one,' she said. 'How did you know?'

'She had a little word with Aunty Rose about sending you off alone with the pig hunter,' I said. 'So Aunty Rose told her Andy's family owns most of Hawkes Bay.'

Although this ploy appeared not to have worked; perhaps even pig hunters with rich land-owning parents were too low-class to associate with.

'They do?' said Kim.

'Goodness only knows. So how come you're not on the school bus?'

'I got off again.'

'Do you think that was wise?' I asked.

'I don't give a rat's *arse*,' said Kim, borrowing a phrase from her brother. 'Josie, she was *awful*. I brought Andy home for a cup of tea – I was just being polite, since he's your friend . . .'

'How kind,' I said.

'Shut up.'

'Sorry.'

'She acted like he'd come to nick the TV. She went all icy and upper-crust, and put on her horrible classy English accent. It was *so* embarrassing. And – and it wasn't like he was even *faintly* interested in me anyway. I'm just some dumb little school kid who threw up in his nice car.' She became less irate and more mournful as she spoke, and swiped a hand across her eyes with a touchingly childlike gesture.

'I'm pretty sure he doesn't think you're a dumb little school kid,' I said gently.

'Well, even if he didn't he'll never want anything to do with me ever again,' said Kim. 'Not now that he knows I'm related to *that*.'

I fished in my desk drawer and found my emergency

Kit Kat. It was half gone – I had needed two rows after my last encounter with Bob McIntosh – but I passed the other half over. 'You know what?'

'What?' asked Kim as she unwrapped the chocolate. She divided it carefully into two and passed half back to me.

'Thanks,' I said. 'I reckon that any bloke who makes a lame excuse to come out and see you after you threw up in his car, braving Aunty Rose and Matt and me, probably isn't going to be that easily put off.' Kim looked up at me with eyes of hope, and I added, 'But, Kimlet, don't forget to pass your exams, will you? I know boys are more exciting than school work, but – oh, I'm sorry. I won't tell you how to run your life anymore.'

'Yes you will,' said Kim resignedly. 'But I forgive you.'

'You're so kind.'

'I am,' she agreed. 'And if it makes you feel better, I have no intention of failing my exams or getting pregnant or piercing my nipples or *any* of the things you all seem to think I might do.' She swallowed the last of her Kit Kat and added, 'Aunty Rose says she'll come back and haunt me if I don't behave myself.'

'She would, too,' I said.

I USHERED OUT my four-thirty appointment, blew my nose for about the seven hundredth time since breakfast, removing the last remaining skin cell from its tip, and dug through my desk drawer to find a cough lolly. The packet was empty but I ran one to ground in a far corner, stuck to a paper clip and a random piece of fluff. Inserting it into one cheek (I had bought savage menthol cough lollies by mistake and if you sucked them directly they seared the taste buds off your tongue), I grimaced in distaste and opened my email inbox.

There was a message from Stu, which was the first nice thing to happen that day.

Angel, I hope you haven't frozen to death yet. My toes have finally thawed after the Extreme Survival Experience, and I don't think I'm going to lose any after all. Fabulous to see you, and give my love to Aunty Rose and the delectable Matthew.

Young Chrissie has finally decided on a date for the society wedding of the year, or whatever the hell it's going to be. A beach ceremony, the second Saturday of next February. With any luck she'll be bitten by a crab. She asked me to be bridesman in a lavender silk suit, but I have politely declined to be the funky gay talking point of her bridal party. Just quietly, I suspect she's having difficulties finding enough girls – if you're going to run off with your best friend's man the rest of your gal pals tend to get a bit wary. I am cynically awaiting the announcement that she's decided against bridesmaids in favour of making the ceremony that much more intimate.

Not meaning to hurt you, sweetie, but I figure it's better to know these things. Come over for a weekend

when the backblocks start to get you down, and we'll do
designer drugs and go clubbing till dawn. Take care.

I expect he was right, and it was better to know the details
than to wonder. But as I transferred my nasty cough lolly
from one cheek to the other and blew my nose for the seven
hundred and first time I wondered drearily what the hell
I'd done to deserve that. I closed down the computer and
picked up my bag from under the desk.

'I booked a five o'clock appointment,' said Amber as I
closed the consulting room door behind me.

'Did you have to?' I asked wearily. 'I just want to go
and crawl into a hole somewhere.'

Heather Anne's sign next door creaked as the wind
stirred it on its rusty hooks, and the niggling repetitive
squeak grated like fingernails down a blackboard.

'Bob McIntosh. He said it was urgent.' Amber rubbed
the back of her hand across her nose, leaving a glistening
trail. She wiped the hand against the fabric seat of her
chair, and sudden fury swept over me like a wave.

'Ring him back,' I snapped. 'I'm sick, and I'm going
home. And for Christ's sake, use a tissue! If I see you wipe
your nose on your hand one more time I swear I'll cut it
off!' I neither knew nor cared whether it was the hand
or the nose I would be severing; whichever was closest
would do.

Amber looked completely unmoved by this threat.
'But I don't know his number,' she complained.

I shoved the local phone directory towards her across

the desk. 'There.' I jabbed a finger at the advertisement on the front cover for McIntosh Farming Solutions.

'But it's such short notice – he'll already be on his way.'

'Then *call his mobile*! Could you just try for one *second* not to be so fucking *useless*?' After which stunningly unprofessional outburst I burst into tears, turned on my heel and stormed out of the building, slamming the door behind me.

Chapter 26

A T THE END of that evening's meal Aunty Rose's plate looked pretty much the same as it had at the beginning. It held a very modest serving of one chicken drumstick, three kumara chips and a tablespoon of peas — not the most exciting meal in the world, but considering the mental state of the cook this evening it could have been much worse. 'Could you eat a little bit?' I pleaded.

'No,' said Aunty Rose as she pushed her chair back. She lay down full-length on the chaise longue, mouth thinned with pain, and closed her eyes.

Hazel arrived as I dried the last of the dishes. 'Good evening, girls,' she trilled, putting her head around the kitchen door. 'Rosie, darling, I've brought a book you might enjoy.'

Aunty Rose opened one eye. 'I hope it's a trashy novel,' she muttered.

Hazel gave a little rippling laugh. 'No, no,' she said. 'It's all about the macrobiotic diet — suggestions for natural healing.'

The eye closed again. 'Thank you,' said Rose dully.

The kettle shrieked and switched itself off, and I poured boiling water into an ancient rubber hot-water bottle with a crocheted cover. 'It might help,' I said, handing it to Aunty Rose.

'I doubt it,' she said, but she took it and tucked it into the small of her back.

'Rosie,' said Hazel reprovingly, 'it's very kind of Josie to try to help.' Her words were greeted with silence and she continued, 'People *are* kind, aren't they? Myra Browne – dear Cilla's mother – lent me the book. *Her* friend had a very rare form of skin cancer, and apparently the doctors had given her up for lost when she discovered this macrobiotic diet. And now she's completely cancer-free.'

'Hazel,' said Aunty Rose tiredly, 'I wish you'd stop this.'

'At the very least it can't possibly hurt.'

'I very much doubt I'll live any longer if I subsist on mung beans and tofu. Although it may well resign me to death.'

'Don't talk like that, Rosie!'

'I have secondaries right through my lungs and a lump on my liver the size of a cricket ball that I can feel through the skin.' I looked at her sharply; this was news to me. 'My body is being taken over by this revolting disease. It's like being chained to a rock below the high-tide mark and waiting for the water to come in. And *surely* by now you know my views on people who peddle useless cures to the terminally ill.'

'Oh, Rosie,' said her sister helplessly, her eyes filling with tears.

'*Don't* weep all over me,' said Aunty Rose. 'Not tonight; I don't feel strong enough.'

I sneezed into a tissue – the side of the box had assured me it was aloe vera–impregnated and gentle on the skin, but it felt like sandpaper on my skinless nose – and Hazel said worriedly, 'I don't know if Josie should be here, with that cold. She might give it to you.'

'I probably passed it on a week ago,' I said. 'Too late to do anything about it now.'

'Just be careful with hygiene, won't you, dear?' Hazel told me. 'Wash your hands carefully and try to cover your mouth rather than coughing over Rose.'

The response on the tip of my tongue was one I would no doubt regret, so I got up silently and went to have a shower.

'Perhaps,' Aunty Rose suggested as I left the room, 'she could ring a little bell and shout "unclean, unclean" as she approaches.'

A head cold is not a very serious ailment, but mine had now reached that unhappy stage where you feel as if your eyeballs have been left out in the sun and your sinuses filled with concrete. I stood limply for some time under the miserable dribble of water that comes out of Aunty Rose's shower, and then climbed into my onesie, took two Pan-adol tablets and went back down the hall. Hazel was still in the kitchen, mopping her eyes in a way that suggested she had indeed been weeping all over her sister.

'For the love of God, Josephine, please take off that hideous thing!' said Aunty Rose, eyeing me with distaste.

'You're just jealous of the – the *awesomeness* of the onesie,' I replied.

The onesie and I had been together for a week now. Cold feet in bed? Not when you have a onesie, my friend. Troubled by uncomfortable pyjama-leg ride-up? Hell, no! That onesie was the nicest thing to happen to me for months. The morning after our first glorious night together I sent the man who had brought it into my life a text from work: *Onesie brilliant. So are you*.

Glad u like it, he sent back.

'I fail to understand why you feel this uncontrollable urge to make the least possible of yourself,' Aunty Rose said.

'I'm not going to start wearing it in public,' I protested, and pulled the hood up defiantly.

Aunty Rose shut her eyes as if my appearance caused her actual pain. 'Josephine,' she said, 'it is *criminal* to be blessed with naturally blonde hair and legs to your armpits, and then go and swathe yourself in that thing.'

I smiled at her, touched. 'It's warm and comfortable,' I told her, 'and I love it very much. So there.'

'Oh, don't be so wet,' she snapped. 'If Matthew gave you a potato sack you'd treasure the bloody thing. I'm going to bed – goodnight.'

She left one of those awful, pregnant silences behind her in the kitchen. At length I managed to unpeel my tongue from the roof of my mouth, and said, 'Thank goodness you're taking her to the pain clinic on Friday.'

'Yes,' said Hazel. 'Yes, thank goodness.' She was silent for a moment and then added carelessly, 'I'm glad Matthew didn't feel he had to come over tonight. He's so devoted to Rosie and has *such* a strong sense of duty, but I know it's a strain. It's nice for him to have a chance to spend time with Cilla.'

'JOSEPHINE?' AUNTY ROSE called as I went down the hall towards bed later that evening. I continued past the door of the Pink Room to look round her door. She was propped on her pillows with *The Sentimental Bloke* and *Persuasion* beside her on the covers and a torrid bodice-ripper in her hands. Nice Marty Holden from the Book Exchange had been bringing romance novels by the boxful and she was getting through two a day, switching to Jane Austen when her brain needed decontaminating.

'What's that one about?' I asked.

'Beautiful orphan cheated out of inheritance and raped by wicked uncle,' said Aunty Rose succinctly.

'But rescued by disturbingly attractive stable hand who turns out to be laird of the neighbouring castle?'

'No doubt,' she said. 'I've only just started it. I'm sorry – what I said was completely uncalled for.'

'That's okay,' I said. 'Hazel's just been letting me down gently by telling me how much in love Matt and Cilla are.'

'I expect you enjoyed that.'

'Very much.' I leant against the doorframe and said, 'That's the first time you've ever been mean to me.'

'I fear, Josephine, that it may not be the last.'

'Bitterness and rage kicking in, huh?'

'Indeed,' said Aunty Rose. 'Goodnight, sweet pea.' And as I turned to go she began to laugh weakly.

'What?' I asked.

'The ghastly thing's got a *tail*. Please get it out of my sight.'

I looked back over my shoulder – she was quite right: the onesie did indeed have a little white bunny tail sewn onto the back. I don't know how I'd overlooked it.

'Bloody marvellous,' I said, and closed the door softly behind me.

✿

WHEN I GOT to work the next morning at ten to eight Amber's red car was already there. Normally she drifts in at five past – this was not, I felt, a good sign. Perhaps she'd come in early to hand in her notice, and I was about to be sued for abuse in the workplace. I went up the hall some-what apprehensively and found her swabbing the front desk with a damp cloth, which was another first.

'Good morning,' she said cheerfully. 'I vacuumed.'

I was bemused. 'Who are you?' I asked. 'And what did you do with Amber?'

This weak sally was greeted by a merry peal of laughter. 'You're so funny,' she said.

I opened my mouth to apologise for shouting at her the previous evening, suddenly thought better of it and closed it again. This new Amber was a vast improvement on the old one; there was no telling how long the transformation would last, and it would be foolish to say anything that might shorten its duration. Amber paused in her cleaning to wipe her nose on the shoulder of her cardigan and I was unexpectedly relieved. She had not, after all, been replaced by a robot whose programming might at any time default to Massacre Mode.

The new and improved Amber lasted all through the morning. She inputted files and phoned tomorrow's clients to remind them of their appointments and didn't once remove her nail polish, and I wondered if I had perchance slipped through the fabric of my life into some parallel universe.

Andy came in at midday, the epitome of the rural young professional in his beige moleskin trousers and glossy chestnut leather boots, with his shirt collar standing up almost as crisply as the gelled spikes of his hair. You wouldn't have wanted to snuggle up to that hairdo; you might have lost an eye.

'Hi,' breathed Amber, opening her eyes very wide and sucking on the end of a pen. Unfortunately this didn't make her look alluring, but merely as if there was a very real risk that her eyes might fall out of her head. 'Hello, Andy.'

'Oh, hi, Amber,' he replied, and then lifted his chin about five degrees in my direction. 'Jo.'

'G'day,' I said.

'I've got some pork for you in the freezer at home,' he informed me.

'You keep it,' I said. 'You're the one who's done all the work.'

'I thought maybe you guys might like some chops and a couple of little roasts. I'll bring it up after work, if you're going to be around.'

'About seven-thirty's usually a good time,' I suggested. 'Matt and Kim come over after dinner most nights.'

'Right,' said Andy uncomfortably. 'Look, Jo, could I have a word?'

'Sure,' I said. 'Amber, you must be due for a lunch break about now.'

Amber looked somewhat crushed, but she pushed back her chair and ferreted under the desk for her hand-bag. 'Can I get you guys anything?' she asked.

'No, thanks,' said Andy. He smiled at her fleetingly and she went pink. It occurred to me that we might well be on the verge of another outbreak of unrequited love, and that I'd better lay in some extra chocolate biscuits. Not Tim Tams, though; something less complicated to eat.

Amber pulled on a pink nylon coat with grubby faux fur around the sleeves, picked up her bag and let herself out into the wintry sunlight. We watched her drift up the street towards the Bake House, and Andy shuffled his feet and looked unhappy.

I waited for a little while, and when there were no signs of imminent speech said, 'It's lovely up the back of the Kings' place, isn't it?'

'Mm.'

After another pause I tried again. 'I hear you met Kim's mother the other day.'

'Mm,' said Andy again, carefully examining the nails of his left hand. Evidently satisfied with their appearance he shoved the hand into his trouser pocket and began to whistle tunelessly through his teeth.

I laughed – I couldn't help it – and he jumped like a startled rabbit. 'Andy! I've got a client in ten minutes.'

'Sorry,' he muttered. 'Um, Jo . . .'

There was another, even longer pause, and I sat down in Amber's chair and rested my elbows on the desk and my chin in my hands. 'Whenever you're ready,' I remarked. 'Just in your own time.'

'Oh, stop it,' said Andy crossly. 'Look, if I ask the girl out are you going to think I'm a dirty old man and run me out of town?'

'By "you" do you mean Matt?'

'Mphmm.'

'Well, he did send Kim off with you up the back of the farm, so I wouldn't think so. And you're employed and not in a rock band, so you're already looking pretty good compared to the last one.'

'I'm five years older than her,' said Andy. '*She'll* probably think I'm a dirty old man.'

Anything less like a dirty old man than Andy with his pink cheeks and sticking-up hair would have been hard to imagine. He looked about twelve. 'That'd be why she wanted your phone number and bought you a stack of Picnic bars and offered to walk up a hill,' I said. 'And if you'd asked me I would have said Kim would rather put lemon juice on a paper cut than go walking through a patch of wet scrub.'

'I don't think her mother thought much of me,' he said glumly.

'No,' I agreed. 'She thought you were probably casing the joint. Aunty Rose told her your family own about half of Hawkes Bay, but I'm not sure she believed it.'

'Only seven thousand acres,' Andy corrected.

'Near enough.' Way to go, Aunty Rose. 'Are you fifth generation?'

He looked at me in a perplexed sort of way. 'We moved there from Feilding when I was six. Does it matter?'

'It's just that I told Hazel you were fifth generation. That kind of thing impresses her.'

'Thank you,' he said. 'I suppose. Right, I'd better go and do some work.'

'Andy?' I asked.

'Mm?'

'Be careful with Kim, won't you? She's having a pretty rough time at the moment.'

'I know,' he said.

Chapter 27

THE PHONE RANG, and I put down the bluntest vegetable knife in recorded history and crossed the kitchen to pick it up. 'Hello, Jo speaking.'

'Hello, love,' said my mother. 'How are things today?'

'Awful,' I said flatly.

'Oh.'

I retreated to the chaise longue and curled up at one end, hugging my knees. 'She won't eat, Mum. I think she's trying to starve herself to death.'

'Oh, sweetie.'

'She didn't eat anything yesterday, and the day before she only had half a little pot of yoghurt when Matt stood over her and made her eat it. She snaps at us and then cries and apologises – and that's a million times worse. Mum, can you come up for a bit? I know it's a lousy time of year, but it might not be much longer and – and I'm not managing very well.'

'I was planning to come for a few days next month,'

said Mum slowly. 'I don't like to leave your father when the goats are still kidding, but I'm sure he can cope if he has to.'

'Sooner would be better. Mum, I'm sorry . . .'

'Stop it,' she said. 'Take deep breaths. I'll talk to your father and we'll see what we can do.'

'Thank you. I've been leaving work early when I can, and the others all drop in every day, but it would be such a relief if you were here too.'

'Isn't Hazel helping?'

'She prefers just having hysterics,' I said. 'You'd think Aunty Rose was only dying to spite her.'

'We can't be doing with *that*,' my mother declared. I expect Boadicea said something very much the same, in similarly ringing tones, when discussing the Roman occupation of Britain a couple of thousand years ago. 'Now, is Rose awake, love?'

'I'll go and look.' I got to my feet and went down the hall to peep through her bedroom door. She was lying back with her eyes closed, but she opened one at my approach. I covered the speaker of the phone and mouthed, 'Mum?'

Aunty Rose nodded and held out her hand for the phone.

'Here she is,' I said into the receiver. 'Love to Dad.' And feeling somewhat invigorated after talking to Edith Donnelly, Woman of Action, I went down the hall and dug through the kitchen drawers for a sharpening stone with which to deal with that useless knife.

IT WAS NEARLY dark when I turned into Aunty Rose's driveway at half past five the following evening. The lights were on in the cowshed across the road, and little angry spats of rain hurled themselves at the windscreen. I dodged the pothole halfway up, swerving towards the orchard fence (in wet weather you had to take Aunty Rose's driveway like a rally driver), and the headlights caught a small pale body lying between two plum trees.

If I'd stopped there I'd have had to let the car run back to the bottom of the hill before tackling it again, so I continued up the drive and parked on the gravel sweep outside the kitchen. Then I zipped my polar fleece vest right up under my chin, got out into the wet dusk and unwillingly went back down to investigate. Only three dogs appeared from under the house to accompany me – Spud had decided, after a taste of indoor life, that exposure to the elements really wasn't his cup of tea.

I climbed the orchard fence, catching my jeans on the barbed wire and ripping a little triangular hole through both the denim and the tender skin of my inner thigh. A brand-new lamb lay stretched on its side under the Red Doris plum tree. I bent and prodded its little eye, but it didn't blink. A nicer person would have mused sorrowfully on the futility of being born only to slip straight out of life again, but I was just relieved not to have to add lamb-rearing to my list of jobs for this evening.

Presumably the lamb belonged to Mildred, although its paternity was a mystery – Edwin lacked the necessary equipment. I stood up and peered through the gathering dusk, and at the far end of the orchard saw two sheep-sized glimmers of white. 'Sit,' I ordered without any real hope of being obeyed, and began to slither down the hill.

As I got close the sheep exchanged a wild-eyed look and made a run for it, one to either side of me. They showed an impressive turn of speed considering they were both as wide as they were high, but the fleeting glimpse I got of Mildred's rear end revealed two little hooves and a nose. 'Bugger you, Mildred,' I said, and went after her.

Normally, if you want to catch a sheep, you head it towards a fence somewhere to cut off at least one possible direction of escape. Then you slink closer, feinting to left and right until you're a few metres away, and make a wild tackle. I'm not a bad sheep-tackler but Mildred, the miserable slapper, refused to be headed. She thundered from one end of the orchard to the other, weaving around trees with the grace and agility of a gazelle while I stumbled behind.

The dogs were wildly excited by this evening's entertainment and frolicked joyously around me. On about our ninth lap of the orchard Mildred miscalculated and ran into the corner, where I might have been able to catch her had the pup not chosen that moment to run between my legs and trip me up. I sat down hard in the wet grass and, as Mildred skipped past, swore with impressive fluency. I hadn't even realised I knew some of those words.

As I climbed grimly to my feet the pup took one look at me and slunk behind a handy pear tree just as Matt's quad bike came up the hill and stopped on the other side of the fence.

'Help!' I called.

'I thought I'd better, before you strangled that poor dog with your bare hands,' he said, climbing off the bike and stepping over the fence. He left the headlights on and they lit the falling raindrops prettily, although I would have enjoyed the effect more from somewhere dry.

'Did you hear me swearing at it?'

'They probably heard you in town.' He smiled. 'And I thought you were a nice girl.'

'Surely you didn't,' I said. 'Mildred needs lambing, and I can't catch her.'

'How the hell did *that* happen?' he asked.

'Immaculate conception?'

'Probably. Either that or some mongrel ram that lives up in the scrub.'

'It would have had to be a pretty desperate ram,' I said. 'She's an eight pinter, at least.' (The pint scale of sex appeal, for those who are not familiar with it, refers to the number of pints of beer a man has to drink before starting to think a woman is pretty.)

We advanced on Mildred, who sagged visibly as she calculated the decreasing odds of escape. She looked wildly from one of us to the other, lost her head and bolted between us. Matt grabbed her as she passed and she promptly collapsed in a heap. I don't know why sheep do that when caught, but it's quite a handy reflex. In this case, though, it would have been handier had she not collapsed halfway down a little clay bank. 'Get up, you lousy animal,' he said, trying to heave eighty kilograms of dead weight up onto the flat.

I took two handfuls of wool on her other side and together we lugged her a couple of metres up the hill into a little grassy depression.

Matt wiped his wet face on the wet sleeve of his raincoat, which achieved not much at all. 'You do it,' he said, 'your hands are smaller.'

'I haven't lambed a ewe for about ten years.'

'It's just like riding a bike.'

I wiped my hands on the thighs of my jeans and pushed my sleeves up to the elbow. The lamb had vanished back out of sight during our invigorating little run, but I found a foot just inside the vulva and caught it between the second and third fingers of my right hand. I pulled it gently out straight, held it in my left hand and reached back in for the second foot. As I grasped it the lamb pulled away from me – fair enough, too; who would want to come out into weather like this?

'It's still alive,' I said.

'But what are the chances of Mildred feeding the bloody thing?'

'Slim to none,' I said. 'Maybe we can palm it off onto Clare.'

I drew the second foot out straight and pulled them both together, and the lamb slid out onto the grass.

It lay quite still, but when I pressed two fingertips to the little wet chest under its elbow I felt a faint heartbeat.

'Come on, little dude, breathe.' I plucked a blade of grass and tickled its nose, and then rubbed its little chest vigorously with my knuckles.

'I don't think it's going to be a starter,' said Matt.

'It's got a heartbeat.' I pinched its nose again to prompt a breath, but the lamb lay limp and lifeless. I felt again for the heartbeat – nothing. 'Oh, crap.'

'Better check in case there's another one in there,' he said.

I wiped my hand again and inserted it back into the vulva. 'No.' I got slowly to my feet. 'Mildred, you lousy mongrel sheep, you didn't even *try*.'

Matt pulled Mildred up onto her sternum and nudged her with the toe of his gumboot. 'Go on, then,' he said. 'Bugger off.' She lurched to her feet and hared off to the far end of the paddock. 'Never mind, Jose.'

I sighed. 'It would just have been nice to make something better, for a change.'

'You do,' he said quietly, bending to pick up the pathetic little corpse. 'I'll take it home and put it in the offal hole so the dogs won't retrieve it. Unless you were wanting to perform a little burial service?'

'Oh, be quiet.' I leant my head against his shoulder for a weak second. 'Thank you.'

'Any time.' He gave me a brief one-armed hug. 'Jo, you look like a drowned rat.'

'You silver-tongued devil,' I said. 'There's another dead lamb just near the fence, by the way.'

'Okay. See you in a bit.' He turned back towards the

fence and I went the other way, straight up the hill, to come out on the lawn beneath the porch.

Seeing as I was out there I went round to the woodshed and scooped a pile of dog biscuits out of their drum into the plastic bucket that sits on top. I fed the three younger dogs and shut them away, carried Spud's ration up the path and let myself in at the kitchen door. The stove had gone out and the kitchen was bleak and cold. I turned on the lights and opened the hot-water cupboard for an old towel, and heard Aunty Rose quaver, 'Josephine?'

'Coming!' I wiped my face with the towel and ran my hands under the tap. 'Sorry I'm late.'

Halfway up the hall the smell hit me like a brick. Aunty Rose was lying on the edge of her bed in a tangle of filthy bedding, tears streaming down her wasted cheeks. 'Oh, Josie,' she wept. 'I'm so sorry. I couldn't get up.'

'It's fine,' I said, racked with pity. 'It doesn't matter – I'm so sorry I was late.'

The sheer *awfulness* of Aunty Rose, that epitome of cleanliness and hygiene, having to lie helpless in a puddle of crap with nobody there to help her was almost too much to bear. I lifted her to a sitting position – goodness knows she wasn't much of a weight these days – and peeled off her filthy nightie. 'I'll just turn on the shower.'

'Where were you?' she asked weakly when I came back into the room.

'Mildred was lambing, and Matt and I had to catch her.'

'He's not here, is he?' Her voice was shrill and anxious.

'No.' I picked her up and carried her down the hall to the bathroom, just a pitiful skeleton with skin stretched over the top and a great red scar across her chest. She sank onto the plastic seat we had got from the hospital and closed her eyes as I washed her, leaning her poor bald head back exhaustedly against the back of the shower cubicle.

'I'll just change the sheets,' I said. 'I won't be a minute – would you rather sit under the water, or shall I turn it off and wrap you up in a towel?'

'Under the water,' she whispered.

I had to strip the bed entirely, and two of the pillows were saturated. I replaced them with pillows from my bed, and while I was at it my duvet as well. Then I propped the poor woman up against the bathroom sink to dry and dress her, picked her up and carried her back to bed. Never have I been so grateful to be, after all, a strapping wench rather than a delicate wisp of a girl.

As I pulled the covers up under her chin she opened her eyes, looked at me sternly and said with nearly her old decision, 'This is *not* the way I wish to be remembered, Josephine.'

'I know,' I whispered, the tears spilling unchecked down my cheeks. Nurses are supposed to be bright and matter-of-fact about these things: my bracing professional manner left a lot to be desired. 'I'll get you some dinner.'

'No,' she said. 'Just my pills, love.'

Back in the kitchen I stood for a moment in a trance of indecision, wondering where the hell to start. It didn't really matter – when you're overcome with lethargy you just have to do *something*. And then the next thing, and then the next, and eventually, although you'd have sworn you were far too tired and depressed to accomplish anything, you're finished. I turned on the tap above the big concrete sink by the back door and began to scrub sheets and blankets.

Chapter 28

TWENTY MINUTES LATER I was splitting kindling on the back porch with Percy at my side when Matt's ute came up the driveway. 'Haven't you made it in yet?' he asked as he crossed the gravel.

'I have been,' I said. 'But the stove's gone out – Kim mustn't have come in after school.'

'How's Rose?'

I pushed a hank of wet hair that had escaped its tie back off my face. 'Not very good. Could you go in and see her while I do this? Maybe she'll eat something if you feed her.'

He patted the pig, collected up the cut kindling and opened the back door, and I followed him in. He paused at the laundry sink and looked down at the sodden heap of dirty blankets for a second, then sighed and rubbed his face with his hands as he continued on up the hall.

I opened the door of the stove and fished in the wood box for a decent-sized piece of wood to use as a back log.

As I balled up sheets of newspaper Matt came back into the kitchen and said, 'She's asleep. I'll do that – you go and have a shower.'

I stood up. 'Thanks.'

'This is crap,' he said. 'You've already got a full-time job, and then you get home and start again here.'

'That doesn't matter,' I said. 'You're working much longer hours than I am. But she was lying there in the dark, crying, and she couldn't get up by herself . . .' I stopped to force the tears back down. 'This isn't working anymore.'

'Then either Mum'll have to do the day nursing, or Rose will have to go into hospital,' he said. He began to screw up sheets of newspaper with rather more violence than was required. Hazel would probably do it, but she would need effusive thanks about seventeen times a day and perform her duties with such nobly repressed suffering that it would be intolerable to witness.

'I could quit my job. Cheryl can just get over it. It's not going to be for very l-long.' My voice broke and the tears welled up inexorably.

'Jose, you can't,' he said gently. 'You've got a mortgage to pay, for a start.'

I wiped my eyes on my damp sleeve. 'With any luck the house has sold by now. And if it hasn't, Graeme'd probably cover it for a while – he's being quite nice at the moment.'

'Look, go and get dry, and then we'll talk about it.'

He was filling the kettle when I re-entered the kitchen after my shower, and Spud sat in front of the newly lit stove with a reproachful look on his face. Clearly he was unimpressed by the chill in the room and thought poorly of whoever was responsible for letting the fire go out.

'Dinner's in the microwave,' Matt said. 'Coffee?'

'Oh, dear God, yes.' I had put on three layers of wool and still felt like an icicle.

'How many sugars today?'

I considered. 'Two, please.' I took the milk out of the fridge, unscrewed the top of the bottle and sniffed warily. It wasn't good. 'Bugger. I hate powdered milk.'

'I can get some from the vat,' he offered.

'Of course not! Just make it three sugars.'

He looked at me with amusement. 'Right you are.' He reached down a pink china jug with a gilt rim from its high shelf and began to mix up milk powder and water.

I came up to the bench beside him and upended the milk bottle over the sink. There was a long pause, and then a gelatinous white lump slithered from the bottle to sit, quivering in a sullen sort of way, in the sink. *Definitely* not good.

'How was your day?' I asked.

'About normal for this time of year. Cow down in the swamp, twelve calves to pick up and I had to tube five of the little bastards because they wouldn't suck, raincoat leaking – that sort of thing.' The microwave beeped. 'Grub's up.'

'Thank you,' I said, poking lumps of milk down the plughole with the handle of a wooden spoon. 'You're a legend.'

'I know,' said Matt. 'It was pretty taxing. You'll

appreciate the way I spread the food out so it would heat more evenly.'

I turned to retrieve an enormous plate of super-heated lasagne from the microwave. 'Hey, Matt, I was thinking – I could start leaving work at two or three if your mum could come over for the mornings. I'll have to run it by Cheryl, but she'll be fine with it.' She probably wouldn't be, in actual fact, but she wasn't in any position to argue. A part-time employee is better than none at all.

'I'll talk to Mum.' The kettle boiled, and he poured hot water into two mugs.

I put down the plate and opened the drawer beside him to find a fork. 'Thanks. It'll be better if you ask her.'

He sighed. 'Yeah.' He stirred my over-sweetened coffee with deep concentration. 'Jo . . .'

'Mm?'

He turned and cupped my cheek in one big hand, ducking his head to kiss me. My heart gave a great bound of exhilarated amazement that lasted all of half a second before my brain caught up, and then plummeted like a stone.

'Don't do that,' I said unhappily, twisting away from him.

Matt stood quite still for a moment. 'Sorry,' he muttered. 'I thought – oh, *fuck* it.' He sounded exhausted and utterly miserable.

'You've got a girlfriend,' I said bitterly. 'Remember?'

'No I haven't,' he said. 'Broke up months ago.'

'*Months* ago?'

'That night she decided you and I were having an affair.'

A tiny, painful stab of hope pricked me in the chest. I opened and closed my mouth like a goldfish for a while, and then managed, in a sort of croak, 'Why didn't you say?'

'I – I thought you knew,' said Matt. 'I thought Kim would have told you.'

'But I saw Cilla in the supermarket buying *Bride and Groom* magazine,' I said to my feet.

There was a short silence, and then he began to laugh. 'Jo,' he said affectionately, 'you womble.'

These romantic words caused the little gleam of hope to swell and blossom. I sat down abruptly on a kitchen chair and burst into tears of sheer blessed relief.

Poor Matt was completely nonplussed. 'Oh, hell,' he said helplessly. 'Jo, I'm sorry. I'm a moron and – and you probably want me to go take a running jump, but I love you so much.'

In response I merely cried harder, burying my face in my hands. I had been trying so hard to come to terms with the dismal truth that Matt was just never going to feel the same way about me as I felt about him – I had decided that when Aunty Rose died I'd better move to the other end of the country so at least I wouldn't have to see him every bloody day. And now he had suddenly turned everything upside down, and it was all just too much.

After a little while he came to stand in front of me, wordlessly pulling my head up against the solid warmth of his body and stroking my damp hair. I couldn't stop crying but I put my arms around his waist and hugged him fiercely.

'Shh,' he said softly. 'Come on, love, it's okay.'

'S-sorry,' I gasped. 'Trying . . .'

He detached me and mopped my eyes with the hem of his shirt. Then he pulled me to my feet and kissed me.

Matt had been my kissing gold standard ever since the night before he went overseas all those years ago. He had kissed me with a sort of skilful and leisurely enjoyment that reduced me to a quivering heap of nerve endings, and nobody since had ever turned me on quite like that. Tonight was completely different. He wasn't slick and practised at all but almost savage – he held me too tightly and I could feel him shaking as his lips found mine – and it blew that nine-year-old memory into the weeds.

I took his face in my hands and kissed him back with the sort of fervour you'd expect from a really impassioned TV evangelist. And about thirty seconds later the kitchen door opened, and Kim tumbled in out of the rain with Andy in tow.

TO BE DISCOVERED attached like a sucker fish to Kim's brother brought me back down to earth at speed. I tried to jump back but was foiled in my attempt to retreat – preferably to the other end of the house, if not the district – by Matt's arms tightening implacably to pull me back against him. I looked at him, puzzled, and then realised that little though he enjoyed being caught with me in his arms he would be much, much unhappier showing his little sister his erection. I stopped trying to escape and rested my forehead against his shoulder.

'*Well*,' said Kim. 'Well, well, well.'

'Oh, shut up,' her loving brother said.

'Kim, leave them alone,' said Andy, deeply embarrassed. But Kim wouldn't recognise embarrassment if it jumped up and hit her over the head. She shook her sleek brown head to dislodge the raindrops, perched on the edge of the table and asked, 'How long has this been going on?'

'About a minute,' I said with some bitterness. It would have been nice to enjoy it for just a *little* longer without anybody else's input.

'Excellent,' said Kim approvingly. 'Good stuff. Took you long enough, but then neither of you is all that bright.'

'Kim,' I said, 'go away, or I will beat you with a stick.'

'She doesn't mean it,' Kim told Andy.

Matt gave me a little thanks-I'm-good-now squeeze, and I let him go.

'Josie, you're a mess,' his sister informed me.

'I know.' I turned and went out of the room. In the bathroom I turned on the cold tap, looked in the little mirror above the sink and winced. The face looking back at me was red and puffy with wild hair and swollen eyes – I looked like someone fresh from a gruelling bout of Chinese water torture. Washing my face wasn't going to be enough to make me into a thing of beauty, but I did it anyway, brushed my hair into something resembling order and went to peep into Aunty Rose's bedroom.

She was still asleep, her head turned away on the pillow and her skin as pale as wax. Having spent five minutes entirely absorbed by the miracle of Matt actually loving me back, it was a fresh shock to see her. I moved her water glass within easy reach and smoothed a pillow and then, because I really couldn't put it off any longer, I went slowly back down the hall to the kitchen.

'Josie,' said Kim, prodding my cooling lasagne in distaste, 'why are you having jellymeat for tea?'

'Dinner,' her brother corrected, and smiled at me over her head with an expression that nearly made me throw myself back into his arms regardless of the audience.

'Isn't it the same thing?' Andy enquired, crouching down to scratch Spud between the ears.

'Aunty Rose always corrects us,' I told him. 'And she makes us say "white" not "wite", and "milk" not "moolk". If you really want to wind her up you just have to say "youse guys".'

'How is she?' Kim asked.

'Asleep.'

'Does she know about you two?'

'No.'

Kim looked speculative, and Matt said, 'Wake her and die, Toad.'

'I wouldn't,' she protested, all wounded dignity.

'Come on,' Andy told her, standing back up. Spud

nosed his ankle hopefully in case he might start scratching again. 'I'll take you home.'

She made a face. 'Nah, let's hang out here for a bit.'

I sympathised; being chaperoned by the lovely Hazel would have to be fairly painful.

'I'll pay you to take her away,' Matt said to Andy. 'I don't care where – your place is fine – just anywhere that isn't here.'

Andy grinned. 'Okay,' he said. 'Let's go, Kim, I think we're kind of in the way.'

'Fine,' said Kim. 'I can take a hint.' She bounced up on tiptoe to kiss my cheek. 'Be gentle with him, Josie.'

I put my arms around her and hugged her. 'Sometimes I'm not at all sure why I like you, Kimlet.'

'Sometimes I'm not sure *if* I like her,' Matt said.

The two of them pulled up their collars and went out into the wet dark, and then Andy poked his head back round the door to say awkwardly, 'I won't – um – do anything.'

'Good luck with that,' said Matt, trying not to smile and failing completely.

Andy muttered something inaudible and pulled the door closed.

I wondered briefly what sort of state Andy's new flat was in. When I lived with him the dirty socks had tended to mount up in the corners of his room and fester, and Kim is a fastidious sort of girl. And then Matt pulled me back into his arms and I stopped thinking about anything except him.

'I've wanted to do this ever since you came home,' he said at last.

'Then what on *earth* were you doing with Cilla?' I asked.

He winced. 'It wasn't serious,' he said. 'And I didn't think you'd be interested. You were damn near married to that pillock.'

I shivered. I *was* damn near married to Graeme – last year we had been talking in a half-hearted way about starting a family. And Graeme superintended my wardrobe and was snobbish about the wines he drank and when we went out for dinner he used to send back his meal two times out of three. *And* he sneered at Dolly Parton. No, Chrissie was welcome to him. 'What a horrible thought.' I leant my head into the comfortable hollow of his shoulder.

The dogs outside launched into their welcome chorus and I realised that the wind must have dropped for us to be able to hear them. 'Why can't everyone just piss off?' I said savagely.

Matthew smiled and released me. 'You need to eat something, anyway,' he said. 'Go and sit down.'

WHEN HIS MOTHER opened the door I was forking up mouthfuls of lukewarm lasagne while Matt pulled clean washing out of the machine in the opposite corner of the kitchen.

'Hello, dears,' she said, brushing the rain from the shoulders of a very smart red woollen coat. 'I'm just on my way home from my Reiki class, and I couldn't pass without popping in to see Rosie.'

'She's asleep,' said Matt. 'She's had a pretty awful day.'

'Oh,' said Hazel vaguely. 'Oh dear. I'll come over in the morning. Perhaps she'll feel better by then.'

Neither of us said anything in response to this – what planet was the woman inhabiting? Matt finished putting clean sheets in the washing basket and began to load dirty ones into the machine.

'Goodness, Josie, that's a hearty plateful!'

'I'm very hungry,' I said, feeling like a beefy peasant wench. 'How was Reiki?'

'Marvellous. So calming. It's a great comfort.' She smiled wanly. 'Kimmy's home, is she?'

'She's at Rachel's place,' said Matt with no hesitation at all. 'She rang and asked me to let you know.'

'That will be nice for her. It might take her mind off poor Rosie.'

'I hope so,' I murmured, seeing that Matt wasn't going to bother to reply.

'Matthew, love,' said his mother, 'I've got a leaking kitchen tap. Could you pop up and have a look at it?'

'How about you call a plumber?'

'I'm sure it will only be a teensy little job,' she said. 'I wake and hear it in the night and it's *so* annoying.'

'Mum,' he said tightly, 'I got up at four-thirty this morning, I had ten minutes for lunch and I've got to go and check a heifer before I go to bed. Call a plumber.'

Hazel's lip trembled ominously. I didn't think we could bear her broken-hearted sobbing tonight – I had been doing quite enough sobbing as it was.

'It's shattering, isn't it?' I said sympathetically. 'You lie there waiting for the next drip to fall and you can't get back to sleep. But if you put a facecloth in the sink underneath you can't hear it anymore.'

Matt rolled his eyes, picked up the wood basket and vanished outside.

'He doesn't realise how much it hurts me when he's so curt,' his mother said sorrowfully.

'He doesn't mean it,' I said. 'It's just calving. I expect every dairy farmer in the country is being rude to his mother just now.'

'It's Rose, too,' she told me. 'He's such a dear boy, Josie; it's tearing him apart to see her so unwell. Perhaps –' she paused and looked at me with a Madonna-like expression of patient and loving reproach – 'perhaps it might help if you didn't expect him to dance attendance every spare minute, hmm?'

My hand clenched on the handle of my fork as I considered throwing it at her like a spear. I've got pretty good aim – I'd probably be able to get her in the side of the head from here. But the consequences wouldn't be worth the fleeting satisfaction. I dropped my eyes to my plate and nodded.

'You're a sweet girl. I know you don't mean to be selfish.' Matt opened the door again and she stretched up to kiss his cheek, which must have been particularly annoying when he was holding an enormous load of very dense, heavy gum wood. 'Goodnight, darling. I hope you feel better in the morning.' And off she trotted.

'Am I not feeling well?' he asked, putting down the wood basket.

'You mustn't be, to be so curt with your adored and adoring mother.'

'Ah.' He opened the door of the stove and slung in a few more bits of wood, and Spud thudded his tail up and down on the floor in approval.

'We'd better ring Kim and tell her she's at Rachel's so she can get her story straight,' I remembered.

'I'll send her a text from across the road.' He yawned widely. 'I'd better go and look at my calving heifer. Will you still be up in an hour if I come back?'

'I expect so,' I said. 'But you should go to bed – you'll fall asleep on the tractor or something awful.' I got up and went to put my arms around him.

'I could come back and sleep with you,' he said very quietly into my hair, and I shivered.

'How much sleep d'you think we'd get?'

'Some,' said Matt cautiously. Then he sighed. 'Better not. It's not our house.' He kissed me again, in a serious sort of way. 'Oh, well. See you tomorrow.'

''Night,' I said, somewhat unsteadily. And then, as he went out the kitchen door, 'Matt?'

He turned and looked back at me. 'Yeah?'

'I love you.'

He didn't say anything but smiled slowly, a smile of pure uncomplicated happiness. Then he pulled the door closed behind him.

278

AT TEN, WHEN I pushed open the door of Rose's bedroom, she was lying awake with *Verse Worth Remembering* open beside her, looking at nothing in particular.

'Hello, love,' she said.

'Hello.' I pulled up a kitchen chair that stood against the bedroom wall for visitors to use and sat at her elbow. 'You couldn't eat something, could you?'

She shook her head. 'I'll eat in the morning. Promise.'

'Had your pills yet?'

'Not just yet. I wanted to find a poem first.'

I tucked my onesie-clad knees up under my chin. 'Something all deep and meaningful, like "Crossing the Bar"?'

'Never could bear Tennyson,' she said weakly. 'What a dreadful thing to admit. No, "The Walrus and the Carpenter". My grandfather used to read it to me when I was small.'

'I remember you reading it to Matt and me.'

'Yes.'

'Thank you,' I said. 'You did so many nice things for us.'

'I always wanted to make pleasant memories for you children. Things are so much more magical if you discover them when you're small.'

We had hunted Woozles and made gingerbread houses and pricked barbary flowers to make the stamens close up and put grass straws down penny-doctor holes, waiting for them to tremble before carefully pulling out a small indignant insect.

'You did,' I said, and felt the tears prickle at the back of my eyes. 'Aunty Rose, you said you didn't want to be remembered like this. But we won't – we'll remember digging Heffalump traps and licking cake bowls and gin and tonic without the tonic.'

'Good,' she said, and closed her eyes.

'Take your pills first,' I suggested. 'Are your pillows okay?'

'Fine.'

She accepted the tablets and I settled back to wait while she went to sleep.

'Go to bed, Josephine,' she whispered a few minutes later.

'I will in a minute. Aunty Rose?'

'Mm?'

'It turns out Matt's in love with me too.'

She moved her head sleepily against the pillow. 'Of course he is,' she said. 'Has been for years. Foolish children.'

Chapter 29

URING AMBER'S LUNCH break the next day I was sitting behind the front desk in a warm, pink-tinged frame of mind that even the weather did nothing to dispel. The hiss of car tyres through the puddles was such a pleasant, cosy sound, and Heather Anne's sign next door creaked in a friendly fashion as it swung on its rusted hooks. Aunty Rose had managed nearly a whole bottle of yoghurt for breakfast, and the district nurse, a good friend of hers, was due this afternoon. And tonight I would see Matt. Not even the unfortunate fact that Amber had spilt nail polish remover through the stationery drawer on her way out could take the sheen off my day.

I looked at the clock on the wall – it was ten past twelve. I thought for a moment and then picked up the phone.

Matt answered on the third ring. 'Hello?' I could hear the clatter of the bale feeder behind the tractor, slowing as he turned it off so as to be able to hear the phone.

'Hey,' I said. 'It's me.'

His voice warmed in an extremely gratifying manner. 'Hey, you. What's up?'

'I was just wondering if there was any chance you'd have time for a lunch break today.'

'Only four calves this morning,' he said. 'And no disasters yet, so it's not impossible.'

'Should I bring you a pie at about ten past one?' I asked.

'Two, please.'

'Mince and cheese?'

'Of course.'

'Custard square?'

'Need you ask?'

'Very good,' I said. 'See you soon.'

As soon as Amber opened the door I leapt to my feet and bolted from the building. I had to wait an interminable two minutes at the bakery while the woman in front of me hunted through her purse in a futile search for the correct change – it was all I could do not to shout, 'Eftpos! Have you not heard of eftpos, you stupid tart?' I bought two mince and cheese and one potato-top pie, a custard square and an apple turnover, pretended not to see Clare strapping a small child into a pushchair on the other side of the street and dived back into the car.

It was sixteen past one when I got to Matt's place. He opened the back door as I came across the lawn.

'Hello,' I said, handing him the lunch bag and feeling, quite suddenly, completely terrified.

'Hello.' He took my hand and pulled me inside out of the rain.

I hadn't been inside this house for about twenty years. Back then it was rented to an elderly couple who kept Angora rabbits on the lawn – they used to let us feed the rabbits and then give us Nice biscuits and plastic beakers of tonic water, which I thought was delightfully exotic.

It hadn't changed a lot. Matt's gumboots and overalls were in a pile beside the door, and a row of coats and hats hung from nails hammered into the wall. The washroom led into a poky kitchen, the benches tiled in those nasty little olive-green tiles that form an uneven surface almost impossible to keep clean, and through the kitchen doorway I could see one corner of an equally small lounge papered in orange geometric designs. The seventies produced such awful home furnishings.

'You were lucky,' I told him, kicking my shoes off. 'I got the last custard square.'

'Thank you.' He began to unpack the lunch. He had set the table with two plates, two knives and a plastic billy of milk, and a pair of mugs with the teabags already in place sat waiting on the bench beside the kettle. A great pile of accounts and Livestock Improvement folders that almost certainly covered the table a foot deep when he wasn't entertaining had been stacked on the floor in a corner. Touched by this thoughtful hospitality, I slid one hand sideways along the kitchen bench and hooked my little finger over his.

He promptly turned and put his arms around me, and I relaxed against him with a little sigh of happiness. He pushed my chin up and kissed me for quite a long time. 'Jose?'

'Mm?'

'Are you very hungry?'

'No,' I said dreamily. 'Oh – have you talked to your mother yet?'

'Not yet.'

'I haven't called Cheryl either. We're very slack.'

'I agree, but can we not talk about it right now?'

'Sorry,' I said, and kissed him again. His stubble was almost past the prickly stage – shaving, in calving season, is for special occasions only – and when he slid his hands up my bare arms the calluses on his palms were rough against my skin. Graeme had soft smooth hands with carefully maintained fingernails, and I wondered irrelevantly how I had ever been able to bear it.

'When do you have to go?' he asked several minutes later.

'Hmm? Oh – quarter to, I suppose.'

He moved an arm to look at his watch. 'One-twenty now,' he said thoughtfully. 'That's a reasonable amount of time.'

I smiled. 'A reasonable amount of time for what?'

'Bed,' said Matt succinctly.

I LATER DISCOVERED that his bedroom was as small and dingy and horribly wallpapered as the rest of the house. But that day I never even saw it. He had removed my Waimanu Physiotherapy vest and shirt by the time we reached the doorway, and I was trying, with hands that shook in an extremely frustrating way, to undo the zip on his jeans. We fell backwards across his unmade bed and tried to kiss and wriggle out of our clothes and press ourselves together as tightly as possible, all at the same time.

'Hang on,' he said breathlessly, rolling away from me. 'Hang on, we can do better than this.'

'*I'm* enjoying it,' I protested.

He laughed and sat up. 'I've been thinking about this for a really long time. I want to do it right.' He slid both hands behind my back to find the catch on my bra.

'I don't think there'd be a wrong way to do it at this point.' I ran my hands up his lean brown forearms, over all the little sharply defined muscles and tendons. To be honest, if he'd jerked his chin at me and barked, 'You there! Legs apart!' that would have been just fine.

'At least –' he broke off to kiss the hollow of my throat, which you wouldn't have thought was a particularly sensitive spot, but it made me want to writhe and moan like someone in a tacky B-grade movie – 'I want to take all your clothes off and look at you properly. You're so lovely.'

I looked up at him and my heart contracted painfully. Of course I had loved Graeme – you don't move in with someone you don't care a lot about, or at least you shouldn't – but this scruffy friend of mine with his slow voice and lazy crooked smile was the kindest, most attractive, *best* man I had ever known. 'Whatever you want,' I whispered. 'Just say, Matt, I'll do whatever you want.'

His pupils dilated abruptly, so that his eyes looked almost black. 'God, Jo,' he said, and pulled me tightly against him.

'WHAT TIME IS it?' I asked weakly.

'Don't know,' Matt said. He sounded at least three-quarters asleep. 'Can't see, can't move . . .'

With a truly heroic effort I pulled my left arm out from under his shoulders and squinted at my watch. It was, apparently, one fifty-two. '*Crap!*' I leapt to my feet like an Olympic high-jumper and began to hunt feverishly for clothes.

'What time is it?' Matt asked, not moving at all.

'Ten to two. Matt, *help* me, I've lost my shirt.'

'Hall,' he murmured, rolling onto his stomach.

He had managed, by the time I'd scrambled into my clothes, to push himself up to sit on the edge of his bed. 'Come here.'

'I can't – I'm *late* . . .'

'Jo, love, you can't go back to work like that.' He pulled me back towards him, unbuttoned my shirt and began to do it up straight. 'Better do something about your hair, too.'

'Where's your hairbrush?' I asked, pulling down the tangled snarl of hair that had been, half an hour before, a tidy and professional knot at the nape of my neck.

'Haven't got one.'

'Ah. That would explain this sexy unkempt look you've been working.'

He grinned. 'Thank you. You're doing quite a good job of sexy and unkempt yourself.'

'You're really not all that helpful,' I told him severely. I scraped my hair back into a ponytail, took his face in my hands and kissed him. 'I love you.' I turned and dashed up the hall.

He ran down the back steps as I started the car, wearing his jeans but no shirt and carrying two little paper bags. I wound down the window and he passed in my pie and apple turnover. 'You can eat them on the way,' he said, and leant in the window to kiss me. 'See you tonight.'

I backed the car round, put it into first and looked up to see Bob McIntosh, his face a mask of shock, opening the door of his little truck. *Oh, shit*, I thought, followed by, *Well, I don't know how else I was ever going to get rid of him.* Feeling like the kind of person who kicks puppies for fun, I waved as I sped past.

Chapter 30

I T WAS ONE of those nerve-racking afternoons when you start off running quarter of an hour late and then everything you do takes longer than you think it will. Somewhere between Mrs Mayhew's thoracic spine pain and Greg Turner's torn calf muscle I heard Kim's voice, but I didn't have time to stick my head out and say hello.

At three minutes past five I farewelled my last client and hurriedly shut down the computer in the consulting room. 'Amber,' I said, going out the front, 'can you call Ben Frazer and tell him his brace has arrived? Maybe you could leave it at the petrol station for him – I'd better run.'

Amber nodded, and Kim picked up her school bag and asked, 'Can I have a lift home?'

'Yep,' I said. 'But I've got to go to the supermarket first.'

'That's cool. See you, Amber.'

Amber jerked one shoulder in what could perhaps have been construed as a farewell.

'What's her problem?' Kim asked as she climbed into the car. 'She's acting really weird even for her.'

I threw the car into reverse and executed a rapid three-point turn. 'Crush on your boyfriend.'

Kim squirmed, cat-like, to get comfortable. 'I guess he is,' she said with satisfaction. 'He introduced me to his flat-mates last night.'

'Good sign,' I remarked.

'Yeah. Hey, Josie?'

'Mm?'

'You do know Matt'll be still milking? You've got time to get home and shave your legs; there's no need to drive like a maniac.'

'I just don't want to leave Aunty Rose by herself for too long, Miss Smarty Pants. I was late last night, and it wasn't good.'

Kim pulled her knees up to her chin and hugged them. 'She's got so sick so fast,' she said unhappily. 'Just like Dad.'

I took my left hand off the steering wheel for a second and touched her arm. 'Oh, Kim.'

'Yeah, well, life's a bitch.' She scrubbed at her eyes with the back of her hand. 'At least you and Matt are here this time.'

❦

WE FLEW AROUND the supermarket, Kim pushing the trolley and me hurling in groceries. 'Vanilla custard,' she ordered. 'Aunty Rose likes it.'

I plucked a carton from the shelf along with two tubs

of Greek yoghurt, and we sped around the corner into the bakery section to run smack into Bob McIntosh. I couldn't believe it – twice in one afternoon. He had a basket over one arm containing three tins of the very cheapest brand of cat food and a jar of marmalade, and he ricocheted gently off the front of the trolley into a perspex-fronted cabinet full of muffins.

'Sorry!' said Kim.

Bob shot me one miserable, accusing look, hunched his shoulders and scuttled off Gollum-like towards the frozen goods.

'I didn't hit him *that* hard,' Kim said. 'He's really strange.'

'Yes,' I said. Bob must truly have thought, despite all evidence to the contrary, that one of these days I would fall gratefully into his arms. I should have realised, and tried harder to discourage him.

As we turned up the valley, leaving the last of Waimanu's streetlights behind us, Kim said conversationally, 'So you *were* in love with Matt the whole time. You dirty rotten liar.'

'Unless you're prepared to walk, you shouldn't insult the driver.'

She completely ignored this empty threat. 'All that "stop it, you guys, he's one of my best friends and you're ruining it".' This was said in a simpering little bleat that bore, I devoutly hoped, no resemblance whatsoever to my actual voice. 'Josie, you should be ashamed of yourself.'

'One day I hope you'll find it in your heart to forgive me,' I said.

'I may,' said Kim regally. 'Eventually. Can't have been much fun watching him go home with Cilla.'

I gave a little snort of laughter. 'Not much.'

'Josie?'

'Mm?'

'Don't be too hard on him, will you? He was only going out with her because she'd have kicked up such a stink if he'd broken up with her, and he didn't think you liked him anyway.'

'I know,' I said. 'It's okay.'

'Good,' said Kim. 'Hey, Josie?'

'Yeah?'

'Are you on the pill?'

'Kim!' I protested.

'I'm not asking about your sex life. I was just wondering . . .'

'Oh,' I said. 'No, I'm not at the moment. Are you thinking about going on it yourself?' I hoped I didn't sound as dismayed as I felt.

'Well, yeah, maybe.' She pulled the tie out of her sleek dark plait and shook her head vigorously. 'Does it make you get really fat?'

'No,' I told her. 'I think the old-fashioned pills might have, but not these days.'

'So I just go to the chemist?'

'You've got to go to the doctor. They take your blood pressure and explain it all – what to do if you miss a pill, and all that kind of stuff. But most people use condoms to start with.'

Kim drummed her fingers against the window moodily. 'I don't know why I'm asking. He won't have sex with me anyway.'

'Won't he?' I asked. I wasn't at all sure I was equipped to be Kim's confidante and romantic adviser.

'He won't even *kiss* me until I've done my homework.'

I tried so hard to stay gravely sympathetic that it hurt, but alas, my efforts were in vain.

'It's not funny!' Kim wailed.

'Yes,' I gasped, 'it is. Sorry – sorry, I'm stopping.'

'Rachel says boys *always* want to. Maybe he doesn't like me very much.'

I pulled myself together with an effort. Nobody in their right mind would ask Hazel for boyfriend advice, Aunty Rose was terminally ill and Rachel's knowledge had been gleaned from the pages of *Cosmopolitan*. Equipped or not, I was it. 'Of course he likes you,' I said. 'Come on, you must be able to tell.'

'Well, I thought he did, but . . .' She stopped and sighed heavily.

'Kimlet, you've only been going out for a week.'

'Ten days,' she corrected.

'Don't you think that any bloke who wanted to sleep with you after you'd been going out together for ten days would be a bit dodgy?' I said.

Kim shrugged one shoulder and said nothing.

'Why the rush, anyway? What's wrong with just hanging out together for a while and seeing if it's going to be a good thing?'

'It's just – Josie, I don't want him to think I'm a silly little kid and go and find someone else instead!'

Ah, of course. Like the last one did. 'Well,' I said, 'I don't think Andy would do that, but if he *was* to wander off and find someone else I reckon you'd feel worse about it if you had slept with him.'

Kim muttered something inaudible in the direction of her feet.

'If he's supervising your homework, he obviously thinks you're going to be together for a good long time,' I said bracingly.

'How do you come to *that* conclusion?'

'Well, if you get a good education you'll be able to get some incredibly well paid job, and he'll be able to give up work entirely and go hunting while you support him. I'm sure he's thought it all out.'

'Josie,' she said, 'do you realise you're a complete idiot?'

'Your brother points that out quite often.'

'Well, he's right.'

'Don't tell him that; it might go to his head.' We were driving up the last straight, a thicket of wet black poplar trunks on one side and Matt's dairy supply sign reflecting back at us on the other. 'Are you coming up to Aunty Rose's now, or do you want me to drop you at home?'

'Aunty Rose's. I'll make dinner while you have a shower and condition your pubic hair.'

I opened my mouth to reply, thought better of it and closed it again.

'I saw it on an old episode of *Friends*,' Kim explained. 'I reckon it sounds like quite a good idea.'

❀

LADEN WITH GROCERY bags we threaded our way through the welcoming crowd of dogs and pig, and let ourselves into the kitchen. Aunty Rose was standing at the kitchen bench with a block of cheese in her hand, but her movements as she grated it were halting and very, very tired. This was no longer the brisk and energetic cook who, with sleeves trailing through the gravy, served sausage and prune bourguignon to her hapless guests.

'Sweet peas,' she said, turning to smile at us. Percy gave a wistful grunt through the open door behind us and she moved slowly across the room to pat him. 'I have neglected you, dear boy. Josephine, where is the pig-scratching fork?'

I fished through the fruit bowl, filled with power bills and notifications of road closures for the Targa Rally and other random bits of paper, and found the fork at the bottom.

'Thank you,' said Aunty Rose. Leaning against the doorframe, she applied herself to Percy's back.

'What's for tea?' I asked, kissing her cheek and beginning to unpack the groceries. There was a most enticing smell of roasting meat.

'Dinner. One of Andy's pork roasts, and I thought I'd make that lovely potato dish with the sour cream and garlic.'

I cast a wary eye at the earthenware dish on the bench. 'What did you use instead of sour cream?'

'Yoghurt,' said Aunty Rose.

I stood quite still for a moment, a bag of peanuts in one hand and a tin of spaghetti in the other. 'Honestly?'

'Would I lie to you, Josephine?'

'It's almost as good,' Kim said from the bench where she was tipping loose tea leaves into the battered tin caddy. '*And* it's healthier.'

'But we only had strawberry yoghurt.'

'I added a little lemon juice to cut the sweetness,' Aunty Rose assured me.

Kim and I looked at one another and collapsed into hysterical laughter.

🌹

'SMELLS GOOD,' MATT said, opening the kitchen door just before seven. My heart gave a ridiculous little lurch and I wanted to leap across the room into his arms, but managed to limit myself to smiling at him over a pot of peas. He grinned back as he crossed the room to kiss Aunty Rose.

She laid a hand on his cheek for a moment, and then held it out so he could help her to her feet. 'It will be,' she said. 'Contrary to what these ill-bred young strumpets imply.'

'That's a bit harsh,' I said. 'Will you carve, or should we get Matt to do it?'

'I'll do it,' said Kim. 'He just hacks lumps off. Aren't you going to kiss Josie, Matt?'

'All in good time,' said Matt. 'What's for dinner?'

'Roast pork, garlic bread, a green vegetable medley and potato and strawberry gratin,' I told him.

'That's novel,' he remarked.

'It's a shame you're all so unadventurous,' said Aunty Rose mournfully.

'I resent that,' I said. 'I've eaten deep-fried crickets.'

'It's your own fault,' said Matt to his aunt. 'We've been scarred by years of Mussel Surprise.'

'So many surprises,' I reminisced. 'And almost all of them nasty.'

'You weren't even here for the one with the whole chillies,' he said.

'And that Portuguese fish thing,' Kim added, carving the roast pork in a most professional way. 'The one with the tiny purple octopuses in it, poor little things.'

'Torn kicking and screaming from their mothers,' said Matt, shaking his head.

'Sit down,' Aunty Rose ordered. 'You will all eat up your dinners and be grateful.'

❦

I WOULDN'T RECOMMEND potato and strawberry gratin, although Percy liked it. Aunty Rose sat carefully erect in her chair and pretended to enjoy her dinner while the rest of us pretended not to notice the effort it took. Kim told us a very funny (and I expect entirely fictitious) story about her latest run-in with her geography teacher, and Matt and I concentrated on not grinning at one another across the table like a pair of feeble-minded idiots.

Hazel came into the kitchen as we finished. 'Here you all are,' she said with a sorrowful and faintly wounded air. 'Having a lovely little dinner party.' The casual observer would have assumed she had just cooked a nutritious dinner for her family and they hadn't bothered to let her know they didn't want it, rather than that she had been getting her roots redone in town.

'Percy's eaten all the potato and strawberry bake,' said Matt, 'but have some pork. It's beautiful.'

'No, no,' said Hazel. 'Don't worry about me. I'll throw something together at home. Rosie, darling, don't you think you should lie down? You don't look at all well.'

'How very unflattering,' said Aunty Rose.

'You children shouldn't have let her cook for you,' Hazel added. 'You won't attempt the dishes, Rosie?'

'Of course not, with three slaves.'

'I think Matthew has got quite enough to do, and it's time you started your homework, Kim darling.'

'I've done it,' said Kim. 'Did it at the physio clinic.'

'Even homework looks good compared to conversation with Amber,' I observed.

Matt pushed back his chair. 'Right,' he said, 'I've got to look round the cows before bed. Want a ride home, Toad?'

'Yes, please,' said Kim. 'Aunty Rose, that was lovely. Thank you so much.'

I picked up the wood basket and accompanied them outside. Matt held out a hand for it, but I shook my head. 'I'll do it – you've got cows to check.'

'Close the door!' Hazel called.

Kim pulled it to, not slamming it but with a certain decisive crispness. 'Sorry to leave you with the dishes, Josie.'

'It's fine,' I said, putting down the wood basket and reaching up to finally kiss her brother. 'I don't mind.'

'You wouldn't mind *anything* at the moment. I could put you in a sack and beat you against a trough.' There was something touching about Kim's adoption of her brother's sayings.

'True,' I admitted, and Matt's arms tightened around me.

'You'd better go back in and get on with the dishes, Cinderella,' he said, kissing the tip of my nose and then letting me go.

'Come back, if you're not too tired.'

'I will.'

'You guys are so cute,' said Kim.

'Put a sock in it, Toad,' he ordered, but as they went across the gravel he slung an arm around her shoulders and she rubbed her head against his shoulder like a kitten.

'CALVING COW?' I asked as he let himself back into the kitchen. He had been gone an hour and a half and I had reached new heights of housewifely accomplishment in his absence. The dishes were done, the dogs fed and put to bed, a week's worth of kindling had been split and a pot of vegetable soup, complete with pork bone, was simmering on top of the wood stove for the next day. Spud lay curled on his beanbag, paws twitching just a little as he chased rabbits in his sleep.

'Two,' said Matt. 'Both breech.' He had a long smear of mud across one cheek, and I crossed the kitchen and wiped it off with the tea towel. He made a face at me. 'Sexy.'

'It could have been worse – I could have spat on a hanky.'

He slid his arms around my waist. 'How's Aunty Rose?'

'Asleep,' I said. 'Or she was twenty minutes ago. Want to go and check?'

'In a minute.' He bent his head and kissed me in an unhurried, expert sort of way, and it was touch and go between staying upright and slithering bonelessly to the floor between his feet.

'Bloody hell,' I whispered, stepping back and leaning against the table for support.

'What?'

'It's a bit frightening, feeling like this.'

'I know,' he said. He reached out and ran the side of his thumb very softly down my cheek. 'I can't quite believe I'm allowed to touch you.'

I turned my head and kissed his hand in blatant adoration. Just then there was a low growl from the other side of the kitchen, and Spud gave a short hoarse bark. 'What's up, mate?' I asked.

'Perhaps he doesn't approve,' said Matt.

But Spud wasn't looking at us; he was staring fixedly across the kitchen.

'It must be a possum,' I said. 'He scared me half to death a couple of weeks ago, growling in the middle of the night. I just about rang you to come and chase away the axe murderer.'

'Charming,' he remarked. 'You weren't worried that the axe murderer might get me?'

'Never occurred to me,' I said. 'It's because you're so strong and manly.'

'Flattery,' said Matt, 'will get you nowhere at all.' He kissed me again, let me go and went up the hall to look in on his aunt.

He was only gone a few moments, and as he came back into the kitchen he pulled the hall door closed behind him. 'Asleep. Come here.'

I went, putting my arms around him, but when he ran both hands up under my top I protested weakly, 'It's not our house.'

'Yeah,' he said, 'but it's over eight hours since I had sex with you, and I can't hold out any longer.' He cupped my breasts in his hands and I very nearly whimpered.

'Someone might come,' I whispered.

'Who? And the dogs would bark.'

'The griffon's watching. *And* Spud. Not to mention the axe murderer.'

'Don't you want to, Jose?'

'Oh, dear Lord, yes,' I admitted. I pulled his sweatshirt up over his head and threw it neatly over the griffon's.

'He was probably quite keen to see,' Matt remarked.

'In that case I *really* don't want him watching.'

'Spoilsport.' He kissed me again. 'I love you.'

'Same. Oh – I haven't got any condoms.'

'I have,' he said. 'I came prepared.'

I looked at him with deep admiration. 'And you weren't even a Boy Scout. What a legend.'

Chapter 31

AT TWO TWENTY-NINE on Wednesday afternoon, Cheryl, wearing her blue Waimanu Physiotherapy shirt, manhandled an enormous and lavishly chromed all-terrain mountain buggy through the front door. 'Afternoon, girls,' she said.

'Hi,' said Amber, coming out from behind her desk to peer at the baby. 'Hi, Max. Can I get him out?'

'Absolutely,' Cheryl said. 'Just don't paint his toenails again – Ian's mother got all worked up about it. Jo, can you have a look at my back before you go? Amber said there was a slot.' She went ahead of me into the consulting room and began to unbutton her shirt without bothering about the door. 'T6, I think,' she said over her shoulder. 'Subluxated the bastard.'

I followed her in and shut the door. 'You must watch your back when you're lifting Max in and out of the car,' I lectured in my best professional voice. 'Try to use your knees, and make sure you put his capsule in on one side and then the other.'

'Thank you *so* much,' she said. 'None of those things had occurred to me.'

'Lucky I reminded you then. Hands on opposite shoulders, please, and rotate to your left.' Cheryl twisted obediently. 'That would be your right.'

'Oh, shut up, or I'll dock your pay. That's catching, there.'

'Right. Other way? Crikey, there's not a lot of movement.'

'Which would be why I'm here,' she said.

'Be quiet. Bend forward.'

'How's Rose today?' she asked, bending.

'Not very good. Yesterday was a bit better, but she's just shrinking to nothing and we can't do anything to help – now back.'

'I'm so sorry,' said Cheryl to the ceiling. 'If you need more time off we'll figure something out.'

'Thank you,' I said. 'You're wonderful. Okay, lie on your back and we'll see if we can get this thing to move.'

'I normally do thoracic manipulations with them on their fronts,' she demurred.

'I don't. Lie down and stop arguing.'

'I'm not at all sure about your bedside manner,' she said, lying down and crossing her arms.

I stood at her head and slid one arm under her, holding her across the shoulders with the other. 'Don't complain – you're in a very vulnerable position. Breathe in . . . and all the way out.' I pressed her back down against the table and there was a most satisfying crunching sound. Customers *love* satisfying crunching sounds; they really feel they're getting their money's worth. Physiotherapists the world over are plagued by people who think that spinal manipulations are an instant cure for chronic injuries and that strengthening exercises and improved posture are for losers.

'That's got the little bastard,' said Cheryl with satisfaction. 'Right, what do I need to know about this afternoon's lot?'

'I think everyone's files are up to date,' I said. 'I'm not sure whether you'll want to strap Paul Moss's ankle – he sprained it really badly a few months ago and it was doing well, but he called this morning to say he'd tweaked it again. And if you can manage to put the fear of God into Keith Taylor so he'll look after his reconstructed shoulder you'll be doing better than me.'

'I'll try,' said Cheryl, 'but I've got a horrible feeling that since the baby I've forgotten everything I ever knew.' She pushed herself up to sit and shrugged her shoulders experimentally. 'Oh, well, we'll see. Off you go.'

THAT EVENING MATT picked up *Pirate's Lady* from his aunt's bedside table and examined the front cover. 'That dress defies the law of physics.'

I looked over his shoulder at the picture of the impossibly buxom girl draped across a man who, judging by his white blouse and the parrot on his shoulder, was supposed to be the pirate. 'The dress is the least of her problems. Look at her breasts.'

'I am,' he said. 'They look pretty good to me. Very perky.'

'But they're in the wrong place,' I pointed out. 'Does it mention in the story that she's deformed, Aunty Rose?'

'Oddly enough, no.' She shifted her head on the pillows.

'Pills?' I asked. The top-up pain pills, which she took when her morphine wasn't cutting the mustard, made her very sleepy and she avoided them if she could.

She sighed. 'I think I'd better. I can't seem to get comfortable this evening.' Which meant that the pain was all but unbearable. This *fucking* disease.

I lifted her so she could swallow her tablets, and Matt shook up her pillows before she lay back. 'Should I read something?' he asked. 'Or would you rather I didn't?' He pulled *The Oxford Book of English Verse* towards him across the bedclothes.

The corner of Aunty Rose's mouth twitched. 'How about a bit of that pirate book?' she suggested. 'I'm sure you'll enjoy it.'

Matt picked it up and held it at arm's length, as if it smelt bad. 'Really?' he asked plaintively.

Aunty Rose looked severe. 'Consider it penance.' She had already told me at some length what she thought of presumptuous youngsters who took time off work and reorganised nursing arrangements without even bothering to consult the patient.

I curled up in the armchair at the end of the bed and

listened with enjoyment to the gurgle of the oil heater and Matt's slow-voiced rendition of *Pirate's Lady*. (Calling the woman a lady, considering she seemed to have the morals of an alley cat and the sex drive of a teenage bull, seemed a bit of a stretch, but then *Pirate's Strumpet* just didn't have quite the same ring.)

'"Eyes hot with desire,"' Matt read with increasing misery, '"MacAdam cleared the table with one thrust of his powerful right arm. Grasping the girl's slender wrist he drew her towards him. Her breath caught on a little sob, half of fear and half of desire, as he lowered his head to graze one exposed nipple with his teeth..."' He put down the book and looked at his aunt pleadingly. 'Don't make me keep going. I'm not old enough.'

I ceased sniggering into a cushion and looked up. 'But we've got to find out what happens next,' I complained. 'You can't stop now.'

'Oh yes I can,' he said.

I laughed. 'Wimp.'

'I think you've suffered enough,' said Aunty Rose sleepily. 'You may stop.'

'Thank you,' he said, putting the book face down beside her on the bedclothes. 'Reading this kind of carry-on to your aunt is just wrong.'

'Like watching porn with your grandparents?' I suggested.

'Why is it,' Aunty Rose murmured, 'that every generation believes that they were the ones to invent sex? Go away and let me sleep.'

I lingered behind Matt to rearrange the water glass and hand bell at her elbow. 'You will ring, won't you?'

''Course,' she whispered. 'Go away, Josephine – the boy needs his sleep and he won't leave until you've kissed him goodnight.'

He was lying on the chaise longue when I entered the kitchen, looking up at the griffon with his arms folded behind his head. 'Hey,' he said, and smiled at me sleepily.

I went and sat beside him, bending to kiss him. 'You should go home to bed.'

'It's only eight-thirty. I'll go and check the cows at nine.' He turned onto his side and hooked the index finger of his free hand over the waistband of my jeans, pulling it down an inch.

'What are you doing?' I enquired.

'Just wondering if you're wearing the pink lacy knickers.' He peered down. 'Nope. Bugger.'

'I was wearing them yesterday.'

'I didn't notice.'

'That's nice,' I said. Then, 'My darling, how about not doing that?'

He grinned and opened the second button on my jeans. 'You love it.'

'I would so much rather *not* have your baby sister find you taking off my jeans,' I said.

'Oh, alright.' He did the buttons up again and lay down, pulling me comfortably back against him.

I squirmed round within the circle of his arm to lie down too, using his bottom arm as a pillow. 'Stu said you looked interested when he mentioned the pink knickers,' I remarked, 'but I didn't believe him.'

'He was right,' said Matt, running his free hand lightly up and down my arm.

'He refers to you in his emails as "the delectable Matthew".'

'I'm not quite sure how I feel about that.'

'You should be flattered. Stu is only attracted to good-looking men; he's very shallow.'

A sleepy sort of silence fell, and I lay in his arms and felt perfectly content. Falling embers hissed in the stove and Spud's tail thumped once or twice against the floor as he stirred and then settled back to sleep. I could feel the slow rise and fall of Matt's chest as he breathed and his hand was warm against my stomach.

'Do they all call you JD in Australia?' he asked suddenly.

'Mostly just Stu,' I said. 'Graeme did sometimes, when he particularly approved of me. Which wasn't very often, come to think of it.'

'Why not?'

I sighed. 'Childish sense of humour, using the bread knife to cut cheese, biting my nails, wearing jeans with jandals, being too scared to get my ears pierced – that kind of stuff.'

'Life with him must have been a barrel of laughs.'

'I'm exaggerating,' I admitted. 'But the last few months weren't much fun.' In a way it had been a relief to walk in on Graeme and Chrissie. It's unspeakably horrible to know you're irritating the person who is supposed to love you and not know why things have changed or how to make them right again. At least that had explained it.

Matt didn't say anything, but his arm tightened around my waist.

I was going to tell him it didn't matter – that even at our best Graeme and I hardly had the kind of love the poets dream of, that apart from Stu and shoe shops Melbourne contained not one thing I missed. But he breathed out on a long sigh and his grip slackened as he slid into sleep. If you want conversation with a dairy farmer in August it pays not to leave silences of over thirty seconds. He knew all those things anyway; I threaded my fingers down between his and closed my eyes too.

❧

'MATTHEW *PATRICK*!' HAZEL shrilled.

I went instantly from deeply asleep to more awake than I had ever been in my life, and leapt to my feet. This was a mistake; blackness boiled in front of my eyes at the sudden shift from horizontal to vertical and I had to lean against the table and clutch my head in both hands.

Matt has far better nerves than I do, and was considerably more sleep-deprived – he didn't leap anywhere. He merely frowned, opened one eye a fraction and said, 'What?'

'What are you *doing*?' his mother cried.

'Sleeping,' he murmured, and prised the other eyelid open. 'Hi.'

'And *what* would Cilla think if she saw this?'

'Oh, for God's sake,' said Matt wearily. He sat up and ran both hands backwards through his hair, which gave him the same coiffeur as the eccentric professor in *Back to the Future*. 'I haven't seen Cilla for weeks.'

'Oh, *Matthew*,' his mother lamented. 'That delightful girl.' And putting her smart black clutch down on the table beside me the woman actually wrung her hands.

I was struck by a most inappropriate urge to giggle, and caught my bottom lip firmly between my teeth. Matt met my eye above his mother's head and said, carefully grave, 'Never mind, Mother, this one's delightful too.'

'Well, yes, of course she is,' said Hazel mechanically. But she sank into a chair as if the effort of remaining on her feet, under the weight of this heavy blow, was too much to bear. 'Oh, Matthew, I *do* wish you'd settle down instead of flitting from girl to girl.'

'Like a butterfly?' I suggested helpfully.

'Watch it,' ordered the love of my life, scowling at me in an only half-successful attempt not to laugh. 'Don't worry, Mum, my flitting days are over.'

'You need to remember, Matthew, that you're the only male role model your sister h-has, now.' Her voice gave an affecting little hitch at this reference to her dead husband. 'It's not good for her to see you picking up and discarding girls as if they were . . .' She paused in search of a suitable simile, and I managed to fight down the urge to suggest one. Avocados, perhaps; you have to palpate them individually to find one at the perfect stage of ripeness. Or jeans – buying the right pair is a solemn undertaking and the experienced shopper expects to have to try on quite a number before finding a good fit.

'Settle down, Mum,' Matt said. 'Anyone would think I'd spent the last ten years working my way through every woman in the district.'

'Have you?' I asked with interest.

He shot me a withering look.

'Of course you've only been home for four,' I murmured.

'True,' said Matt. He stood up and stretched. 'Right, I'd better go and check my cows. Goodnight.'

'You don't need to run away, Matthew,' said Hazel.

'I'm not,' he said shortly. 'I'm checking the cows and going to bed.' He kissed his mother's cheek and then my mouth, a brief hard kiss that was really just to make a point. 'See you tomorrow.'

'Goodnight,' I said as he opened the kitchen door.

''Night,' he said to me. ''Night, Mum.'

'Goodnight, love.' She watched him pull the door closed behind him, then turned to me with a small sad smile. 'Let's go and see how Rosie is, shall we?'

'It's only been a day or two,' I said impulsively. 'We haven't been sneaking around behind your back.'

Her smile became even sadder. 'Thank you, dear,' she said, and I felt like a complete worm. That's the remarkable thing about Hazel: you might consider her the silliest woman of your acquaintance, but she can still play you like a virtuoso. It's quite a gift.

Chapter 32

AFTER SENDING MY eleven o'clock appointment on her way, handbag swinging precariously from the handle of her right crutch, I wandered out of the consulting room to find that Amber had vanished. She had been replaced by a tall, greying man in his fifties with a snub nose and very blue eyes. His glasses, without which he can only see about three feet, were balanced on top of his head.

'Afternoon, young Jo,' he said, graciously inclining his head. His glasses fell forward onto Amber's computer keyboard.

'Dad!' I threw my arms around his neck and hugged him, and he patted my shoulder in a sheepish sort of way. 'Where's Amber?'

'She said something about a cup of tea,' he said, picking up his glasses and replacing them carefully on top of his head. Why he doesn't keep the things on his face and look through them I have no idea.

'And Mum?'

'Supermarket.'

'The house is full of food,' I said.

Dad shrugged. 'The woman is fundamentally unable to visit anyone without taking groceries. You know that.'

I did indeed know that – on her last visit to see me in Melbourne she had brought toilet paper and washing-up liquid with her as well as enough food for a large hungry family. Graeme had looked at these offerings for a while and then enquired just what sort of a household she had thought she was coming to.

'I thought you were going to stay at home and look after the goats,' I said.

'Bloody animals,' said Dad morosely. 'No, I've left Maurice from next door a list of instructions as long as your arm. It sounded as if I'd better not put it off if I want to see Rose?' He made the last sentence into a question.

'No,' I said. 'I don't think it'll be very long. And I hope it won't.'

Dad grimaced, and turned in his seat as Amber came back down the hall bearing a mug of tea. 'Thank you,' he said.

'Chocolate biscuit?' Amber offered, sniffing as she handed over the mug.

'No, thanks,' said Dad. 'Jo treating you right, is she?'

Amber pondered this. 'She's grumpy sometimes,' she said at last. 'But not as grumpy as Cheryl.'

'Thank you,' I said doubtfully.

'And sometimes she's really funny.'

'Funny peculiar or funny amusing?' Dad wanted to know.

'Both,' said Amber. 'She sings along with the radio, even though she can't sing at *all* – and yesterday she did cartwheels all across the car park.'

Dad raised an eyebrow. 'Sounds to me as if she's mentally unstable.'

'Oh, no,' Amber assured him. 'She's a really good physio. She's really strong – she cracks people's backs just like *that*.' She attempted to snap her fingers and failed.

'And if I get too enthusiastic and break them right in half there's a skip just outside the back door,' I said.

Amber giggled at this lame joke, and the sensor above the door buzzed as my next appointment, a delicate little elderly lady dressed all in beige, pushed it open.

'Like a lamb to the slaughter,' said my father under his breath.

✿

HE WAS GONE when I had finished with my beige patient and her sciatic nerve. As I emerged, Amber blew her nose *on a tissue* and said, 'You look like your mum.'

'Thanks!' I said. I don't, particularly – Mum has that classical, timeless beauty that depends on bone structure and so doesn't diminish with age, and I look like an amateur sort of copy beside her. But at least I got the legs, and according to Chrissie I might not be all that pretty but you didn't realise it when you were with me (which was such a nice compliment it almost made up for stealing my boyfriend).

When I got home at three both Hazel's car and a teeny-weeny silver thing that was doubtless the very cheapest hire car you could get were parked beside the woodshed. I got out of the car and patted each member of the welcoming committee then, turning towards the house, spied my father kneeling on the roof with a hammer in his hand.

'Have you been put to work already?' I called.

'Hmm?' he asked distractedly. 'This is like patching a sieve. Throw me up a handful of those nails there?'

There was a box of roofing nails on the path. I filled my pockets and went round the side of the house to climb the plum tree. The corrugated-iron roof was blotched with rust, and looking at it I was surprised it kept out as much of the rain as it did. I made my way carefully across to Dad and he held out a hand for the nails.

'Thank you,' he said. 'Better go in and see your mother, hadn't you?'

'I will in a minute. Why don't you come? It must be time for a cup of tea.'

'I think I'll carry on here for a little while,' said Dad.

I smiled. 'Is it all a bit heavy-going inside?'

'Just ever so slightly,' he admitted, removing his glasses and putting them on top of his head. 'Rose isn't looking good, is she?'

'Every time she falls asleep I wonder if she's still breathing.'

'And you'd almost hope she wasn't.'

'Mm.'

'Go on in,' said Dad. 'Your mother wants to see you. I won't be long.'

I climbed back down the plum tree and went around the side of the house to let myself in the kitchen door. Hazel was actually folding washing at the kitchen table and Mum had both hands in the sink. She pulled them out and dried them on the tea towel she had tucked into the waistband of her jeans, then crossed the kitchen to take my face in her hands and inspect me. I laughed at this painstaking scrutiny, and she gave a satisfied nod.

'Hello, love,' she said.

I put my arms around her and hugged her tightly – I adore my mother, although I reserve the right to laugh at her a little bit from time to time. 'Is Aunty Rose asleep?'

'Yes,' said Hazel. '*Don't* go in and wake her, please, Josie dear.' She pulled my black lace bra out of the washing basket and looked at it with distaste before folding it in half and laying it on the table. I wondered how she'd react when she came across the matching g-string – perhaps well-bred girls are supposed to wear flesh-coloured cotton knickers.

'I won't,' I said. 'Cup of tea, guys?'

'Yes, please,' said Mum, but Hazel shifted her shoulders wearily and shook her head.

'Not for me. I've not even *looked* at my own housework yet.'

As she backed her white car round, Aunty Rose appeared in the kitchen doorway, steadying herself against the doorframe with one hand. 'Is she gone?' she hissed.

AFTER HER SHOWER that evening Aunty Rose sat on the edge of her bed and tipped her jewellery box out beside her in a glittering heap. Frowning, she picked up a wide and only slightly tarnished silver bangle and slipped it over her left hand. It dangled pathetically from her skeletal wrist. 'Perhaps not,' she murmured, taking it off again.

I knelt at the edge of the bed, passing her the green satin cap. 'How about the pearls?'

She nodded, and held out her hand so I could do up the catch of the little bracelet. 'That's better,' she said. Then, very quietly, 'Josephine?'

'Mm?'

'Is it getting too pitiful, like poor old Barbara Cartland?'

I took her hand gently – she was so fragile now. 'No,' I said. 'It's like a – a warrior chief putting on his war paint.'

'Right,' said Aunty Rose. 'Very good.' She twitched the lapel of her dressing-gown straight. 'And my silver brooch, I think.' She fastened the brooch, dabbed perfume onto her wrists and held out an imperious hand for her stick. As a lesson in courage it was unsurpassed.

In the kitchen Kim was mixing mustard powder and water to a paste in the little green china mustard jug. Aunty Rose felt that buying one's mustard already made up was a slovenly, immoral sort of way to run a kitchen. Dad was setting the table, Mum was on her knees feeding the wood stove and Hazel, looking distinctly put upon, stood at the sink washing dishes.

Aunty Rose had just lowered herself onto the chaise longue when the phone rang.

'I'll get it,' said Mum, standing up and dusting her hands on her jeans. She plucked the portable phone off the kitchen table. 'Hello?' Then, 'Matthew, it's Edith here. What can we do? Really? Are you sure? Well, then, we'll see you when we see you.' She put the phone back down. 'Matthew's been held up – he'll be another forty-five minutes.'

HE WAS AN hour, and it was past eight when his ute came up the driveway. Kim and I were clearing the table and our elders had retired to the lounge, but as the dogs sped barking to meet him his mother bustled back into the kitchen to retrieve his plate from the oven.

'Stop!' said Kim as she opened the microwave door, plate in hand. 'That plate's got gold edging – it'll spark.'

'The poor boy can't work all day and have his dinner lukewarm!' Hazel protested.

I held out a plain china plate, freshly dried. 'You could put it on that.'

'Hi, guys,' said Matt, opening the door. He met my eyes for just a second with a fleeting, lopsided smile. 'That looks good.'

'I'll just heat it up for you, darling,' said Hazel tenderly.

'Don't worry – I like it better cold.' This was true, come to think of it. I've never known anyone else who would cheerfully tuck into a bowl of cold porridge.

'Nonsense.' She took the plate from me and began to transfer potatoes and slices of pot roast with a fork. 'Now, Matthew, sit down and your sister will bring you a drink.'

'And then she can fan me while I eat,' he agreed, and Kim, who had looked ever so slightly sour at being pressed into service, grinned.

Mum came into the kitchen with a smudge on her nose and her hair escaping its bun. 'Matthew, love,' she said warmly, reaching up to kiss him. 'I presume you're well, under all that hair?'

'I was thinking about shaving today,' Matt admitted. 'But thinking's about as far as I got.'

'Fair enough,' I said. 'It's a big decision. You wouldn't want to do anything hasty and then regret it later.'

'Besides, the hairier he gets the less of him we can see, which has got to be a good thing,' said Kim.

'Kimmy!' said Hazel reprovingly. 'Don't listen to them, darling, you have *such* lovely hair. Now, would you like a cup of tea or a cold drink?'

'Neither,' he said, taking the still-unheated plate out of her hands. 'Thanks, Mum.' He rummaged in the cutlery drawer for a knife and fork and escaped into the lounge with Hazel hard on his heels.

Mum looked after them thoughtfully, then put her arms around Kim and hugged her. 'It's okay,' said Kim, her voice muffled in the folds of Mum's jumper. 'It's worse for Matt than me.'

Mum laughed and let her go. 'Good girl,' she said.

LIKE THE THEATRE nurse at the surgeon's elbow, I handed a hot-water bottle in a hideous purple crocheted cover to my mother. She slid it deftly beneath the small of Aunty Rose's back, rearranged a pillow and lowered the patient down with delicate precision.

'Thank you,' Aunty Rose murmured.

Hazel and Kim had gone home to watch the Living Channel and phone Andy respectively. With any luck Matt was in bed rather than calving a cow, and Dad was sitting in front of the kitchen stove with a pile of local newspapers beside him and Spud asleep on his feet. The sequins on the bedspread gleamed in the light of Aunty Rose's bedside lamp and a mouse skittered about in the ceiling.

Mum sank into the armchair and I sat cross-legged on the edge of Rose's big bed. A companionable sort of silence fell.

'Josephine,' said Aunty Rose suddenly.

'Yes?'

'Make sure Matthew has a colonoscopy in the next twelve months, will you?'

I smiled at this unromantic request, and then sobered. When your aunt and your father have both succumbed to cancer you'd be an idiot not to have yourself checked over every few years. 'I will. Kim too.'

'Every five years after the age of twenty-five.'

'It shall be done,' I promised, lying back beside her and looking up at the India-shaped watermark on the ceiling.

'You might persuade him to shave and cut his hair while you're at it,' Mum put in. 'The boy has such a nice face – it's a shame not to be able to see it.'

'I think there's a sort of default period before you're supposed to start trying to change them,' I said.

'Nonsense,' Mum said briskly. 'Start as you mean to go on.' Then, 'I could always give him a bit of a trim myself. You've still got those clippers, haven't you, Rose?'

'No!' Aunty Rose and I said at the same time.

Mum laughed.

'I mean it, Edith,' Aunty Rose continued. 'I'm not having a nephew who looks like he had his hair cut in prison standing up at my funeral to read my eulogy.'

Mum's eyes filled. 'Alright, alright,' she said. 'Keep your hair on.' And we all three giggled weakly at the utter inappropriateness of the words.

🌹

'THAT'S A GORGEOUS piece of clothing,' Dad remarked, coming into the bathroom behind me half an hour later.

I spat out my toothpaste and pulled the hood of my onesie up to give him the full effect. 'Did you notice the tail?'

He looked at it with a sort of horrified fascination, but words failed him and he merely shook his head.

'You scoff now,' I said, 'but we'll see who's laughing in the morning when I'm toasty warm and you've got frostbite.'

He shook his head again. 'I think I'd go for the frostbite.'

'Be nice, or I'll confiscate your heater,' I said sternly.

Dad smiled and reached out for the toothpaste. 'Sold that house yet?' he asked.

'No. I think I'll have to go over and throw my toys for a while.'

'He really is a first-class waste of space, isn't he?'

'Thank you,' I said. It's nice when the people you love share your opinions.

'You're welcome,' Dad said. 'And the cartwheels would seem to imply that the new model's a good thing?'

I looked at him with something close to shock. My father and I have a very satisfactory system in place, based on the unspoken agreement that I won't tell him about my love life and he won't ask. All that sort of carry-on is Mum's department, and she advises Dad on a need-to-know basis. 'Um, yes,' I said.

'Very good,' said Dad and, clearly appalled at having strayed so far into this emotional minefield, he began to brush his teeth with most unnecessary vigour.

Chapter 33

A T SIX O'CLOCK on Friday night Kim came up the driveway in her mother's car and dragged at the handbrake to spin around and shower the lawn in gravel.

'Very cool,' I remarked, picking up the washing basket and propping it on my hip. Especially if you're not the one who mows the lawn.

'I know,' said Kim. 'Matt taught me. How's Aunty Rose?'

'Just the same.' We started back towards the house. 'Are you staying for dinner?'

She shook her head. 'Andy's cooking for me,' she said proudly. 'I'm going to his place.'

'That sounds really nice,' I said.

'Is he a good cook?'

'Well,' I said, 'when I lived with him he alternated between tins of Just Add Mince and Just Add Sausages. But I expect he'll lift his game a little bit for you.'

AUNTY ROSE WAS very tired by dinner time, and as she took her seat at the table I saw that her mouth was tight with pain. I dished her up a spoonful of risotto and she looked at it unhappily for a moment before pushing the plate away.

Matt, cleanshaven this evening although still shaggy as to hair, got up silently and went to the fridge for the vanilla custard. He poured some into a cup and microwaved it for twenty seconds, stirred it with a teaspoon and handed it to his aunt.

'I can't,' she whispered.

'Three spoonfuls,' he said matter-of-factly, taking the cup back and offering spoonful number one.

'Horrible boy,' Aunty Rose murmured, but she opened her mouth.

She managed four teaspoonfuls of custard in total, before pushing herself up to stand with an effort that hurt to watch. 'Don't *fuss*, Edith,' she said between her teeth as Mum got up too.

'I'm not fussing,' said Mum serenely. 'I'm trying to get out of doing the dishes.' She handed Rose the stick that had slid under her chair.

'Well, I must be off,' said Hazel, kissing her sister's cheek. She had dined with us so as not to miss anything, but she preferred to exit gracefully before the clean-up began. 'Goodnight, everyone. Sleep well, Rosie. Matthew, my love, why don't you have an early night seeing as Eric and Edith are here to hold the fort?'

My mother's smile tightened with annoyance at this

slur on her daughter's fort-holding abilities. 'What a good idea!' she said brightly. 'Go home, Matthew, and take Jo with you. Do you think you can put up with being nursed by a couple of amateurs for a night, Rose?'

'I expect I shall muddle through,' said Aunty Rose.

'Very good. Run along, then, kids; we'll see you tomorrow.' And having trumped Hazel she smiled in exactly the same way as the picture of the Cheshire cat in my old copy of *Alice in Wonderland*.

I looked at Matt in mute apology for my parent and saw that he looked not embarrassed but frankly delighted. 'Thanks!' he said. 'Goodnight, guys. Come on, Jose.'

I blushed hotly before two amused smiles and one frozen stare (Dad was carefully inspecting the bottom of the pepper grinder so as to avoid meeting anyone's eye). It was like being a teenager again, and the first time had been bad enough. ''Night,' I muttered, and fled outside without so much as pausing for my toothbrush.

Matt followed me onto the porch at a more leisurely pace, and bent to put on his boots. A morepork called through the dark from somewhere up the hill and the elderly plumbing gurgled as someone turned on the kitchen taps.

'Smooth,' he murmured.

'Oh, shut up,' I whispered back, picking up a gumboot and shaking it hard to dislodge potential wetas before putting it on. The other one had mysteriously vanished – after a brief search Matt discovered it under an ancient tweed coat that had fallen off its nail on the wall.

'Never mind, Hazel,' said Mum, her voice carrying

beautifully from inside. 'They're big kids now.' That woman is not above putting the boot in when her opponent is already down.

'That's all very well,' replied Hazel bitterly. 'But when Josie leaves I'm going to be the one picking up the pieces.'

Her son looked somewhat startled at this prediction, and I giggled as he handed me my second gumboot. He made a face at me.

'Why on earth would she leave?' Mum asked.

'Of course she'll leave! She's used to life in a big city – eating in restaurants and going to nightclubs – she's hardly going to settle down with Matthew on a little dairy farm in Waimanu.'

'Oh yes she will,' said Aunty Rose, her voice a little slurred with pain and tiredness. 'She's pining to.'

I closed my eyes in silent horror. Day five of the relationship is *not* the appropriate time for these revelations.

'Are you?' Matt asked quietly, and I opened my eyes again. He wasn't looking at me but towards the ragged black outline of the woodshed roof against the sky, and he very nearly pulled off a tone of mere idle curiosity.

I started to say something light and dismissive, and then abruptly decided not to. If he'd asked, it was because he wanted to know. 'Yes.'

He looked at me, then, and smiled crookedly. I would cross boundless wastes and scale cliffs for that smile – on reflection it was probably best that Matt didn't know it. Although on further reflection I was pretty sure he did. 'Come on,' he said. 'God only knows what they'll say next.'

We scrunched across the gravel to his ute, ignoring dogs and pig. There was a chainsaw and at least three jumpers in the passenger-side footwell, and an assortment of fencing tools on the seat. 'Really should empty this stuff out, one day,' he said. 'Hang on, I'll chuck it all on the back.'

'It'd be easier to chuck me on the back,' I suggested, picking up a set of wire strainers.

He grinned. 'Tempting,' he said. 'Especially since our mothers'll be watching out the kitchen window.'

We drove the short distance between Aunty Rose's house and his without speaking, got out of the ute and went across the unkempt lawn. A little square of apricot light shone from the tiny washroom window where he had left a light on. We went silently up the back steps; once inside, Matt shut the door behind us and we fitted ourselves neatly together, mouth to mouth and arms tight round each other.

'Twelve whole hours,' I said when I could talk again. 'All by ourselves.'

'I love the way your voice goes all shaky when I kiss you,' he said, resting his forehead against mine. 'You sounded like that the very first time, and I couldn't believe I could do that to you when I'd spent most of my life trying to impress you.'

I smiled, and kissed him again. 'But you were so much cooler than me. Let's face it, you still are.'

'Rubbish,' he said. 'I'm a scruffy dairy cocky who tucks his jeans into his socks.'

'Only slightly scruffy. You did shave.'

'Only because I'm scared of your mother.'

'Very wise,' I said. 'But don't let her cut your hair, will you?'

'God, no! You smell nice, Jose.'

'Like peppermint?' I asked.

He sniffed me. 'No, just like you. Like – like sunshine or something.'

I tightened my arms around his waist. 'What does sunshine smell like?'

'You. *Do* pay attention, Josephine.' He got Aunty Rose's inflection perfectly.

I laughed and kissed him again. 'Can we go to bed now, or do we need to check the cows?'

'We'd better, but maybe we could put it off for a little while.' He detached me and led the way into the kitchen, turning on a few more lights. The place felt chilly and unlived in, the mail was piling up on one side of the counter and the sink was half full of dishes. 'Sorry about the mess,' he said. 'I'd have cleaned the place up a bit if I'd known you were coming.'

'It's fine.'

'Cup of tea before I start taking off your clothes?' he asked politely. 'Except I think I'm out of milk.' He opened the fridge and peered in – inside was the end of a block of cheese, half a pound of butter and the ubiquitous softening carrots that collect at the bottom of everyone's fridge. You probably don't even need to buy them; they just arrive by some mysterious process of inter-refrigerator travel. 'That's poor, for a dairy farmer.'

'Lucky you've got a couple of thousand litres just up the hill,' I said. I shut the fridge door and turned him round to face me, undoing the top button of his jeans. 'No thank you.'

'No thank you?' he repeated blankly.

'I don't want a cup of tea,' I explained.

'Fair enough,' said Matt weakly. And then, as what sounded like a medium-sized tank turned off the road to storm the hill towards the house, 'You have *got* to be kidding.' He vanished hurriedly around the corner into his tiny lounge.

'It's not Cilla, is it?' I hissed, appalled.

'No! It's bloody Scott.'

Scotty wasn't on the bike this evening but driving an enormous jeep-like thing. He is always buying cars off mates, tinkering with their innards and selling them to other mates – you never know from week to week what he'll be driving. He parked, turned off the headlights and clambered out to cross the lawn, a box of bourbon and cola pre-mixes under one arm.

'I suppose he'll stay and drink that entire box of Woodstock he's carrying?' I said.

'Usually. And then he's over the limit, so he sleeps on the couch. Don't worry. We'll tell him to bugger off.'

'We can't,' I said glumly. When it comes down to it you can't actually ask your friends to please go away so you can have sex. Seeing me through the window Scotty waved, and I waved back.

'Watch me.' He came back into the kitchen with his

329

jeans restored to seemly heights as his friend climbed the back steps.

'No, we really can't. He asked me out a few weeks ago.'

'Did he? Sneaky sod.' He sounded amused.

'Evening, people,' said Scotty cheerfully, opening the door and letting himself in. 'Hey, Jo, fancy meeting you here.'

'Hey, Scotty,' I replied. Matt said nothing – being male he was under no obligation to actually be nice to his best mate. 'How's the rat's tail?'

'Mint,' Scott said, stroking the back of his neck. 'Thanks for asking. Shit, it's cold in here. Jo, you wouldn't be able to have a look at my back, would you? I did something funny to it at motocross last weekend.' And without further ado he began to shrug off his denim jacket.

'What d'you think this is?' Matt protested. 'Some sort of free physio clinic for the mentally impaired?'

His friend ignored him. 'Do you want me to take off my shirt too?' he asked.

I laughed helplessly. 'Go on then.'

'You can touch the rat's tail if you want,' Scotty offered, pulling a particularly nasty purple T-shirt over his head.

'Wow,' I said. 'What an offer.'

Matt sighed and went into the laundry, picking his overalls up off the floor and beginning to put them on. 'I'm going round the calving mob,' he said. 'If you could restrain yourself from hitting on my girlfriend while I'm away that'd be nice.'

Scotty twisted round to look at me. 'Is this true?' he demanded. I nodded, and he shook his head in sorrow.

'And you could have had all this,' he said, gesturing towards himself. His chest was very pale and quite hairy, and he had the beginnings of a little potbelly from excessive Woodstock consumption.

'You *are* gorgeous,' I said gravely. 'There's no denying it.'

'Thank you.'

'Lucky she didn't see you without your shirt earlier,' Matt remarked, doing up the zip on his overalls. 'I'd have had no show. Right, chaps, see you in ten minutes.'

'Hang on!' I said. 'Milk.'

'There's a plastic jug somewhere under the sink – that's the one.' He took it, smiled at me and let himself out into the dark.

'Right,' I said briskly. 'So where's it sore?'

'All down the left side.'

'Just when you're up and moving, or does it hurt in bed too?'

'Only when I roll over,' said Scott. 'Then it catches.'

Outside Matt started the quad bike and headed up towards the shed.

'So,' Scott continued, 'you've gone for the King, eh? There's just no helping some people.'

'Scotty,' I said impulsively, 'you're a star.'

'Yep. Hey, you haven't got any hot single friends, have you?'

AN HOUR LATER Scotty put down his second empty bottle of Woodstock, rearranged his pleasant features into a frightening leer and said, 'I'm guessing you two would quite like me to piss off so you can have some alone time?' He put air quotes around 'alone time' with his fingers.

Matt, who was lying full-length on his shabby sofa with his legs across my lap, grinned. 'You guess right,' he said. 'Go on, bugger off.'

'I just hope you'll spare a moment to think of me, going home alone to an empty house . . .'

'With only your rat's tail for company,' I said sadly.

'I'll probably cry myself to sleep.'

'Either that,' Matt agreed, 'or you'll put in a couple of solid hours downloading porn off the internet.'

'I don't know how you could suggest anything so disgusting,' said Scotty piously. 'It hurts, Matthew.' He got up and stretched, revealing an inch of pallid stomach below the edge of his T-shirt. 'Oh, well, goodnight.'

''Night, Scotty,' I said. 'Don't lift anything heavy for a week or two, will you?'

Matt rolled off the couch and followed him out into the kitchen. As the roar of Scott's jeep split the night he came back and held out a hand to help me to my feet.

'Who do you think will pop in next?' I mused.

He smiled. 'They'll be right out of luck. I've locked the door.' And he pulled me down the hall to his room.

❧

MATT ROLLED ONTO his side and reached out to pull me more snugly up against him, finding my mouth with his and kissing me with sleepy contentment. 'What's wrong, love?'

'Nothing.' I ran a hand lightly down his spine and back up again.

'Your face is wet.'

'Just happy.'

'So happy you're crying?'

'Yep,' I said.

'Girls are weird,' he observed.

It was ten forty-seven according to the fluorescent face of the alarm clock beside his bed, and he had to get up at four-thirty. A really nice person would have let him go to sleep, but I couldn't bear to just yet.

'Why did you kiss me on Monday?' I asked.

I felt him smile against my skin. 'Rose told me to.'

'Huh?'

'She told me to stop devouring you with my eyes across the room and jolly well do something a bit more productive,' said Matt.

'Devouring me with your eyes,' I murmured. 'Crikey.'

'I think we'd better cut back her Mills and Boon quota.'

'You might be right.'

'Then,' he continued, 'she said that after your lousy ex-boyfriend's shenanigans you had the self-confidence of a flatworm, and that if I thought I could just say it with hideous nightwear I'd better think again.'

I considered that for a while, wondering whether to be offended. And then I decided that, seeing as I was currently the happiest girl in the observable universe, Aunty Rose could liken me to any invertebrate she liked.

'Thank you for doing what you were told,' I said.

'Never been so scared in my life,' he said. 'And then you looked at me like I was some slimy prat who'd tried to pick you up in a bar.'

'I did not!'

'You did too. It's a bit depressing to find that the girl you love thinks you're a cheating scumbag.'

'Only for about ten seconds,' I said feebly. 'It had been a particularly bad day.'

'Hmph,' said Matt.

I pinched the tender skin under his arm, which was nice and handy. 'Don't you *hmph* me, Matthew King. I've spent the last six months watching you go home with Farmer Barbie, remember.'

'Farmer Barbie?' he repeated.

'Yeah, it's childish, but I was bitter.'

'Jose, I'm really sorry.'

I felt a sudden fierce pang of guilt. Aunty Rose was dying. His mother was of minimal use, so it was Matt who taught Kim to drive and shouted at her and worried about her and generally did all the things parents are supposed to do. He was the adored son and heir, and all his life he had known he'd have to take over the family farm or break his father's heart. I don't think it ever even crossed anyone's mind to ask him if it was what he wanted. He worked twelve hours a day, seven days a week, and he never complained – he just quietly got on with it. It's inexcusable to give someone like that a hard time for failing to guess the state of your emotions.

'It doesn't matter,' I whispered. 'I'm sorry.' I rolled us

both over so that I was lying on top of him, and hugged him fiercely. 'You know that Rudyard Kipling poem "If"?'

'What about it, you strange and random woman?'

'It's you. It describes you.'

Matt laughed. 'Sometimes, Josephine,' he said, 'I wonder about you.'

IT FELT LIKE about two minutes later when his radio alarm clock clicked on, and we were woken by some pillock assuring us that nothing beats a car from McGuire's super-cheap imports. I fell out of my side of the bed and groped blindly for clothes.

'Don't get up,' he said thickly. 'It's Saturday. Stay in bed.'

I banged my head on the corner of his dresser and sat down hard. 'Shit.'

Matt turned on the light and we blinked at each other painfully. 'You don't have to come,' he said, reaching for a shirt.

'I want to. Have you got a spare pair of overalls?'

'Yeah.' He dug through the heap of clothes in the corner of the room and tossed me a pair, along with a polar fleece. 'Socks?'

'Yes, please.'

It was very dark outside, still and crisp and starless. Matt stopped the quad bike at the cowshed to turn on the lights, and then taking a big torch from the box on the front played the beam slowly across the neighbouring paddock. Cows' eyes glowed green in the torchlight, and one very new calf was just staggering to its feet.

'Good,' he said. 'Nobody lying upside down in the hedge. Shut the gate across the track, Jo?'

SEVERAL HOURS LATER I kicked off my gumboots and went into Aunty Rose's kitchen, newspaper in hand.

'Good morning, love,' said Mum, pouring tea into her cup. 'Did you have fun?'

'Good grief, Edith, what a question!' Aunty Rose said. She was reclining on the chaise longue with a pen in one hand and pad in the other, wrapped in a fluffy green blanket. 'Is that the paper, sweet pea?'

'It's a bit damp,' I said, peeling off the wrapping and handing it over. 'He got it right into the drain this morning. Where's Dad?'

'In the ceiling,' said Mum. 'Looking for leaks. Oh, Graeme rang.' She cradled her teacup in both hands and looked at me over the top with a wicked smile.

'What about?' I asked.

'Grammar, Josephine,' Aunty Rose murmured.

'I've no idea what he wanted,' said Mum. 'His exact words were: "Babe, we need to talk."'

Babe? I think the last time I was addressed as 'babe' was after about seventeen tequila shots at the Martini Lounge the night Graeme got his residency. Maybe Chrissie had traded him in.

'Personally I prefer "love",' Mum said. 'That's what

Matthew calls you when *he* rings. Anyway, I told Graeme you were spending the night with Matthew and he'd have to call back another time. Rose, what time is Art Cooper coming to get the chickens?'

'Mid-morning. Do you think he might like a dog to go with them?' She spoke lightly, but kept her face down to hide her expression.

'Don't split them up,' I said impulsively. 'I'll look after them, I promise. And Percy.'

'Sweet pea,' said Aunty Rose gently, 'you don't want four dogs and a pig on your hands.'

'I do.' Well, I'd rather that than have Aunty Rose break her heart trying to rehome them.

'Matthew *certainly* won't.'

I smiled at her. 'He'll learn to love it.'

'My goodness, Josephine, you grow more like your mother every day,' said Aunty Rose.

'That was a compliment,' said Mum. 'Just in case you didn't notice.' She reached for my hand and pressed it for a moment.

There was an ominous-sounding crash from above, and a shower of plaster fell.

'Eric?' Mum called. 'What *are* you doing up there?'

'Trying not to fall through the ceiling, dear,' Dad answered, his voice just a little curt.

'Jo, love, why don't you take him to town?' said Mum. 'I've written out a list – it will be good for him to get out for a while.'

'WHAT DID ANDY make you for dinner?' I asked that afternoon.

Kim sat back on her heels and smiled. We were picking daffodils for Aunty Rose's room, the old-fashioned ragged double kind that grow along the orchard fence. 'Pasta,' she said. 'Lemon and chicken pasta, with salad and garlic bread.'

'Wow.' I hadn't realised Andy was capable of such lofty culinary heights.

'It was burnt,' Kim said. 'It all stuck on the bottom, and so he scraped it off with a wooden spoon and there were little flakes of charcoal all through it. And the garlic bread was still frozen in the middle when he unwrapped it.'

Ah. So he *wasn't* capable of such lofty culinary heights. 'How was the salad?'

'Fancy lettuce leaves out of a bag, but they were a bit old and they'd gone sort of slimy.' She laid down her daffodils and abandoned herself to laughter. 'So we went to McDonald's.'

'It does sound like he tried really hard.'

'Yeah,' said Kim, smiling in a misty sort of way. 'And I like chicken nuggets, anyway.'

Chapter 34

'BYE, MUM.' I hugged her hard, hiding my face for just a second in her warm shoulder. I was grown up, and presumably fairly capable by now, but it had been such a relief *not* to be the one who's supposed to know what to do when things go wrong, just for a little while. 'Thank you.'

Mum smiled at me, tucking the hair back behind my ears like she used to when I was six. 'We are so proud of you,' she said. 'Aren't we, Eric?'

'Hmm?' Dad said vaguely, slotting the last suitcase into the tiny space available in the boot of a Toyota Yaris. 'I suppose she's moderately satisfactory, as daughters go.'

'There you are,' said Mum. 'Fulsome praise from your father. I am confidently expecting an epitaph reading "Could have been worse".' She sighed. 'Well, love, I'll be back in a few weeks. Or maybe earlier.' She wiped her eyes impatiently on a scrap of tissue.

'I've put a bit of money in your account to help with the flights,' I said.

'Jo, love –'

'Look, you can pay me back if it turns out you don't need it.' Early spring is a particularly lean time of year for those who earn their living from seasonal milk production. 'You'd better go, or you'll miss your plane.' I kissed Dad's cheek as he opened the driver's-side door. 'See you soon.'

A FEW DAYS later I went down the hall from Aunty Rose's room to check the progress of tonight's casserole and found Matt leaning against the living-room sideboard, reading something in the dim light from the hall.

'Hey,' he said, closing his book hastily and standing up straight. 'How's the wood situation?'

'We've got heaps.' I looked round him towards the faded cloth cover of the book, and he stepped sideways to block my view.

'Nosy, aren't you?' he murmured, bending his head to kiss me.

I smiled and kissed him back, slipping my hands up under his sweatshirt against the warm skin of his back. Then, attempting to emulate a sexy undercover KGB agent from a Bond movie, I eased one hand back down again and grabbed the book behind him. 'Hah!' I said in triumph, twisting out of his arms to examine it.

'You're such an egg,' Matt informed me.

I put Aunty Rose's *Kipling's Verse* back on the sideboard

and leant my forehead against his shoulder, touched by his actions if not his words. 'I love you.'

'You're still an egg.' He kissed the side of my neck. 'Is Rose awake?'

'She's going to get up for dinner – she's just having a nap first.'

WE WERE SHARING the chaise longue and the paper when a car roared up the hill.

'Finished with the sports section?' Matt asked.

'Trade you for world news.'

'Libya's still a mess, and the French farmers are rioting.'

'Why?' I asked, handing over the rugby page.

'Didn't bother to read that far,' he said. 'Just to pass the time, I expect.'

Kim opened the kitchen door and came in, Andy behind her. 'How's Aunty Rose?' she asked.

'Getting up for dinner, she thought,' I said. 'Just napping in the meantime.'

She nodded. 'Cool. Is there enough for us?'

'Heaps. Hi, Andy.' I swung my legs over Matt's to stand up. 'Anyone got any objection to peas and carrots?'

'Peas are such a cop-out vegetable,' Kim remarked. 'Remove from freezer, put in pot, boil for about three minutes.'

'You forgot the most important step,' her brother told her. 'Add butter.'

'Just about every known food can be improved by adding butter,' I said dreamily. 'Or lemon juice and sugar. Or both.'

Andy shook his head. 'Not pizza,' he said. 'Or ice cream.'

'Have you never buttered the back of a piece of cold pizza?' Matt asked, reshuffling the paper into some form of order. 'You should. Jo, what have you done with the TV guide?'

'You had that section,' I said. 'Look harder.'

Kim snorted. 'Man, you two are pathetic. You've been going out for a week, and you act like you've been married for twenty years.'

I made my way to the freezer to hunt for frozen peas. 'Yes,' I agreed, 'but you forget, Kimmy, that by the time you get to our age passion comes a distant second to companionship.'

As he located and perused the TV guide, Matt tucked the corners of his mouth in firmly, and managed quite a reasonable impression of a man who would never *dream* of deflecting someone into the woodshed on her way in from the washing line to have sex against a stack of logs. A little splintery, but entirely worth it.

'Would you like me to cut up a carrot or two?' Andy offered.

'That'd be great,' I said, opening the oven door and prodding a baked potato to see how soft it was. Aunty Rose's bell rang and I straightened up again, but Kim had already whisked down the hall.

Andy unearthed a bag of carrots from the recesses of

the fridge and put them on the table. 'Where's the chopping board?'

Matt passed it to him and began, in a leisurely sort of way, to set the table. 'Did you get anything last night?' he asked. Andy had, to the amazement of those who knew her, convinced Kim that crawling around in the wet dark with a spotlight and a rifle would be a fun way to spend Tuesday evening.

'One rabbit and four possums,' said Andy. 'The possums were all hanging out around that pond below the cowshed, eating the new willow growth.'

'How many did you see?'

Andy smiled as he began to decapitate carrots. 'One rabbit and four possums,' he repeated with quiet satisfaction. 'It's a lovely little pond – do you go out after ducks?'

'Scotty and I usually wander out on opening morning,' said Matt. 'We're not very serious about it.'

'Serious duck shooting has a few major drawbacks,' I observed.

'Like having to eat ducks?'

'That's one. And pluck ducks.' Of course, turkeys are worse; not only are they as ugly as sin but more often than not they're crawling with lice. And they're bigger than ducks, which means more of them to eat.

'I like duck,' said Andy mildly.

'Come out next year, if you like,' Matt offered.

Andy smiled, presumably at this vote of confidence in his chances at still being around next May. 'Cool,' he said.

343

IT WAS AFTER eight and Andy had gone home when Hazel opened the kitchen door and came in with a rush, not bothering to remove her shoes. 'Is Kim here?' she demanded, with most un-Hazel-like crispness.

'She and Matt are in Aunty Rose's room,' I said, giving the table top a final swipe with a cloth and going to the sink to rinse it out.

Hazel trotted purposefully across the room. She paused as she reached the hall and looked back for a second. 'Josie, dear, do you really think you should let that dog eat table scraps off the good china?'

I probably shouldn't, but he had looked at me with big brown eyes brimful of hope, and I'm a sucker. I hung up my dishcloth, left Hazel's muddy footprints in the hope she might notice them on the way out and feel ashamed, and followed her up the hall.

'*There* you are, Kim,' she said as she reached Aunty Rose's door. 'Come along – we're going home. Hello, Matthew, love.'

Kim had been reading aloud, curled on the bed beside her aunt. She put the book face down on the peacock-coloured bedspread and frowned at her mother. 'It's okay,' she said. 'I handed in my English assignment today.'

'I don't want to argue about it; I want you to do as you're told. Say goodnight to your aunt.'

'What on *earth* is your problem?' Kim demanded.

Stretched in the armchair at the foot of the bed, Matt winced.

'I don't appreciate that tone of voice, young lady. If I ask you to do something I expect it to be done.'

'What's the matter, Hazel?' Aunty Rose asked tiredly.

Hazel drew herself up to her full five foot three and reached into her handbag. '*This* is the matter,' she said, flourishing a box of condoms before our startled eyes.

'*Mum!*' Kim cried.

'Well?'

Kim opened and shut her mouth for a while without making any sound, and finally managed in an indignant croak, 'How dare you go through my drawers?'

'You're living under my roof, and the contents of your drawers are my business.'

'That's right,' said Matt unexpectedly. His sister gaped at him, and he continued, 'Drawers are fair game. I can't believe you haven't got a better hiding place than that.'

'Matthew, be quiet,' snapped his mother. 'Kim, I am *extremely* disappointed in you. Now get up, and come home.'

'No,' said Kim, not defiantly but with a calm consideration that must have made her mother want to slap her.

'You listen to me, young lady –' Hazel started.

'Mum, settle down,' said Matt. 'I gave them to her.'

'*You* gave . . .' She trailed off, shoulders bowed in despair. 'Really, Matthew – your poor father would be spinning in his grave.'

'It would have to be in his urn,' murmured Kim, heaping fuel on the flames of her mother's wrath. 'Just like a tiny little dust storm.'

Aunty Rose frowned at her and she had the grace to look ashamed of herself.

'I doubt he's spinning at all,' said Matt. 'He gave a box to me, so I thought I'd better continue the tradition.'

'It's a *completely* different situation!' Hazel cried. 'You're a man, you're expected to –' She stopped abruptly.

'Sow his wild oats?' I suggested, unable to help myself.

Kim giggled, and Aunty Rose frowned at me in turn.

'Let's have a cup of tea,' she said. 'Kim, you can make it, seeing as you're in disgrace.'

Hazel sank into a chair. '*What* am I to do with that child?' she demanded. 'She doesn't confide in me – she *certainly* doesn't listen to a word I say . . .'

'Of course not,' said Aunty Rose. 'You're merely her mother.' And because she was Aunty Rose she didn't add that storming into a sickroom brandishing a box of condoms is unlikely to induce a girl to go to her mother for relationship advice.

Chapter 35

'WHAT A DAY,' said Matt the following evening, stretching out beside his aunt on top of the bedspread and folding his arms beneath his head.

'What happened, sweet pea?'

'Hmm,' he said. 'Two heifers with mastitis, the met weather reckons we'll get a hundred mil of rain overnight, lost a silage bale through a fence . . . oh, and the pump's playing up.'

Aunty Rose smiled, just a twitch at one side of her mouth. 'And yet people extol the virtues of the farming lifestyle.'

'What people?' Matt asked.

I tucked my feet up under me in the chair. 'The same people who come for lunch and stand on the lawn telling you about the peace and tranquillity of the countryside, when you got up at five in the morning to get all the stock work done before they arrived.'

'Yeah,' he said. 'I know those people. They have every weekend off and go home at five o'clock every night, and tell you they're exhausted by the rat race and that they envy you.'

The wind rose sharply and the first raindrops hit the window with angry-sounding splats. 'Here comes your storm, Matthew,' said Aunty Rose.

'Goody,' he said morosely.

I smiled at him. 'If you're really nice I'll let you borrow the onesie to wear underneath your waterproof leggings.'

'Excellent plan,' said Aunty Rose. 'Take it off her and drop it down a deep hole. She's wedded to the horrible thing.'

'Do you wear it, Jose?' he asked.

'Damn straight. I'd wear it to work if Cheryl would let me. Want to see it?' I got up without waiting for an answer and went to put it on.

He raised his head when I came back into the room, looked me up and down and began to laugh.

'Do you like it?' I asked, doing a little twirl.

'It surpasses all my wildest hopes.'

'Thank you,' I said demurely, sitting back down and crossing one mustard polar fleece–clad leg over the other.

Aunty Rose sighed and shifted her head on the pillow.

'Pills?' I asked.

'Not yet,' she said, and there was a comfortable silence while we listened to the wind howling round the eaves of the old house.

'I believe the boy's asleep,' she said softly not long after.

'He looks very peaceful, doesn't he?' I said. 'Should we wake him up and send him out into the rain?' This had settled, now, into a persistent steady downpour – I wondered how the newly patched roof would hold up.

'Not just yet.' She turned her head painfully and looked at the lean brown face beside her. 'I used to get up to him in the night when he was tiny. It doesn't seem very long ago. He was such a funny scrap – bald as an egg with great surprised brown eyes, and he would hold his little arms out to me and coo.' A tear ran down each wasted cheek. 'I used to pretend he was mine.'

My heart gave a little savage twist. 'He was,' I said. 'He still is.'

'Sometimes Pat was getting up to milk, and he would make a cup of tea while I gave Matthew his bottle.'

I blinked hard. They would have sat in Pat and Hazel's ugly kitchen, not talking; drinking their tea and cuddling the baby and pretending for just a little while that there was no Hazel sleeping down the hall.

'Sweet pea,' said Rose gently. 'It was all a very long time ago. Don't look so tragic.'

I nodded, and pressed my eyes against my fuzzy mustard-coloured knees.

She raised her voice. 'Matthew, my love, wake up. You'd best go and see to your cows.'

'Don't want to,' he muttered, not opening his eyes but stretching his arms above his head.

'Life is hard,' said Aunty Rose. 'Chop chop.'

'Alright, woman, I'm getting there.' He rolled to his feet and came around the edge of the bed to kiss her cheek. 'And now will you take your bloody pills?'

'I will,' she said, reaching up with a shaky hand to touch his cheek. 'Goodnight, sweet pea.'

''Night, Aunty Rose,' said Matt. 'See you tomorrow.' He reached for my hand and pulled me to my feet.

In the kitchen he took my face in his hands and kissed me, and then held me tight against him. 'You weren't asleep, were you?' I asked, and he shook his head. I hugged him, hard.

'Thank you,' he said.

'You're welcome. Why?'

'For – for understanding that not everything needs to be discussed.'

'That's what comes of being raised by a man who tries never to discuss *anything*.'

'Good man, your father.'

I smiled. 'I'm sorry you had such a lousy day.'

He rested his forehead against mine. 'It wasn't,' he said quietly. 'I was thinking about you.'

Having kissed me goodnight in a comprehensive sort of way, he let himself out into the rain. I took an armful of stock pots and preserving pans and went on a little tour of the house, ending back in Rose's room. 'Dad's fixed the leak in the hall,' I announced, 'but the one in the end toilet is much worse.'

'Don't tell him,' Aunty Rose said. 'He was trying so hard to be helpful. Help me to the bathroom, sweet pea?'

I did, weaving our way around pots, and then helped her into one of the adult nappies we had got from the district nurse. 'Not very dignified, is it?' she remarked.

'Who cares? No-one can see it, and your nightie's pretty.'

'You're a good nurse, Josephine.'

'Now *that*,' I said, 'is a serious compliment, coming from you.'

'Like having Delia Smith praise your scones?'

Aunty Rose's scones were small windowless buildings – if you could manage to worry one down it sat and sulked at the bottom of your stomach for hours, impervious to the processes of digestion. I giggled, and she said haughtily, 'My scones are very nice.'

'We could bury you with a batch,' I suggested as we went slowly back down the hall. 'And if archaeologists opened your grave thousands of years in the future they'd find them there, just as good as on the day they were cooked.'

'Ill-mannered wench,' Aunty Rose said. She sank onto the edge of her bed and reached up to touch my cheek as she had Matt's. 'I'm glad the pair of you finally sorted yourselves out.'

I smiled at her. '*You* sorted us out, didn't you?'

'I swore I wouldn't interfere, but I couldn't stand it any longer.'

'Thank you,' I said soberly.

'You're welcome. Honestly, Josephine, for an intelligent girl you can be appallingly dim at times. Couldn't you have fluttered your eyelashes at the poor boy?'

'He had a girlfriend!'

Aunty Rose dismissed poor Cilla with a flick of the wrist. 'He would have sent her packing months ago if you'd given him any encouragement. However.' She lowered herself back against her pillows with a little grunt.

I had learnt by now not to remark on her pain, and merely pressed two pills out of their wrapping in an off-hand sort of way.

'I *said* I'd take them,' said Aunty Rose. 'Leave them on the bedside table.'

'Yes, Aunty Rose,' I said meekly.

'Humouring the invalid?'

'Yep.'

'Go away and let the invalid sleep,' she said. And then, as I reached the door, 'Josephine, I can't tell you what it's meant to me to have you here.'

Chapter 36

I WAS WOKEN by a long, drawn-out, fingernails-down-a-blackboard screech that cut through the background roar of the storm. For a few seconds I lay listening to the insistent slam made by a sheet of corrugated iron that had shed most of its nails and was making a bid for freedom from the roof. Then I opened my eyes, which made not the slightest difference to the view, sat up and groped for the bedside light switch.

Nothing happened, and I flicked the switch back and forth a few times before gathering enough wit to realise it wasn't going to work. I got up instead and felt my way towards the door of the Pink Room. The main light switch by the door didn't work either, which meant the power must be out. Presumably at least one tree was down across the line.

Trailing the fingertips of one hand along the wall I made my way down the hall to the kitchen. Of course the lights didn't work there either, but embers flared in the glass-fronted wood stove as gusts howled down the chimney, filling the room with a flickering pinkish light. Spud met me at the door and pushed a wet nose into my hand.

'I hope we're not going to lose the whole roof,' I told him, and he gave a short hoarse bark.

I would have to go out there and look, I supposed, and probably call Matt to come and help pin the roof back down again. Lucky Matt. But first I would go and see Aunty Rose – even after her pills she couldn't possibly be sleeping through that demented crashing overhead.

I retrieved the big torch from its cupboard above the microwave and turned it on, then went down the hall to the end bedroom.

'Aunty Rose,' I hissed, opening the door and thinking for about the three hundredth time that I really must oil it so it didn't squeak like something in the Addams Family home. I aimed the torch at her feet rather than her head so as not to blind the poor woman. 'Are you awake?'

Her eyes were closed and her velvet-capped head lolled on the pillow. It looked horribly uncomfortable.

'Aunty Rose?'

It was then that I noticed the bottle on the floor, lying on its side in a little dark puddle and filling the room with the rich alcoholic smell of port. And quarter of a second after that I saw the scatter of empty foil pill-sheets on the bedspread beside her right hand. *Oh, dear Lord*, I thought. *She wouldn't. Aunty Rose wouldn't do that* . . . The torch fell from a hand made clumsy by shock. I bent to retrieve it and dropped it again before finally managing to force my stiff fingers to grasp the thing. Straightening, I took her by a fragile bony shoulder and shook her gently.

She was limp and unresponsive. 'Aunty Rose!' I said sharply.

From somewhere above came another rending metallic screech as, presumably, the loose sheet of corrugated iron parted company with the roof. At the same time a flurry of raindrops hurled themselves at the window.

Putting the torch down on the bedside table I picked up her hand and felt for the pulse in her wrist. I couldn't find it, but she might still be alive. I could try CPR, and mouth to mouth, and call an ambulance . . . I had placed both hands, one on top of the other, on her chest before it occurred to me not to be so bloody stupid.

Aunty Rose loathed the indignity of her illness – she had waited this long merely to organise her affairs and ours to her satisfaction. And then, in the capable, orderly manner she applied to everything in her life (with the obvious exception of cookery), she had left us. Even if it were possible to resuscitate her – and knowing Aunty Rose, she'd have made damned sure it wasn't – I couldn't do it.

Stepping back, I pointed the torch at her chest. I watched for quite a long time as the storm howled around the old house, but there was no movement of breath under the peacock-coloured bedspread. I straightened her head on the pillow and carefully rearranged her cap before bending to pick up the bottle on the floor.

There was a piece of folded notepaper beside the port bottle, half hidden by the satin fringe of the bedspread. Spud was barking down the hall and another sheet of corrugated iron slapped insistently on the roof, but I ignored the noise and sank into the armchair to read the note.

Aunty Rose had written to me quarterly ever since I left home for university, keeping me up to date with her skirmishes with the mayor ('the man's a complete tit, Josephine'), Matt's latest adventures and the state of her tomato crop. Her letters were always scrawled firmly on that flimsy blue airmail paper that is almost a collector's item in this age of email, and due to the author's habit of dealing with her correspondence over breakfast they were usually filled with toast crumbs. The writing of this letter, though, was faint and thready, as if the effort of holding the pen had been almost too much for the writer.

My dear Josephine,

This is not suicide; it is simply the desire to spare us all the discomfort of my final nose-dive towards the grave. I have thoroughly enjoyed my life. I rather expected to enjoy another thirty years, but there you have it.

Having already asked far more of you than is reasonable, I do not hesitate to ask still more. Please remove the evidence before calling Rob Milne to pronounce me dead. I do not envisage him asking any awkward questions, but if he does, show him this note. He is a decent chap with far too much sense to subject you all to a coroner's inquiry.

Matthew will inherit the house and land, and Kim my

jewellery and savings. My only specific bequests to you are four
dogs and one pig, but mentally I have bracketed you with Mat-
thew. I confess I have bracketed you with Matthew for some time.
    My best love to you all,
    Rose

I laughed through my tears and, carefully refolding the
note, put it into the pocket of my much-maligned onesie.
Trust Aunty Rose to sweep out of life with a last grand gesture rather than just dwindling into oblivion. Never have
I known a person with such flair or courage or kindness,
or with such boundless tolerance – or, come to think of it,
such a boundless capacity for wine. We were going to miss
her terribly.

Torch in hand I strode down the hall to the kitchen.
I collected a black plastic rubbish sack, a bar of Sard Wonder Soap, an armful of towels and the kettle, and went
back to Aunty Rose's room to remove the evidence.

Ten minutes later I sat back on my heels and shone my
torch at the piece of carpet that had been stained with port.
I had wet it and soaped it and jumped up and down on
a towel to wick up the moisture, and now not the merest
trace of a stain remained. I was quite a good accessory
after the fact – perhaps if I tired of physiotherapy I could
turn to crime. Or, more realistically, to carpet cleaning.

I collected up the empty foil sheets of pain medication
and the port bottle, peered under the bed in case I'd missed
any foil sheets, and played the torch slowly around the
room. Everything was peaceful and neat, and the sequins

on the bedspread glinted softly in the torchlight. I bent
and kissed the still face on the pillow, swiped the back of a
hand across my wet eyes and pulled the door shut behind
me. I would put the towels in the wash and the pill packets
down the offal hole, and then discover the body at seven
and call the doctor.

From outside there was another of those ghastly
screeches that sounded like someone trying to dismember
a live piglet with a hacksaw, but I had lost all interest in the
state of the roof.

When I came back into the kitchen Spud was at the
door, still barking. 'It's okay, Spud, I can hear it too.' And
shooting back the bolt on the kitchen door I opened it and
stepped out onto the porch, black plastic rubbish bag in
one hand and torch in the other.

Spud pushed past me and stopped dead, growling.

'*Spud!*' I protested, stepping into my gumboots and
dragging Aunty Rose's ancient oilskin off its peg. A gust of
wind caught it as I tried to put it on and it flapped wildly.
'Would you please *move*, idiot dog?' The torch beam swept
across the back lawn as I wrestled with the oilskin, briefly
catching a figure that cowered away from the light, and I
screamed in terror.

It barely looked human. It was some kind of malevolent goblin, and beside it crouched a shapeless dark blot
like the gebbeth in *A Wizard of Earthsea*. I clutched at my
chest just like a heroine in one of Graeme's over-acted
cult horror films before realising that the blot was in fact
covered with ginger bristles. It was just Percy, and Percy

wouldn't be consorting with the forces of evil. I steadied my torch hand and the goblin turned into the drenched figure of Bob McIntosh, spotlighted against the wood-shed door.

'Bob?' I called. I dropped my incriminating black sack and stepped off the porch into the driving rain, pulling Aunty Rose's oilskin tight around me.

I thought for a moment he was going to turn and flee, but instead he shrank back against the side of the wood-shed. Spud stood stiffly at my side, and Percy waddled forward to snuffle at the pocket of the oilskin for possible treats. As a guard pig he was a miserable failure; surely the very first rule is *not* to fraternise with the prowler. Of course the price of Percy's cooperation is pretty low – my estimate would be one chocolate biscuit.

'What are you doing here?' I demanded, shining the torch at Bob. He put up a shaking hand to block the light, and I lowered the torch just a fraction.

'I – I just came to see if you were alright,' he quavered.

'And how is skulking round the house going to tell you that?'

'I just wanted to check . . .'

'To check *what*?' I spat.

'Your roof,' said Bob, his eyes lifting to the house behind me in sudden inspiration. 'You've lost some iron off the roof. The rain will come in.'

'Yes,' I said coldly. 'Thank you. Go away.'

He took a sudden step forward and I retreated, star-tled. 'You shouldn't be outside in this awful weather, Josie.

359

Now, let's go inside and have a nice cup of tea, hmm?' He reached out as if to lay a hand on my arm and I backed off another step.

'Josie,' he said, 'I just want to look after you.'

'Bob,' I said firmly, 'skulking round in the dark isn't looking after someone. It's *sick*. Go *away*!' And I think I even stamped my foot for extra emphasis.

His smile never wavered, although the rain was streaming off the end of his nose and plastering his sparse hair against his scalp. 'Now, now, Josie. Don't let's get worked up, or we might wake your poor sick aunty. And we wouldn't want that, would we? We wouldn't want to scare the poor lady.'

At that, I got properly angry. 'Get away from me,' I said bitingly. 'Go away, you poisonous little worm, or I'll call the police.'

'The phone's sure to be out,' Bob informed me. 'Now, Josie . . .' He reached out and grasped me by the elbow, and I kicked him squarely in the groin. He crumpled onto the wet grass, and I felt nothing but satisfaction.

Bob made a high-pitched wheezing noise then pushed himself shakily onto his hands and knees before staggering to his feet. He tottered around the side of the woodshed and let himself out through the wooden gate under the walnut tree. I watched him vanish into the rainy dark without the smallest twinge of remorse.

I marched back to the house, picked up the rubbish bag and carried it across to the offal hole. Dragging back the heavy concrete cover I dropped it in. Evidence removed.

Turning, I shone the torch up at the roof. At least two sheets of iron had been peeled back to expose the naked beams beneath and a trailing length of guttering flapped scarf-like in the wind. It was as if the old house, without its mistress, lacked the heart or strength to defy the elements any longer and was giving up the unequal struggle. I shivered, suddenly tearful and forlorn rather than invigorated by righteous fury, and Spud pressed his wet body comfortingly against my leg.

I stroked the broad grizzled head and followed him across the lawn to the kitchen door. I opened it and he trotted in, stopping in the middle of the floor to shake himself briskly before retiring to his Spiderman beanbag by the stove. I snatched my keys and phone off the bench and ran down the path to my car. Matt was only just across the road, warm and reassuring and entirely capable of dealing with the situation. He would know what to do about the roof, and if Bob managed to extract his testicles from somewhere up by his liver and came back bent on revenge he would know what to do about that too.

Chapter 37

I BARRELLED DOWN Aunty Rose's drive in my little car, shot out across the road and spun left up Matt's tanker track. As I breasted the last slope something loomed out of the darkness in front of the car. I stamped hard on the brakes and slid to a halt about a foot away from the quad bike, abandoned at the edge of the track.

Leaping out of the car I scanned the immediate surroundings and failed to find Matt either lying unconscious in the ditch or wandering the open hillside. *Bob*, I thought wildly. *Bob's got him.* And a vision presented itself to my overwrought brain, of Matt lying in a patch of scrub with blood from his multiple stab wounds congealing around him.

Or, I thought, dragging myself back from the brink of hysteria, *the bike stopped and he had to leave it there*. It might pay to at least check he wasn't safe in bed before falling to my knees and rending the onesie in grief and despair.

I leapt back into the car, attempted a handbrake start

and promptly stalled. Idiot. Okay, handbrake engaged, clutch in, turn the key – *there* you go. Around the bike, turn in at Matt's gate, pull up behind the ute, just here . . . Again I leapt out of the car, and dashed across the lawn to hammer breathlessly on the back door. 'Matt! *Matt!*'

The door was unlocked, and kicking off my gumboots I stumbled in, torch in hand. 'Matt!'

There was no answer, and when I reached his bedroom door to shine the torch across the empty unmade bed I nearly *did* crumple despairingly to my knees. He had left Aunty Rose's at nine, and he must have got home because the ute was here, but he hadn't made it back in after checking the cows. It was – I checked my watch in the torchlight – quarter to four now. Where the hell *was* he?

I went slowly back up the hall to the untidy kitchen and leant against the bench with my head in my hands. The wind had dropped and the only sound was the steady relentless drumming of rain on the roof. There must of course be some perfectly logical explanation for Matt's absence, if I could only think of it. Of *course* Bob McIntosh hadn't murdered him in a frenzy of insane jealousy – that sort of thing doesn't actually happen to ordinary people. *I bet*, said a small cold voice inside my head, *that* everyone *who ends up in the middle of a homicide investigation thought it could never happen to them.*

I suppose it was only a minute or so before I pushed myself up straight and wiped my nose Amber-like on the back of my hand. I would go to the cowshed. Perhaps Matt was calving a cow. Or – or cleaning the vat. At quarter to four in the morning. And from the shed I'd go next door to his mother's, and if he wasn't there – although I realised with a spasm of relief that of *course* he would be; she'd have summoned him to deal with some storm-related crisis – we'd call the police.

THE COWSHED WAS dark, and silent except for one calf that bawled sleepily back when I shouted. I drove far too fast back down the wet track, my fingers clenched white on the steering wheel. I swerved around the bike and out onto the road, and lost control for a terrifying second as I met a sheet of surface water. Grimly I straightened the car and continued up the road to the King homestead.

The house was dark, and I realised suddenly that if Matt was here he'd surely have come in the ute. Which was still at his place. But I got out, seeing as I was here, and ran up the path to the back door.

I pounded on the door and then grabbed the handle to try it. They'd never hear me over the rain – I'd have to bang on bedroom windows and frighten them out of their skins – but the door opened beneath my hand and pitched me forward into the hall. 'Hazel! *Hazel!* Kim! *Matt!*' I groped for a light switch and found that the power was out here too.

Torch in hand I searched the house, carefully opening every door although it was obvious nobody was home. The curtains were drawn and the beds neatly made up, and in

Kim's room a battalion of stuffed animals looked incuriously back at me from the armchair under the window.

With shaking hands I pulled my phone out of my pocket and scrolled through the numbers. Matt's number rang out, so I tried Hazel. 'Hello?' she said tremulously, answering on the second ring, and I nearly dropped the phone in relief.

'Hazel,' I said, 'it's Jo.'

'Oh, *Josie*,' Hazel wailed.

'Where are you?' I asked.

'At the hospital. Waikato.'

'Where's Matt?'

Hazel began softly and piteously to cry. I slid down the wall of her hallway – my legs didn't seem to want to hold me up. 'Is – is he dead?' My voice came out as a hoarse croak, which was all I could manage from a throat stiff with horror. His mother continued to sob brokenheartedly into the other end of the phone, and I wondered dully just how on earth I was going to keep breathing without him.

'*Josie! JOSIE!*'

I started, and picked up my phone from where it had dropped into my lap.

'*JOSIE!*' Kim howled into my ear.

'What?' I asked numbly.

'Matt's been hurt. He's just come out of surgery.'

Hurt. Not dead. The relief rose up in my throat and nearly choked me.

'Josie? Are you there?'

365

'He's not dead?' I gasped.

'No. *No!* He's got some broken ribs, and they were worried about internal bleeding or something, but they seem to think it's stopped. Liver lacerations, the doctor said.'

'It was Bob,' I told her.

'Bob? What was Bob?'

'Who hurt Matt,' I said stupidly.

'It wasn't Bob,' said Kim. 'It was Cilla.'

'Cilla?' I repeated blankly. What on earth was Cilla doing lurking in the stormy darkness, bent on murder? I wouldn't have thought she'd have it in her.

'She hit him on the drive.'

'What with?' Scythe? Spade? Manicure scissors? Nothing in this whole horrible nightmare made any sense whatsoever.

'Her ute,' Kim said, in a careful voice. 'She didn't see him in time – she ran into the bike. Josie, are you alright?'

'No!' I said wildly. 'I couldn't find Matt, or you guys, and Aunty Rose is dead, and – and Bob McIntosh was skulking round outside the house, and . . .' And at that point I lost it completely and burst into tears.

It was an inexcusable thing to do to an eighteen-year-old who was already propping up a hopeless mother. There was a brief pause on the other end of the line, and then Kim murmured very softly, 'Is she really?'

'Y-yes,' I wept. 'Kim, I'm s-sorry . . .'

'Oh, thank God,' whispered Kim, which was unexpected. But then she added, 'She'd have been so worried.'

From somewhere behind her came Hazel's voice, shrill with anxiety. 'Kimmy? What's wrong?'

'Hang *on*, Mum,' said Kim impatiently. 'Josie, what did you mean about Bob?'

'It's okay,' I said, taking a long shaky breath. 'I kicked him, and he ran away.'

'You *what*?'

'Kicked him. In the balls. I think he's been hanging around the house at night.' I shuddered; the idea of having Bob McIntosh observe my love life made me want to take a nice hot bath with caustic soda and a wire brush.

There was another pause as Kim digested this. 'Where are you now?' she asked.

'At your place.'

'Lock yourself in – Mum, be *quiet*, I'll tell you in a *minute* – Josie, I'll call you as soon as we've spoken to Matt's doctor, okay?'

'Okay,' I said obediently.

I put down the phone, rested my forehead on my knees and cried. It seemed, just lately, to be my only response to good news. I've always felt that dissolving into tears is one of the feebler and less useful ways of dealing with a situation, but sometimes nothing else will do.

At length I picked up the phone again and scrolled to Andy's number. He answered straight away. 'Kim just rang,' he said by way of greeting. 'Jo, are you okay? Do you want me to take you up to Waikato?'

'No, thank you,' I said, not without regret. 'Andy, how would you feel about helping me milk two hundred cows?'

Chapter 38

ANDY'S FLATMATE WADE came along to help with the milking. His first act was to catch the toe of one gumboot on the half-step leading into the milk room and fall heavily against the hot-water cylinder. 'Turn on the fucking lights, would you?' he roared. His voice was barely audible over the rain pelting against the corrugated-iron roof.

'The power's out,' I shouted back, pointing my torch in his direction. 'There's a generator in the implement shed.' Or at least there had been fifteen years ago, when last I'd milked here in a power cut.

Sure enough, the generator was still there, underneath three hessian cow covers and about a thousand electric-fence standards. But it weighed one metric tonne (a conservative estimate) and the implement shed was across the tanker loop from the cowshed. We manoeuvred it painfully through the deluge and hooked it up in a laborious and amateurish sort of way. To my astonished delight it actually started, with a roar like a 747 taking off, and I turned on the lights.

'Right,' Andy bawled into my left ear. 'Where are the cows?'

I had been enjoying a little glow of satisfaction at my own competence. It vanished abruptly. 'No idea.' The prospect of searching for them over ninety acres of wet hill in the howling darkness was not particularly attractive. 'I'll ring Kim.'

'She won't know.'

'But Matt might be awake by now.' I looked at my watch – it was just before five.

We had to turn the generator off to hear the phone, which meant we were plunged back into darkness lit by one failing torch battery.

'Josie?' said Kim.

I pressed the phone hard to one ear and blocked the other in an attempt to hear over the rain. 'How is he?'

'He's waking up,' she said. 'He's going to be okay.'

'Could you ask him where the cows are?'

'Oh!' she said, clearly surprised at this prosaic question. 'Are you milking?'

'We will if we can find the cows,' I said. 'Andy and Wade are helping.'

There was a long pause, broken by incoherent voices on the other end of the line, then Kim asked, 'Did you get that?'

'Nope. Not a word.'

'They're in the Long Swamp – you know, up the hill from the shed and take the race that goes round to the left.'

'I know the one. Thank you.'

'And the dry cows are in the second hay barn paddock.'

'Which hay barn is the second?' I asked.

'The old wooden one with the big hedge just behind it,' said Kim. 'And Matt says you'll have to drench them with causmag, and they get two squirts, and you use – how much was it again? Yes, o*kay*, Matt. They get half a bag, and then fill the drum on the drenching unit with water up to two-thirds full. Settle down, you loser! Sorry, Josie, not you. He's being a nob.'

Well, that was reassuring. You don't call people nobs *or* losers unless you're confident they're going to make a full recovery.

'Tell him we promise not to milk any antibiotic cows into the vat,' I said. 'And – and tell him I love him.'

'Will do,' said Kim cheerfully, and hung up.

Wade clasped his hands girlishly together. 'Tell him I wuv him,' he repeated in a quavering squeak. 'Aww. Here, give me that torch and I'll go get the bike.'

IT WAS ALMOST nine when I drove back up Aunty Rose's driveway and climbed wearily out of my car. The dogs stood at the doors of their runs, complaining in a body at this departure from their standard morning routine, and Percy came bustling out of the woodshed to meet me.

I let the three dogs out, patted Percy and walked slowly up the path. It was still raining, although the wind had dropped, and the place looked indescribably sodden and dreary. About half the roof was missing, and a loose sheet of rusting corrugated iron slapped half-heartedly against the timber underneath.

I took off Aunty Rose's wet oilskin and hung it on a nail by the front door. It had long since given up the struggle to keep the rain out and my poor maltreated onesie was soaked from shoulder to knee. As soon as I opened the door Spud passed me like a medium-sized black and tan lightning streak, two hours overdue for his morning pee.

I padded gingerly across the kitchen floor, bundled the filthy onesie into the washing machine and wrapped myself in a towel from the adjacent cupboard before continuing up the hall. Aunty Rose's room was cold and dark and silent – of course it was, but it felt unexpected and wrong. I pulled back the heavy velvet curtains to let in what little light there was outside and turned to look at the still face on the pillow.

I had never seen a dead person before. Well, not before the small hours of this morning. Novels had led me to expect an expression of unearthly peace on the face of the deceased, and perhaps the sort of smile that suggests the beholding of a beautiful vision. But Aunty Rose just looked exhausted. Her skin was waxy and her mouth sagged a little, and if I hadn't seen her in the last three months I would have been hard pressed to recognise her. I made a fierce abrupt resolution to do as she had asked and *not* remember her like this.

'I'm sorry,' I told her softly. Her death was a tragedy, and yet for the last few hours it had been just another drama, something that piled still more tasks onto the towering heap of things I had to do before even *thinking* of getting to see Matt.

Hot on the heels of this lowering reflection I remembered I had an appointment with Hannah Dixon's left supraspinatus muscle right about now, and I hadn't even rung to say I couldn't make it. And that I needed to call Dr Milne, and the undertakers, and Mum, and the power board, and someone to come and do something about the roof, and we hadn't got in today's calves yet, and I was cold and filthy and dressed only in a small towel, and –

'Sorry,' I repeated helplessly. Brushing the still cheek with a fingertip I left the room.

Closing Aunty Rose's bedroom door I went back down the hall, keeping my eyes resolutely away from the end toilet whose leak would surely have increased from dribble to torrent during the night. Then I had a small brainwave and turned back that way.

The leak had indeed overflowed the big stock pot and the end toilet had become a lake. This was depressing, but at least I had a brimming stock pot full of clean water (albeit freezing cold) for washing in. I dipped an end of my towel into it and started scrubbing – it was no hot shower, but it did at least remove a fair number of green smears. Then I went along the hall to the Pink Room, cast a sorrowful eye over the heap of sodden plaster that had fallen from the ceiling onto the foot of my bed, and got dressed.

I lifted the handset of the hall phone without much hope, but there was actually a dial tone and I sagged with relief; I had envisaged having to take my mobile halfway up the hill behind the house in the rain. Right, start at the beginning, Jo – you're about twenty-five years too old to go back to bed and put your head under the covers – and call Amber.

'HELLO?' SAID AMBER. She was supposed to answer the phone with a sprightly 'Waimanu Physiotherapy! Hello, this is Amber!' but she almost never did.

'Hi, it's Jo,' I said, and there was a clatter as she dropped the phone and bellowed, 'Cheryl! Cheryl, it's Jo!'

There was a second clatter as the phone was retrieved. 'Good morning,' said my employer grimly.

I winced. 'Cher, I'm really sorry.'

'How soon can you get here?' she asked crisply.

'I can't.'

There was an ominous pause before she asked, 'What's happened?'

'Aunty Rose died in the night,' I started.

'Oh, Jo, I'm sorry.'

'And Matt's been in an accident, and he's in Waikato being sewn up again, and the power's off, and the roof's come off the house.'

'Oh,' said Cheryl. There was a wail behind her and she snapped, 'Pick him *up*, Amber!'

'I'm so sorry. I completely forgot to call.'

'Damn it,' she said tiredly. 'I was going to yell at you, and now I can't.'

Poor Cheryl – it sucks to be bursting with righteous indignation and then denied your opportunity to vent it. 'Go ahead, if it makes you feel better.'

'No, that's okay. It's just I've been up half the night with Max, and two people have already told me they would rather have seen you.'

***

I HAD CALLED the medical centre and Copelands Funeral Services and was on hold to the power company (listening with very little pleasure to Aaron Neville, who in my opinion should never have been allowed to sing anywhere but the privacy of his own shower) when Andy arrived back from taking Wade to work.

'Jo?' he called. Then he stuck his head round the hall door and grimaced in apology.

'It's alright,' I said. 'I'm on hold. Are you honestly okay taking the day off?'

'Yeah, it's fine. Do you want sugar in your coffee?' He held up a paper cup with a lid.

'Andy, I love you. Three, please.'

'It's not very warm anymore.'

'Doesn't matter. *Thank* you.' It could have been brewed sometime last week and stored in a gumboot for all I cared.

'Roof's pretty buggered,' Andy remarked over Aaron Neville's warbling, coming up the hall with the cup in one hand and a pie in a paper bag in the other. 'Have you got a tarpaulin?'

I drank about half the lukewarm coffee in one ecstatic

gulp, and shook my head. 'Not that I know of. Who would I ring to come and do something about it?'

'A builder, I suppose. But I don't know if anyone'll come at such short notice.'

'I thought I'd try crying,' I said. Close observation of Hazel King had taught me never to underestimate the effect of judiciously applied tears.

'Might work,' he said doubtfully. 'What d'you want me to do?'

I hesitated. Lighting the fire? Sopping up one of the indoor lakes? Getting in today's new calves? 'Can you drive a tractor? Or is there anyone we can call to come in and take over the farm work at this time of year?'

Aaron Neville's wailing stopped abruptly. 'Waimanu Energy, how can I help you?' said the bored young man on the other end of the phone, and the dogs began to bark as another car came up the driveway.

'Hi,' I said. 'It's Jo Donnelly here – we've got no power up Puketutu Valley Road – sorry, hang on a second.' I covered the receiver and hissed, 'That'll be the doctor. Could you show him in?'

❧

DR MILNE BENT for only the briefest of moments over Aunty Rose's bed before straightening up again. 'Rigor mortis,' he said. 'She died some time ago then.'

'I found her after three,' I said nervously. 'I didn't want to call you in the middle of the night, and – and then I – we – had to milk . . .' I was horribly afraid he would detect some sort of foul play and that I would have to show him Aunty Rose's note, which incidentally I had forgotten about and would have to fish from the depths of the washing machine. And I was by no means as convinced as Rose that he wouldn't feel the need for a coroner's inquest.

'You had to milk?' he repeated blankly.

'Matt's in hospital. He was in an accident last night.'

'What sort of an accident?'

'Someone ran into his bike on the driveway,' I said. 'I'm sorry I didn't call sooner.'

'My dear, it wouldn't have made the slightest difference. We'll put the time of death as three am, and that will be close enough.' He took a step away from the bedside and then paused. 'Oh, and you'll have some fairly serious opioids that we'd better not leave lying around the place. I'll take them away with me.'

I jumped like a startled rabbit, and hastily opened the drawer of the bedside table to hide it. 'Everything's in here – this box is empty . . .' I balled it up with shaking hands as I spoke – it had only been prescribed at the beginning of the week and there should have been four days' worth remaining. It occurred to me suddenly that Aunty Rose had swallowed more than four days' worth of pills last night, and that to ensure a decent overdose she must have been saving them up for weeks instead of using them for pain relief.

'That's fine, Josie,' Dr Milne said gently, relieving me of several little bottles. 'She was a wonderful woman, wasn't she?'

'Mm,' I agreed.

'She told me more than once how much she appreciated having you here.'

'Don't,' I said shakily, 'or I'll weep all over you.'

He looked at me over the tops of his glasses. 'And why shouldn't you?'

I gulped. 'T-too much to do.'

'I'll help,' said Andy from the doorway. 'I'll go and feed out now, and then I'll come back.'

'Stay on the flat,' I said worriedly. 'It's so wet.'

'The problem with you,' Andy told me, 'is that you don't believe anyone else can do anything.'

'Sorry.'

The doctor and I followed him down the hall. 'Nice boy,' Dr Milne remarked, watching him cross the gravel.

'Very,' I said.

'Would you like me to call the undertakers?'

'I already have,' I said. 'They're coming at eleven.'

'Very good. Now, Tim Reynolds is the man you want for that roof. Tell him you need him today, and if he argues you let me know and I'll sort him.'

I nodded. 'Thank you so much.'

'Pleasure, my dear.' He reached out and tweaked the end of my nose as if I were a little girl again. 'My goodness, you're a carbon copy of your mother. I always thought she showed very poor taste in preferring your father to me.'

Chapter 39

IT WAS NEARLY four o'clock when I found a park high up in the Waikato Hospital parking building. According to Kim's latest text message I needed ward twelve, general surgical, where Matt had been transferred from intensive care at lunchtime. This was encouraging news, and I was further encouraged by finding the right ward without getting lost even once.

I paused at the desk, and a nurse in her forties with the look of a woman whose day was *not* going well glanced up. 'Yes?'

'I'm looking for Matthew King.'

'Right down the end.'

'Thank you,' I said, but she had already turned away and picked up the phone.

I made my way down the corridor, dodging several abandoned wheelchairs, a cleaning trolley and a man in fluffy socks and a hospital gown who was pushing his drip pole in front of him as he shuffled along. The end room had four beds, all occupied, and a bank of big windows along the far wall. In the furthest bed, with his eyes closed and looking heartrendingly pale and battered, was Matt.

I expect I would have clung to his hand and sobbed – which, let's face it, is more than anyone should have to put up with on top of liver lacerations and broken ribs – if I could have only got near him. But Hazel was in a chair at his right hand and a small piteous Cilla in a chair at his left, while a third woman, whom I didn't recognise, arranged a bunch of orange gerberas on a table at the foot of the bed.

'Josie!' said Kim from the hallway behind me. She put a cardboard tray of disposable coffee cups down on the seat of a handy wheelchair and threw her arms around me.

I hugged her back tightly. 'Hey, Kimlet.'

'You've had a *horrible* day,' she said into my shoulder.

'So have you,' I pointed out.

'Yeah.'

'But hey,' I said. 'Matt's alive.'

Kim sighed and detached herself. 'True. And I suppose we'd probably have missed him a little bit.'

'We'd better not tell him that; he'll get all uppity.' And we smiled shakily at one another.

'It's awful,' said Kim suddenly. 'I keep forgetting about Aunty Rose.'

'I reckon she understands,' I said. My confidence in the whole notion of life after death is a trifle wobbly – 'Because I really want it to be true' seems such a weak argument for the existence of heaven – but the idea of Aunty Rose being gone entirely was frankly ridiculous. 'She'd be disgusted if we just collapsed in a heap instead of getting on with things.'

'Mm,' said Kim, her gaze wandering thoughtfully towards her mother. She turned and picked up her tray of coffee again. 'Come on.'

She led the way across the room and plonked the tray on the wheeled table at the foot of the bed, digging in her jeans pocket for coins. 'Two dollars forty,' she said, handing it to the unknown woman.

'Thank you, dear. Daylight robbery, isn't it? Just like in an airport.' She looked past Kim to me. 'And this must be Josie.'

'Hi,' I said. Matt opened his eyes with an effort and found mine over the end of his bed. 'Hey, Matt.' Because you just *can't* say, 'My darling, I love you more than anyone has ever loved anybody in all the histories of all the worlds, and when I thought you were gone I wanted to die too' in front of an audience. Actually, I don't think anyone related to my father can say it at all.

'Hey, Jose,' he whispered.

'I'm Myra Browne,' said the woman. 'Cilla's mother.'

'Oh, of course,' I said. 'Nice to meet you.' It wasn't, but 'What the hell are you and your miserable daughter doing here?' is another of the things you just can't say.

Hazel looked up, her face crumpling like a child's. 'Oh, Josie,' she wailed, and held out her arms. This was surprising, but I gathered her up obediently and patted her small trembling form. 'He so nearly d-didn't pull through. My baby boy – and R-Rosie has p-passed . . .'

'In her sleep,' I said soothingly. 'It was very peaceful.'

'Have a coffee, Hazel,' said Myra Browne. 'You'll feel better for it. Was it cinnamon or chocolate on your cappuccino?'

Hazel sighed and released me, sinking back into her chair at Matt's elbow and neatly cutting off access. 'Cinnamon,' she said. 'Thank you.'

'Cilla?' Her mother held out a cup. 'Come on, love, drink up while it's hot.'

Cilla took a long shuddering breath and shook back her smooth pale hair. Her eyes were red and her face puffy with crying, and she had a long graze across one cheek. And yet she still looked like a little porcelain doll. 'I'm sorry,' she whispered.

'He knows that, love!' said her mother heartily. 'Matthew knows it was an accident.'

Matt grunted painfully in the affirmative. Cilla hid her face again and I felt a twinge of pity – which was unexpected, since the girl was responsible for damaging my very favourite person. But imagine the remorse at having landed someone in intensive care combined with the writhing shame of providing the district with such a delicious snippet of gossip: *Jilted Ex-Girlfriend Flattens Local Farmer!* Let she who has never paid that late-night, ill-reasoned visit to the boy who dumped her cast the first stone. Or something to that effect.

'Jo?' Matt croaked.

'Yes?'

'Is everything . . . okay?'

'The farm, you mean?'

'Mm.'

I smiled. 'Yeah.' If it's affection in public you're after, Matthew King is never going to be your ideal man. 'No major dramas. Three new calves this morning, and milking went fine.'

'Good,' he said. 'Where'd you put . . . cows?'

'The milkers are in paddock forty.' We'd had to leave the cows standing in the race after milking this morning until it was light enough to find them a paddock with sufficient grass in it. They had been most indignant about this treatment and returned in a body to the shed to complain.

'Shit,' said Matt, which was discouraging.

'Why?' I asked.

'Spread . . . effluent . . . there,' said Matt.

'But we had about a hundred mil of rain last night,' I said. 'It'll all have washed off, don't worry.'

Cilla raised her head and looked at me with scorn across Matt's bed. 'Grass that's been spread with effluent is very high in potassium,' she explained. 'And potassium inhibits the uptake of magnesium, so the cows are more likely to go down. Especially in bad weather.' *You dumb townie*. She didn't actually say that last bit, but I could hear her thinking it.

Cheers, Farmer Barbie, I thought back. 'Well, we did drench them with causmag. Andy's putting them in that long narrow paddock with the poplars tonight – is that okay?'

'Yeah,' said Matt. His eyelids drifted shut, the effort

of keeping them open being more than he could manage. 'Thanks.' Then, 'You'll have to do a . . . hot wash . . . tomorrow.'

'Matthew, darling,' his mother said tenderly. 'Don't think about the farm. You just need to rest and get better.'

He paid her not the slightest attention. 'Remember how, Jose?'

'Not really,' I said. 'But it's written down on the back of the milk room door, isn't it? And Andy'll help me figure it out. Where do you want the cows tomorrow?'

'Josie,' said Hazel quietly.

'Sorry, but I need to ask.'

'It's hardly important right now, is it?' she said. 'Matthew's very weak – he's lucky to be a-alive . . .' She pulled a hanky from the sleeve of her cardigan and pressed it to her eyes.

'Milkers in seventeen,' said Matt. He moved his head restlessly. 'Springers have two more breaks, but give them both and don't worry about feeding out. And . . . call Kevin Goulding about . . . relief milking.'

'We did. He's busy this weekend, but he'll come on Monday.'

'Good girl.' He opened one eye just the merest sliver and smiled at me crookedly.

❧

'JOSIE,' SAID KIM, 'you muppet.'

'Be nice to me,' I said defensively. 'Or I'll cry. It'll be the next level down.'

We located the car eventually, five minutes after I announced it must have been stolen. It was two levels up from where we had started, behind a pillar that I was privately certain wasn't there when I parked it.

'Give me the keys,' Kim ordered.

I fished for them in my bag. 'No.'

'And why not?'

'Because I'm older and uglier than you. And I had at least some sleep last night, which is more than you can say.' I unlocked the car, and we climbed in.

'I reckon I got at least half an hour on a chair in the waiting room.' She sighed and leant her head back against the seat. 'The surgeon told us he's lucky to be alive. They couldn't get the rescue helicopter in through the storm, and he could easily have bled to death during the ambulance ride.'

I gulped, started the car and backed smartly into the pillar. There was a short, shocked pause.

'Shall I drive?' Kim suggested.

I swallowed. 'Okay.'

Chapter 40

'G ET OUT OF it,' I said, gently because after all they were orphans now.

Nobody paid the slightest attention.

'*Get out of it!*' Kim roared, and dogs and pig fell back, abashed. 'You've got to say it like you mean it, Josie.'

I passed her the takeaways and patted Percy. He leant his full weight against my leg and squinted up at me lovingly. 'Traitor,' I told him, scratching him behind his left ear.

It was very nearly dark, and the cloud had lifted just a little to sit on the shoulders rather than the knees of the ranges. It looked like it hadn't rained for at least half an hour, which made a pleasant change, and smoke curled up lazily from the kitchen chimney. Kim went in while I fed the dogs and gave Percy three apples from the shelf in the woodshed. Then I went slowly up the path and let myself in at the kitchen door.

The kitchen, bleak enough when I left it to depress even the most determined optimist, now radiated warmth and comfort. Kim was unwrapping fish and chips at the table while across the room Andy crouched in front of the roaring stove, critically adjusting the damper. His hair, lacking its normal half-kilogram of wax, stuck up at the back like duck fluff and he had missed that tricky spot just below the elbow while scrubbing, so that he had a green stripe on the back of each forearm.

'How did the afternoon go?' I asked, opening the fridge to hunt for the tomato sauce.

'Fine,' said Andy. He closed the door of the stove and stood up. 'A bloke from the bike shop came out with an old quad bike to use until Matt's is fixed. Or written off.'

The bike had actually started when Chris went to retrieve it that morning, only to stop halfway up to the shed as the last of its oil drained out of the crack in the tank. And retrieving a hundred and fifty cows from a two-hectare paddock on foot – in the rain, mind, and with only the light of a torch – made Dallas Taipa's socks look pretty good.

'Thank goodness,' I said. 'I wasn't looking forward to walking all the way to the back of the farm to get the cows in the morning.'

'I thought you liked that sort of thing,' mocked Kim. 'You're always heading off up some random hill to feel the wind on your face.'

'I like it less at half past four in the morning in the rain,' I said.

Kim served our fish and chips off Aunty Rose's favourite silver platter with the wart-like grapes. She had set out the good crockery and the silver salt and pepper shakers in silent tribute to her aunt, and filled a little lattice-work china bowl with lemon wedges. Aunty Rose was fond of quoting the late Isabella Beeton at meal times, and used to inform us that a well-laid table was one of the refining influences that home should bring to bear upon the young mind. And this from a woman who died at the ripe old age of twenty-eight – I bet *she* was the life and soul of every party. Of course, Mrs Beeton wouldn't have approved of me either. I have spent years perfecting the art of simultaneously straightening my hair, moisturising my legs and slurping yoghurt straight from the pot.

'How's Matt?' Andy asked.

'Three broken ribs,' said Kim. 'Internal bleeding, a hole in his liver, a catheter because he can't get up to pee – is that all, Josie?'

'I think so,' I said. 'He's a sort of pale grey colour and they've got him on so much morphine he can hardly keep his eyes open.'

'Bloody hell. He's not going to be farming for a while, is he?'

'According to him,' said Kim, 'he'll be fine by Monday.' She ate a chip in a pensive sort of way. 'Idiot. He's *awful* when he's sick.'

'Oh, well,' I said. 'We'll tie him to the chaise longue by the ankle, or something. Andy, did you get a look at the roof before it got dark?'

Andy nodded. 'The builder came over to the shed on his way home. He said he's just tacked it down and covered it with a tarpaulin, but he thinks it'll keep out more water than it has for years. He didn't want to do anything more serious, since the whole place is bug—' Realising a little too late that this was hardly a tactful remark when the house's owner was not yet cold in her grave, he stopped abruptly and took a large bite of fish burger instead.

'Poor old house,' said Kim softly. 'Dad always said the only thing keeping it together was the borers holding hands. But Aunty Rose didn't care.'

AFTER DINNER I left the two of them washing dishes and withdrew to the swamp at the end of the hall to continue the happy job of sopping up water with a towel, wringing the towel out over a bucket and every now and then getting up to empty the bucket into the bath. Half an hour later I was cold and wet and getting fairly sour about the whole thing, but the swamp had not noticeably diminished. I wasn't sure why I was bothering anyway – the sensible thing to do would be to remove the books and crockery and about a tenth of the furniture from the house and bulldoze the rest flat. A smidgeon callous, perhaps, but it was that or plant rice along the hall, because at the current rate of progress I'd be here till sometime next year.

'Josie!' Kim called.

I dropped my sodden towel into the bucket and went back into the kitchen to see Andy and Scott nodding to one another and exchanging gruff and manly greetings, about an octave below their normal voices.

'Mate.'

'Mate.'

'How's it going?'

'Beauty.'

These formalities having been observed, Scotty put down his motorbike helmet and turned to Kim. 'I'm sorry about your aunt,' he said.

'Thanks,' said Kim.

He unzipped his leather jacket and shrugged it off. 'She was a top lady.'

Kim nodded. 'Y-yes,' she whispered. Andy tore a paper towel off the roll on the windowsill and wordlessly passed it over, and she wiped her eyes. 'Thank you.' She rested her cheek against his shoulder, and he put his arms around her.

The tenderness in this little display made my throat ache, but Scotty was affected quite differently. He tightened his mouth into a disapproving line, hooked his thumbs through the belt loops of his jeans and did his best to look scary. His best wasn't bad, just quietly.

'So,' he said. 'Andy, wasn't it? You're in a band, I hear.'

Andy looked somewhat taken aback. 'Uh, no,' he said.

'That was the last one,' I explained. 'We quite like this one.'

'Hmm,' said Scotty.

'Scott,' Kim said wearily, 'don't be a dick.'

'Don't you get fresh with *me*, young lady. I remember the day you laid an enormous turd and painted a window with it.'

'*Scotty!*'

'That was mean,' I observed.

'I wasn't even a year *old*!'

'Man, it was disgusting,' Scotty continued reminiscently. 'Were you there, Jo?'

'No,' I said. And as punishment for that exceptionally low blow I added, 'I wasn't there when you got caught short on that bus in Jordan, either.' Matt had, however, described the incident in vivid detail over the phone.

'I was sick,' he protested. 'And the bastard driver wouldn't stop. It could have happened to anyone.'

'I heard he stopped, alright. And you had to get changed on the side of the road, and you tried to scrape your clothes clean with a stick, and then he made you leave them behind anyway.'

Scott grinned, unembarrassed. 'Pissed me right off,' he said. '*And* it was my Rip Curl boardies. They cost me a fortune, and I had to leave them in that miserable desert.'

Andy smiled and picked up his keys, looking somewhat relieved that he wasn't, after all, going to be beaten up by a rat-tailed thug. 'What time are we starting in the morning?' he asked.

'Cups on at five?' I suggested. 'Sorry.'

'See you at the shed at four-thirty, then,' he said gallantly.

'Nah,' I said. 'Make it five. I'll get the cows.'

'Sure?'

'Yep. Thank you so much for all of this, Andy.'

'It's nothing,' he said, ducking his head in embarrassment.

'No it isn't,' Kim said softly. She reached up and kissed his cheek.

'Ahem!' said Scotty pointedly.

'Shut up, Scotty.'

'I'll take you home to get a change of clothes and then drop you back here,' Andy offered. 'Okay, Jo?'

'Sure,' I said. 'But why don't you just return her in the morning?'

Scotty's eyes fairly bulged with horror.

'That's okay,' said Kim, and they retreated back into their sockets.

'Good girl,' he told her approvingly.

Andy looked somewhat downcast.

'I'm not leaving you here by yourself,' Kim told me.

'I have Spud,' I pointed out.

Kim looked across the kitchen at Spud, who was stretched flat on his side in front of the stove, snoring gently. 'Yeah, but he's about a hundred years old. And he doesn't have any teeth.' She thought for a moment. 'Hey, Scotty?'

'Mm?'

'Want to stay the night and look after Josie?'

'What, while you traipse off with this seedy-looking bugger? No offence, mate.'

'None taken,' said Andy cordially.

'Good man.' He sighed. 'Oh, alright, then. Piss off.'

'Cup of tea?' I offered as Andy's car vanished down the drive at high speed – in case the chaperones changed their minds, presumably.

'Why not?' said Scotty idly, leaning back against the kitchen bench. 'What happened to your car?'

'I ran into a pillar in the hospital car park.' I hefted the kettle experimentally, found it was nearly full and switched it on.

'Blinded by tears as you rushed to Matt's bedside, were you?'

'Shut up, Scotty.'

'Well, *there's* a nice thankyou for dropping all my Friday-night plans and rushing over to make sure you were alright.'

'I'm sorry,' I said repentantly. 'Did you have Friday-night plans?'

'Of course I did,' said Scott. 'You know me. Booked up for months in advance – new woman on my arm every week . . .'

'Waimanu's most eligible bachelor,' I agreed.

'There's no need to be sarcastic.'

'I wasn't!' I said. 'Chocolate biscuit to go with your cup of tea?'

'You can't just buy my forgiveness with chocolate biscuits, you know.'

'Not even Jaffa Thins?'

'Nope.' He looked pensive. 'Mallowpuffs, perhaps.'

'I *am* sorry,' I said. 'Thank you for coming over. How did you know Matt was in hospital?'

'He rang just before,' Scotty said.

'How did he sound?'

'Like a bloke who's been run over by a truck.'

I winced.

'He'll be alright,' said Scott comfortingly. 'Very hard man to kill. He asked me to come and check up on you.'

'Oh,' I said, slightly taken aback. 'Thank you.' It's funny how when you become the girlfriend you are instantly transformed in the eyes of your partner from reasonably capable adult to delicate blossom. It's sort of sweet, I suppose.

'So, *are* you okay?' he asked.

'Yes,' I assured him. 'Although Aunty Rose's house feels all wrong without Aunty Rose in it.'

'I always liked coming up here,' Scott said. 'You always got put to work, but you didn't mind. She was a very cool lady.'

'She was,' I agreed, hunting through the biscuit cupboard and finding that we had neither Thins nor Mallowpuffs. Very poor form from the grocery shopper – we would have to settle for Shrewsburys, and jam in a biscuit is a poor substitute for chocolate.

'When's the funeral?' Scotty asked.

'I don't know. Wednesday, perhaps. But they might put it off if Matt's still in hospital. Hey, Scotty, would you mind coming round the cows with me before you go?' I would probably be able to find the calving cow by myself, but my chances of cutting her out and getting her to the shed without bringing everyone else too were slim to none.

'I'm staying the night, aren't I?'

'I wouldn't,' I said morosely. 'Every bit of this house except the kitchen is freezing, and most of it's underwater.'

We had our cup of tea, went round the cows and decided that any more work on the swamp in the hall was above and beyond the call of duty. So we had a brief argument about whether or not I was fit to be left alone for the night, and then retired to bed.

'Hey, Jo?' Scotty called as I went down the hall from the bathroom.

I looked around the kitchen door. He was stretched on the chaise longue with a blanket, and he lifted his head and said, 'I know a bloke who'll fix your car up for you. Panels, paint – the lot. Under the table.'

'Does this bloke spend most of his time repainting stolen cars?' I asked.

He grinned. 'That would be telling.'

I grinned back. ''Night, Scotty. Thanks for staying.' I didn't really believe the man lurked on the fringes of the criminal underworld, but he liked us thinking he did.

Chapter 41

I WENT DOWN the corridor of ward twelve, turned expectantly into the end room – and found the far bed occupied by an elderly Indian man with his leg in traction.

'King?' repeated the nurse on reception. She shook her head. 'Not in here. Perhaps he's in a different ward.'

'He was here this morning,' I said. 'I talked to him on the phone. I've come to take him home.'

'Ah,' she said. 'Then he'll be waiting in reception.'

It took me another fifteen minutes to locate him, during which I think I toured most of the hospital. But finally, more by accident than design, I stumbled into a reception area and found Matt reading *The New Zealand Gardener*, wrapped in a dark green velvet dressing-gown and with a lock of hair falling most artistically over his brow. 'G'day,' he said.

'G'day. How are you feeling?'

'Better.'

I bent and kissed him. 'You look a bit like Hugh Hefner.'

'Thanks,' said Matt, somewhat sourly. 'You didn't bring me a change of clothes, by any chance?'

'Never even occurred to me. I'd better go and get you a wheelchair; it's a fair distance to the car.'

'I can walk,' he said. 'I'm alright once I'm up. It's just getting there that's the problem.'

I helped him to his feet and picked up his bag, and we began to make our way slowly across the room. 'Your mum and I played paper-scissors-rock to decide who'd get to come and pick you up,' I told him. 'Best of three. It went to the wire.'

'I'm honoured,' said Matt.

'I lost.'

'Don't make me laugh,' he said. 'It hurts.'

'No, I did lose, but then the vicar rang wanting to go over the music for tomorrow. So I was allowed to come after all.'

'Ah.'

We progressed in silence through the doors and along a corridor, hugging the wall as official-looking people bustled past.

'I don't really believe she's dead,' he said suddenly.

'Me neither. I think of something I want to tell her a dozen times a day, and each time it comes as a shock that I can't.' We were passed by an obese woman with a walker and a moon-boot, which was a little discouraging. 'Wheelchair?'

'No, thank you,' said Matt with dignity. 'I'm coming along nicely.'

'So's Christmas,' I murmured.

'Oh, shut up. I thought women were supposed to be gentle and nurturing.'

'Bad luck,' I said sympathetically. 'You must just have got a dud one.'

Matt sighed. 'Yeah,' he agreed. He reached for my hand, and I slid my fingers down between his.

'Can you remember the accident?' I asked.

'Most of it, I think. The ambulance ride – God, that's a lousy way to travel – and poor Cilla trying to get me out from under the bike.'

'Hmph,' I said.

'Hmph?'

'*Poor* Cilla? She made quite a good job of flattening you.'

Matt smiled tiredly. 'Well,' he said, 'fair enough, I suppose. I haven't treated her very well.' He stopped and leant against the wall. 'Might need that wheelchair after all, Jose.'

❧

'ERIC!' CALLED MUM. 'Eric, where are you?' She rammed a final bobby pin into the knot of hair at the nape of her neck and frowned at it critically in the bathroom mirror. 'Where *is* the man? We need to go. Josie, are you ready?'

I was, and having winkled Dad out of the bedroom, undone and retied his tie and removed a rogue stain from the lapel of his only jacket, we departed for the church.

It was a huge funeral. The Presbyterian church was crammed full, with people shoulder to shoulder all round the walls and another thirty on the steps outside.

Matt gave the eulogy (as requested by his aunt), white-faced and with great dark smudges under his eyes. His shaky progress to and from the podium, coupled with that careless lock of hair tumbling Byronically across his brow, gave a beautifully dramatic effect. Aunty Rose would have loved it. I could almost hear her appreciative murmur, 'Simply dripping with pathos, isn't it, Josephine? Marvellous stuff.'

We didn't, after all, sing 'Another One Bites the Dust' as the coffin was carried out; Hazel and the vicar had settled instead on the more traditional 'How Great Thou Art'. And Aunty Rose's old adversary the mayor was pressed into service as a coffin bearer to replace Matt.

Rose Adele Thornton, born in Bath, England, died in Waimanu, New Zealand, a mere fifty-three years later. Adept and compassionate nurse, fervent advocate of animal welfare, champion of correct diction and tireless crusader against the misuse of apostrophes. Experimental chef, peerless aunt, brave sufferer and true friend. She had the grace and courage to thoroughly enjoy a life which denied her everything she most wanted. The bravest woman I ever knew.

WHILE MOST OF the district applied themselves to club sandwiches and apple shortcake in the draughty

Presbyterian church hall, I slipped away to look for Matt. I found him perched on the low brick wall bordering the neighbouring park. It was cold, with a brisk southerly wind stirring the new leaves of the oaks across the park and whisking the petals from a blossoming plum tree next door.

His cheeks were wet and he didn't turn as I sat down beside him, but he put a hand out silently and took mine. We sat there for a while, looking at the vivid green of the oak trees and the two small boys kicking a soccer ball half-heartedly beneath them, before he said, 'Déjà vu, huh?'

I squeezed his hand. 'Yep.' Last time we'd sat here like this was on an afternoon in February, four years earlier, and the oak leaves were the tired dusty green of late summer. And Matt had been pale and jet-lagged and wretched, and I'd wanted desperately to hug him, or say something sympathetic, or do *something*, but with a five-year gulf between us I couldn't.

Kim came along the path behind us and sat down on his other side, tucking her skirt under her thighs. 'Hey,' she said.

'Hey, Toad,' said Matt.

'How's it going inside?' I asked.

'Great,' she said bitterly. 'Social event of the decade.'

Matt lifted his right arm with a little grunt of effort and put it round her shoulders.

'Everyone says how wonderful she was,' Kim continued. 'Funny how none of them bothered to go and see her while she was alive and tell her to her face.'

399

'That's funerals for you.'

'If one more person tells me that cancer's a cruel, horrible way to die I'll throw something at their head,' she said savagely. 'Do they think we didn't notice?'

'She didn't,' I said abruptly, having agonised for days before deciding that sharing this information wasn't going to help anyone and I'd better keep my mouth shut. A wise decision, but unfortunately I'm completely crap at keeping my mouth shut.

'Huh?' Matt said.

'She didn't die of the cancer; she took every pill she could find and washed them down with forty-year-old port. She left a note.'

Both Kings turned to stare at me.

'She said it wasn't suicide,' I continued. 'It was just sparing us all any more deathbed scenes. And could I please remove the evidence, and she thoroughly enjoyed her life, and she loved us all very much. So I collected up the pill packets and the bottle and put them down the offal hole.'

There was a long frozen silence, broken at length by Kim. 'Way to go, Aunty Rose,' she said softly.

'WHAT WOULD YOU like for dinner?' Mum asked wearily, elbows on Aunty Rose's big kitchen table and chin in her hands.

'Not hungry,' I said. 'You?'

'Not really. Eric?'

'Hmm?' Dad said absently, turning a page of his book.

'Are you hungry?'

'Hmm?'

'Do you want dinner now?'

Dad merely resettled his glasses on his nose, giving no sign whatsoever that he had heard a word she said.

'Are you up to the bit where he deflowers her in the crow's nest, Dad?' I asked. As well as the obligatory enormous willy, that pirate was blessed with extreme suppleness and a head for heights.

My father reddened and thrust *Pirate's Lady* down the back of the chaise longue. 'Load of rubbish,' he said. 'Jo, be a good slave and put the kettle on, would you?'

I straightened from where I had been leaning against the stove and crossed the kitchen to fill the kettle. 'Are you guys going home tomorrow?'

'Yes,' said Mum. 'Our flight leaves at two-thirty.' She rubbed at her eyes with her hands. 'We've been thinking of selling the goat farm.'

'And doing what?' I asked, startled.

'Dry stock, probably,' said Dad. 'The goats are a huge tie.'

'Oh,' I said. 'Fair enough.' But I was a little puzzled, because my parents, when told (by me) that they should be out there seeing the world and spending my inheritance, have always said firmly that travel is not for them and that they like nothing more than staying at home. 'Anywhere in particular?'

'Somewhere up this way, we thought,' said Mum

casually. 'We miss the district – most of our friends are here – and then we don't want to be too far from the grandchildren.'

'Grandchildren?' I repeated faintly.

'Yes please, dear.' She stood up. 'If you have a little girl you might like to call her Rose, don't you think?'

'But no pressure,' Dad said. He put a hand down the back of the chaise longue and gave a fairly poor impression of surprise as he encountered a book. And then, with an even poorer impression of detached curiosity, he pushed his glasses back up his nose and reopened *Pirate's Lady*.

Chapter 42

'**M**ATTHEW *PATRICK*!'

He jumped about a foot in the air, slopping colostrum down his gumboot. 'Jesus, Jo!' he said crossly.

'What the *hell* do you think you're doing?'

'What does it look like I'm doing?'

'Trying to pull out all your stitches, by the look of it.'

'Settle down, woman, I'm not stupid.'

I climbed off the bike and picked up the twenty-litre bucket at his feet. 'Exactly what part of "Just wait here a minute while I shut the cows away" did you not understand?'

'I was being careful,' he argued.

I scowled at him. 'You nearly bled to death a week ago. You could rupture your liver or something, you idiot.'

'Just because you used to go out with a doctor,' said Matt, 'you seem to think you're some sort of medical expert.' He stepped out of his left gumboot, tipped out the milk and put it back on with a grimace of distaste.

'I think most people would agree that lifting heavy

403

buckets a week after major abdominal surgery probably isn't the best plan,' I pointed out.

Realising that he was on shaky ground, he altered his line of attack. 'You sound like your mother.' His tone of voice was exactly the same as the one in which, twenty years ago, he used to tell me that I had girl germs.

'Take that back,' I said indignantly. I poured the milk he hadn't tipped down his gumboot into the feeder hanging on the gate, put the bucket down and climbed into the pen to prevent the moronic white-faced calf that liked to butt the feeder from sloshing most of it out again. Kevin the relief milker was attending his niece's wedding today, which meant I was farming while Matt supervised. This would have been more enjoyable if only he would have refrained from climbing fences, lifting sacks of calf meal and otherwise contravening the doctor's orders. And if he had refrained from pointing out (kindly, because he's quite fond of me, but it was still painful) the many areas in which my dairy-farming practices failed to meet his high standards.

Matt sighed, and scuffed the gravel moodily with the toe of his gumboot. 'This is doing my head in,' he said.

I clamped the white-faced calf between my knees and managed *not* to tell him that he wasn't the only one. I once met a little saying – probably in one of those books of potted wisdom you find in waiting rooms – which said that the key to a successful relationship is to leave half a dozen things a day unsaid. So true.

'Have you sorted out where you want Kevin to put the cows next week?' I asked. I pushed a teat into the calf's mouth and he spat it out as if it was poisonous. I was starting to wish it was.

'Yep.'

'Put all the calving information into the computer?'

'Yep.' He leant over the gate and scratched the nearest calf between the ears.

'Just one more week,' I said encouragingly. My calf took two sucks, let the teat go and pushed his neighbour off too. 'You revolting animal. You could always resort to housework, if all else failed.'

Matt smiled. 'Shit, it's not *that* bad,' he said. 'Oh, alright. I'll go and do something about tea.'

I smiled back. 'Dinner.'

'Dinner.' He stretched across the feeder and kissed me. 'Wash the teats out with hot water, okay?'

He went slowly across the tanker loop to the ute, slightly stooped and with one hand holding his sore ribs. I had a small epiphany as I watched him go; even though he'd been pushed into living the life his family wanted him to rather than the one he'd chosen for himself, he had ended up just exactly where he was meant to be. But my soulful musings were interrupted by the little white-faced calf, who chose that moment to bunt me firmly from behind and nearly pitch me into the feeder.

❦

'PLEASE TELL ME you're kidding,' said Matt, looking up from the *Dairy Exporter* as I came into the Pink Room that night.

'Not at all. Stylish yet functional – why don't you order another one for yourself, and then we can match?' I pushed the eared hood of the onesie back off my head and climbed into bed beside him.

'Great,' he said sourly. 'Let's get matching Gore-Tex jackets and backpacks too, and walk up hills with those gay ski-pole things.'

'Mum and Dad have matching Gore-Tex jackets,' I remarked. 'They found them in a bargain bin at Kathmandu.'

'Awesome,' said Matt.

I wriggled out of the onesie, which I had only put on to get a reaction, and pulled the covers up under my chin. Matt tossed his magazine onto the floor and reached out with a little grunt to turn off the bedside light, plunging the room into velvety darkness.

'Hey, Jose?' he asked.

'Mm?'

'D'you still reckon it would be unbearable to be called Jo King?'

For some time I merely lay on my back and gulped. 'I reckon,' I managed at last, 'that I could probably learn to live with it.'

Matt gave a little sigh of satisfaction. 'Bloody marvellous,' he said. Followed, as I rolled over and hugged him enthusiastically, by, '*Ow!*'

Epilogue

IN THE END I did have to go to Melbourne and jump up and down before Graeme would buy me out of the house. We spent a very long afternoon sitting one on either side of the kitchen counter with a pile of bank statements between us, and by the end of it only the knowledge that if he didn't pay me something I'd have to spend the next five years without a roof stopped me from just giving him the lot.

The one bright spot in this encounter was when Graeme slid his bare foot up my shin under the counter, and I got to use the what-the-hell-do-you-think-you're-doing-you-sleazy-little-philanderer look I had worked up during the drive to the airport in hope of just such a moment. I must have nailed it, because he went a dirty puce colour and accused me of taking the remote-control garage-door opener with me when I left. (I didn't, but I would have if I'd thought of it.)

Kim is studying Media Arts at Waikato University.

On reflection Otago, while it had the benefit of being a long way away from her mother, was also a long way away from Andy. Last time she came home her hair was bright crimson. However, she points out that she has yet to pierce her nipples, fail her exams or fall pregnant, so it could be much worse.

Hazel has given up on Reiki and started a pottery course at the high school. For my birthday I got an earthenware ashtray. It was going to be a coffee cup, but she hasn't mastered cups yet. We use it to hold the pig-scratching fork.

Stu is going out with a Scandinavian personal trainer called Bjorn. Apparently he's not all that bright, but he looks like a Norse god and helps little old ladies across the street and is hung like a stallion. The mind boggles.

Brett and Clare's fourth baby is due any day. Clare is resigned; she says she's forgotten what a good night's sleep is like anyway so it won't make any difference. Brett says that if one more person claps him on the back and says, 'Haven't you figured out what causes that yet?' he will fly into a berserker rage. He will also beat Scott to a pulp if he dares make one more joke about the irony of impregnating your wife the day before your vasectomy.

Scotty is still looking for the girl of his dreams. However, he *has* cut off his rat's tail, which can only increase his chances.

I hear that Cilla is going out with a nice young sheep farmer from the coast. She waves to Matt on the road, but when she and I meet she mostly pretends not to have seen me.

Matt and I live in Aunty Rose's house. We've got a new roof and a new shower, and one of these days we might even be able to afford insulation. It would be much more sensible to flatten the place and start again, but we couldn't do it. And even if we could have brought ourselves to do it, just think of the possible psychological damage to Percy and the dogs.

Sometimes I am sure I catch a whiff of Aunty Rose's perfume, or see just a flicker of crimson satin as her dressing-gown whisks around a corner. And she must have been responsible for me coming home at Labour Weekend with two tiny, feeble courgette seedlings from Mitre 10. We've been getting about twenty-seven bloody courgettes a day for the last three months and Matt threatens divorce if I ever make another courgette quiche. I'm pretty sure he doesn't mean it.

Acknowledgements

THANK YOU VERY, very much to Louise Thurtell and Ali Lavau for being the kindest, most constructive publisher and editor anybody could ever ask for.

Thank you to Kelly Forster for wanting to read, and then liking, my writing. Giving a friend your manuscript is even worse than bringing your new boyfriend home for parental inspection, and if she hadn't been so encouraging I'm sure I would never have got any further.

And most of all thank you to Jarrod for being so nice about me spending any spare time bent over the laptop, and for managing the first fifty pages and quite enjoying them even if there weren't any battle scenes.